Danse Macabre

"Highly charged, well-written, no-holds-barred erotica . . . jaw-dropping . . . it's an almost sure bet that there will be plenty of readers ready to enjoy the 'good parts'—sexual and otherwise—of each successive Anita Blake novel for years to come."
—*The Denver Post*

"Fans will find plenty here to sink their teeth into."
—*St. Louis Post-Dispatch*

"[A] fabulously imagined series."
—*Publishers Weekly*

Micah

"An exciting, erotic, and evocative paranormal romantic suspense thriller that will thrill her fans and send new readers scrambling for her backlist."
—*The Best Reviews*

"Highly palatable . . . equal portions hot sex and supernatural crime fighting—with a dollop of old-fashioned male-female melodrama."
—*Publishers Weekly*

"A tightly plotted, fast-paced romp."
—*Romantic Times*

Incubus Dreams

"Hamilton maintains a terrific pace with suspense, revenge, and heart-pounding endings."
—*Detroit Free Press*

"Gruesome, action-packed scenes and episodes . . . Hamilton really does come off like the genre's answer to Henry Miller."
—*The Denver Post*

"[A] thrill ride."
—*St. Louis Post-Dispatch*

continued . . .

SKIN TRADE

LAURELL K. HAMILTON

JOVE BOOKS, NEW YORK

THE BERKLEY PUBLISHING GROUP
Published by the Penguin Group
Penguin Group (USA) Inc.
375 Hudson Street, New York, New York 10014, USA
Penguin Group (Canada), 90 Eglinton Avenue East, Suite 700, Toronto, Ontario M4P 2Y3, Canada
(a division of Pearson Penguin Canada Inc.)
Penguin Books Ltd., 80 Strand, London WC2R 0RL, England
Penguin Group Ireland, 25 St. Stephen's Green, Dublin 2, Ireland (a division of Penguin Books Ltd.)
Penguin Group (Australia), 250 Camberwell Road, Camberwell, Victoria 3124, Australia
(a division of Pearson Australia Group Pty. Ltd.)
Penguin Books India Pvt. Ltd., 11 Community Centre, Panchsheel Park, New Delhi—110 017, India
Penguin Group (NZ), 67 Apollo Drive, Rosedale, North Shore 0632, New Zealand
(a division of Pearson New Zealand Ltd.)
Penguin Books (South Africa) (Pty.) Ltd., 24 Sturdee Avenue, Rosebank, Johannesburg 2196,
South Africa

Penguin Books Ltd., Registered Offices: 80 Strand, London WC2R 0RL, England

This is a work of fiction. Names, characters, places, and incidents either are the product of the author's imagination or are used fictitiously, and any resemblance to actual persons, living or dead, business establishments, events, or locales is entirely coincidental. The publisher does not have any control over and does not assume any responsibility for author or third-party websites or their content.

SKIN TRADE

A Jove Book / published by arrangement with the author

PRINTING HISTORY
Berkley hardcover edition / June 2009
Jove mass-market edition / June 2010

ISBN: 978-0-515-14805-3

JOVE®
Jove Books are published by The Berkley Publishing Group,
a division of Penguin Group (USA) Inc.,
375 Hudson Street, New York, New York 10014.
JOVE® is a registered trademark of Penguin Group (USA) Inc.
The "J" design is a trademark of Penguin Group (USA) Inc.

PRINTED IN THE UNITED STATES OF AMERICA

10   9   8   7   6   5   4   3   2   1

To Jonathon,
who understands that I'm a moody bastard,
but loves me anyway.
Some days he loves me because of it.
Of course, it takes one to know one.

ACKNOWLEDGMENTS

To everyone who keeps hanging in there: Darla, Sherry, Mary, and Teresa. Merrilee, my agent, for never giving up. Susan, my editor, who often surprises me with her insights. Everyone at Marvel who works on the Anita Blake comic series. A team, at last. Shawn, who answered nearly endless questions about police work, and when he didn't know the answers, admitted it and helped me find other experts to talk to. Thanks for having our backs in Vegas. Robin, who helped calm me down. Blessed be. Thanks to Kathy, who helped us out at the last Wolf Howl. Charles, we'll miss seeing you at all the events, but life moves on, and new goals need pursuing. Good luck in getting your degree. Daven and Wendi, thanks for the hospitality and the hugs. Sharon Shinn, because no one else understands the panic. To all the rest of the Alternate Historians: Deborah Millitello, Tom Drennan, Mark Sumner, and Marella Sands—good friends, good writers, what more could one ask for? To Las Vegas Metro SWAT, thanks to all of you, because I was told that it's about the team, not the individuals, and who am I to argue with a team that works this well. Thanks to Bill, Alane, Nicole, and REM, who showed us around the Clark County Coroner's office. It was great meeting everyone in Vegas; you all made us feel very welcome. Thank you. Any mistakes in the book are mine and mine alone, because there wasn't time for everyone to read over the manuscript, but the help I received in Vegas helped keep the mistakes to a minimum. Thanks, everyone.

Sudden and swift and light as that
The ties gave,
And he learned of finalities
Besides the grave.

—From "The Impulse" by Robert Frost (*The Hill Wife*, 1922)

1

I'D WORKED MY share of serial killer cases, but none of the killers had ever mailed me a human head. That was new. I looked down at the head, ghostly, through the plastic bag it was wrapped in. It sat on my desk, on top of the desk blotter, like hundreds of other packages that had been delivered to Animators Inc., where our motto was *Where the Living Raise the Dead for a Killing*. The head had been packed in ice, looking for all the world like some employee of the postal service had done it. Maybe they had; vampires can be very persuasive, and it was a vampire who had sent the package. A vampire named Vittorio. He'd included a letter with my name written on the envelope in lovely calligraphy: *Anita Blake*. He wanted me to know who to thank for my little surprise. He and his people had slaughtered over ten people in St. Louis alone before he fled to parts unknown. Well, not unknown now, maybe. There was a return address on the package. It had been mailed from Las Vegas, Nevada.

Either Vittorio was still there, or it would be another of his disappearing acts. Was he in Las Vegas, or had he mailed it from there and would be somewhere else by the time I gave the information to the police there?

No way to know. I could still hear our daytime secretary, Mary, being hysterical in the other room. Luckily we had no clients in the office. I was about thirty minutes away from my first client of the day, and my appointment had been the first of the day for Animators Inc.; lucky. Mary could have her breakdown while our business manager, Bert, tried to calm her. Maybe I should have helped, but I was a U.S. Marshal, and business had to come first. I had to call Vegas and tell them they might have a serial killer in town. Happy fucking Monday.

I sat down at my desk, the phone in my hand, but didn't dial it. I stared at the pictures of other people's families on my desk. Once the shared desk had been empty, just files mingling in the drawers, but first Manny Rodriguez brought in his family portrait. It was the one that every family seems to have, where people are too serious, and only one or two manage a good smile. Manny looked stiff and uncomfortable in his suit and tie. Left to his own devices he always forgot the tie, but Rosita, his wife, who was inches taller than he, and more inches wider than his slender form, would have insisted on the tie. She usually got her way on stuff like that. Manny wasn't exactly henpecked, but he wasn't exactly the voice of authority in his house either.

Their two girls, Mercedes and Consuela (Connie), were very grown-up, standing tall and straight with their father's delicate build, and their faces so pretty, they shone in the shadow of Rosita's older, heavier face. His daughters made me see what he might have seen all those years ago when Rosita, "little rose," must have matched her name. Their son, Tomas, was still a child, still in elementary school. Was he in third grade now, or fourth? I couldn't remember.

The other picture was a pair of photos in one of those hinged frames. One picture was of Larry Kirkland and his wife, Detective Tammy Reynolds, on their wedding day. They were looking at each other like they saw something wonderful, all shiny and full of promise. The other photo was of them with their daughter, Angelica, who had quickly become simply Angel. The baby had her father's curls, like an auburn halo around her head. He kept his orange-red hair cut so short there were no curls, but Tammy's brown hair had darkened Angel's, so that it was auburn. It was a little more brown, a little less red, than Nathaniel's auburn hair.

Should I bring a picture of Nathaniel and Micah and me in, to put on the desk? I knew that the other animators at Animators Inc. had pictures of their families on their desks, too.

But, of course, would I need more pictures? If I brought a picture of me with the two men, then did I need to bring a picture of me with my other sweeties? When you're sort of living with, at last count, four men, and dating another five or six, who goes in the pictures?

I felt nothing about the package on my desk. I wasn't scared or disgusted. I felt nothing but a huge, vast emptiness inside me, almost like the silence that my head went to when I pulled the trigger on someone. Was I handling this really well, or was I in shock? Hmm, I couldn't tell, which meant it was probably some version of shock. Great.

I stood up and looked at the head in its plastic wrap and thought, *No pictures of my boyfriends, not at work.* I'd had a handful of clients who had turned out to be bad guys, and girls. I didn't want them seeing pictures of people I loved. Never give the bad guys ideas; they find enough awful things to do without giving them clues.

No, no personal photos at work. Bad idea.

I dialed Information, because I'd never talked to the Las Vegas police force before. It was a chance to make new friends, or piss off a whole new set of people; with me, it could go either way. I didn't do it on purpose, but I did have a tendency to rub people the wrong way. Part of it was being a woman in a predominantly male field; part of it was simply my winning personality.

I sat back down, so I couldn't see inside the box. I'd already called my local police. I wanted forensics to do the box, find some clues, help us catch this bastard. Whose head was it, and why did I get the prize? Why send it to me? Was it a sign that he held a grudge about me killing so many of his vampires when they were slaughtering people in our town, or did it mean something else, something that would never, ever, occur to me to think?

There are a lot of good profilers working on serials, but I think they miss one thing. You can't really think like these people. You just can't. You can try. You can crawl into their heads so far that you feel like you'll never be clean again, but in the end, unless you are one, you can't really understand what motivates them. And they are selfish creatures, caring only about their own pleasure, their own pathology. Serial killers don't help you catch other serial killers unless it helps their agenda. Of course, there were people who said that I was a serial killer. I still had the highest kill count of all the legal vampire executioners in the United States. I'd topped a hundred this year. Did it really matter that I didn't enjoy my kills? Did it really change anything that I took no sexual pleasure from it? Did it matter that in the beginning I'd thrown up? Did the fact that I'd had an order of execution for most of my kills make them better, less brutal? There were serial killers who had used only poison, which caused almost no pain; they'd been less brutal than me. Lately, I'd begun to wonder exactly what set me apart from people like Vittorio. I'd begun to question if to my oh-so-legal victims it mattered what my motives were.

A woman answered the phone in Las Vegas, and I began the process of getting passed up the line to the person who might be able to tell me whose head I had in the box.

2

UNDERSHERIFF RUPERT SHAW had a rough voice; either he'd been yelling a lot, or he'd smoked way too much, for way too many years. "Who did you say this was?" he asked.

I sighed, and repeated for the umpteenth time, "I am U.S. Marshal Anita Blake. I need to talk to someone in charge, and I guess that would be you, Sheriff Shaw."

"I will kick the ass of whoever gave your name to the media."

"What are you talking about, Sheriff?"

"You didn't hear about the message from the media?"

"If you mean television or radio, I haven't had either on. Is there something I should know?"

"How did you know to call us, Marshal?"

I sat back in my chair, totally puzzled. "I get the feeling that if I hadn't called you, you'd be calling me, Sheriff Shaw."

"How did you know to call us?" he said again, each word a little more defined, an edge of stress, maybe even anger in his voice.

"I called you because I've got a package sitting on my desk that was mailed from Las Vegas."

"What kind of package?" he asked.

Was it time to tell the whole story? I hadn't earlier because once you tell someone certain things—say, you got mailed a human head in a box—they tend to think you're crazy. I was in the media enough for someone to pretend to be me, so I'd wanted them to take me seriously before they discounted me as some crackpot psychotic.

"Someone mailed me a human head. The return address is your city."

He was quiet for almost a minute. I could hear his raspy breathing. I was betting on the smoking. About the time I was going to prompt him, he said, "Can you describe the head?"

He could have said a lot of things, but that wasn't on my list. Too calm, even for a cop, and too practical. The moment he asked me to describe it, I knew he had someone in mind, someone who was missing a head. Shit.

"The head is in plastic, packed in ice. The hair looks dark, but that could be partially from the way it was packed. The hair looks straight, but again, I can't be sure that it's not some leakage making the hair appear straight. Caucasian, I'm sure of, and the eyes look pale. Gray, maybe pale blue, though death can steal color from the eyes. I have no way of telling time of death, so I don't know how much discoloration could have taken place."

"Have you searched the box for anything else?"

"Is your man missing more than just a head?" I asked.

"A badge, and a finger. The finger should have a wedding band on it."

"I'm sorry to hear that last part."

"Why?"

"Telling the wife, I don't envy you that."

"You have to do that yourself much?"

"I've seen the grieving families of the vampire vics often enough. It always sucks."

"Yeah, it always sucks," he said.

"I'm waiting for forensics to look at it before I touch anything. If there are any clues, I don't want to fuck them up because I got impatient."

"Let me know what they find."

"Will do." I waited for him to add something, but he didn't. All I had was his breathing, too rough, too labored. I wondered when was the last time he'd had a physical.

I finally said, "What happened in Vegas, Sheriff Shaw? Why do I have a piece of one of your officers on my desk?"

"We aren't sure that's who it is."

"No, but it would be an awfully big coincidence if you've got an officer who's missing a head, and I've got a head in a box sent from your town that superficially matches your downed officer. I just don't buy a coincidence that big, Sheriff."

He sighed, then coughed; it was a thick cough. Maybe he was just getting over something. "Me either, Blake, me either. I'll go you one better. We're holding back the fact that we've got a missing head and badge. We're also holding back from the media that there's a message on the wall where my men were slaughtered. It's written in their blood, and it's addressed to you."

"To me," I said, and my voice sounded a little less certain of itself than I wanted it to sound. It was my turn to clear my throat.

"Yeah, it reads, *Tell Anita Blake I'll be waiting for her.*"

"Well, that's just . . . creepy," I said, finally. I couldn't think of what else to say, but there was that electric jolt that got through the shock for a second. I knew that jolt; it was fear.

" 'Creepy,' that's the best you can do? This vampire sent you a human head. Will it mean more to you if I tell you it's the head of our local vampire executioner?"

I thought about that for a few breaths, felt that jolt again—somewhere between an electric shock and the sensation of champagne in your veins. "What word would make you happy, Shaw? Did he take any souvenirs from any of the other officers?"

"You mean, did he decapitate anyone else?"

"Yeah, that's what I mean."

"No. He and his monsters killed three operators, but the bodies were not used for souvenir hunting."

"Operators . . . so the vamp executioner was with your SWAT?"

"All warrants of execution are considered high risk, so SWAT helps deliver the message."

"Yeah, they're talking about that in St. Louis, too." I was still unsure how I felt about them forcing me to take SWAT on vampire hunts. Part of me was happy for the backup, and another part was totally against it. The last time SWAT had backed me, some of them died. I didn't like being responsible for more people. Also, it was always a chore to convince them

I was worthy to put my shoulder beside theirs and hit that door.

"If our men killed any of the monsters, we don't have any evidence to prove it. It looks like our people dropped where they stood."

I didn't know what to say to that, so I ignored it. "How long ago did all this happen?"

"Yesterday, no, night before last, yeah. I've been up for a while; it starts to make you lose track."

"I know," I said.

"What the hell did you do to this vampire to make him like you this much?"

"I have no idea. Maybe let him get away and not chase him. Oh, hell, Shaw, you know there's no logic to these nut-bunnies."

"Nut-bunnies," he said.

"Fine, serial killers. Dead or alive they operate on a logic all their own. It doesn't make sense to the rest of us because we're not nut-bunnies."

He made a sound that I think was a laugh. "No, we're not nut-bunnies, yet. The papers and television say you killed a bunch of his people."

"I had help. Our SWAT was with me. They lost men."

"I've looked up the articles, but frankly, I thought you'd take credit and not mention the police."

"They went in with me. They risked their lives. Some of them died. It was bad. I don't think I'd forget that."

"Rumor has it that you're a publicity sl— hound," he said, changing the word he was going to use to something less offensive.

I actually laughed, which was a good sign. I wasn't completely in shock, yea! "I'm not a publicity hound, or a publicity slut, Sheriff Shaw. Trust me, I get way more media attention than I want."

"For someone who doesn't want the attention, you get a hell of a lot of it."

I shrugged, realized he couldn't see it, and said, "I'm involved with some pretty gruesome cases, Sheriff; it attracts the media."

"You're also a beautiful young woman and are dating the master of your city."

"Do I thank you for the *beautiful* comment before or after I tell you that my personal life is none of your concern?"

"It is if it interferes with your job."

"Check the record, Sheriff Shaw. I've killed more vampires since I've been dating Jean-Claude than I did before."

"I heard you've refused to do stakings in the morgue."

"I've lost my taste for putting a stake through the heart of someone chained and helpless on a gurney."

"They're asleep, or whatever, right?"

"Not always, and trust me, the first time you have to look someone in the face while they beg for their life . . . Let's just say that even with practice, putting a stake through someone's heart is a slow way to die. They beg and explain themselves right up to the last."

"But they've done something to deserve death," he said.

"Not always; sometimes they fall into that three-strikes law for vampires. It's written so that no matter what the crime is, even a misdemeanor, three times and you get a warrant of execution on your ass. I don't like killing people for stealing when there's no violence involved."

"But stealing big items, right?"

"No, Sheriff, one woman got executed for stealing less than a thousand dollars of shit. She was a diagnosed kleptomaniac before becoming a vampire; dying didn't cure her like she thought it would."

"Someone put a stake through her heart for petty theft?"

"They did," I said.

"The law doesn't give the preternatural branch of the marshal program a right to refuse jobs."

"Technically, no, but I just don't do the stakedowns. I had stopped doing them before the vampire executioners got grandfathered into the U.S. Marshal program."

"And they let you."

"Let's say I have an understanding with my superiors." The understanding had been that I wouldn't testify on behalf of the family of the woman executed for shoplifting if they simply wouldn't make me kill anyone who hadn't taken lives. A life for a life made some sense. A life for some costume jewelry made no sense to me. A lot of us had turned down the woman. In the end they'd had to send to Washington, DC, for Gerald Mallory, who was one of the first vampire hunters ever who was still alive. He still thought all vampires were evil monsters, so he'd staked her without a qualm. Mallory sort of scared me. There was something in his eyes when he looked at any vampire that wasn't quite sane.

"Marshal, are you still there?"

"I'm sorry, Sheriff, you got me thinking too hard about the shoplifter."

"It's in the news that the family is suing for wrongful death."

"They are."

"You don't talk much, do you?"

"I say what needs saying."

"You're damn quiet for a woman."

"You don't need me to talk. I assume you need me to come to Vegas and do my job."

"It's a trap, Blake. A trap just for you."

"Probably, and sending me the head of your executioner is about as direct as a threat gets."

"And you're still going to come?"

I stood up and looked down at the box and the head staring up at me. It looked somewhere between surprised and sleepy. "He mailed me the head of your vampire executioner. He mailed it to my office. He wrote a message to me in the blood on the wall where he slaughtered three of your operators. Hell, yes, I'm coming to Vegas."

"You sound angry."

In my head I thought, *Better angry than scared.* If I could stay outraged, maybe I could keep the fear from growing. Because it was there in the pit of my stomach, in the back of my mind like a black, niggling thought that would grow bigger if I let it. "Wouldn't you be pissed?"

"I'd be scared."

That stopped me, because cops almost never admit that they're scared. "You broke the rule, Shaw, you never admit you're scared."

"I just want you to know, Blake, really know, what you're walking into, that's all."

"It must have been bad."

"I've seen more men dead at one time. Hell, I've lost more men under my command."

"You must be ex-military," I said.

"I am," he said.

I waited for him to say what service; most would, but he didn't.

"Where were you stationed?" I asked.

"Classified, most of it."

"Ex–special teams?" I made it part question, part statement.

"Yes."

"Do I ask what flavor, or just let it drop, before you have to threaten me with the old if-I-tell-you-then-I-have-to-kill-you routine?" I tried for a joke, but Shaw didn't take it that way.

"You're making a joke. If you can do that, then you don't get what's happening."

"You've got three operators dead, one vamp executioner dead and cut up; that *is* bad, but you didn't send just three operators in with the marshal, so most of your team got away, Sheriff."

"They didn't get away," he said, and something in his voice made that tight, black pit of fear rise a little higher in my gut.

"But they're not dead," I said, "or you'd say so."

"No, not dead, not exactly."

"Are they badly hurt?"

"Not exactly," he said.

"Stop beating the bush to death and just tell me, Shaw."

"Seven of our men are in the hospital. There's not a mark on them. They just dropped."

"If there are no marks on them, why did they drop, and why are they in the hospital?"

"They're asleep."

"What?"

"You heard me."

"You mean comas?"

"The doctors say no. They're asleep; we just can't wake them up."

"Do the docs have any clues?"

"The only thing close to this is those patients in the twenties who all went to sleep and never woke up."

"Didn't they make a movie years back about them waking up?"

"Yes, but it didn't last, and they still don't know why that form of sleeping sickness is different from the norm," he said.

"Your whole team didn't just catch this sleeping thing in the middle of a firefight."

"You asked what the doctors said."

"Now, I'm asking what you say."

"One of our practitioners says it was magic."

"Practitioners?" I made it a question.

"We've got psychics attached to our teams, but can't call them our pet wizards."

"So operators and practitioners," I said.

"Yes."

"So someone did a spell?"

"I don't know, but apparently it all reeks of psychic shit, and when you run out of explanations that make sense, you go with what you got."

"When you've eliminated the impossible, whatever remains, however improbable, must be the truth," I said.

"Did you just quote Sherlock Holmes at me?"

"Yeah."

"Then you still don't get it, Blake. You just don't."

"Okay, let me be blunt here. Something about my reaction wasn't what you expected, so you're convinced that I don't get the seriousness of the situation. You're ex–special teams, which means to you, women are not going to measure up. You've called me a beautiful woman, and that, too, makes most cops and military underestimate women. But special teams, hell, you don't think most other military men are up to your level, or most cops. So I'm a girl; get over it. I'm petite and I clean up well; get over that, too. I'm dating a vampire, the master of my city; so what? It has nothing to do with my job or why Vittorio invited me to come hunt him in Vegas."

"Why did he run in St. Louis? Why didn't he run here when

he knew we were coming? Why did he ambush our men and not yours?"

"Maybe he couldn't afford to lose that many of his vampires again, or maybe he's just decided to make his last stand in your city."

"Lucky fucking us."

"Yeah."

"I called around, talked to some of the other cops you've worked with, and some of the other vampire executioners, about you. You want to know why some of them thought this vampire ran in St. Louis?"

"I'm all ears."

"You, they thought he ran from you. Our Master of the City told me that the vampires call you the Executioner—that they've called you that for years."

"Yeah, that's their pet name for me."

"Why you? Why you, and not Gerald Mallory? He's been around longer."

"He's been around years longer than me, but I've got the higher body count. Think about it."

"How can you have the higher body count if he's been doing this for at least ten years longer than you?"

"One, he's a stake-and-hammer man. He refuses to go to silver ammo and guns. That means he has to totally incapacitate the vampires before he can kill them. Totally incapacitating a vampire is really hard to do. I can wound one, bring it down from a distance. Two, I think his hatred of vampires makes him less effective when hunting them. It makes him miss clues and not think things through."

"So you just kill them better than anyone else."

"Apparently."

"I'll be honest, Blake, I'd feel better if you were a guy. I'd feel even better if you had some military background. I've checked you out; other than a few hunting trips with your dad, you'd never handled a gun before you started killing monsters. You'd never owned a handgun at all."

"We were all newbies once, Shaw. But trust me, the new is all worn off of me."

"Our Master of the City is cooperating fully with us."

"I'll just bet he is."

"He says bring you to Vegas, and you'll sort it out."

That stopped me. Maximillian, Max, had met me only once, when he came to town with some of his weretigers after an unfortunate metaphysical accident. The unfortunate accident had ended with me pretty much possessing one of his were-tigers, Crispin. He'd taken Crispin back to Vegas with him, but it wasn't because the tiger wanted to leave me. He was disturbingly devoted to me. It wasn't my fault, honest, but the damage was still done. Lately, some of the powers I'd gained as Jean-Claude's human servant seemed to translate into attracting metaphysical men. Vampires, wereanimals, so far just that, but it was enough. Some days it was too much. I didn't remember doing anything that impressive when Max was visiting.

I'd spent most of his visit trying to be a good little human servant for Jean-Claude, and whatever became mine, like a weretiger, became my master's, too. We'd done some fairly disturbing metaphysics, my master and I, for our guest's benefit. We'd left him kind of creeped, unless he was way more bisexual than he'd ever admit.

"Blake, you still there?"

"I'm here, Shaw, just thinking about your Master of the City. I'm flattered that he thinks I can sort it out."

"You should be. He's old-time mob. Don't take this wrong, but if you think my opinion of women is low, then old-time mobsters think worse."

"Yeah, yeah, you just think women can't cut it on the job. Mobsters think we're just for making babies or fucking."

He made another laugh sound. "You are one blunt son of a bitch."

I took it for the compliment it was; he hadn't called me a daughter of a bitch. If I could get him to treat me like one of the guys, I could do my job.

"I am probably one of the most blunt people you will ever meet, Shaw."

"I'm beginning to believe that."

"Believe it, warn the other guys. It'll save time."

"Warn them about what, that you're blunt?"

"All of it—-blunt, a girl, pretty, dates vampires, whatever. Get it out of their system before I hit the ground in Vegas. I don't want to have to wade through macho bullshit to do my job."

"Nothing I can do about that, Blake. You'll have to prove yourself to them, just like any . . . officer."

"Woman, you were going to say *woman*. I know how it works, Shaw. Because I'm a girl, I gotta be better than the guys to get the same level of respect. But with three men dead in Vegas and seven more in some sort of a spell, ten dead here in St. Louis, five in New Orleans, two in Pittsburgh, I'd like to think your officers will be more interested in catching this bastard than giving me a hard time."

"They're motivated, Blake, but you're still a beautiful woman and they're still cops."

I ignored the compliment because I never knew what to do with it. "And they're scared," I said.

"I didn't say that."

"You didn't have to; you're special teams and you admitted it. If it's spooked you, then it's sure as hell spooked the rest. They're going to be jumpy and looking for someone to blame."

"We blame the vampires that killed our people."

"Yeah, but I'm still going to be the whipping boy for some of them."

"What makes you say that?"

"The message on the wall was for me. The head came to me. You already asked me what I did to piss Vittorio off. Some of your people are going to say that I pissed him off enough to make him do all this, or maybe even that he did it all to impress me in that sweet serial killer sort of way."

Shaw was quiet, only his thick breathing on the phone. I didn't prompt him, just waited, and finally he said, "You're a bigger cynic than I am, Blake."

"Do you think I'm wrong?"

He was quiet for a breath or two more. "No, Blake, I don't think you're wrong. I think you're exactly right. My men are spooked, and they'll want someone to blame. This vampire has made sure that the police here in Vegas will have mixed feelings about you."

"What you need to ask yourself, Shaw, is did he do it on purpose, to make my job harder, or did he not give a damn about the effect it had on you and your men?"

"You know him better than I do, Blake. Which is it—on purpose, or didn't give a damn?"

"I don't know this vampire, Shaw. I know his victims, and the vampires he left behind for killing. I thought he'd resurface because most of these guys can't stop once they get to a certain level of violence. It's like a drug, and they are addicted. But I never dreamed he'd send me presents or special messages. I honestly didn't think I'd made that big an impression on him."

"We'll show you the crime scene when you land. Trust me, Blake, you made an impression on him."

"Not the impression I wanted to make," I said.

"And what was that?"

"A hole in his head, and a hole in his heart big enough to see daylight through."

"I'll help you do it."

"I didn't think undersheriffs did fieldwork."

"For this one, I'll make an exception. When can you get here?"

"I'll have to check the airline schedule, and I'll have to check the regulations for my vampire kit. Seems like the rules change every time I have to fly."

"Our marshal didn't carry anything special on him that you couldn't get on a plane with if you've passed the air marshal test."

I thought to myself, *Maybe that's why he's dead*. Out loud, I said, "I'm bringing phosphorus grenades if I can get them on the plane."

"Phosphorus grenades, no shit."

"No shit."

"They work on vampires?"

"They work on everything, Shaw, and water makes them burn hotter."

"You ever seen a man dive into water, thinking it will put it out, but it just flares?" Shaw asked.

I had a sudden picture in my head of a ghoul that had run through a stream trying to get away. He, or one of his pack, had killed a homeless man who'd fallen asleep in the cemetery where the ghouls had come out of the graves. They'd never have attacked him awake, but they still ate him, and that still earned them an extermination. I'd just been backup for a flamethrower team of exterminators. But ghouls that are brave enough to attack and kill the living rather than just scavenge the dead can turn deadly. Which means you don't send civilians in without badges to back them. It'd been the first time I'd used the grenades. They worked better than anything I'd ever used on ghouls. When they go bad, they are as strong as a vampire, faster and stronger than a zombie, immune to silver bullets, and almost impossible to kill with anything but fire. "I saw some run through a stream. The phosphorus flared up around them like a hot, white aura everywhere the water splashed. So bright, the water sparked in the light."

"And the men screamed for a long time," Shaw said.

"Yeah, ghouls, but yeah, they did." I heard my voice utterly cold. I couldn't afford to feel anything yet.

"I thought modern phosphorus didn't do all that," he said.

"Everything old is new again," I said.

"I'm beginning to see why the vampires think you're scary, Blake."

"The grenades aren't what make me scary, Shaw."

"What does?" he asked.

"That I'm willing to use them."

"It's not being willing to use them, Blake. It's being willing to use them again."

I thought about that, and finally said, "Yeah."

"Call me when you have your flight arranged." His voice was unhappy with me, as if I'd said something else that wasn't what he wanted to hear.

"I'll let you know as soon as I know. Give me your direct number, if you're my go-to guy."

He sighed loud enough for me to hear it. "Yeah, I'm your

go-to guy." He gave me his extension and his cell phone number. "We're not going to wait for you, Blake. If we can catch these bastards, we will."

"The warrant of execution died with your vampire executioner, Shaw. If you guys kill them without me or another executioner with you, then you'll be looking at charges."

"If we find them, and we hesitate, they'll kill us."

"I know that."

"So what are you telling me to do?"

"I'm reminding you of the law."

"What if I said I don't need a fucking executioner to remind me of the law?"

"I'll be there as soon as I can. I have a friend with a private plane. That's probably the fastest way to get to you."

"Your friend, or your master?"

"What did I say to piss you off, Shaw?"

"I'm not sure; maybe you just reminded me of something I didn't want to remember. Maybe you just made sure I know what may have to happen in my town before this is over."

"If you want pretty lies, you have the wrong marshal."

"I heard that about you, that and that you'll fuck anything that moves."

Yeah, I'd pissed him off. "Don't worry, Shaw, your virtue is safe."

"Why, not pretty enough for you?"

"Probably not, but I don't do cops."

"What *do* you do?"

"Monsters." I hung up. I shouldn't have. I should have explained the rumors, and how it wasn't true, and how I had never let sex interfere in a case, much. But there comes a point when you just get tired of explaining yourself. And, let's face it, you can't prove a negative. I couldn't prove I didn't sleep around. I could only do my job to the best of my ability and try to stay alive, oh, and try to keep everyone else alive. And kill the bad vampires. Yeah, mustn't forget that part.

I had other phone calls to make before I could leave town. Cell phones are wonderful things. First call was to Larry Kirkland, fellow U.S. Marshal and vampire executioner. He answered his own cell phone on the second ring. "Hey, Anita, what's up?" He still sounds young and fresh, but in the four years we'd known each other, he'd acquired his first scars, along with a wife and baby, and was still the main person for the morgue stakings. He had also refused to kill the shoplifter. In fact, he'd been the one who called me from the morgue to ask what the hell to do about it. He's about my height, with bright red hair that would curl if he didn't cut it so short, freckles, the works. He looks like he should be going out with Tom Sawyer to play tricks on little Becky, but he's stood shoulder to shoulder with me in some bad places. If he had one fault, other than that I wasn't entirely a fan of his wife, it was that he wasn't a shooter. He still thought more like a cop than an assassin, and sometimes that wasn't good in our line of work. Oh, and what did I have against his wife, Detective Tammy Reynolds? She didn't approve of my choices in boyfriends, and she kept wanting to convert me to her sect of Christianity, which was a little too Gnostic for me. In fact, it was one of the last Gnostic-based forms of Christianity to have survived the early days of the church. It allowed for witches, read psychics in this case. Tammy thought I'd be a fine Sister of the Faith. Larry was now a Brother of the Faith, since he, like me, could raise zombies from the grave. It's not evil if you're doing it for the church.

"I've got to fly to Vegas on a warrant."

"You need me to cover while you're gone?" he made it a question.

"Yep."

"Then you're covered," he said.

I thought about giving him more details, but I was afraid he'd want to come with me. Endangering myself was one thing, endangering Larry was another. Part of it was that he was married and had a baby; the other part was that I just felt protective of him. He was only a few years younger than me, but there was something still soft about him. I valued that, and feared it. Soft either goes away in our business or gets you killed.

"Thanks, Larry. I'll see you when I get back."

"Be careful," he said.

"Aren't I always?"

He laughed. "No."

We hung up. He'd be pissed when he learned the details about Vegas. Pissed that I hadn't confided in him, and pissed that I was still protecting him. But pissed I could live with; dead, I wasn't sure about.

I also called New Orleans. Their local vampire hunter, Denis-Luc St. John, had made me promise that if Vittorio ever resurfaced I'd give him a chance to get a piece of the hunt. St. John had almost been one of Vittorio's victims. Months in the hospital and rehab after had made him pretty adamant about helping kill the vampire that put him through all that.

It was a woman's voice on the other end of the phone, which surprised me. To my knowledge, St. John didn't have a wife. "I'm sorry, I'm not sure I have the right number. I'm looking for Denis-Luc St. John."

"Who is this?" the woman asked.

"U.S. Marshal Anita Blake."

"The vampire executioner," and she made it sound like a bad thing.

"Yes."

"I'm Denis-Luc's sister." She said *Denis-Luc* with an accent I couldn't match.

"Hi, could I speak to your brother?"

"He's out, but I'll give him a message."

"Okay." I told her about Vittorio.

"You mean the vampire that nearly killed him?" she asked.

"Yes," I said.

"Why would you even call him?" Her voice was definitely hostile now.

"Because he made me promise that if this vampire resurfaced I would call him and given him another crack at it."

"That sounds like my brother." Again, she didn't sound happy about it.

"Will you give him the message?"

"Sure." Then she hung up on me.

I wasn't sure I believed that the sister would give him the message, but it was the only number I had for St. John. I could have called the local police and probably gotten a message to him, but what if I did, and this time Vittorio killed him? What would I say to his sister then? I left it in her hands. If she gave him the message, fine; if she didn't, then not my bad. Either way, I'd kept my promise and wouldn't be getting him killed. It seemed like a win-win to me.

3

IN THE MOVIES, you always see the hero just getting on a plane and going off to fight the bad guys; in reality, you've got to pack first. Clothes I could probably have bought in Vegas, but the weapons . . . those I needed.

Home, for the moment, was underneath the Circus of the Damned. Sort of like the old idea of a store owner living above his shop, except when you're shacking up with a vampire, windows are bad; cavernous underground, good. Besides, it was also one of the most defensible places in all of St. Louis. When your vampire sweetie is also the Master of the City, you have to worry about defense. Not humans anymore, but other vampires wanting to take a bite of your action. Okay, once it had been a group of rogue shapeshifters, but the problem was the same. Monsters outside the law were as dangerous as humans outside it, but with more skills.

Which was why I knew there were guards watching me as I parked and went to the back door. I always had to resist the urge to wave. It was supposed to be a secret that they were watching, so waving was out.

My cell phone rang as I was digging out my keys for the back door. The music had changed again; now it was "Wild Boys" by Duran Duran. Nathaniel found it amusing that I couldn't figure out how to program my own ring tone, so he changed it periodically without warning. Apparently, this was my default ring tone now. Boys.

"Blake here."

The voice on the other end of the phone stopped me dead in the parking lot. "Anita, it's Edward."

Edward was an assassin who specialized in killing monsters because humans had become too easy. As Ted Forrester he was a U.S. Marshal and fellow vampire executioner. By any name he was one of the most efficient killers I'd ever met. "What's wrong, Edward?"

"Nothing on my end, but I hear you're having a hell of an interesting time."

I stood there in the summer's heat, keys dangling from my hand, and was scared. "What are you talking about, Edward?"

"Tell me you were going to call and have me meet you in Vegas. Tell me you weren't going to hunt this one without inviting me to come play."

"How the hell did you know about it?" Once upon a time, not that long ago, if anyone died, especially spectacularly, Edward was a good bet for it. I had a moment to wonder if he knew more about Vegas than I did.

"I'm a U.S. Marshal, too, remember?"

"Yeah, but I only found out less than an hour ago. How did you rate a call, and from whom?"

"They killed one of our own, Anita. Cops take that hard." In one sentence he'd said *our own* and then talked about the police like he wasn't one. Edward was like me; we had a badge, but sometimes we didn't quite fit.

"How did you find out about it, Edward?"

"You sound suspicious."

"Don't fuck with me, just talk to me."

He took in a deep breath, let it out. "Fair enough. I live in New Mexico, remember? It isn't that far from Nevada. They'll probably call up all the western-state executioners."

"How did you know to call me?" I asked.

"They're only holding the message back from the media, not from other marshals."

"So, you know about the writing on the wall; that's why you called me." The question was, did he know about the head? How good were his sources these days? Once he'd been like a mysterious guru to me. All-knowing, all-seeing, and better at everything than I was.

"You telling me that you aren't going to fly to Vegas to hunt this bastard?"

"No, I'm definitely going."

"There's something you're not telling me," he said.

I leaned against the side of the building and said, "You know about the head?"

"That the vampires took the head of Las Vegas's executioner, yeah. I've been wondering why they took his head. They're vampires, not ghouls or a rogue zombie. They don't eat flesh."

"Even ghouls that cache food almost never take the head. They prefer meatier bits."

"You've seen ghoul food caches?" he asked.

"Once," I said.

He gave a small laugh. "Sometimes I forget that about you."

"What?"

"That you are one of the only people who run into weirder shit than I do sometimes."

"I don't know whether to be insulted, flattered, or scared," I said.

"Flattered," he said, and I knew he meant it.

"They didn't take the head for eating," I said.

"You know what happened to it?"

"Yep."

"What, I need to ask?"

I sighed. "No," and I told him about the little present I'd gotten at work this morning.

He was quiet for so long that I continued talking. "We're just lucky it came in on the only morning that I do client meetings all day. God knows what Bert, my business manager, would have done with it if I hadn't been there to make him wait for forensics."

"You really think it was coincidence that the package got there on the only morning that you'd be in?" Edward said.

I leaned a little harder against the wall, clutching the cell phone with one hand and my keys with the other. I suddenly felt exposed out there in the parking lot, because I understood exactly what Edward meant.

"You think Vittorio's been monitoring me. That he knows my schedule." I looked out into the daylit parking lot. There was no place to hide. Daylight meant there weren't that many cars. I had this sudden desire to be inside, out of sight.

I put my key in the door and used my shoulder to hold the phone while I opened the door.

"Yes," he said. That was Edward: high on truth, low on comfort.

I spilled in through the door and got it closed behind me before the two guards inside could do much more than push themselves off the wall. They were both in black T-shirts and jeans, only the guns and holsters ruining the casual look. They tried to talk to me, and I waved at them that I was on the phone. They went back to holding up their section of wall, and I went for the far door. The door was one of only two ways into the underground area where Jean-Claude and his vampires slept. It was why we had two guards in the storage room at all times. Boring duty, which meant they were two of the newer hires; I remembered that one of them was Brian, but for the life of me I couldn't remember the other one's name.

"Anita, you still there?" Edward asked.

"Give me a minute to find some privacy."

I opened the door leading down and closed it behind me. I was standing at the head of stone steps that led down and down. I kept one hand on the wall as I started down. High heels were not meant for these steps. Hell, they seemed carved for something that didn't walk quite like a human being at all. Something bigger than a person, with different legs maybe.

"Vittorio wouldn't have come back to St. Louis," I said.

"Probably not, but you know better than most vampire hunters that the vampires have other resources."

"Yeah, I'm Jean-Claude's human servant, so Vittorio could have one, too."

"Hell, Anita, he could have humans with just a couple of bites. You know that once a vampire uses its gaze on someone and does the whole bite thing, they'll do anything for their master."

"I wouldn't sense a human with a few bites on them. They hit the radar as just human."

"So, yeah, I think you've been spied on. I'd tell you not to come, Anita, but I know you won't listen."

I stumbled on the steps and had to catch my balance before I said, "You honestly would tell me to stay home on this one?

You, who are always inviting me out to hunt bigger and badder monsters?"

"This one's made it personal, Anita. He wants your head."

"Thanks for that imagery, after my little present this morning."

"I said it on purpose, Anita. You're like me now; you've got people you love, and you don't want to leave them. I'm just reminding you, like you remind me, that you really do have a choice. You can sit this one out."

"You mean stay safe in St. Louis while the rest of you guys hunt this bastard?"

"Yes."

"And you can tell me, honestly, that you wouldn't think less of me for playing it that safe?"

He didn't answer for so long that I was almost at the blind corner turn at the halfway point of the stairs. I didn't prompt him. I just listened to him breathe and concentrated on my heels on the uneven stones.

"I wouldn't blame you for staying home."

"But you would think less of me," I said.

He was quiet. "I'd try not to."

"Yeah, and the rest of the cops who already think I'm a girl, and that I'm sleeping with vampires, and that I'm sleeping around with other cops, they wouldn't think less of me?"

"Don't get yourself killed because of pride, Anita. That's a guy reason to die. You're a girl; think like a girl for once."

"Edward, if they've been watching me in St. Louis, I may not be safe here, either."

"Maybe, or maybe he's luring you out, Anita. Maybe he would have come back to St. Louis for you, but with all the people Jean-Claude has around him he couldn't get to you."

I walked around the corner, thinking about that. "Shit, I hope you're wrong about that."

"You knew it was a trap, Anita."

"Yeah, but knowing Vittorio is throwing down the gauntlet in Vegas is one thing. Believing that he's picked somewhere far away so I'll be away from Jean-Claude and his guards is . . . frightening."

"Good, I want you scared on this one, because you should be."

"What's that supposed to mean?"

"It means Vittorio has been watching you, or having someone else do it. He sent the head on a day you'd be there. He sent it early in the morning before your vampire lover will be awake, so no one can tell you to take guards, or not to go. In St. Louis, if Jean-Claude is still down for the day, you're in charge."

"We've been working really hard at making me more human servant and Jean-Claude more master."

"Yeah, so hard that you've moved into the Circus with him. The other marshals don't think much of you shacking up with the master of your city."

"Prejudiced bastards." I was at the big cell-like door that led into the underground proper.

"I also heard that Jean-Claude and your boyfriends have come out of the closet. I take it that the idea that Jean-Claude is fucking you and your boyfriends was to explain why he was letting you fuck other men."

"We told the vampire community that, not the marshals. How do they know all this?"

"You aren't the only one who's a little close with their local vampires, Anita."

"I've met your local vampires, and I know that you are not talking to Obsidian Butterfly. She's so scary that the worldwide vampire community has made Albuquerque, New Mexico, off limits."

"I live in Santa Fe."

"Yeah, and it's still too close to Obsidian Butterfly and her group. It's why you have to travel out of state to hunt vampires; your local master is too scary to share."

"She thinks she's an Aztec goddess, Anita. Gods don't share."

"She's a vampire, Edward, but she may actually be what the Aztecs worshipped under her name."

"She's still a vampire, Anita."

"I don't like the tone in your voice, Edward. Promise me if

you ever get a warrant of execution against her or any of her vampires that you'll let me come help."

"You'd have flown to Vegas without me."

"Maybe, or maybe getting a human head in a box was weird even for me. Maybe I am afraid of Vittorio, and I don't like running into a trap like some rabbit. Maybe I just hadn't had time to think to call you."

"That's a lot of *maybe*s, Anita."

"I may lose the phone signal if I go any farther underground, Edward, but I have to pack, so . . ."

"It's a shorter flight for me to Vegas, so I'll see you on the ground."

"Edward," I said.

"Yeah."

"Do you really think Vittorio planned me to have to fly to Vegas before Jean-Claude could be awake to argue with me, or make me take guards?"

"I don't know, but if he did plan it this way, then he's afraid of your guards. He's afraid of you with Jean-Claude. He's afraid of you with all your shapeshifter friends. But he's not as afraid of you on your own."

"I won't be on my own," I said.

"No, you won't be," he said.

"I don't mean just you, Edward. Vittorio killed police officers. I don't think he understands how serious that can be."

"We'll explain it to him," Edward said, voice gone empty of accent, empty of almost anything. It was the voice that he used when he was at his most deadly.

"Yes," I said, "we will."

Edward hung up.

I hung up and went through the door into Jean-Claude's living room.

4

TWO OF MY lovers were dead in the bed that we all shared. They'd be alive again later in the day, or earlier in the night, but for now, Jean-Claude and Asher truly were dead. I'd touched enough dead bodies to know that sleep does not mimic death. There is a looseness, an emptiness, to the dead that not even coma can imitate.

I stared down at them. They lay in a tangle of white silk sheets. Jean-Claude all black curls and that beautiful face; a line less or more, and he'd have been too beautiful, too feminine, but you never looked into his face and thought *girl*. No, he was all male no matter how pretty he looked. It helped that he was naked on top of the sheets. Nude, there was no mistaking him for anything but oh so male.

Asher's golden waves spilled across his face, hiding one of the most perfect profiles that had ever existed. I had some memories from the vampire who had made him: Belle Morte, Beautiful Death. She was over two thousand years old, and she still thought that his left profile was the most perfect she'd ever seen in a man. His right profile was marred, in her eyes, by the acidlike scars of the holy water that the Church had used to try to burn the devil out of him. The scars didn't take up that much of his face, just from midcheek to chin on one side. His mouth was still as kissable, his face still had that heartrending beauty, but to Belle, the scars had covered everything.

His neck was untouched, but from chest to groin to part of the thigh, the right side of his body was covered in the holy water scars. It looked as if the flesh had melted and partially reformed, like wax. The skin was textured differently from the unscarred half of him, but it wasn't ruined. He could still feel my touch, still be licked and caressed, and bitten. It was just different. It was Asher, and I loved him.

It wasn't the same way I loved Jean-Claude, but I'd learned that love could mean many things, and no matter how similar it looked from the outside, inside it could feel very different. Good still, but different.

I was packed, though I was going to get some of the bodyguards to help carry the equipment bags of weapons up the stairs for me. I needed to get to the airport and the jet that was fueled and waiting for me. I wanted to be on the ground in Vegas while it was still daylight. If Vittorio had intended to get me out of St. Louis before Jean-Claude could wake and maybe insist on guards going with me, then fine, I'd get to Vegas while Vittorio was still dead to the world, too. It was the great leveler, that vampires were helpless during the day. I would take every advantage of it that I could. Of course, Vittorio knew that about me, if he'd been spying on me. The thought that he probably had daylight eyes and ears waiting for me in Vegas wasn't comforting.

I stared down at the two vampires and wished that I could have said good-bye.

The bathroom door opened and Jason came out, wearing a robe that he hadn't bothered to tie shut, but he'd been completely nude between the two vampires when I'd first entered the room. Besides, it wasn't like I hadn't seen it all before. He was Jean-Claude's *pomme de sang*, his apple of blood, sort of part kept woman and part morning snack. Most people didn't actually fuck their *pommes de sang*, and Jean-Claude didn't either, but Jason's reputation had fallen to the need to make our shared master look more powerful in the eyes of the larger vampire community. He was also going to have the fun job of telling Jean-Claude where I was and what I was doing when the vampire woke.

Jason was my height, maybe an inch more, short for a man and I guess short for a woman. His blond hair was to his shoulders now. He'd started letting it grow back out, though truthfully he was one of the few men I thought actually looked better with the short executive haircut. But I was just his good friend and lover, not his girlfriend, so his hair length was his own business.

He smiled at me, his spring-blue eyes shining with some joke that only he knew. Then the look changed, from joking to serious to . . . I was just suddenly aware that he was naked, and the robe was covering precious little, and . . .

"Stop it, Jason," I said, softly. I don't know why you always whisper around sleeping vampires, as if they were truly asleep, but you do; unless you stop yourself, you treat the ones you know like they can hear you and you don't want to disturb them.

"Stop what?" he asked, in a voice that was a little lower than it needed to be. I couldn't have told you what he was doing differently with his walk, but he suddenly made me aware that his day job was as a stripper.

"What's with the serious flirting, Jason? You know I don't have time for it."

He came to the end of the bed, and I had to either back up or stand my ground while he flirted. Backing up seemed cowardly, and once I could have withstood Jason's attentions, but since I'd accidentally made him my werewolf to call, he seemed to have more pull on my libido. He didn't usually take advantage of it, so why was he upping the heat now?

I stood my ground, but was almost painfully aware of how close he was to me. "You know Jean-Claude is going to go apeshit when he wakes up," he said.

"Jean-Claude never goes apeshit."

"Vittorio has set a trap for you, Anita. You're walking into it." He was behind me now, so close that the edges of his robe brushed against the back of my body.

"Jason, please, I have to go," and this time I didn't whisper so as not to wake the vampires. I whispered because it was the best I could do. One of the real downsides to moving into the Circus and living with all the men who were tied to me metaphysically was that all of them seemed to be gaining power—power over me. Jean-Claude I could understand; he was the Master of the City. Asher even, because he was a master vampire. But Jason was a werewolf, a blood donor, and my wolf to call. I should have been master here, and I wasn't.

He moved around me, so close, so very close, so that not having our bodies touch took more effort than just closing that small distance. I kept one hand on the bedpost like it was my anchor to reality. He stood in front of me, his eyes a little below mine because I was still in the heels.

"Then go," he whispered.

I swallowed hard but didn't move away. I had a moment to wonder if I could move away, and the thought was enough. I closed my eyes and stepped back. I could do this. It was Jason, not Jean-Claude; I could do this.

Jason caught my arms. "Don't go."

"I have to go." But having to keep my eyes closed took a lot of the punch out of the statement.

He pulled my hands in toward his body, so that I touched the muscled smoothness of his stomach. He put one hand to his groin, and he was already happier to be near me than last I'd looked. He filled my hand, and he was thick and perfect again. Two months ago, some very bad men had captured the both of us. They'd tortured him with cigarettes, fire, the only thing a lycanthrope can't heal. They'd marked up a very nice body and damn near killed him.

My hands slid over him, under the robe, so I held him close, feeling how very naked he was, in my arms. I held him, and he held me back. I held him and remembered holding him while he bled. Holding him while I thought he was dying.

His voice was normal, not seductive, when he said, "Anita, I'm sorry."

I drew back enough to see his face. "Sorry you tried to use your new powers over me to get me to stay home?"

He grinned. "Yeah, but I do like you admiring the newly healed me."

"I'm just glad that Doc Lillian figured out that if they cut away the burned bits you'd heal on your own."

"I'm just glad they found anesthesia that worked on our faster metabolism. I would not have wanted that much of me cut away without being put under."

"Agreed."

"You know, they're talking about trying to cut away some of Asher's scars and see if he heals on his own."

"He's a vampire, not a shapeshifter, Jason. Vampire flesh doesn't heal quite the same."

"You can heal fresh wounds on all sorts of dead flesh, including vampires."

"That's fresh wounds, Jason, and never a burn."

"Maybe if the doctor cuts away the scars, it'll count as a fresh wound, then you could heal him."

"And what if it doesn't work? What if Doc Lillian cuts away part of Asher and I can't heal it, and it doesn't heal on its own? He just goes around with a big hole in his side, or wherever?"

"You know, we have to try."

I shook my head. "All I know for sure is I've got a plane to catch, and I need to call some guards down to help me carry up the weapons."

"You know, the guards are scared of you now."

"Yeah, they think I'm a succubus and I'll eat their souls."

"You feed off sex, Anita, and if you don't feed often enough, you die. That's pretty much the definition of *succubus*, isn't it?"

I frowned at him. "Thanks, Jason, that makes me feel *so* much better."

He grinned and shrugged. "Who are you going to feed on in Vegas?"

"There's Crispin," I said.

"You can't feed on one little weretiger for long."

"I can feed on anger now, remember?" I'd discovered that ability only recently. Jean-Claude couldn't do it, and neither could anyone in his bloodline, which meant if I were only gaining powers through him, I shouldn't have been able to do it either, but I could.

"You know, you haven't got that down to a science yet," he said.

"No, but it works."

"And whose anger are you going to feed on in Vegas?"

"I'll be hanging around with cops and suspects; please, we're an angry bunch."

"If you feed off them without their permission, it's illegal. I think it's even a felony."

"If I fed blood, yes, but the law hasn't caught up to the vamps who can feed through other things. If I fed on sex involuntarily, then it would be covered under the date-rape psychic and magic ability law, but if I feed on anger, it's a gray area."

"What if they find out? The cops already think you're one of us."

I thought about it, then shrugged. "Honestly, the way most warrants are worded, I'm sort of encouraged to use any metaphysical abilities in pursuit of the bad guys."

"I don't think feeding off them is what the warrant means," he said.

"No"—I smiled—"but it's the way it's written. The law is all about how it's written and how you can interpret it."

"What happened to the girl I met a few years back who believed in truth, justice, and the American way?"

"She grew up," I said.

His face softened. "Why do I feel like I should apologize on behalf of all the men in your life for that?"

"Don't flatter yourselves; the police helped toughen me up, too."

"You've only fed on anger a few times, and it's not usually as good a feeding as the *ardeur.*"

"Jean-Claude can divide my *ardeur* up among all of you while I'm gone. He's done it before when I've worked with the police."

"Yeah, but that's only a temporary measure, and it works better if you've had a really good feeding before he tries it."

"You offering?" I asked.

He gave me a wide grin. "And if I say yes, what then?"

"This is a trick to delay me until Jean-Claude wakes up, because you think with him awake I won't be able to just fly away."

"I think you have a hard enough time saying no to just little old me; if our master wakes and says, 'Don't go,' could you defy him?"

I was suddenly afraid. Because Jason was right; whatever was happening with me and the men, Jean-Claude was the hardest to resist. It was almost as if it hadn't been my necromancy that kept me safe from him controlling me but my lack of proximity. It was almost as if simply being too close to him too much of the time was wearing my resistance and my independence away.

"Thanks, Jason," I said.

He frowned. "For what?"

"Now I am going, because I don't know if I could go if he woke up and told me to stay. That's not cool. I'm a U.S. Marshal and a vampire executioner. I have to be able to do my job, or what am I?"

"You're Anita Blake, Jean-Claude's human servant, and the first true necromancer in a thousand years."

"Yeah, his pet necromancer." I went for the door to tell the guards to send more guards to help tote and fetch.

Jason called after me, "You're one of my best friends, and I'm afraid for you in Vegas."

I nodded, but didn't turn around just in case seeing one of my best friends nude made me change my mind. "I'm afraid, too, Jason—of Vegas, and Vittorio, but I'm beginning to be afraid to stay here." I wrapped my hand around the door handle and said, "When he's awake, when he looks at me, I'm having more and more trouble saying no. I'm losing myself, Jason."

"I'm your animal to call, Anita; touch me and you gain strength to resist other vampires."

"Problem is, Jason, that you're one of the people I'm losing myself to. It's not just Jean-Claude, it's all of you. I can fight one or two of you, but I can't fight six of you. I'm outnumbered."

I opened the door and told the black-shirted guards that I needed bellmen. I didn't go back into the bedroom. I didn't want to talk to Jason anymore, and I didn't want to gaze down at the bed with the two beautiful vampires in it. If I hadn't been convinced that Vittorio wanted to kill me and mail my head somewhere, I'd have looked forward to the trip to Vegas. I needed some distance between me and the men in my life.

5

THE PLANE LANDED in Vegas without me having hysterics. Brownie point for me. The really sad thing was that I flew better now if I had someone next to me, so while I was happy for some privacy, I also missed a boyfriend's hand to hold. I couldn't want to run away from them all *and* miss them, could I? I mean, that made no sense even to me.

St. Louis is hot, but Vegas is hotter. They can say it's a dry heat, but so is an oven. It was so hot that it took my breath away for a second. It was like my body just went, *You're joking, right?* No, unfortunately, we were not only serious, but we'd be hunting vampires in this heat. Great.

I slipped on sunglasses, as if that would make any difference to the heat, but it did help with the brightness.

The pilot was helping me unload my luggage when I spotted a big man in uniform coming our way. He had a few other uniforms at his back. They kept a respectful distance, and I didn't need to see the nameplate that read *Undersheriff* to make me guess it was Sheriff Shaw.

Shaw was a big guy, with a hand that swallowed mine when we shook. His eyes were lost to me behind mirrored sunglasses, but then my eyes were lost to him, too. Sunglasses may look cool, but they hide one of the best ways to decipher another person. People can lie with a lot of themselves, but eyes can give a lot away—sometimes not by what they show you but when they go their most hidden. You can judge a lot by what a person wants to hide. Of course, we were all standing in the middle of a desert, so maybe the glasses weren't for hiding anything, just for comfort.

"Fry and Reddick will get your bags," Shaw said. "You can drive ahead with me."

"Sorry, Sheriff, but once a warrant of execution is in effect and the hunt begins, I'm legally bound to keep my kit in sight, or secured by me, or with me watching, in an area out of sight of the general public."

"When did that change?" he asked.

It was Grimes who answered, "About a month ago."

I nodded at the lieutenant. "I'm impressed you know that."

He actually smiled. "We've been going in with our local executioner for a year. It's our job to know if the law has changed."

I nodded again. I didn't say out loud that a lot of police still treated the preternatural branch of the marshal service as a lesser unit, or maybe an embarrassment. I couldn't really blame the attitude; some of us were little better than assassins with badges, but the rest of us did our best.

"What caused the change?" Shaw asked.

I liked that he asked. Most wouldn't. I answered this time. "A vampire hunter in Colorado left his bag of tricks on the backseat of his car, where some teenage joyriders stole it. They probably had no idea what was in it, but they did sell the guns, and one of them was used in a holdup where there was a death."

Shaw looked at the heavy equipment bags. "You can't carry all that on a hunt. Some of those bags must weigh more than you do."

"I'll store them, then take what I need for the hunt. I'll get it down to a backpack and some weapons."

Grimes said, "We can store them at our place. We'll be with you when you serve the warrant, so you can come back and load up with us."

I nodded. "Sounds good."

Grimes gave me that smile again; I still wasn't sure if it was a real smile or his version of cop face. Some give a blank face, some give smiles, but all police have a face you cannot read. I might not even learn which it was on this visit, because the lieutenant would not be going in to help serve the warrant. He'd be back at the command center, commanding.

"Sonny will drive us back, then you can stow your gear." I wasn't sure who Sonny was, but I'd figure it out when someone got behind the wheel.

"I'll need to be taking Marshal Blake for debriefing," Shaw said.

"You want to ride with us, Sheriff?" Grimes asked.

Shaw seemed to think about it for a second or two. He took his hat off and wiped some of the sweat, showing that his haircut was shorter than the SWAT. He had what the marines call a high and tight, nearly shaved on the sides, and not much longer on top, as if he'd never left the service, or at least not its barbers.

"I'll follow you; let's just get out of the heat."

They all nodded, and I just waited for someone to move toward the car we'd be taking. I'd expected more speed when I hit the ground. Everyone was being way too calm, but then, so was I. Whatever we were feeling inside, outside it was all business. There'd be time for emotion later, maybe. Sometimes you keep putting off an emotional reaction until it just becomes moot. It becomes just one more thing that you couldn't afford to let yourself feel.

I picked up one of the big equipment bags and started to reach for another, but Rocco got there first. I let him get it. Hooper reached for the last bag, and I was okay with that, too. It was when Grimes started to reach for the bag I was carrying that we had problems.

"I've got it, Lieutenant, thanks."

We had a moment where he hesitated, and we looked at each other. I finally said, "You can get the luggage if you want."

He gave a little nod and went for the luggage. I learned that Hooper was Sonny, because he was the one who opened the back of an SUV. The back was full of his own equipment. His assault vest was visible, as well as two different helmets. There was a lot of stuff, but no guns were visible.

He answered as if I'd asked, "Gun safe." He moved the pile enough for me to see it.

"Aftermarket add-on?" I asked.

He nodded.

"I'll have to look into that. It would satisfy the new law, as written, and be a heck of a lot more convenient."

"We have to be ready to roll at any time."

"Me, too."

There was enough of his equipment already in there that adding my bags stuffed it full. Grimes joined us with my single suitcase in tow. "The pilot said this is all the luggage."

"It is," I said.

"Three bags, longer than you are tall, full of weapons, but only one suitcase for clothes," Rocco said.

"Yep," I said.

They all sort of nodded as they worked to find room for the suitcase in the back. I'd learned a long time ago that if you packed like a girl, you lost brownie points with the police. The idea was to try to be one of the guys; that meant you did not bring your entire wardrobe on a job. Besides, it was the continental United States; there'd be a mall somewhere if I ran out of clean clothes.

Hooper aka Sonny got in the driver's seat. Grimes rode shotgun. Highest rank usually rode in front, or in back. Depended on the officer. Sergeant Rocco got in beside me. The mound of weapons and bags seemed to sort of press in from behind, as if the potential for destruction could leak out of the bags, or maybe it was nerves? I knew I had grenades in the bags. Yes, Mr. Grenade is your friend until you press, pull, or otherwise activate it, but still, boomy and fiery things were fairly new for me to carry. Part of me didn't exactly trust it; no logic, just nervous. I didn't like explosives.

We pulled out, and Shaw was still standing there in his ring of uniformed officers. He'd been the one to suggest we get out of the heat, but he was still standing in it, watching me from behind his mirrored shades. I realized I'd never seen his eyes, not once. I guess, to be fair, he'd never seen mine.

"He does know we can still see him, right?" I said as we drove past.

"Yes," Grimes said, "why?"

"Because suddenly he looks unhappy."

"We lost men," Grimes said.

I looked at him and found that the pleasant face had slipped a little. Some of the pain that had to be in there showed around the edges. Pain, and that thin edge of anger that we all carry around with us.

"Nothing I can do will bring them back, but I will do everything I can to kill the vampire that did it."

"We're about saving lives, Marshal, not taking them," Grimes said.

I opened my mouth, closed it, and tried to say something that wouldn't upset him more. "I don't save lives, Lieutenant, I take them."

Rocco said, "Don't you believe that killing the vampires saves their future victims?"

I thought about it, then shook my head. "I used to, and it may even be true, but it just feels like I kill people."

"People," he said, "not monsters."

"Once I believed they were monsters."

"And now?" Rocco asked.

I shrugged and looked away. I was seeing a lot of empty land and the beginnings of strip malls. It might have been Vegas, but the landscape was more Anywhere, USA.

"Don't tell me the infamous Anita Blake is going soft?" This from Hooper.

Grimes said, "Hooper," in a voice that clearly meant he was in trouble with the boss.

Hooper didn't apologize. "You've told me my team is her go. I need to know, Lieutenant. We all need to know."

Rocco didn't so much as move or even wince; he went very still, as if he wasn't sure what was about to happen. Just that reaction from him let me know that they didn't question their looie much, if ever. That Hooper did it now showed just how upset they all were about the men they'd lost and the men in the hospital. That moment was Hooper's way of grieving.

I sat beside Rocco and let the weighted silence stretch in the truck. I was going to follow the sergeant's lead.

Grimes finally said, "You don't learn if you can trust someone from asking questions, Sonny."

"I know that, Lieutenant, but it's all we have time for."

I felt tension slide out of Rocco as he sat beside me. I took that as a good sign, and waited.

Grimes looked at me. "We can't ask if you've gone soft, Marshal. That would be rude, and I think you'd answer it the way any of us would: no."

I smiled and shook my head. "I'll kill your vampire for you, Grimes. I'll kill anyone who helps him. I'll kill everyone the warrant lets me kill. I'll get revenge for your men."

"We aren't about vengeance," Grimes said.

"I am," I said.

Grimes looked down at his one big hand where it lay on the seat. He raised brown eyes up to me then, face solemn. "We can't be about vengeance, Marshal Blake. We're the police. We're the good guys. Only the criminals get to do revenge. We uphold the law. Vengeance takes the law away."

I looked at him and saw that he meant it, down to the bottom of his eyes. "That is a brave and wonderful sentiment, Lieutenant, but I've held people I cared about while they died at the hands of these things. I've seen families destroyed." I shook my head. "Vittorio is evil, not because he's a vampire but because he's a serial killer. He takes pleasure in the death and pain of others. He will keep killing until we stop him. The law gives me the legal right to do the stopping. If you don't want it to be about revenge for your men, then that's your concern. He'll be dead no matter whose death I'm avenging."

"And whose death will you be avenging?" Hooper asked.

No one told him to stop this time.

I thought about it, and I had my answer. "Melbourne and Baldwin."

"The two SWAT you lost in St. Louis," Grimes said.

I nodded.

"Were you close to them?" he asked.

I shook my head. "Met them once."

"Why vengeance for two men you met once?" Rocco asked it, and there was the first trickle of energy from him. He'd lowered his psychic shields just a little. Was he an empath, wanting to read how I really felt?

The truck was pulling in, and Hooper was parking. I looked

into Rocco's dark eyes, darker than the lieutenant's. Rocco's were so dark, they almost crossed that line from brown to black. It made his pupils hard to find, like the eyes of a vampire when its power begins to fill its eyes, all color of the iris and no pupil.

"What flavor are you?"

"Flavor of what?" he asked.

"You're too tall to play coy, Sergeant."

He smiled. "I'm an empath."

I gave him narrow eyes, studying his face. His pulse had sped, just that tiny bit, some parting of the lips. I licked my bottom lip and said, "You taste like a lie."

"I am an empath." He stated it, very firm.

"And?" I said.

"And what?" he asked.

"An empath and . . ." I said.

We stared at each other in the backseat, the air growing thicker, heavier, as we peeled our shields down.

"Can we move this inside?" Grimes asked.

"Yes, sir," Rocco said.

"Sure," I said.

"Are you willing to have him read you?"

"Grimes said it, questions won't tell you if I'm for real, but something tells me that the part of Rocco here that's not empath will tell you a hell of a lot more."

"We want to know about the last time you hunted this vampire, Marshal. Are you ready to relive that?"

I didn't even look at Grimes; I just held that dark, steady gaze from my fellow psychic, because I knew something that the lieutenant probably didn't know about his sergeant. Rocco was eager to try me. It was part that male instinct to see who's the bigger dog, but it was more than that. His power was eager, as if it had an edge of hunger to it. I couldn't think of a polite way to ask if his psychic ability fed on the memories he collected. If it did, if he could, then I wasn't the only living vampire in Vegas.

6

ROCCO AND I slipped our shields back up the way others would have shrugged their jackets on. We were both professionals; nice.

Grimes told Hooper, "Take us in through the garage. The briefing room should be ready for the meeting."

Hooper pulled out of the parking spot and maneuvered around to a really big garage door. We drove the whole SUV inside, and suddenly I could see why the door was big.

I would say the garage was full of trucks, but the word didn't do them justice. I'd seen the equipment that St. Louis SWAT had, and I was suddenly filled with serious equipment envy.

We all got out. I noticed sort of peripherally that there was a carpeted exercise area to the left, but I mostly looked at the vehicles. I recognized the Lenco B.E.A.R., because St. Louis had one, but the rest were new to me. There were two smaller trucks that looked like the little brothers of the B.E.A.R., and probably were, but the rest of them, I had no idea. I mean, I could guess what they did, but I didn't know the names. They had one of the biggest RVs I'd ever seen. The vehicles alone were intimidating and strangely masculine. I know that most men talk about their favorite cars as if they were beautiful women, but there was nothing feminine about anything sitting in that garage.

"Marshal Blake," Grimes said, with some force to it.

I turned and looked at them, clustered and looking back at me. "Sorry, Lieutenant, but I just had a minute of equipment envy."

He smiled. "If there's time before you leave, we'd be happy to give you a tour."

"I'd appreciate it."

The garage door lowered. "Your weapons are secure in the back of Sonny's truck."

"Agreed," I said.

He motioned. "Briefing room then."

I nodded, and followed them around the edge of the exercise area. I noticed the beige storage lockers with locks against the wall. I was guessing weapons lockers, and eventually we'd lock up my stuff, but frankly, if the bad guys got in here, I was betting on us. The back of Sonny's truck was dandy.

The briefing room was a largish room with long tables and chairs in rows. There was a whiteboard at the front of the room. It was all very classroom. The six men waiting in the room for us didn't look like students, though. No one had called from the truck, so either Rocco was even more psychic than I thought, or they had planned on introducing me to their practitioners from the beginning. I couldn't decide if I felt ambushed or would have done the same thing in their place. Would I have trusted me?

They all had the same short haircuts as the rest, as if they went to the same barber, but I had Shaw's high and tight to compare them to, which meant they all had plenty of hair, it was just short. They were all tall, the shortest maybe five-ten, most six feet or above. They were all broad of shoulder, and the uniform couldn't hide that everyone worked out. But they were SWAT; either they stayed in shape or they lost their spot. The main difference between them all was the color of hair, eyes, and skin tone. Even just standing there, doing nothing, they were very much together, a unit, a team. Did I feel left out? Naw. Did I feel like I was the exhibit for show-and-tell day? A little.

Sergeant Rocco stepped into the room and introduced me. The lieutenant and Hooper stayed by the door, which was now closed. "This is Davis, Davey."

Davey was yellow-blond, with clear blue eyes and a cleft in his chin that helped frame a nice mouth. Should I have not noticed Davey's mouth? Probably.

I offered my hand; he took it and shook it nice and solid. Since his hand was at least twice the size of mine, it was nice that he didn't hesitate on the shake. Some big men have trouble with my small hands, as if they're afraid to break me. Davey seemed confident he wouldn't hurt me. Good.

"This is Mercer, Mercy."

Mercy had medium-brown hair and large, pale eyes that couldn't decide if they were blue or gray. Looking right at me as he shook my hand, they were blue, but it was an uncertain color, as if the light would change it. He had a good hand-shake, too. Maybe they all practiced.

The next man's hair was almost the same color, but it had more curl that even the short haircut couldn't hide completely. His eyes were a pure, solid milk-chocolate brown. There'd be no color change here.

When he was introduced as Rusterman, I'd have expected his nickname to be Rusty, but it wasn't. "Spider."

I fought the urge to ask, *Why Spider?* and let Rocco move me down the line. Next up was Sanchez, who matched the name, but still managed to look so much like all the other men that it was like looking at Army Man, now in new Hispanic. It wasn't just that they were all tall and athletic, but there was a sameness to them, as if whoever hired for the unit had a type he liked and stuck to it.

Sanchez's name was Arrio, and I wasn't sure if it was his real first name or another nickname. I didn't ask because, frankly, it didn't matter. They were giving me their names, and I took them.

Sanchez's hand in mine gave a little spark, like a small jolt of electricity as we touched. We both fought not to jump, but the others noticed, or maybe they felt it. I was standing in a room full of trained psychics.

"You spiked her, Arrio; bad practitioner, no cookie," Spider said. The other men gave that masculine chuckle that women, even butch women, can never quite imitate.

"Sorry, Marshal," Sanchez said.

"No harm, no foul," I said.

He smiled and nodded, but he was embarrassed. I realized that the handshake had been a test not just for me but for all of us. Just as the men would test their bodies in weight training, the gun range, drills, this was a test, too. Could you hide what you were, hand to hand with another psychic? I'd met a lot who couldn't have done it.

"You need to work at your contact shielding, Arrio," Rocco said.

"Sorry, Sarge, I will."

Rocco nodded and moved to the next man. He was Theodoros, very Greek sounding and looking, but he was Santa, though Santa never looked like that when I was a little girl. His hair was straight and as black as Sanchez's and my own. He was the proverbial tall, dark, and handsome, if you were into jocks. I wondered how in hell he'd earned the nickname "Santa." It was Spanish for *saint*, but somehow I didn't think that's what they were going for.

Santa didn't have any trouble shaking my hand and not letting me feel anything but a firm handshake. It would be a point of pride for him and the last man. Sanchez had blown it; they'd work harder because of it.

The last man was also ethnic, but I wasn't entirely sure what flavor. His short hair was curly enough to be African American, but the skin tone and facial features were not quite that. He, too, was tall, dark, and handsome, but in a different way. His eyes couldn't decide if they were dark brown or black. They were somewhere in between my dark brown and Rocco's almost black. But either color, they were framed by strangely short but very, very thick lashes, so that his eyes looked bigger and more delicate than they were, like something edged in black lace.

"Moonus, Moon," Rocco said.

We smiled; we shook. Rocco motioned me to follow him to the front of the room. We stood in front of the whiteboard. "I'm Cannibal." Like Spider, Cannibal made me wonder why that name.

"If we're doing first names and nicknames, then I'm Anita."

"We heard you had a nickname," Cannibal said.

I just looked at him, waited for him to say it.

"The Executioner."

I nodded. "The vampires call me that, yeah."

Davey called out, "You look a little short to be the Executioner."

"Everyone looks short to you, Davis," I said. "What are you, six-four?"

"Six-five," he said.

"Jesus, most of the human population must look short to you, unless you're at work."

They laughed at him, and with me, which was good. The sergeant quieted the laughter with a gesture and said, "We do use nicknames, Marshal; do you want us to use yours?"

I looked at him. "You mean have you guys call me the Executioner, instead of Anita or Blake?"

He nodded.

"No, hell no. First, it's too long for a call sign. Second, it's not a name that I've ever heard spoken in a happy way."

"Are you embarrassed by the name?" he asked.

"No, but it's like Ivan the Terrible. I doubt seriously that anyone ever called him that to his face."

"The vampires call you that to your face," and Cannibal said it like he knew for sure. Maybe he did.

I nodded. "Sometimes they do, but it's mostly Executioner when they're talking to me. They just leave off the *the*."

"We can call you Executioner," he said.

I sighed. "I'd rather you didn't, Sergeant. I've had too many bad guys call me that while they tried to kill me. They look at the package and call me Executioner to make fun of me. How small, how delicate, how not deadly looking."

"And after they make fun of you?" he asked, voice serious, eyes studying my face.

I met his gaze. "Then they die, Sergeant, or I wouldn't be here."

"I promise never to call you short again," Davey said.

That broke the serious mood, and I was happy to laugh with everyone else.

"Anita, then, if you go out with us."

"Whether you let me go with your team depends on how this little test goes, doesn't it?"

"Yes."

Lieutenant Grimes spoke from the door, and everyone swiveled to give him attention. It was automatic for them. "There are a lot of psychics in the world, Marshal Blake, but there aren't many that are powerful enough to be useful and controlled enough to take into a firefight with you. We need to know how good your control is, and exactly what type of psychic you are. Some types of abilities clash, and if you clash with one of the men in this room, we'll make certain you aren't put on the same team."

"I appreciate all the thought you've put into this, Lieutenant, but I also know that Cannibal here is testing your men at the same time he tests me. He wants to know if they can stay in the room while he tastes my power and not be affected. Yeah, you want to know if my powers clash with your men's, but it's also another test for your own practitioners."

"We lost one of them, Marshal. One of our best. We have precious little time to get you up to speed, and for you to get us up to speed. You hunted this vampire before, and we need to know what you know."

"It's in the reports," I said.

He shook his head. "Cannibal's abilities will tell us whether your reports were accurate."

"You mean, if I lied."

He smiled and shook his head. "Left out things, not lied. You're dating the master of your city, Marshal, living with him; we need to know if that has compromised your loyalties."

"Thanks for the politeness, Lieutenant; the last Vegas cop who asked me accused me of fucking everything that moved."

Grimes made a face of distaste. "None of my men would ever have said that to you, but I apologize to you for the abuse of our city's hospitality."

"Thank you, Lieutenant, I appreciate that."

"Wizard was Cannibal's second-in-command for this squad."

"Wizard was the man you lost," I said.

He nodded. "We need to see how you fit in here, and we have maybe an hour to do it, before we have to deliver you back to Shaw." Not Sheriff Shaw, I noticed; I wondered if he'd figured out who'd insulted me.

Cannibal spoke, turning me back to look at him. "If you were like our own executioner and just used weapons, we'd try to find time to put you on the range, but it's your psychic abilities that will mess us up the most. We can always take your weapons away, but we can't take the rest."

"If I don't pass your test, what then?"

"I won't endanger my men," Grimes said, "if you are the danger, Marshal Blake."

"If I do pass?" I asked.

"Then we'll help you serve your warrant," Grimes said.

"If you don't pass, there are other vampire hunters in town," Cannibal said, "ones that aren't psychic enough to be a problem."

"They also won't be psychic enough to be a help, either," I said.

"We can help ourselves," Cannibal said.

"Can any of you sense the living dead?" I asked.

"None of us has a talent with vampires in particular, no."

I stared into Cannibal's dark eyes as I said, "The dead come in lots of flavors, not just vampires, Cannibal." I took that small step closer to him, not quite invading his personal space. I spoke low. "Just as vampires come in different flavors, too."

Cannibal smiled, and again I got that flash of anticipation from him. "Let's do this, then."

"Let's."

Louder, for the room—his lieutenant and his men—he said, "Are you ready, Anita?"

"How ready do you want me to be?"

"What do you mean?"

"Do you want me to try to keep you out, or do you want me to cooperate with your little mind-reading act?"

"I'd love to try to breach your shields sometime, but we don't have time, and the last psychic who played that game with me had to be taken out in an ambulance."

"Are you that good, or that bad?" I asked.

One of the men made a noise, like *ooh*. We ignored him.

"I'm good," Cannibal said, "unless you fight me; then it's bad for you."

"If we had time I'd make you prove that, but we don't, so I'll drop my shields enough to let you in, but I won't drop them completely. Please, don't try to force them all the way down."

"Why not?" he asked.

"Because not only can I sense the dead, but sometimes they can sense me. If you breach all my shields, I'll shine like a beacon, and all the vampires in the area will know something supernatural is in town. I'd rather not advertise quite that loudly yet."

"I don't think you're lying about that, which means you're not exaggerating."

"I try not to exaggerate, Sergeant; the truth is strange enough without that."

"I'll be careful of your shields, Anita."

"Okay, how do we do this?"

"Sitting down," he said.

"In case one of us falls down," I said.

"Something like that."

"You really do believe you're the strongest psychic in this room, don't you?" I asked.

"Yes."

I shrugged. "Fine, let's get chairs."

The men handed us up a chair apiece. We sat down facing each other. I lowered my shields a little, like partially opening a door. Not only could I feel Cannibal's energy humming along my skin now, but there were buzzes and flashes and heat from some of the other men. I fought not to concentrate on them, just to ignore it the way I did ghosts. Ignore it and it will go away.

"It works better if I can touch you," he said.

I gave him a look.

He smiled. "So young to be so cynical."

I held out my hands, still frowning. "Fine."

He took my hands in his, and only then did he lower his own shields, only then did he reach out to me with that humming energy of his. Only then did I realize that touch makes all vampire powers worse, more, even if the vampire in question wears a uniform and has a heartbeat.

7

HIS POWER FLOWED through the hole in my shields like something warm and alive. Shapeshifter energy was warm, but it held an edge of electricity, like your skin couldn't decide if it felt good or hurt. Shapeshifters rode that edge of pain and pleasure, but this power was just warm, almost comforting. What the hell?

His hands felt warmer in mine than they had been a moment ago, as if his temperature were rising. Again, I kept trying to equate it to a lycanthrope, because it was so not the cool touch of the grave.

I realized I was staring at our hands. I was treating him like a real vampire. You don't look one of them in the eye, but that was years ago for me. I hadn't met a vampire that could roll me with its gaze in a long time. One very alive, psychic vampire wasn't going to be able to do it, was he? So why didn't I want to meet his eyes? I realized I was nervous, almost afraid, and I couldn't have told you why. Short of someone trying to kill me, or my love life, my nerves were rock steady. So why the case of nerves?

I made myself look away from his hands on mine and meet his eyes. They were just the same almost black, the pupils lost to the color, but they weren't vampire eyes. They hadn't bled their color into shining fire across the whole of his eyes. They were human eyes, and he was only human. I could do this, damn it.

His voice seemed lower, soothing, the way you see people talk when they're trying to hypnotize someone. "Are you ready, Anita?"

I frowned at him. "Get on with it, Sergeant; the foreplay's getting tedious."

He smiled.

One of the other psychics in the room, I didn't know their voices well enough to pick who, said, "Let him be gentle, Marshal; you don't want to see what he can do."

I met Cannibal's dark, dark eyes and said the truth: "Yeah, I do want to see what he can do."

"Are you sure?" he asked, voice still low, soft, like he was trying not to wake someone.

I spoke low, too. "As much as you want to see what I can do."

"You going to fight back?"

"You hurt me, and I will."

He gave that smile that was more fierce than happy. "Okay." He leaned in, drawing down all that extra height from his much longer waist to bring our faces close, and he whispered, "Show me Baldwin, show me the operator you lost. Show me Baldwin, Anita."

It shouldn't have been that easy, but it was as if the words were magic. The memories came to the front of my head, and I couldn't stop them, as if he'd started a movie in my head.

The only light was the sweep of flashlights ahead and behind. Because I didn't have a light, it ruined my night vision but didn't really help me. Derry jumped over something, and I glanced down to find that there were bodies in the hallway. The glance down made me stumble over the third body. I only had time to register that one was our guy, and the rest weren't. There was too much blood, too much damage. I couldn't tell who one of them was. He was pinned to the wall by a sword. He looked like a shelled turtle, all that careful body armor ripped away, showing the red ruin of his upper body. The big metal shield was crushed just past the body. Was that Baldwin back there? There were legs sticking out of one of the doors. Derry went past it, trusting that the officers ahead of him hadn't left anything dangerous or alive behind them. It was a level of trust that I had trouble with, but I kept going. I stayed with Derry and Mendez, like I'd been told.

I was left gasping in the chair, staring at Cannibal, his hands tight on mine. My voice was strained as I said, "That wasn't just a memory. You put me back in that hallway, in that moment."

"I needed to feel what you felt, Anita. Show me the worst of that night."

"No," I said, but again, I was back in the room beyond the hallway. The one vampire that was still alive cringed. She pressed her bloody face against the corner behind the bed, her small hands held out as if to ward it off. At first it looked like she was wearing red gloves, then the light shone on the blood, and you knew it wasn't opera-length gloves—it was blood all the way to her elbows. Even knowing that, even having Melbourne motionless on the floor in front of her, still Mendez didn't shoot her. Jung was leaning against the wall, like he'd fall down if he didn't concentrate. His neck was torn up, but the blood wasn't gushing out. She'd missed the jugular. Let's hear it for inexperience.

I said, "Shoot her."

The vampire made mewling sounds, like a frightened child. Her voice came high and piteous, "Please, please, don't hurt me, don't hurt me. He made me. He made me."

"Shoot her, Mendez," I said into the mic.

"She's begging for her life," he said, and his voice didn't sound good.

I peeled shotgun shells out of the stock holder and fed them into the gun as I walked toward Mendez and the vampire. She was still crying, still begging, "They made us do it, they made us do it."

Jung was trying to hold pressure on his own neck wound. Melbourne's body lay on its side, one hand outstretched toward the cringing vampire. Melbourne wasn't moving, but the vampire still was. That seemed wrong to me. But I knew just how to fix it.

I had the shotgun reloaded, but I let it swing down at my side. At this range the sawed-off was quicker; no wasted ammo.

Mendez had glanced away from the vamp to me, then farther back to his sergeant. "I can't shoot someone who's begging for her life."

"It's okay, Mendez, I can."

"No," he said, and looked at me; his eyes showed too much white. "No."

"Step back, Mendez," Hudson said.

"Sir . . ."

"Step back and let Marshal Blake do her job."

"Sir . . . it's not right."

"Are you refusing a direct order, Mendez?"

"No, sir, but—"

"Then step back and let the marshal do her job."

Mendez still hesitated.

"Now, Mendez!"

He moved back, but I didn't trust him at my back. He wasn't bespelled; she hadn't tricked him with her eyes. It was much simpler than that. Police are trained to save lives, not take them. If she'd attacked him, Mendez would have fired. If she'd attacked someone else, he'd have fired. If she'd looked like a raving monster, he'd have fired. But she didn't look like a monster as she cringed in the corner, hands as small as my own held up, trying to stop what was coming. Her body pressed into the corner, like a child's last refuge before the beating begins, when you run out of places to hide and you are literally cornered, and there's nothing you can do. No word, no action, no thing that will stop it.

"Go stand by your sergeant," I said.

He stared at me, and his breathing was way too fast.

"Mendez," Hudson said, "I want you here."

Mendez obeyed that voice, as he'd been trained to, but he kept glancing back at me and the vampire in the corner.

She glanced past her arm, and because I didn't have a holy item in sight, she was able to give me her eyes. They were pale in the uncertain light, pale and frightened. "Please," she said, "please don't hurt me. He made us do such terrible things. I didn't want to, but the blood, I had to have it." She raised her delicate oval face to me. "I had to have it." The lower half of her face was a crimson mask.

I nodded and braced the shotgun in my arms, using my hip and my arm instead of my shoulder for the brace point. "I know," I said.

"Don't," she said, and held out her hands.

I fired into her face from less than two feet away. Her face vanished in a spray of blood and thicker things. Her body sat up very straight for long enough that I pulled the trigger into the middle of her chest. She was tiny, not much meat on her; I got daylight with just one shot.

"How could you look her in the eyes and do that?"

I turned and found Mendez by me. He'd taken off his mask and helmet, though I was betting that was against the rules until we left the building. I covered my mic with my hand, because no one should learn about someone's death by accident. "She tore Melbourne's throat out."

"She said the other vampire made her do it; is that true?"

"Maybe," I said.

"Then how could you just shoot her?"

"Because she was guilty."

"And who died and made you judge, jury, and ex—" He stopped in midsentence.

"Executioner," I finished for him. "The federal and state government."

"I thought we were the good guys," he said.

"We are."

He shook his head. "You aren't."

And through all of it, I could feel Cannibal's energy like a song that you can't get out of your head, but I could feel that this song was feeding on the pain, the terror, even the confusion.

I pushed at the power, shoved it away, but it was like trying to grab a spiderweb when you run through it. You feel it on your skin, but the more you pull off, the more you find, until you realize that the spider is still on you somewhere making silk faster than you can get it off you. You have to fight the urge to panic, to simply start screaming, because you know that it's on you, crawling, ready to bite. But the memory receded like turning down a radio, still there, but I could think again. I could feel Cannibal's hands in mine, and I could open my eyes, look at him, see the now. Through gritted teeth, I said, "Stop this."

"Not yet." His power pushed at me again; it was like drowning, when you think you've made it to the surface, only to have another wave hit you full in the face. But the trick to not drowning is not to panic. I would not give him my fear. The memory couldn't hurt me; I'd already lived through it.

I tried to stop the memory, but I couldn't. I pulled on my hands, still in his, and got a flicker of image, like flipping channels on a television. The briefest image of him, his memory.

I pulled on my hands and got more, a woman under his hands, him holding her down. She was laughing, fighting not for real, and I knew it was his wife. Her hair was as dark as his, and curled like mine. It flung across the pillow, and her tan looked wonderful in the red silk. Sunlight spilled across the bed as he leaned down for a kiss.

I was suddenly back in that other bedroom, in the dark with the dead. I turned my hands in Cannibal's, caressed a finger across his wrist, just where the skin is thinnest and the blood flows close. We were back in the sunlit memory, and red silk on cotton sheets, and a woman who looked at him as if he were her world.

I felt her body underneath him, felt how much he wanted her, how much he loved her. The emotion was so strong, and just like that, I fed. I drew in the emotion of the moment.

But Cannibal didn't give up; he pushed back, and I was in my bedroom at home. Micah's face was above me, his green-gold eyes inches from mine, his body buried deep inside mine, my hands traced down his bare back until I found the curve of his ass, so I could feel his muscles working, pumping him in and out of me.

I shoved the power back at Cannibal, chased him out of my memory, and found us back in his sunlit bedroom. There were fewer clothes now, and I got a confused glimpse of his body inside hers, and then he threw me out. He jerked his hands out of mine, and the moment he stopped touching me, it was over, done. I was back in my own head, with my own memories, and he was back with his.

He got up too fast and knocked his chair to the floor with a loud clang. I sat where I was, hugging myself, huddling around the feeling of his power inside me, rifling through my head, though that didn't cover how it felt. It felt intimate, and it wasn't about the sex; it was about having his power force its way into me.

Cannibal went to the far side of the room, facing the wall and not looking at me.

"Sergeant Rocco," Lieutenant Grimes said.

I heard Cannibal's voice but wasn't ready to look at him yet, either. "The reports are accurate. She felt the loss of the operators. She's tired of killing."

"Shut up," I said, and got to my feet, but didn't knock my chair over. Point for me. "That was private. That last memory had nothing to do with the deaths of the two men."

He turned around, lowering his arms, as if he'd been hugging himself, too. He looked at me, but I saw the effort of that on his face. "You killed the vampire that killed Melbourne, you killed her while she begged for her life, and you hated doing it, but you killed her for him. I felt it; you took her life because she took his."

"I took her life because I am duty bound by the fucking law to take it."

"I know why you did it, Anita. I know what you were feeling when you did it."

"And I know what you were feeling in that other room, Sergeant. Do you want me to share that?"

"That was personal, not the job," he said.

I strode over to him, past the lieutenant. The men were on their feet, as if they felt that something was about to happen. I got close enough to hiss into Rocco's face, a harsh whisper, "You overstepped the bounds and you know it. You fed off my memories, off my emotion."

"You fed off mine," he said. He kept his voice as low as mine. Technically what we'd done hadn't been illegal, because the law just hadn't caught up to the fact that you could be a vampire and not be dead. By legal definition, neither of us could be a vampire.

"You started it," I said.

"You took my ability and used it against me," he said. He was talking low, but not whispering now. I understood; we needed to talk about some of what had happened.

"If a vampire uses an ability against me, sometimes, I can borrow it," I said.

"Explain, Cannibal," Grimes said.

We both looked at him, then back at each other. I always hated trying to explain psychic ability to people who didn't have it. It never translated quite right.

Cannibal started, "All I can sense, most of the time, is violent memories, fear, pain. When Anita tried to stop me, she drew a memory from me, and it wasn't about violence. How did you do that?"

Grimes asked, "If it wasn't violence, what was the memory?"

Cannibal and I exchanged another look. I shrugged. "It was personal, about my family." He looked from the lieutenant to me and asked again, "How did you do that?"

"In real life I do violence, but for psychic stuff I do other things better." There, that was cryptic enough; one thing I did not want the police to know was that I was a succubus. The only thing that would keep Cannibal from spilling the beans was that he didn't want me to tattle on him. We'd keep each other's secrets, if we were smart.

A look passed over his face, as if he were trying to decide what expression to show me. "She showed me love, tenderness, like the girl version of what I can do." Again, he'd told the truth, but not too much of it.

"You learned fast enough, Cannibal. The last memory you got from me wasn't about violence, either."

He nodded. "So you peeked at mine and I peeked at yours."

"Yes."

"Peeked at what?" Grimes asked.

"The people we love," Cannibal answered.

Grimes frowned from one to the other of us.

"The man in your memory wasn't a vampire," Cannibal said. "I thought you were living with the Master of the City."

"I am."

"Then who is he, the man? I saw his eyes; they weren't human."

"He's a wereleopard," I said.

"Don't you have any human men in your life?"

"No," I said.

"Why not?" he asked.

I thought of a lot of answers, but settled for, "Did you plan on falling in love with your wife?"

He opened his mouth, then closed it, and said, "No, she was supposed to be a one-night stand." He frowned, and the look was enough; he hadn't meant to say that out loud. "If you were a man, I don't know what I would do right now."

"What, you'd hit me?"

"Maybe."

"You drag me through one of the worst kills of my recent past, and you stand there and bitch because I made you re-member something wonderful. I think I'm ahead on karmic brownie points here. Don't you ever mind-fuck me like that again."

"Or what?" he asked.

"I can't shoot you, but if you ever touch me and do that again, I will figure out something very unpleasant to do to you that will be just as legal as what you just did to me."

We glared at each other. Grimes came beside us. "Okay, what went wrong, Cannibal?"

"She caught my power and turned it on me. I got it back, but I had to fight for it."

Grimes's eyes widened, then he looked at me. He looked at me the way he might look at a new weapon, or another shiny new truck to put in his garage from testosterone hell. "How good is she?"

"Good," Cannibal said, "and controlled. We could have se-riously hurt each other, but we were both careful. Honestly, Lieutenant, if I'd known she was this powerful I'd have been gentler. If she had been less in control of her abilities, you might be carting both of us off to the hospital for the day."

Grimes continued to look at me, as if he'd only just seen me, but he talked to Cannibal like I wasn't there. "You saw her range scores when she qualified for the badge."

"Yes, sir."

"Is she as good psychically as she is with a gun?"

"Better," Cannibal said.

Grimes looked pleased. "Better, really."

"You know, Grimes, it's a little unnerving to have you looking right at me but talking like I'm not here."

"I'm sorry, really, that was inexcusable, but I've just never seen anyone take Cannibal on like that. He is the best practitioner of his kind we have."

"Yeah, I bet he's hell on wheels at an interrogation."

"He gathers information that helps us save lives, Marshal Blake."

"Yeah, I've felt how he gathers his information, Grimes, and I don't like it."

"I told you if you fought me, you might get hurt," Cannibal said.

"No, you said if I fought to keep my shields up so you couldn't get through, it might hurt me. I let you in, and frankly, I consider what you just did the equivalent of having an invited guest steal the silver."

"Am I missing something?" Grimes asked.

"No, sir."

"You're missing the fact that you aren't psychic and you're trying to be in charge of men who are. Nothing personal, Lieutenant, but if you don't have abilities, then you are going to miss things."

"I'm not a doctor either, Marshal, which is why each team has one, plus a med tech that goes out on every run. Since we added practitioners to our teams, we've saved more lives with no injuries to anyone involved than any unit in the country. I may not understand everything that just happened between you and Cannibal, but I do know that if you're as good as he is, then you can help us save lives."

I didn't know what to say to that. He was so sincere. He might even be right, but that didn't change the fact that Cannibal had mind-fucked me and enjoyed feeding on my pain. Of course, I'd fed on the energy of his memory of sex with his wife, and we'd both fed on the memory of me with Micah. Had I found another way to feed the *ardeur*, or without Cannibal's abilities would I never be able to repeat it again? Didn't know, wasn't sure I cared.

She's tired of killing, Cannibal had said. That was the worst insult of all because he was right. I had six years of blood on my hands, and I was tired. I could still see the vampire with her bloody hands, begging me not to kill her. I'd dreamed about her for days afterward, waking up to Micah and Nathaniel, having them pet me back to sleep or take turns getting up with me and drinking endless cups of coffee and waiting for dawn, or waiting until it was time to get ready to go to work so I could raise the dead or get a new warrant and maybe kill someone else.

I'd pushed it all back in that part of myself where all the other ugliness gets shoved, but whatever Cannibal had done had raked it up like having a scar start to bleed again. I thought I'd dealt with it, but I hadn't. I'd just tried to ignore it.

"We have to take you to Sheriff Shaw now, Marshal," Grimes said, "but we want to take you to the hospital, let you see our men. All our practitioners, and all our doctors, have come up empty on what's wrong with them. I trust Cannibal, and he's impressed. He's not easily impressed."

"I'd be happy to go to the hospital and look at them. If I can help, I'll do it."

He gave me the full weight of his sincere brown eyes, but there was a weight to them. It wasn't psychic power, but it was power. The power of belief, and a sort of purity of purpose. This unit of SWAT was Grimes's calling, his religion, and he was a true believer. One of those frightening ones whose faith can be contagious, so you find yourself believing in his dreams, his goals, as if they were your own. The last person I'd met who had that kind of energy to him had been a vampire. I'd thought Malcolm, the head of the Church of Eternal Life, had been dangerous because he was a master vampire, but I realized as I met Grimes's true-brown eyes that maybe it hadn't all been vampire powers in Malcolm either. Maybe it was simply faith.

Grimes believed in what he did, with no doubts. Though he was older than me by over a decade, I suddenly felt old. Some things mark your soul, not in years but in blood and pain and selling off parts of yourself to get the bad guys, until you finally look in the mirror and aren't sure which side you're on anymore. There comes a point when having a badge doesn't make you the good guy, it just makes you one of the guys. I needed to be one of the good guys, or what the hell was I doing?

8

I'D BEEN RIGHT about the beige cabinets against the one wall, and now I was kneeling in front of the open weapons lockers, going through the three bags to decide what to keep with me. I was back to just Grimes, Hooper, and Rocco. The other practitioners had been dismissed, but they hadn't gone far. Most of them had simply moved to the weight-lifting area and started working out. I dug through the bags to the clink of weights and the small noises that people make when they do the work. The large open space seemed to swallow the noise more than most gyms, so it was very subdued.

Hooper spoke over my shoulder. "Wait, what is that?"

I looked down into the open bag and said, "What are you looking at, and I'll tell you."

He squatted beside me and pointed. "That."

"Phosphorus grenade."

"Not like any one I've ever seen."

"It's based on the older models."

Now I had their attention. They all squatted or knelt by the bag. "How old is that thing?" Hooper asked.

"It's not old; it's actually newly manufactured. It comes from a specialty weapons house."

"What kind of specialty weapons house?" Grimes asked; he looked positively suspicious.

"One that understands that the older idea of phosphorus works better for the undead."

"How is it better?" Hooper asked.

"I don't want them to be able to run into water and put it out; I want the bastards to burn."

"Has it got the same radius as the real old ones?" Rocco asked, and he studied me with those too-dark eyes.

I fought to keep that gaze but wanted to look away. I didn't like him much right at that moment. "Actually, no. You don't have to try to be fifty feet away so you don't get fried with your target. It's a ten-foot danger zone, easier to set it and get the fuck away." I reached in and drew out an even smaller one. "This is only five feet."

"Phosphorus were never grenades, they were markers," Hooper said.

"Yeah, a marker that if you were fifty feet or closer, you would be vaporized, or wished you were. Let's call a spade a spade, gentlemen. This is a weapon."

Grimes said, "It was decommissioned. You shouldn't be able to get new tech with that material in it."

"The government has made an exception for the undead and shapeshifters."

"I didn't hear about that." Grimes sounded like he would have, if it were true.

"Gerald Mallory, Washington, DC, head vampire hunter, got a special weapons bill pushed through for us. We had a couple of preternatural marshals get killed when the newer grenades got doused by water."

"I did hear about that," Grimes said. "The vampires burned them alive and filmed it."

"Yep," I said. "They put it on YouTube before it got yanked. It was used to get the warrant for them and to get us some new toys."

"Did you watch the film?" Rocco asked, and again there was too much weight to his gaze. I met it, but it made me fight not to wiggle. You'd think I was uncomfortable around him now. Nay, not me.

"No," I said.

"Why not?" he asked.

I expected Grimes to tell him to stop, but no one came to my rescue. I was pretty sure they were still kicking my tires. Something about what I'd done in the other room with their head psychic had made them more serious about me.

I switched my gaze to Grimes to answer. "Been there, done that, didn't want the T-shirt."

"Explain," Grimes said.

"I've seen people burned alive before, Lieutenant; I didn't feel like seeing it again. Besides, once you've seen and smelled it in person, film really can't compare." I knew my gaze had gone a little angry, maybe even hostile. I didn't care. I wasn't interviewing here; I was here to do my job.

I went back to sorting through my bag.

"They are not going to let you walk into homicide with explosives," Grimes said.

I spoke without looking up, "Not even a small one?"

"I doubt it," he said.

"I'll leave them here then," I said, and started getting out things I thought they might allow me to carry.

I ended up with the guns lying in a line on the floor. The Mossberg 590A1 Bantam shotgun; a sawed-off that I'd had made, cut down from an Ithaca 37; Heckler & Koch's MP5, my favorite submachine gun; and Smith & Wesson's MP9c. I was still wearing the Browning BDM, which had replaced my Browning Hi-Power for concealed carry. The BDM had fewer knobbly bits to catch on clothing. Though honestly, the S&W was the best of the three for concealed carry, but then that was one of the niches it was built to fill.

I laid the blades out next. The machete that was my favorite for beheading, mostly chickens, but I'd used it on vampires a time or two. The two smaller blades that fitted into wrist sheaths. They had higher silver content than a normal knife. They were also balanced for my hands. They sat on the floor in their custom sheaths, fitted for my muscular but small forearms. I had one extra knife that was an in-between size that I'd started carrying since they made me wear the vest. It fitted into the Velcro straps of the MOLLE system on the vest.

Ammunition next, laying out extra magazines for each gun. I liked to have at least two per gun. Three was better, but it was a matter of space. For the shotgun I had a stock mag attached to the butt of the Mossberg that held extra shells. I had a box of shells per shotgun, too.

The last thing was two wooden stakes and a small mallet. That was all that would fit on me and in the backpack.

"That's not a lot of wooden stakes," Hooper said.

"I don't use the stakes unless it's a morgue execution; then legally that's one of the approved methods for carrying out the warrant. But honestly, you just have to take the heart and the head, even in the morgue. Most executioners use blades or metal spikes; they go through meat and bone easier than wood."

"You don't use the stakes for hunts?" Grimes asked.

"Almost never," I said.

The three men exchanged a look.

"I take it from that look that your local executioner was a stake-and-hammer man."

"We were told that most of them are," Grimes said.

I smiled and shook my head. "That's the official line, Lieutenant, but trust me, most of us are silver-bullet-and-blade men."

"Tony didn't believe that any vampire was really dead until he staked them," Rocco said.

I picked up the Mossberg. "All you have to do is take the heart and head. Trust me, every gun sitting here will do the job."

"Even the Smith and Wesson?" Rocco asked.

"I'd have to reload, but eventually, yeah."

"How many times would you have to reload?" Grimes asked.

I looked down at the Smith & Wesson. "The Browning has to be reloaded twice, and it holds about twice as much as the Smith and Wesson, so probably I'd have to reload four times, but I could do it. Waste a hell of a lot of ammo, though." I lifted the Mossberg. "The shotguns and the MP5 are my choice for an actual execution, but I can do it with almost everything in my kit." I looked down at everything. "I wouldn't actually want to try to decapitate someone with either of the wrist sheath knives, but they'll reach most vampires' hearts."

I put the shotgun down and opened another bag. I got my vest and helmet out. I really hated the helmet, even more than the vest. I was up against things that could tear my head off my body, so the helmet seemed a little silly to me, but it was part of the new SOP for us. I couldn't wait to see what they'd make us wear, or carry, next.

"So you just have the stakes because they insist on you carrying some of them," Grimes said.

"I follow the rules, Lieutenant, even if I don't agree with them."

"I don't see any metal spikes," Hooper said.

"I don't do morgue stakings if I can help it, and outside that, I trust the guns." I took off my suit jacket and started taking off my shoulder rig. It wouldn't fit under the vest, or rather I couldn't get to the weapons on the rig once the vest went over everything.

"Wait," Grimes said.

I turned and looked at him.

"Move your hair off your back, please."

I moved the nearly waist-length hair so they could see my back. I knew what he'd seen.

"That knife is almost as long as you are from shoulder to waist," he said, "and you've been wearing it the whole time."

"Yep." I let my hair fall back, and like magic, the blade was nearly invisible. Add a suit jacket or a heavy shirt, and it was.

"You have any more surprises on you, Marshal Blake?" he asked.

"No."

"How easy is it to draw?"

"Easy enough that I've had this sheath design redone for me three times, so I could keep carrying it this way."

"Why do you need to have it redone?" Rocco asked.

"Emergency room trips. They always cut everything off if you aren't able-bodied enough to stop them."

"That where you got the arm scars?" Hooper asked.

I looked down at my arms, as if I'd just noticed the old injuries. I touched the mound of scar tissue at my left elbow. "Vampire." I touched the thin scars that started just below it. "Shapeshifted witch." The cross-shaped burn scar was crisscrossed by the scars, so the cross was a little crooked on one side. "Human servants of a vampire. They branded me. Thought it was funny." I turned to my right arm. "Knife fight with a master vampire's human servant." I undid my belt so that I could slip the shoulder rig off, then I held the rig with the gun and knife still on it and used my other hand to lower my shirt from one shoulder. "Same vampire that did my elbow bit through my collarbone, broke it." I pushed the shoulder of my shirt up to show the small shiny scar on it. "Bad guy's girl-friend shot me." Then I smiled, because what else could I do. "We'll have to be better friends for you to see the other scars."

Grimes and Hooper looked a little uncomfortable, but Rocco didn't. We'd passed the point where a little hint could embarrass us. We'd already seen too far inside each other's private lives for that to faze either of us. It was a strange, in-stant kind of intimacy, what we'd done. I didn't like it much. I couldn't tell how Rocco felt about it. He hadn't liked me peek-ing at him and his wife, that was all I knew for sure.

I started to put on the vest.

"Are you about to suit up?" Grimes asked.

I looked at him over the collar of the vest; I hadn't fastened the Velcro yet. "I was, why?"

"Unless the vampire you're hunting is inside with Sheriff Shaw, you'll just have to take it off to talk to him."

"They won't let me wear full gear in the police station?" I made it a question.

"Carrying all that, they'll stop you at the front. You'll never get into an interrogation room dressed for battle," Rocco said.

I sighed and slipped the vest back over my head. "Fine, I hate the vest and helmet, anyway. I'll carry them in a bag."

"The vest and helmet will save your life," Grimes said.

"If I weren't hunting things that could peel the vest like an onion and crush the helmet, with my head in it, like an egg-shell, maybe. I love having a badge and being part of the Mar-shals Service, but whoever is making the rules keeps making us rig up like we're hunting human beings. Trust me, what we'll hunt here in Vegas isn't human."

"What would you wear if you had your choice?" Grimes asked.

"Maybe something that was better at stopping slashing.

Nothing works good enough against a stabbing attack yet. But honestly, I'd carry the weapons and leave the protective gear at home if I were going in with just me. I move faster without the vest, and speed will usually save my life more than the vest."

"Do you have trouble moving in full gear?" Grimes asked.

"The damn thing weighs around fifty pounds."

"Which is what, half your body weight?" he asked.

I nodded. "About that, I weigh one-ten."

"That would be like putting a hundred-pound vest on most of us. We wouldn't be able to move, either."

Hooper was the one to ask it. "How badly do you move in the vest?"

"I can't tell what's going on with you guys. I keep expecting you to rush me to the hospital to see your men, or to Shaw to get this started, but you're checking me out."

"We're about to trust you with our lives on a hunt that's already killed three of our operators. Speed won't bring them back. Rushing things won't wake up the men in the hospital. All speed will do is get more of my team killed, and that is not acceptable. You're a strong and controlled practitioner, but if you can barely move when you're in full gear, you're going to be an obstacle to overcome, not a help."

I looked into Grimes's very serious face. He had a point. The vest was very new, and when I wasn't working with SWAT, I did my best not to wear it, but it wasn't because I couldn't move in it.

I sighed again, laid the vest with my other gear, and walked toward the weight area. The men were using the weights, but they were watching us, too. I went to the weight bench where tall, dark, and handsome Santa was bench-pressing. Mercy of the straight brown hair was spotting him, which meant the weight was heavy for the big man. Both Santa and Mercy had to weigh well over two hundred pounds, most of it muscle.

I watched Santa's arms bulge with the effort to push the bar up and back into its cradle. Mercy's hands hovered nearby, and at the end he had to guide the bar. That meant it was close to the other man's limit on this exercise.

"Can I jump in for a minute? The lieutenant wants to see if I'm going to slow you guys down."

The two men exchanged a look, and then Santa sat up, smiling. "Tell us what weight you want, and we'll put it on."

"What's on it now?"

"Two-sixty; I was doing reps." He had to add that last so I wouldn't think it was the max weight he could bench. It was a guy thing; I got it.

I stared at the weights, thinking. I was about to do something that the guys would both like, a lot, and hate. I knew I could bench-press the weight; I'd done it at home. Thanks to vampire marks and several different kinds of lycanthropy floating around in my body, I could do things that were amazing even to me. I hadn't been this strong long enough for it to lose its novelty. But I'd never showed it off to human cops before. I debated, but it was the quickest way I could think of to make my point.

The other men had started gathering around. Mercy reached for the weights. "What weight do you want, Blake?"

I waved him away. "This will do."

They exchanged a look, all of them. Some of them smiled. Santa stood and waved at the bench as if to say, *It's all yours.*

I went to the back of the bench. Mercy moved out of my way. The others moved back and gave me room. I knew I could bench-press it, and that would impress them, but I knew something that would impress them more, and I was tired of having my credentials checked. I wanted to be done with the tests and be out hunting vampires before it got dark. What I needed was something fairly spectacular.

I put my hands on the bar and braced my legs wide enough to get a good stance. I knew I was strong enough to lift it, but my mass wasn't enough to counterbalance it, so I had to rely on other muscles to keep me steady and upright while my arms did the other work.

I got my grip on the bar, worked my stance.

Santa said, "That's two hundred and sixty pounds, Blake."

"I heard you the first time, Santa." I lifted the bar, tensing my stomach and leg muscles to hold me while I curled it. Making it a controlled, pretty curl was the hard part, but I did it. I curled it, then set it back down with a tiny clink.

My breath was coming a little hard, and my whole body felt pumped and full of blood; there was even a little roar in my ears, which meant I shouldn't try to curl that much weight again. So I wouldn't, but . . . There was absolute silence from the men, as if they'd forgotten to breathe.

I put my hands on my waist and fought to control my breathing; it would all be for nothing if I looked dizzy or unsteady now.

Someone said, "Oh my God."

I looked at the lieutenant and the sergeants where they stood off the edge of the mat. "I can carry my own weight, Lieutenant."

"Hell, you can carry me," Mercy said.

Santa said, "How did you do that? There's not enough of you to lift that much weight."

"Could you do it again?" Grimes asked.

"You mean reps?" I asked.

He nodded.

I grinned. "Maybe, but I wouldn't want to try."

He gave an expression that was almost a smile, then shook his head. "Answer Santa's question, Anita."

"You've heard the rumors. Hell, you checked up on me before I stepped off the plane."

"You're right, I did. So you really are the human servant of your local Master of the City."

"That won't make you this strong," I said.

"I saw your medical records," he said.

"And," I said.

"You're a medical miracle."

"So they tell me."

"What?" Santa asked, looking from one to the other of us.

"So, you really are carrying five different kinds of lycanthropy, but you don't shift."

I nodded. "Yes."

"Wait," Santa said, "that's not possible."

"Actually," Grimes said, "there have been three documented

cases in the United States alone; you would be the fourth. Worldwide there have been thirty. People like you are what gave them the idea for the lycanthropy vaccines."

Someone must have made a movement because Grimes said, "Yes, Arrio."

"Is her lycanthropy contagious?"

"Anita," he said.

"Shapeshifters are only contagious in animal form, and I don't have an animal form, so, no."

"Are you sure?" he asked.

"Not a hundred percent, no. I wouldn't drink my blood, and if you have a cut, you might not want me to bleed on you."

"But you've got five different kinds in your blood, right?" Santa asked.

"Yes," I said.

"Then if you bled on me, I wouldn't get just one, I'd get them all, or nothing, right?"

I nodded. "Yes."

"Would it make me be able to do what you just did?"

"You can do what I just did."

He shook his head, frowning. "Able to curl over twice my body weight, so, six-ninety, seven hundred pounds."

"I've seen a shapeshifter about your size that could do it, but I'm not as strong as a real shapeshifter. If I were, I could do reps easy, and I can't."

"So a shapeshifter your size would be even stronger?" Davey, the tall blond with the nice mouth, asked.

"Absolutely." I looked back at the lieutenant. "That's what I mean about the vest and helmet. It just won't protect you from that level of strength."

"It will protect you if you get hit in the chest or head."

"Some."

"You'll wear the full gear when you go out with us, Anita."

"You're the boss."

He smiled. "Reports say you aren't much for following orders."

"I'm not."

"But I'm the boss."

"For these men, this unit, you are, and if I want to work with you, that makes you the boss."

"You have a federal badge. You could try to be the boss."

I laughed. "I've seen the way the men react to you. I could have a dozen federal badges, and that wouldn't make any of these guys see me as their boss."

"It will let you take all your weapons into the main station if you want to rub their faces in it."

"I'm trying to make friends here, not enemies."

"Then you'll be the most polite Fed we've met in a while."

I shrugged. "I just want to start hunting these vampires before dark. Tell me what I have to do to make that happen, and I'll do it."

"Collect your gear. We'll take you to Shaw."

"Do I wear my gear or just carry it?"

"You asking my opinion?"

"Yes."

"Carrying it is less aggressive, but they may also see it as a weakness."

"If I asked you to just take me to the crime scene, would you?"

"No."

I sighed. "Fine, take me to Shaw. Let him check under my hood, too."

"Why does that sound dirty?" Santa asked.

"Because everything sounds dirty to you," Mercy said.

Santa grinned. "Not everything."

"Why are you called Santa?" I asked.

He aimed that grin at me. "Because I know who's been naughty and who's been nice."

I gave him a look.

He did a Boy Scout salute. "Honest."

"He's not lying," Spider of the curly brown hair said.

I waved my hands, as if clearing the air. "Fine, whatever that means. Let's go." I started walking toward Grimes, Rocco, Hooper, and my gear.

Mercy called out, loud enough so it would carry, "Tell us, Santa, is Blake naughty or nice?"

I felt something prickle along my back. It made me whirl

around and glare at Santa. "I let Cannibal inside my shields; you don't get in."

Santa had a look on his face, as if he were hearing things I couldn't hear. He blinked and looked at me, his eyes a little unfocused, as if he were having to draw himself back from far away. "I can't get past her shields."

"Come on, Blake," Mercy said, "don't you want to know if you're naughty or nice?"

"I'm naughty, Mercer, I've killed too many people to be nice." I didn't wait to see their reaction. I just turned and went for my gear. I'd pack up, and they'd pass me to Sheriff Shaw. Maybe he'd just take Lieutenant Grimes's word that I was okay, but remembering the look on Shaw's face as we drove off, I doubted it. I appreciated everyone's professional caution, but if this kept up, it would be dark before I got to do my job, and I did not want to hunt Vittorio in the dark. He'd mailed me the head of the last vampire hunter who'd tried to kill him; I was betting he'd be happy to cut me up and mail me to someone, too.

9

AN HOUR LATER I still hadn't seen the crime scene. Why? Because I was sitting at a small table in an interrogation room. You can watch all the *CSI* you want, but the Vegas interrogation room was just like all the others I'd seen. The glass and open space on television was so cameras could work and it would look nifty. In real life, it was like everyone else's room: small, dingy, painted a pale but always slightly odd color, as if somewhere there were a list of colors suitable for interrogation rooms but for nowhere else.

There are no weapons allowed in interrogation rooms, so I'd had to put everything in lockers. The fact that being completely unarmed made me nervous, regardless of the situation, said sad things about my state of mind. It wasn't that I thought Shaw or the rest would hurt me; I just liked being armed, especially in a city where I knew a vampire was gunning for me. Shaw had asked me to answer a few questions about the last time I'd hunted Vittorio. I hadn't really understood that he meant to treat me like a suspect. I'd thought I'd be talking to other cops and telling them what little I knew of Vittorio. Instead I was being interviewed, and not in a good, happy way.

Shaw leaned against the door, big arms crossed over his chest. He'd thrown his hat on the table a while back. He was giving me his hard look, and it was a good look, but I knew he wouldn't try to kill me. Lately, unless death or heartbreak was involved, you could look at me as hard as you wanted and I wouldn't fucking care.

"Tell me about the last time you dealt with this bloodsucker," he said.

"I've told you, twice."

"Naw, that's what's in the reports. I want to know what you left out."

"I had our SWAT with us, Shaw, cross-check their reports with mine."

"I've done that, but I don't mean the assault on the condo at the end. I want to know what you and your vampire boyfriend kept secret."

I thought about it for a few moments, and fought the urge to rub my neck. "The only thing that probably didn't make it into a report was the fact that Vittorio could hide from other Masters of the City."

"Can't all the powerful ones do that?"

"No, Masters of the City, especially, have the ability to pick up the energy of other powerful vamps that cross their territory. For someone as powerful as Vittorio was, to be able to hide from every vampire in St. Louis, including the Master of the City, is really unusual."

"And I thought old Max was lying."

"Your Master of the City didn't sense him either?"

"Says he didn't." Again the doubt was clear in his voice.

"He's not lying," I said.

"Or you're lying for him," Shaw said.

"What the hell does that mean?"

"It means what I said."

"I came here to help you."

"You came here because a vampire serial killer painted your name on a wall with our men's blood. You're here because the bastard mailed you the head of our executioner. I need to know what you did to this guy to make him like you this much."

"I hunted him, Shaw, and he got away. That's all."

"Initially the police in St. Louis said they got him, but you said you missed him. How did you know he wasn't one of the dead vampires if you'd never seen him before?"

"Because nothing we killed in the condo was powerful enough to do everything he'd done. If Vittorio had been in that condo, more of us would have died."

"You lost three men, too."

"Trust me, if Vittorio had been there, it would have been a lot worse."

"Bad enough to kill three of our men and put the rest in the hospital?" he asked.

"I put in my report that I thought he would resurface again. He's a serial killer, and being a vampire doesn't make that big a difference to the pathology. Most serial killers have to keep killing; they can't, or won't, stop until they die or are caught."

"The BTK killer stopped for years," Shaw said.

"Yeah. Bind, torture, kill—I always hated that moniker. The fact that he was able to channel that murderous impulse into raising kids and being the local monitor for how tall the grass is, is playing hell with a lot of the profilers. Everyone thought he was dead or in jail on some other charge when he stopped. We're taught that serials can't stop for twenty years. They can stop for a while, or until the pressure builds up again, but not decades. The fact that he could stop means that others could stop, if they wanted to, or it means that for him it was about control. It only looks like a sexual killing to us, but for him it was about control, and once he had enough control in other parts of his life, he could stop."

"You sound like you've thought about it," he said.

"Haven't you? Hasn't every cop? I mean, the BTK killer has thrown a lot of our traditional theories on these guys into the crapper. It's like because of this one guy, we know less than we did before about these fruitcakes."

"You talk like a cop," he said.

"You sound surprised," I said.

"I guess I am. Let's just say I've heard some interesting opinions about you."

"I just bet you have."

"You don't sound surprised."

"I told you on the phone, I'm a girl and I clean up well. That gets the gossip going all on its own. But I'm dating a vampire, and though legally no one can bitch at me, it doesn't stop the other cops from hating me for it."

"It's not dating the vampire, Blake."

"What is it?"

"It's moving in with him, or are you going to deny that you moved in with your Master of the City?"

"Why would I deny it?"

He narrowed his eyes at me. "You're not ashamed of it, are you?"

"You should never be ashamed of loving someone, Shaw."

"You love him, a vampire?"

"They're legal citizens now, Shaw. They have the right to be loved just like everyone else."

A look of distaste crossed his face, so strong that it was unpleasant to look at. That look was enough. Vampires were legal, but that didn't make them good enough to date, or love, in everyone's book. The sad thing was that a few years ago I'd have agreed with Shaw.

We'd moved me into the Circus to help Jean-Claude's reputation among the other vampires, but what we hadn't anticipated was what it would do to my reputation among the cops. I shouldn't have been surprised, and it shouldn't have hurt my feelings, but I was and it did.

The door opened, and the good cop to Shaw's grumpy cop entered, smiling. He had coffee for me, and that made me feel better. Just the smell of it helped brighten my mood.

He'd introduced himself earlier as Detective Morgan, though I suspected he was a little higher rank than a straight-vanilla detective. He had that feel to him of someone in a suit trying to mingle with the common folk, but used to giving orders to everyone else.

Morgan put the coffee in front of me and sat down in the chair that Shaw had vacated. He crossed strong, tanned fingers on the scarred tabletop. His hair was a deep, rich brown, cut short but still too close to his eyes, as if he were overdue for a haircut. I'd put him at about my age, but after an hour of looking at the small lines at his eyes and around his mouth, I'd put him closer to forty than thirty. It was a strong, well-kept forty, but he wasn't the young, friendly guy he was trying to be. But I bet the act had worked on a lot of interviewees over the years, and probably women outside the job.

He waited for me to lift the cup. I inhaled the scent, and it was bitter enough that I knew it had been on the burner too long, but it was coffee, and I'd take it.

"Now, Anita"—he'd established first names a while back; fine with me—"we just want to know why this guy is after you. You can understand that."

I looked into his true-brown eyes and that damn near boyish grin, and wondered if they'd put him in here because I was a woman with a reputation for men. Had they thought he could charm it out of me? Boy, were they barking up the wrong girl.

"I've told you everything I know, Ed"—yeah, Ed Morgan was his name. We were Ed and Anita, and he seemed to think that would win him points. He could have called himself Tip O'Neill and I wouldn't have cared.

The door opened and Lieutenant Thurgood came back in; great. She was a woman, but she was one of those women who seem to hate other women. She was tall and moved with a muscular ease that said she kept in shape. She was older than me by at least ten years, which was how she'd gotten to be a lieutenant. Her hair was short and curled carelessly but attractively around a thin face with great cheekbones—the kind of cheekbones that people pay surgeons for, but hers were natural, because anyone who would pay for cheekbones would have worn a better skirt suit. Hers fit her like it had been borrowed, or like she'd lost a lot of weight and never bothered to replenish her wardrobe.

"Get out, both of you. I think we need some girl talk." She said it like it was something bad.

Morgan gave Shaw a look, like *Should we go?* I was betting they had practiced this little routine before. Shaw nodded, all stoic, and the men left me alone with Thurgood. Perfect.

She leaned over the table, using her height to intimidate. She was tall for a woman, though I knew taller, but height never impressed me. I was used to everyone being taller than me.

"Did you fuck this Vittorio, too? Did you fuck him, then dump him for your Master of the City? Is that why he sent you the head? A little present about old times?" She moved around the table so the last words were hissed into my face.

Most people would have leaned away from her, but I wasn't

most people. I leaned into her, carefully, just my upper body. We were suddenly close enough to kiss, and she jumped back as if I'd bitten her.

She put the table between us, which pleased me; so much reaction to such a little movement from me. She was afraid of me, genuinely afraid of me. What the hell was going on?

"I didn't think you liked girls, Blake."

I stood up.

She moved back to the door.

Interesting, but not interesting enough to put up with it. "Have your little lesbian fantasies on your own time, Thurgood. My crime scene is getting cold while you guys dick me around. Worse yet, we're wasting daylight, and I don't know about you, but I really don't want to be hunting these vampires in the dark if I can help it."

"If we want you here all day, then you'll sit here all day," she said.

That was a mistake. "Are you charging me with something?"

"What do you think we should charge you with?" she asked.

I walked toward her, and she backed away. What the hell? The door opened and Morgan stepped inside, between us. Shaw followed at his heels. They were both pretty good-sized men, and without really threatening me, they backed me up just by walking toward me. I'd done a version of the same thing to Thurgood, so I couldn't really bitch.

Morgan smiled his charming smile and said, "Anita, why don't we sit down and have some more coffee."

"No, thanks, Morgan."

"Ed, call me Ed."

"Look, I've had all the good cop/bad cop I can stand. Either charge me or let me go."

They exchanged looks. "Now, Anita."

"You know, I've changed my mind, Morgan; call me Blake or Marshal Blake. No more first names."

"If you'll just talk to us."

"I'm done talking. I've got a federal badge, and I have every right to this crime scene. So, one more time, charge me or let me go."

Morgan's brown eyes lost some of that friendly shine. "And exactly what would we charge you with, Marshal?"

I smiled back at him, but it wasn't a pleasant smile. "There, that's better; I knew you didn't like me, either."

"You said I wasn't pretty enough for you," Shaw said from the door, "so I thought we'd add Morgan. Or is he not pretty enough for you, either?"

I looked Morgan up and down, slow, the way some men will do to a woman. I made sure to hit his face last, so he'd have time to be pissed. But he wasn't pissed; he was challenging, defiant, but not really angry. "Well?" he said.

I started to say something disparaging, but though not really my cup of tea, he was attractive enough. I sighed, tired of the games already.

"I was going to say something cutting, but you're cute enough. I just didn't know that the Vegas PD put seduction on their list of interrogation techniques."

He looked surprised. "I don't know what you mean."

"Why put you in here with me? Why make a point of you being all cute? What was it supposed to prove, or do?" I waved my hand at him, as if clearing the air. "Never mind, I don't care."

I looked past him to Shaw. "Are you going to charge me?"

"We don't have anything to charge you with—yet." He had to add the *yet*.

"Fine, then get out of my way." I was almost touching him before he deigned to move. He opened the door and held it for me. I just kept walking.

10

SHAW ESCORTED ME back to my weapons. They couldn't keep me from doing my job. They couldn't keep me from having more weapons than God, but they didn't have to like it. Fine with me. I'd gone in with fewer weapons showing to try not to rub their faces in my federal badge. Grimes had said they might see it as a weakness. Next time I'd wear the full gear, and the local cops could deal. I tried to be nice, since I'd had my share of being on the receiving end of federal attitude before they grandfathered us into a federal badge. Today I was beginning to understand what might make the Feds so grumpy. Be arrogant; they don't pick on you as much.

The backpack was new, since I'd gotten more lethal toys than I could carry easily. I'd had to have the straps tailored down to fit snug at my back, and I had to keep it tight so it didn't queer the draw from my shoulder holster with the Browning BDM. When I had to wear the vest, I carried the Browning on a thigh holster. The Smith & Wesson went in straps on the front of the vest. Without the vest, the S&W went at the small of my back. I'd given up on interpants holsters when women's jeans started having so many damn styles and waistlines. I kept holy water, extra crosses, and holy wafers in little slots that had originally been for ammo, but there were enough pockets for extra magazines and other useful things. The backpack was actually pretty useful but awkward once the vest went on, which was another reason I didn't care for the vest. I had to put the guns I was wearing on me before the backpack went on. I'd carry the vest and helmet back out in the big pack like they'd come in.

It was the big knife at the back, with its sheath connected

to the shoulder holster, that made Shaw widen his eyes. I did my best to ignore him. There was room for an extra magazine on the other side of the holster for the Browning, which put me at fourteen rounds in the Browning and another fourteen in the extra magazine, plus the two extra magazines in the backpack. I put the Smith & Wesson at my waist, canted forward so it wouldn't get caught in the other straps. I had a thigh holster that I'd modified to hold extra magazines for the Browning and the MP5, which would go on a tactical sling across my body once everything else was in place. In the backpack there was a Bantam shotgun with extra shells strapped to its butt, and more shells in the backpack. When it was time to hunt vampires, I'd carry the shotgun and leave the MP5 for backup, but not everything would fit in the backpack, so the MP5 just stayed out in the sling.

"If I'd seen you pack your gear, there wouldn't have been an interrogation."

I glanced at Shaw, then went back to ignoring him while I made sure everything was where I wanted it. You did not want things to slide around, because you needed to know where things were when you went to grab them. Seconds counted.

"You going to give me the silent treatment?"

"You treated me like a perp, Shaw. What do you want me to say, that I'm happy you like the way I pack for work?"

"You pack like a soldier."

"She had a good teacher," a voice from the door said.

I stood up, tugging the straps into place, and smiled at Edward. "You can't take all the credit for me."

He wasn't very tall, five foot eight, so that Shaw had him by inches. He was muscular, but not muscled. He'd never have the shoulders that the bigger man had, but I knew that every ounce of him was more dangerous than any human being I'd ever known.

"You were still wet behind the ears when I met you," he said, and he grinned. It was a real smile that went all the way up to his eyes. I was one of the few people on the planet who got Edward's real smile. He had lots of fake ones. He made Detective Morgan look like an amateur at pretend. If Edward hadn't been so terribly blond and blue-eyed, he could have fit in anywhere, but he was just too damned WASP-looking to hide anywhere too ethnic.

"Where the hell have you been . . . Ted? I thought you said the plane ride from New Mexico was shorter than the one from St. Louis."

The smile vanished, and his eyes had that cold winter look to them. One minute happy, the next the real Edward looking out. He wasn't exactly a sociopath, but he had his moments.

"I was being entertained by the Vegas PD."

"They interrogated you, too?"

He nodded.

"You weren't in on the hunt for Vittorio. What could you tell them?"

"They didn't ask me about him." He looked at Shaw when he said the last. It was not a friendly look, and Edward did a better not-friendly look than anyone I knew.

Shaw didn't blanch under the gaze, but he didn't look comfortable either. "We're doing our job, Forrester."

"No, you're trying to scapegoat Anita."

"What did they ask you about me?" I asked.

"They wanted to know how long we'd been fucking."

I gave wide eyes to that. "What!"

He kept looking at Shaw. "Yeah, according to the rumor mill, you're sleeping with me, Otto Jeffries, and a cop in New Mexico, oh, and a few others. Apparently, you've been a very busy U.S. Marshal."

"How're Donna and the kids?" I asked. One, I did want to know; two, I didn't want to talk about the rumors anymore in front of Shaw.

"Donna sends her love, and so do Becca and Peter."

"When does Peter take his black belt test?"

"Two weeks."

"He'll get it," I said.

"I know."

"How'd Becca's dance recital go?"

He gave that real smile again. "She's really good. Her teacher says she has real talent."

"Are you trying to shame me by doing the whole domestic thing?" Shaw asked.

"No," I said, "we're ignoring you."

"I guess I deserved that. But look at it from our side . . ."

I held up a hand. "I'm tired of being treated like one of the bad guys by you, just because I'm better at my job than the rest of the men."

Edward cleared his throat sharply.

"Present company excepted," I said.

He nodded.

"But that's part of the problem. I *am* better than the rest of the executioners. I've got more kills, and I'm a girl. They can't stand it, Shaw. They can't believe that I'm just that good at my job. It has to be because I'm fucking my way to the top. Or that I'm some sort of freak myself."

"You can't be that good," he said.

"Why, because I'm a girl?"

He had the grace to look embarrassed. "You have to have training to be that good."

"She *is* that good," Edward said, in that empty voice he could do—the one that made the hairs at the back of your neck stand up if you knew what you were listening to.

"You're ex–special forces. She doesn't have that kind of training."

"I didn't say she was a good soldier."

"What then, a good cop?"

"No."

Shaw frowned at him. "What then? What is she that good at? And if you say *fucking*, I'm going to be pissed."

"Killing," Edward said.

"What?" Shaw said.

"You asked what she's good at. I answered the question."

Shaw looked at me up and down, not in a sexual way but like he was trying to see what Edward was talking about. "You really that good at killing?"

"I try to be a good cop. I try to be a good little soldier and follow orders up to a point. But in the end I'm not really a cop, or a soldier. I am a legally sanctioned murderer. I am *the* Executioner."

"I've never heard another marshal admit that they were a murderer."

"Technically, it's legal, but I hunt citizens of these United States with the intent of killing them. I have decapitated and torn the hearts out of more people than most serial killers. You want to pretty it up, give me a warrant, great, but I know what I do for a living, Sheriff. I know what I am, and I'm really, really good at it."

"Anyone better?" he asked.

I glanced at Edward. "Only one."

Shaw glanced at Edward and back to me. "I guess I'm lucky to have you both, then," though his voice made sure he was thick on the sarcasm.

"You *are* lucky to have us," I said, and I went for the door. Edward trailed me and held keys out. "I got us a car, so we'll have some privacy."

"Good," I said.

"Oh, and I didn't mention Olaf just for kicks."

I stopped in the hallway and looked at him. "You don't mean . . ."

"Marshal Otto Jeffries is one of the western state marshals. He was on the ground when I got here."

Olaf was a real serial killer. But he, like the BTK killer, could control his urges to a point. He'd never done his worst in this country, to my or Edward's knowledge. We couldn't prove anything, but I knew what he was, and he knew I knew it, and he liked that I knew it.

It was hunting vampires with me that had given Olaf the idea that he could become a marshal and do his little serial killer routine legally. There's no set way to take the heart and head of a vampire. You're just supposed to do it. Once the killing starts, there are no rules to protect the vampire. None. They are at the mercy of their executioner. One of my goals in life was never, ever, to be at Olaf's mercy.

11

EDWARD HAD MANAGED to get us a big SUV. It was black and looked vaguely menacing. I knew he hadn't asked for the color, but it was perfectly appropriate. I approved of the car, because if we had to go out into the desert or even off road, it would still do.

"When did you have time to rent a car?" I asked.

"I was the first one they interrogated. I knew it would take them a while to interrogate three other U.S. Marshals. I knew I had time."

I stopped in midstep. "Did you say three other U.S. Marshals?"

He turned and nodded at me. "I did." He almost smiled, which meant he was hiding something from me. Edward loved being mysterious. My having seen his family and knowing most of his secret identity hadn't cured him of the habit. It just made it harder for him to find opportunities to surprise me.

"Who's number four?" I asked.

He raised his hand. It was a gesture I'd seen him use in the field when he was dealing with people with enough training to know the hand signals. It was the come-ahead gesture.

There was a small cluster of police near the back of the pinkish-tan building. I'd noticed them, in that cursory way you begin to notice everything in our business: people, palm trees, heat, sunshine. Olaf stood up, and he was just suddenly there. He was half a head taller than all but one of them. Had he been slumping? But it was more than that; he was also wearing a black T-shirt and black jeans tucked into black boots. He had a black leather jacket thrown over one arm, revealing bare muscular arms. He had more color to his skin than the last time I'd seen him, as if he'd been out in the sun more, but Olaf, like me, just didn't tan. Most people with a lot of German in their background have trouble tanning.

His head was still completely shaved, so that his black eyebrows stood out on his face in stark contrast. He had a shadow of a beard along his jawline, because he was one of those men who needed to shave twice a day to be truly clean shaven. Made me wonder if he shaved his head or was bald. It had never occurred to me before.

The head, the clothes, the height; it all made him stand out in the group of cops like a wolf among sheep, or a Goth among uniforms. But I'd missed him completely.

Edward could do that, too. That invisible-in-plain-sight shit. I watched Olaf walk toward us, and admitted that for such a large man he moved gracefully, but it was the grace of muscle and violence contained.

The violence was helped along with the shoulder holster, with its H&K P2000 and extra magazines on the other side of the straps. Last time he'd carried his backup gun at the small of his back; I'd check later. There was a knife bigger than my forearm at his side, tied down to his thigh. Most vampire hunters carried blades.

He walked toward me all dark and menacing, then he smiled. It wasn't a friend smile. It was a boyfriend smile. No, more than that. It was the smile a man gives to a woman he's had sex with, good sex, and he's hoping to have it again. Olaf had not earned that smile.

"Anita," he said, and again there was too much emotion when he said my name.

I had to pause and say his fake name: "Otto."

He kept coming until he loomed over both Edward and me. Of course, Olaf was enough over six feet that seven was his next stop, so he loomed over damn near anyone.

He offered me his hand. In the two times I'd met him, had he ever offered to shake hands with me? I had to think, but no, he didn't shake hands with women. But there he was offering his hand, with that too-familiar smile fading a little around the edges, but still there.

The smile made me not want to touch him. But Olaf's pathological hatred toward women made the offer of a handshake a big deal. It meant he thought I was worth it. Besides, we were going to have to work together where police could see us. I did not want to start the hunt with him mad at me.

I took his hand.

He wrapped his big hand around mine, then put his other hand higher up my arm. Some men do that, I've never been sure why, but this time I knew why.

I pulled to move away. I couldn't help it. He tightened his grip, let me know he had me, or that it would be a fight to get away. Just an instant of it, a moment, but it was enough to remind me of the last time we'd met.

Olaf and I had been the ones to take the hearts out of the vampires last time we hunted. They were old and powerful, so you don't just stake the heart. You cut it out of the chest cavity and destroy it with fire later.

I'd gotten the heart tangled somehow on some bit of viscera in the body. He'd offered to help, and I'd accepted. I'd forgotten what he was.

He slid his hand inside the hole I'd made, so that his arm slid up alongside mine in the chest cavity. It wasn't until his hand cupped mine, pressing both our hands into the still-warm heart, that I looked at him. We were both leaning over the body, our faces inches apart, with our arms up the much longer torso of the male. He looked at me over the body, our hands around the heart, blood everywhere. He looked at me as if it were a candlelit dinner and I was wearing nice lingerie.

He'd kept his free hand on my arm, controlling how slowly we eased out of the chest cavity. He made it last, and he stared at my face while we did it. For the last few inches of arm he looked down at the wound and not at my face. He watched our arms emerge from the bloody hole just under the sternum. He kept his hand on my arm and forced our hands upward, so that for a moment we held the heart together, and he looked at me over the bleeding muscle.

He'd stolen a kiss like that, our first and, if I could help it, our last.

"Let go of me," I said, softly, each word very clear.

His lips parted, and his breath came out in a long sigh. It

was worse than the smile. I realized in that moment that I had
become a trophy of that kill. A trophy for a serial killer is
something they take from the victim or the murder scene, so
that when they see it, or touch it, or hear it, or smell it, or taste
it, it brings back the memory of the slaughter.

I did my best not to show fear, but I probably failed. Edward
actually stepped up beside us and said, "You heard her."

He turned his eyes behind the sunglasses toward Edward.
The last time we'd all been together, Edward had done what he
could to protect me, but protecting me from Olaf now wasn't
just a matter of guns and violence. Edward had taken my arm
that last time, as if I were a girl and needed to be led. It was the
first time, ever, that Edward had touched me as if I were a girl,
because I was never just a girl to him. He'd put the idea into
Olaf's head that he, Edward, thought of me as a girl, maybe his
girl. Maybe a girl he'd be willing to protect. I wouldn't have
let anyone else endanger themselves for a lie, but if anyone I
knew could handle Olaf, it was Edward. Besides, he was Edward's friend before he was mine, so it was sort of Edward's
fault that Olaf had a crush on me.

Now, Edward did it again. He put his arm around my shoulders. It was a first. It also wouldn't help my reputation with the
other cops, but I wasn't worried about the cops. All I was worried about in that moment was the man with his hands on my
arm and hand. It was such an innocent touch, but the effect it
had on him, and on me, was about as far from innocent as you
could get.

Edward put his arm across my shoulders, less than a hug
but very much about marking territory. It's something that high
school athletes are fond of doing with their cheerleading girlfriends. Again, a fairly innocent gesture, but it was a sign of
possession. *This is mine, not yours.*

I was so not Edward's, but in that moment I might have
volunteered to be anyone's if it would just get Olaf off me. I
was fighting off the memory of our last kill together, and it was
making my skin run cold even in the Vegas heat.

Olaf gave Edward the full weight of that sunglass-covered
gaze, and then, slowly, he let go of me. He stepped back
from us.

Edward kept his arm across my shoulders and looked up at the bigger man. I just stood there and fought the urge to shiver, and finally lost. In a heat so hot it made it hard to breathe, I shivered.

It made Olaf smile again, and for just a moment I had the very clear thought that someday I would kill him. Maybe not this day, or even this time, but eventually he'd cross a line and I would kill him. The thought helped steady me. Helped me feel more myself. It helped me smile back at him, but it wasn't the same smile. His was damn near sexual; mine was the smile, most unpleasant, that has frightened bad guys across the country.

Olaf frowned at me. Which made me smile wider.

Edward squeezed my shoulders in a one-armed hug, then stepped back.

I caught the glances of some of the cops who were outside the station. They'd watched the show. I doubted they understood everything they'd seen. But they'd seen enough to pick up the tension between Olaf and Edward and me. They'd draw the same conclusion that Olaf did, that Edward and I were a couple and it was hands-off.

They were already convinced that I was fucking all of them, so why did it hurt my feelings to do something that confirmed the rumor?

I looked at the police looking at us, and found two of the cops who weren't looking at us. The moment I saw them, I knew who the fourth marshal was.

Bernardo Spotted Horse was standing very close to a female deputy. She had shoulder-length hair tied back in a ponytail. Her small triangular face was turned up to him, all smiles and almost laughing. Even the uniform couldn't hide that she was petite and curvy.

Bernardo was tall, dark, and handsome, even by the standards that I was used to. His hair was actually blacker than mine, that black that has blue highlights in the sun. He'd tied it back in a braid that trailed nearly to his waist. He said something to the deputy that made her laugh, then walked toward us.

He was still broad-shouldered and slim of waist, and he'd been hitting the gym regularly. It all showed. He was also

American Indian, with the perfect cheekbones genetics can give you. It was a pretty package, and the deputy watched him walk away from her. The look on her face said plainly that if he called her later, there would be a date. But then Bernardo knew that. Lack of confidence with women was not one of his problems.

He smiled as he came toward us, sliding sunglasses over his eyes, so that he looked model perfect by the time he got to us.

"That was quite a show you just put on," he said. "They're more convinced than ever that the big guy here is dating you, or wants to, and that Ted here already is. I've done my best to persuade Deputy Lorenzo that I am not in the running for your affections."

I had to smile, shaking my head. "Glad to hear it."

He got a funny look on his face. "I know you mean that, and let me say that it's an ego blow."

"I think you'll recover, and the deputy there looks like she'll be happy to help ease your pain."

He glanced behind and flashed her that world-class smile. She smiled back and actually looked flustered. This was from a smile yards away.

"This is like Old Home Week," I said.

"It's been what, almost three years?" Bernardo said.

"About that," I said.

Olaf was watching us, not like he was happy about it. "The girl liked you."

"Yes, she did," Bernardo said. His white T-shirt looked good against the tan of his skin. It was the only thing that ruined what I'd started calling casual assassin chic: black jeans, black T-shirt, boots, leather jacket, weapons, sunglasses. His leather was on his arm like Olaf's, because it was too damn hot to be wearing leather. I'd left my leather in St. Louis.

Bernardo offered his hand, and I took it, then he raised my hand and kissed it. He did it because I'd let him know I didn't think he was scrumptious, and part of him hated that. I shouldn't have let him do it, but short of arm-wrestling him, there was no graceful way to stop the gesture once it started.

He shouldn't have done it because of the deputy. I shouldn't have let him because of the other cops and Olaf.

Olaf looked not at me but at Edward, as if waiting for him to do something about it.

Edward actually said, "Bernardo flirts with everyone; it's not personal."

"I did not kiss her hand," Olaf said.

"You know exactly what you did," Edward said.

Bernardo looked at Olaf, then at me; he actually lowered his sunglasses so he could give me the full weight of his baby browns. "There something you need to tell me about you and the big guy here?"

"Don't know what you mean," I said.

"He just reacted like guys react around me and the women they like. Otto's never cared before."

"I do not care," Olaf said.

"Enough," Edward said. "Our escort is ready to go, so everyone in the car." He sounded disgusted, which was rare for him. Letting us hear that much emotion in his voice, I mean.

"I call shotgun," Bernardo said.

"Anita gets shotgun," Edward said, and went around to the driver's side.

"You like her better than you like me," Bernardo said.

"Yep," Edward said, and slid in behind the wheel.

I got in the passenger side. Olaf slid across the seat so he was sitting catty-corner from me. I'd have put Bernardo in that corner, but couldn't decide whether it would bother me more for Olaf to stare at me where I could see him, or to know he was staring at the back of my head where I couldn't see him.

The patrol car in front hit lights and sirens. Apparently, we wouldn't be wasting any more time. I looked up at the sun in a sky so bright the blue was washed out—like jeans run through way too many washes. It was afternoon, maybe five hours until full dark. Another car followed behind us with lights and sirens. I was willing to bet that I wasn't the only one who thought delaying all the vampire hunters had been a bad idea.

12

THE CRIME SCENE was a huge warehouse. It was mostly empty, echoing space. Or it would have been if there weren't cops of every flavor, emergency personnel, and forensics all over the place. It was less full than it had been a few hours ago, but still damn busy for a crime scene from the night before last. But, of course, the dead were their own people. Everyone would want a piece of it. Everyone would want to help, or feel like they were helping. People hate to feel useless; cops get that squared. Nothing drives the police more nuts than not being able to fix something, like the ultimate guy attitude. I don't mean guy in a sexist way, either; it's a cop thing. People would linger looking for clues, or trying to make sense of it.

There might be clues, but there wouldn't be any sense to it. Vittorio was a serial killer who had enough vampire powers to make his less powerful vamps help him get his kicks. A serial killer who could share his pathology with others, not by persuasion but just by metaphysical force. Anyone who he turned into a vampire could be forced to join his hobby and share in his perversion.

I stared at all the markers where bodies had lain. Shaw had said they'd lost three, but that was just a number, a word. Standing there looking at the markers where the bodies had lain, where the blood had spilled, brought it home more. There were a lot of other markers, marking where things had fallen. I wondered what things. Weapons, spent shells, clothing—anything and everything would be marked, photographed, videotaped.

The floor looked like a minefield—so many things marked

that there was almost no way to walk through it all. What the hell had happened here?

"Firefight," Edward said, voice low.

I looked at him. "What?"

"Firefight, spent shells, weapons emptied and thrown down. A hell of a fight."

"If those markers are spent shells, then why aren't there dead vampires? You don't empty this much brass into a space this open and not hit something, especially not with the training these guys had."

"Even the vampire hunter was ex-military," Bernardo said.

"How do you know that?" I asked.

He smiled. "Deputy Lorenzo likes to talk."

I gave him an approving look. "You weren't just flirting, you were gathering intelligence. And here I just thought you were hound-dogging it."

"I like to think of it as multitasking," he said. "I got information and she was cute."

Olaf began to walk out through all the little markers and signs that forensics had left behind. He moved gracefully, almost daintily through it all. He looked somehow unreal, moving that large body through the evidence markers. I wouldn't have been able to do it without moving things out of place, but Olaf seemed to glide. I spent most of my time around shapeshifters and vampires, both of which could define the term *graceful*, but it was still impressive, and unsettling, to watch the big man move through the evidence.

I'd have rather seen the actual evidence and the actual bodies, but I understood not being able to leave the bodies in the heat. I also understood not being able to leave weapons lying around, and you had to take the ammo and casings for evidence in case there was a trial.

"They always gather the evidence as if there's going to be a trial," Edward said, as if he'd read my mind.

"Yeah," I said, "but vampires don't get trials."

"No," Edward said, "they get us." He was gazing out over the crime scene as if he could visualize what had been taken away. I couldn't yet. The pictures and video would help me more than this empty space. Then I'd be able to see it, but here was just things removed, and the smell of death getting stronger in the Vegas heat.

They'd taken the bodies away but not yet cleaned up the blood and other fluids, so the smell of death was still there.

I'd been ignoring it as best I could, but once the front of my head thought about it, I couldn't ignore it. One of the real downsides to having as much lycanthropy running through my veins as I do is that my sense of smell can suddenly go into overdrive. You don't want that happening at a murder scene.

The smell of dried blood, decaying blood, was thick on my tongue. Once I smelled it, I had to see it. The blood had to have been there the whole time, but it was as if some filter had been stripped from my eyes. The floor of the warehouse was dark with blood. Pools of it everywhere. No matter how much blood you see in a movie or on television, it's never enough. There is so much blood in the human body, and the floor was so thick with it, it looked like some sort of black lake frozen there on the concrete floor.

They'd given us little booties to put over our shoes, and I knew now that it wasn't just the standard reason. Without them, we'd have been tracking the blood of Vegas's finest all over.

"They didn't feed on them," Bernardo said.

"No," I said, "they just bled them out."

"Maybe some of the blood belongs to vampires. They could have taken their dead," Edward said.

"In St. Louis he left his people behind as bait, and a trap. He left them to live, or die, and didn't seem to give a damn which. I don't think he's the kind of man to take his dead, if he doesn't protect his living."

"What if these dead would have given something away?" Edward said.

"What do you mean?"

"If he wouldn't take his dead because it was the decent thing to do, maybe he would take them if it was the smart thing to do."

I thought about that, then shrugged. "What could dead vampires tell us that we don't already know?"

"I don't know," Edward said, "it's just a thought."

"How did they ambush a SWAT team?" Bernardo asked.

"Did the dead vampire hunter have ability with the dead?" I asked.

"You mean, was he an animator like you?" Bernardo asked.

I nodded. "Yeah."

"No, he was ex-military, but he didn't raise the dead."

"That means they went in without anyone who could sense vampires," I said. Then I had to add, "I know they had a practitioner with them, who was among the dead, but being psychic doesn't mean you do well with the dead."

"There aren't that many of us who have a talent for the dead like you do, Anita," Edward said.

I studied his face, but he was looking out over the crime scene, or maybe he was watching Olaf kneeling so carefully among the carnage.

"I always wonder how you guys stay alive if you can't sense the vamps."

He smiled at me. "I'm good."

"You have to be better than me, if you don't have my abilities and you stay alive."

"Does that make me better than you, too?" Bernardo asked.

"No," I said, and made it sound final.

"Why is Ted better than you, but I'm not?"

"Because he's proven himself to me, and you're still just a pretty face."

"I got damn near killed the last time we played together."

"Didn't we all," I said.

Bernardo frowned at me. The look was enough to let me know that it really did bug him that I didn't think he was as good as Edward.

"How about Otto? Is he better than you?"

"I don't know."

"Is he better than Ted?"

"I hope not," I said, softly.

"Why say it that way, you hope not?"

I don't know what made me say the truth to Bernardo;

Edward, yes, but the other man hadn't earned that kind of honesty from me yet. "Because if I'm not good enough to kill Otto, it'll be up to Edward to finish it."

Bernardo moved closer to me, studied my face hard. He spoke low. "Are you planning on killing him?"

"When he comes for me, yes."

"Why is he going to come for you?"

"Because someday I'll disappoint him. Someday I won't be able to keep being his little serial killer pinup, and when he thinks I'm less fun alive than I would be dead, he'll try for me."

"You don't know that," Bernardo said.

I looked out at the lake of dried blood and the big, graceful man moving through it. "Yeah, I do know that."

"She's right," Edward said, softly.

"So, the two of you are planning to kill him, but you'll work with him until he crosses the line." He spoke very low, almost a whisper.

"Yeah," I said.

"Yes," Edward said.

Bernardo looked from one to the other of us. He shook his head. "You know, sometimes the big guy doesn't scare me as much as the two of you."

"Only because you're not a petite brunette woman. Trust me, Bernardo, if you fit his vic profile, you'd have a whole new level of creep about the big guy."

He opened his mouth, as if to argue, then closed it. He finally nodded. "All right, I'll give you that. But unless you're going to kill him today, let's get to work." He walked away from us, but not toward Olaf. He wouldn't help us contemplate killing Olaf, but he wouldn't exactly stop us, either.

I wasn't sure where Bernardo fell on the good guy/bad guy scale. Sometimes I wasn't sure Bernardo knew, either.

13

TWO HOURS LATER we'd learned all the warehouse could tell us. There were crates that had been used as coffins. They'd been shot to hell by the M4s that the team had carried. If the vampires had been in the crates at the time it would have been a kill, but there was no blood on the inside of any of the crates.

Olaf had padded back to us, soundless, somehow, in his black boots. "I thought it was an explosion, but it wasn't. It's almost as if there was something here that could bleed and incapacitate, but not kill right away. But whatever did this left no trace on the ground. There are no footprints at the center of the blood pool except for the boot tracks of the police."

"How can you tell that it was designed to bleed and incapacitate, but not kill?" I asked.

He'd given me that arrogant look out of his deep, caveman eyes. It was the old Olaf peering out, the one who'd thought that no woman could be good at this kind of work. Hell, women to him weren't good at anything.

"That look makes me not want to admit this, but I want to solve this more than I want to be cool."

"What look?" he asked.

"The look that says I'm a woman, and that makes me stupid."

He looked away, then said, "I do not think you are stupid."

I felt my eyebrows go up. Edward and I exchanged a look. "Thanks, Otto," I said, "but pretend I can't look at a concrete floor and track the events of a crime on it, and just explain. . . . Please." I added the *please*, because we were both trying to be nicer to each other. I could play nice.

"The blood pattern, the markers on the floor. The pictures and video will confirm it, but this was a trap, not with a bomb or human soldiers but with something that could"—he made a waffling motion with one hand—"hover, but still attack. I saw something similar to this once before."

He had everyone's attention now. "Tell us," Edward said.

"I was on a job in the Sandbox."

"Sandbox?" I made it a question.

"Middle East," Edward answered.

"Yes, it was a group of terrorists. They had a sorcerer," Olaf said, then looked way too thoughtful for comfort.

"Don't say the T-word," Bernardo said, "or they'll bring in Homeland or the Feds, and it will get out of our hands."

"When I do my report, I will have to say what I have seen," Olaf said. The flirting was gone; he was all business. He was colder, more self-contained this way, and once I'd thought scary. Now that I had his version of flirting to compare it to, the business side of him was by far my favorite.

"When you say *sorcerer*, are you using it the way we do in the States?" I asked.

"I do not know."

"*Sorcerer* means someone who gets their magic from dealing with demons and evils here," Edward said.

He shook his head. "No, a sorcerer is just someone who uses their powers to harm and never to do good. We did not have a practitioner, as they say here, with us. So I cannot speak knowledgeably about the magic, other than the damage it caused."

"How similar to this was it?" I asked.

"I need to see the bodies before I can be sure, but the blood pattern doesn't look the same. The bodies in"—he stopped as if he wasn't allowed to say the place name—"where I was were substantially different. The bodies there were torn apart, as if by some unseen force that left no tracks and no physical evidence other than its victims."

"I've never heard of Middle Eastern terrorists being willing to work with magic. They tend to kill any witches they find," Bernardo said.

"They were not Islamic," Olaf said. "They wanted to send their country back to a much older time. They thought of themselves first and foremost as Persian. They felt that Islam had weakened them as a people, so they used older powers that the Muslims with us thought unclean and evil."

"Wait," Bernardo said, "you were working with the locals?"

"You do a lot of that," Edward said.

I glanced at him and couldn't read past the blank face, but he'd admitted he had worked in the Middle East. That was news to me, though not a surprise.

"The men working with us would have gladly killed us a week before, but we were all in danger."

"The enemy of my enemy is my friend," Bernardo said.

We all nodded.

"So this may be some kind of Persian bogey beast, not a demon but something similar."

"As I said, we had no practitioners with us, so I can only say the damage seems similar, but not the same."

"Okay, we'll see if we can find anyone in town who knows more than I do about pre-Islamic Persian magic." I looked at Edward. "Unless you know more than I do, which is nothing."

He shook his head. "Nothing."

"Don't look at me," Bernardo said.

I bit back the first reply, which was, *We weren't*. It would have been mean and not entirely true. He'd found out information from the deputy for us. "Okay, we'll see if there's anyone in town who knows more than we do, or even at some university. There's an expert out there somewhere."

"Academics aren't always good with real-world information," Edward said.

"Right now, we have zero to go on, which means any info is better than where we are." I shrugged. "It doesn't hurt to ask."

The homicide detectives called Marshal Ted Forrester over to talk. Edward went, turning to the more open face of his alter ego. I knew that his "Ted" face actually hid more. It was interesting that none of the rest of us was invited to talk to the detectives.

I turned back to Olaf and Bernardo. "Okay, we'll check into

the Persian angle later, but right now I have another question. Why would they kill them in such a way as to destroy the chance to feed on their blood?"

"Maybe their master didn't like the taste of men," Olaf said.

"What?" I asked.

"Their master's victim of preference is strippers, mostly female, correct?" Olaf said.

"Yeah."

He leaned in and whispered so that only I and Bernardo could hear. "I have simply killed men, cleanly, so that I could take my time with the women. Maybe it is the same for this master vampire. He takes no pleasure from feeding on men."

"He killed a male stripper in St. Louis," I said.

"But was he like these men, trained, a soldier?"

I pictured the body in my mind, and because it had been the only male victim, I could see him fairly clearly. "He was tall, but thin, not that muscular, more . . . effeminate, I guess."

"He likes his victims to be soft; the men killed here were not soft."

"Okay," Bernardo said, "didn't it just creep you out that he talked about killing men so he could take his time with the women? Am I the only one who found that disturbing?"

I looked at Olaf, and we had a moment of a look between us, then we both looked at Bernardo. I said, "I know what Otto is and what he does. Frankly, comments like he just made are one of the few reasons I'm glad he's here. I mean, you have to admit he's got a unique insight into the whole serial killer mentality."

"And you're calm about it?" Bernardo asked.

I shrugged and looked back at Olaf, who looked at me, so calm he looked bored. "We're doing our jobs."

Bernardo shook his head. "You are both weird as hell, you do know that, right?"

"You know, you might want to keep your voice down, Bernardo," Edward said. He was back from talking to the detectives and Sheriff Shaw, who had finally joined us. They were still ignoring the rest of us. Somehow I wasn't hurt that Shaw didn't want to talk to me.

"Sorry," Bernardo said.

"They're going to give us access to the forensics: pictures, video, the stuff they bagged and labeled."

"I might learn more from the photos and film," Olaf said.

"They're hoping we all will," Edward said.

"Just let me see the pictures and video," I said.

"I just want something to shoot," Bernardo said.

"You know, life must be simpler for you," I said.

Bernardo gave me a dirty look. "You're just cranky because we've been here for hours and we don't know anything that will help us find this bastard."

"We know it is similar to the Persian sorcerer I met in the Sandbox," Olaf said.

"I know it would be weird, and too coincidental for real life, but could it be the same sorcerer with a slightly different spell, or whatever?" I asked.

"Not possible," Olaf said.

"Why not?" I asked.

"The sorcerer was not bulletproof."

"So he's dead," I said.

Olaf nodded.

"Well, if we can trace someone in this country who plays with Persian magic, then we need to find someone who went missing from his life."

"What do you mean?" Bernardo asked.

"Someone who knows this type of magic and has suddenly vanished. Someone from work, a wife or family member, whatever, someone who's been reported missing. Then we might be looking for someone who was recently made into a vampire," I asked.

"Why?" Olaf asked.

"Because if they'd had this kind of magic in St. Louis or New Orleans or Pittsburgh, they would have used it. This is a complete change in how they kill. If they didn't have missing strippers who fit the original MO, which is what got the warrant of execution revived, then I would say it was someone signing Vittorio's name to the note on the wall and the note that came to my office, but not him."

"It could still be two different crimes," Edward said.

"What do you mean?"

"Maybe Vittorio is killing strippers in Vegas, but that doesn't mean that our sorcerer and the people who killed these operators are actually Vittorio's vampires. They went in standard op for vampire hunts, during the day."

"I know that with SWAT technology they usually go in at night for human bad guys, but vampires are daylight hunts if possible," I said.

"They went in during the day, Anita. The hovering magic, or whatever, killed three of them, and either that sorcerer or something else put the rest in some sort of sleep."

"I've never heard of anything like that," I said.

"No one has," he said.

"But if it was daylight," Bernardo said, "who wrote the note in their blood? Who took the head and mailed it to you? It was daylight and there are windows in here that aren't covered. The only reason the cops are saying vampires is because Vittorio's name is signed, and this was an old lair of the vampires."

"Are you saying someone has framed Vittorio and his vamps for this?" I asked.

Bernardo shrugged. "Maybe."

"Fuck, I don't know whether to hope you're right or hope you're wrong. If you're right, then we have Vittorio to find before he kills another stripper, and some crazy sorcerer who's trying to blame vampires for this crime. Were there fang marks on the dead?"

"No one's said," Edward said.

"Don't tell me," Bernardo said. "We get to go to the morgue and look at the bodies?"

"Are you afraid?" Olaf asked.

Bernardo gave him an unfriendly look that didn't even faze the other man. "No, I'd just rather not go."

"You are afraid," Olaf said.

"Stop it," Edward said, "both of you. We'll go look at the bodies. Though, Otto, you could start calling around about the Persian angle. You are the only one of us who's seen something similar."

"No, I will go to the morgue with"—he looked at me—

"Anita. But I will call the local university from the truck and see if they have the expert we need."

"We're all going to the coroner's," Edward said.

"Otto just wants to watch me poke around in the bodies," I said.

"No," Olaf said, "I want to help you do it."

In that instant I wanted to say that I'd just sit this one out. I'd just look at the pictures and the video and that would be good enough. I did not want to go to the morgue and look at the recently dead, especially with this much blood on the ground. It was going to be pretty gruesome, but more than that I did not want to have Olaf help me with the bodies. He'd enjoy it. But the bodies were part of the crime scene. They were full of clues. I had to see if I could find anything to help us catch whoever had done this. Whether it was Vittorio with a new sorcerer friend, or someone else, they needed to be stopped. How far was I willing to go to stop them? All the way to the morgue with our very own pet serial killer. Sometimes the things I do for my job worry me.

14

OLAF USED HIS new uber–cell phone to search online for the nearest university or college that might have what we needed. University of Texas at Austin was the winner, with both Persian and Iranian studies and a minor available in Near Eastern mythology. Other universities and colleges had the first two but not the third. He left a message with the Near East Studies Department as we pulled into the parking lot of the Las Vegas/Clark County Coroner's Office.

The building was nondescript, set in the middle of an industrial area, but there was a discreet sign that let us know we were in the right place. There was also a little herd of white cars and trucks against the far side of the lot that had *Clark County Coroner* on the side of them. We got out, and Edward led us to a small door beside a larger garage door. He pushed a button to ring the bell.

"I take it you've been here before," I said.

"Yes."

I spoke low. "Was it Edward or Ted who came to town?"

He gave me that smile that said he knew things I didn't. "Both," he said.

I narrowed my eyes at him. "Are you saying you've come as a marshal and an assa . . ."

The door opened, and questions had to wait. Bernardo leaned forward and whispered in my ear, "He never answers questions for anyone but you."

I threw back over my shoulder, as we followed Edward into a double-doored entryway, "Jealous?"

Bernardo scowled at me. No, I shouldn't have taunted him,

but I was nervous, and baiting him was more fun than what we were about to do.

On television there are drawers. In real life there aren't, or not at any morgue I frequent. I'm sure that somewhere there must be drawers, but have you ever noticed on some television shows that the drawers are so high up, you'd have to get a ladder to reach the bodies? What's up with that?

Olaf and I were in the little backward gowns, with two layers of gloves on his and the pathologist's hands: one pair latex, and one pair of the blue nitrile. The double layer had become standard at most morgues, to protect against blood-borne pathogens. Thanks to Jean-Claude's vampire marks, I probably couldn't catch anything, even bare-handed, so I'd opted for a single layer of the nitrile. One, you sweated less; two, if I had to touch, or pick up anything, I was less clumsy in a single layer. I'd never been comfortable in gloves. I chose nitrile over latex because they were more puncture resistant.

Morgues are almost never dark and gloomy, like they show on television. Clark County was no exception; it was bright and strangely cheerful. It smelled clean, with that undertone of disinfectant and something else. I was never sure what the something else was, but it never made me want to breathe deeper. I suspected that the "smell" was actually imaginary, and not there at all. Morgues actually don't smell of much of anything. Clark County had a second cooler for bodies that would have made the morgue smell of something else. I really appreciated that.

Olaf and I were in the first autopsy suite, which was all red countertops, shiny silver sinks, and walls that were tan and red tile. The color scheme looked like someone's cheerful kitchen. Except that most kitchens don't have bodies in plastic wrap on a gurney near the sink and countertops. I couldn't get the kitchen analogy out of my head, so the body didn't look ghostly behind the layers of plastic wrap but oddly like something you'd take out of the refrigerator.

Once the bodies had bothered me, but that was a while ago. What bothers me about morgues now is thinking of the handful of vampires that were awake while I had to stake them. Awake and chained down to a gurney. The ones who just spit at me or tried to bite me to the bitter end don't bother me. It's the ones who cried. The ones who begged for their lives. Those haunt.

Morgues make me think of tears now, and not my own. Clark County had a small room off to the side of the garage that was just for vampire stakings. It was next door to the room that they reserved for organ harvesting. They were nearly identical rooms, just that one helped people live, and the other helped them die. Oh, there were chains and holy items in the vampire room, that was different. But, thankfully, I wasn't having to use that room today.

Dr. T. Memphis—honest, that was on his name tag—stood over the first body. Memphis was five foot six and a little round around the middle, so that his white coat wasn't happily buttoned, but he'd buttoned it all the way up. He wore his white coat, tie, and collar tight. It must have been hell in the desert heat, but then he spent most of his time in cooler places. His curly hair was beginning to give up the fight to cover all of his head, and gray was winning out over the brown he'd started with. Small, round glasses completed the look.

He looked harmless, and professional, until you looked in his eyes. His eyes were cool and gray and pissed. *Angry* did not cover it; he was pissed, and didn't care that we saw it.

Of course, I didn't have to get to his eyes to know that he was not happy with us. Everything he did was jerky with anger. He snapped his gloves on. He banged the side of the gurney. He jerked the plastic off the corpse's face, but only the face. He made sure the rest stayed covered.

Olaf watched everything impassively, as if the man meant nothing to him. Maybe that was the truth. Maybe Olaf spent his life waiting for someone to interest him, and until then, people just didn't. Was it peaceful inside Olaf's head or lonely? Or, maybe just silent.

Edward and Bernardo were looking at the only body they hadn't had time to finish processing. It was in a different room, so it was just Olaf and me with Dr. Memphis. They'd gotten a female doctor, whose name I hadn't caught. I trusted Edward to find out anything I needed to know, and Bernardo to know everything about the attractive woman from just a few minutes' acquaintance. Either way, we were covered.

I had not chosen to start with the processed bodies; Edward had done the division of labor. He'd tried to separate Olaf and himself into one team, and Bernardo and me into another, but Olaf had put his oversized foot down. The best Edward could do was to give me the bodies he thought would be less interesting to the big guy.

Eventually, we'd have to see the other bodies, but we could delay the part that Edward and I both thought would get Olaf's rocks off the most. Sometimes the best you can do is delay the worst part, for just a little bit.

The man nestled in the plastic had short brunet hair. His complexion was gray with the edges dark, like someone who had a tan but had been bled pale. Just from seeing his face and neck, I knew he'd bled to death, or bled out, before he died. The official cause of death might read something else, but he'd been alive long enough to lose all or most of his blood.

"Is the official cause of death exsanguination?" I asked.

Dr. Memphis looked at me; it was a little less hostile. "This one was; why do you ask?"

"I'm a vampire hunter; I see a lot of bloodless corpses."

"You said this one was. Are there other causes of death on the other men?" Olaf said.

He looked up at the bigger man, and again it wasn't as friendly. Maybe he just didn't like men who were over a foot taller than himself. Short person's disease: attitude.

"See for yourself," Memphis said, and he peeled back the plastic farther to expose the man to his waist.

I knew how he'd bled out—cuts. So many cuts. I knew blade work when I saw it. But so many wounds, like angry mouths everywhere, lipless but gaping wide to show the pale meat underneath.

"It was a blade of some kind."

Olaf nodded and reached out toward the wounds with his gloved hands. I stopped him, just short of touching the body, with my own gloved hand on his arm. Olaf glared at me, his deep-set eyes going back to that first blush of hostility he'd had before he started "liking" me.

"Ask first," I said, "we're in the doctor's house, not ours."

He continued to scowl at me, and then his face changed—

not softened, just changed. He put his other hand over mine, so that he pressed my hand to his arm. It was my turn not to freak. But it sped my pulse, and not from the usual reason a man's touch will speed your heart rate. Fear put my pulse in my throat as if I were choking on candy. I fought not to show my fear in any other way. Not for Olaf's benefit, but so the doc didn't figure out something was weird.

My voice was even as I asked the doctor, "Is it okay if we touch the body?"

"I've gathered all the evidence I can from this . . . body, so yes."

He'd hesitated on the word *body*, not something that most pathologists have problems saying. Then I realized I'd been slow. He knew the men, or at least some of them. The odds were that he'd had to work on people he knew over the last few hours. Hard.

I tried to lift my hand from Olaf's arm, but he kept his pressed over mine, holding me in place. For a second I thought it would be a fight, but then he moved his hand away.

I fought not to step away from him. I fought with almost everything I had not to run screaming. Seeing the corpse cut up like this was romantic to Olaf. Motherfucking shit.

He whispered, "You look pale, Anita."

I licked my dry lips and said the only thing I could think of. "Don't touch me again."

"You touched me first."

"You're right, my mistake. It won't happen again."

He whispered again, leaning over me, "I hope it does."

That was it; I stepped away. He made me flinch first; not many people can say that, but I just couldn't stand there beside the cut-up corpse of this man, this police officer, and know that Olaf thought my touching him over the dead body was foreplay. Oh my God, I could not work with this man. I just couldn't, could I?

"Is there a problem?" Dr. Memphis asked, looking curiously from one to the other of us. He wasn't angry anymore, he was interested. I wasn't sure that was an improvement.

"No problem," I said.

"No problem," Olaf said.

We went back to looking at the corpse, and the fact that I was less bothered staring at the butchered man than at Olaf's living eyes said volumes about both Olaf and me. I wasn't sure what it said, but something. Something frightening.

15

I'D EXPECTED OLAF to be heavy-handed with the corpse, now that he had a green light, but he wasn't. He explored the wounds with his fingertips, delicately, as if he were afraid of waking the man or hurting him. At first I thought he had some respect for the dead. Maybe it was the whole military/police thing. You respect your dead. Then I realized that wasn't it at all.

It was when he was on his third wound, and did the exact same pattern again, that I got a clue. He started by tracing the very edge of the wound with his fingertips; then the next time around the wound, he plunged his fingers a little deeper but was still strangely gentle. The next time around he shoved two fingers into the meat of the wound. It wasn't as smooth a motion, as if he were finding bits that stopped the smoothness of his progress, but he circled the wound again.

He finally plunged those two fingers far enough into the wound that it made a little squelchy sound. When he did that, he closed his eyes as if to listen, as if that sound could tell him something. But I was pretty certain that wasn't it. He wanted to savor the sound. The way you close your eyes for a favorite piece of music. Close your eyes so that your sight doesn't steal away some of your hearing.

When he reached for a fourth wound, I started to say something, but Memphis beat me to it. "Is there a purpose to what you're doing, Marshal Jeffries?" His tone said plainly that he doubted it.

"Each wound that I have explored was made by a different blade. Two of the wounds were made with something that had a pronounced curve to it. The first wound was a more standard blade shape."

Memphis and I both looked at Olaf, as if he'd spoken in tongues. I think neither of us had expected anything useful from the corpse fondling. Damn.

"That is exactly right," Memphis said. The doctor stared up at the big man and finally shook his head. "You were able to tell all that with just your fingers along the wounds?"

"Yes," Olaf said.

"I would have said that was impossible, to tell all that from what you just did, but you are right. Maybe you can help us catch this . . . bastard." I wondered what he'd planned on saying before he picked *bastard*, or was he just one of those people who didn't cuss much and needed practice? I'd be happy to help him practice.

"I know blade work," Olaf said, in his usual empty voice, though when your voice is that deep, *empty* has a growl to it.

"Do you need to see the whole show?" Memphis asked.

"The whole show?" Olaf made it a question.

I said, "He means, do we need to see the rest of the body uncovered?"

Olaf just nodded, wordlessly, face impassive.

I wasn't sure we needed to see the damage below the waist, but I couldn't refuse. What if I went all wussy on them and didn't look, but there was some vital clue on the body? Some metaphysical thing that Olaf wouldn't see, or the doc, but I'd know what it was? Olaf knew blade work, more intimately than I ever would, hopefully. But I knew the metaphysics better. In a way, Edward, who did metaphysics pretty well for someone with no talent for it, and Bernardo, who was strictly a see-and-shoot-it guy, were a good team to look at the bodies, and oddly, so were Olaf and I. We each had skills the other lacked, and we could learn more together than apart; as disturbing as that was to admit in my head, it was true.

The cuts continued down the body. I don't know why damage to the sex organs is always so disturbing, but it is. There was nothing special about the damage there, just a cut that happened to cross his groin. It wasn't mutilation for the sake of mutilating; it was just another cut. It still made me want to look away. Maybe it was all those taboos on nudity that I grew up with, but it seemed wrong to just stare. You'd think I'd get over that part, but I hadn't yet. Sexual mutilation, even accidental, bothered me.

Olaf reached toward the body, and for one awful moment I thought he was reaching there, but he went to a wound in the thigh. He didn't lovingly explore it, like he had the others; he just shoved his fingers in, as if looking for something.

He actually knelt beside the gurney, peering into the wound. He had plunged his fingers as far in as he could and was fighting to go farther. He'd actually managed to find new blood.

"What are you looking for?" Memphis asked.

"This one is deeper, and torn. Did you find the tip of one of the weapons broken off in the wound?"

"Yes," and Memphis sounded completely impressed now.

I was impressed, too, but I also knew where Olaf had gotten his expertise. "You knew the weapon had broken off in that wound, particularly, just by looking at it?" I said.

He looked up at me, his fingers still deep in the wound, the tearing he'd made bringing out what little blood was left. His face was finally turned away from the doctor, so he let me see what he was thinking. His face softened and filled with heat, anticipation; romantic things. Fuck.

"Your fingers are smaller than mine; you might be able to reach farther in," he said, and stood, taking his finger out, letting it make another sound. He closed his eyes and let his face show the shudder he'd been hiding from the doctor because only I could see. It wasn't a shudder of fear or revulsion.

I looked away from his face and back at the body. "I'm sure the doctor has gotten everything out of that wound that he can find, right, Doc?"

"Yes, but he's right. I found the tip of a blade. We'll analyze it and hopefully learn something."

"Are all the bodies like this?" I asked. Olaf was still turned away from the doctor. I'd moved so I couldn't see his face. I didn't want to know what he was thinking, and I sure as hell didn't want to see the thoughts cross his face.

"Are you done with this body?" he asked.

"I am; I don't know about Jeffries here."

Olaf spoke without turning around. "Answer Anita's question before I answer yours."

"The bodies that I've processed are like this, yes; some worse, one not as bad, but mostly worse."

"Then, yes," Olaf said, "we are done with this body." His voice was under control, and he turned around, with his face once again its impassive angry normal.

The doctor covered the body back up. Then we got to see number two. Olaf got to take off his gloves and get fresh ones. I hadn't touched the body, so I got to keep mine.

The next body was almost identical, except the man was a little shorter, more muscled, with paler hair and skin. His body had been nearly shredded. It wasn't just cuts; it was as if some machine had tried to eat him, or . . . With the body cleaned and laid out, you could see the damage, and it was still hard for my mind to take it all in.

"What the hell happened to him?" I asked it out loud before I was sure I wanted to.

"The few wounds I've been able to isolate so far seem to have some of the same edges as the earlier wounds. It's the same kind of weapon, maybe the same weapons; I'll need more tests to be sure."

"But this is different"—I gestured at the body—"this is . . . He's been butchered."

"No, not butchered; there was no intent to take meat for eating," Olaf said.

I looked up at him. "Meat?" I said.

"You said he was butchered, but that was not accurate; the meat is ruined this way."

"It's a figure of speech, Otto," I said, and again didn't know how to interact with him.

He was looking at the body, and this time he couldn't hide everything from the doctor. He was enjoying seeing this corpse.

I looked at Memphis and tried to think about something other than Olaf. "This looks almost mechanical," I said. "There's too much for one human being, isn't there?"

"No," Olaf answered. "A human could do all this damage if

some of it were postmortem. I've seen people cut at corpses, but this is"—he leaned over the body, closer to the wounds—"different from that."

"Different how?" I asked; maybe if I just kept asking questions, he'd answer and not be as creepy.

He traced his finger across some of the wounds on the chest. Anyone else around a body would have motioned above the skin, but he touched the body. Of course he did.

"The first body, the wounds are deliberate, spaced. This is frenzy. The wounds crisscross each other. The first one looks almost like a knife fight; most of the wounds are not killing wounds, as if the killer was playing with him, making him last. These wounds are deep from the beginning, as if the killer meant to finish it quickly." He looked at Memphis. "Did anyone interrupt the scene? Any civilians found among the dead?"

"You think the killer heard something and stopped playing, to just kill?" Memphis asked.

"A thought," Olaf said.

"No, no civilians; just the police and our local vampire hunter."

"Is the last body cut up like this one?" Olaf asked.

I'd have thought of it eventually, but I was having trouble being a good investigator around Olaf. My creep factor was getting in the way of my thinking.

"One other member of SWAT is cut up like this. Only the body you've already seen and the vampire hunter are cut, as you put it, like they were played with, or offered a knife fight."

"Do they have wounds on their hands and arms, like they were armed with a knife and fought back?" I asked.

Olaf asked, "How do you know about wounds like that?"

"When you fight with knives, you still use your arms like shields; it's like defensive wounds, but it looks different. It's hard to explain, but you know it after a while."

"Because you've had the same kind of wounds?" he asked. His voice had the faintest edge of eagerness to it. I almost hated to answer the question, but . . . "Yes."

"Did you see wounds like that on the arms of the other men?" Olaf asked.

I thought back, pictured them. "No."

"Because they were not there."

"So no knife fight," I said.

"Or whatever they were fighting was so much faster than they were, they were not able to use their skills to help themselves."

I looked up at Olaf. "It was daylight, and there were uncovered windows in the warehouse. It couldn't have been vampires."

He gave me a look. "You of all people know that there are more than just vampires that are faster than humans."

"Oh, okay, you mean wereanimals."

"Yes," he said.

I looked at Memphis. "Were any of the more frenzied attacks made with things other than blades? I mean, did you find evidence of claws or teeth?"

"Yes," he said, "and the fact that you figured that out makes me glad you got invited here. These are our men, do you understand?"

"You wanted to solve it without help from a bunch of strangers," I said.

"Yes, we owed them."

"I understand," Olaf said. He was ex-military, so he probably did.

"But you know the monsters better than regular police. I thought that the Marshal Service having a preternatural branch was just some politically expedient way to give a bunch of killers a badge. But you guys really do know the monsters."

I glanced at Olaf, but he was still looking at the body. I answered the doc, "We know monsters, Doc, it's what we do."

"I stopped processing the last body when I found what I thought was lycanthrope damage. I wanted to wait for the preternatural experts, which I guess is you."

"So they tell us," I said.

The door to the autopsy suite swung open, and three new gowned and gloved people entered the room, wheeling another gurney and a new plastic-wrapped figure. This plastic was looser, as if it had been hastily thrown back over the body. Memphis stripped off his gloves and started to put on new ones. New body, new gloves; clean up, move down. I threw my gloves after the doctor's. Olaf followed at my heels, like a game of follow the leader. Olaf loomed behind me, a little too close. I hurried to catch up with Memphis and the new arrivals. Three strangers and a corpse, and I was eager to meet them. Anyone was a step up from Olaf at this point.

16

I EXPECTED EDWARD and Bernardo to trail after the body, but they didn't. I wondered if Edward had gotten the call about the warrants. The three strangers were already suited up and ready to go. Memphis introduced one as Dale and the other as Patricia. Dale had glasses behind his faceplate and short, brown hair. Apparently, he wanted to be extra careful. Patricia wore just the protective glasses. She was taller than me and had her hair in tight, dark pigtails. You didn't see many grown women who wore pigtails. She was a little tall for Olaf's preference, but the hair was right. I'd have rather had all men, or at least a blonde. But I couldn't figure out how to ask without giving away the fact that we had a serial killer in our midst and it wasn't the bad guy we were chasing. Of course, maybe I should stop worrying about other women and just watch my own ass for a change. No, because I knew what Olaf was, and if he hurt someone, I would feel responsible. Stupid, or just true?

The last man in the room had a camera in his gloved hands.

Memphis said, "This is Rose."

"Rose?" Olaf made it a question.

"It's short for something worse," Rose said, and that was all he said. I wondered what could be worse, for a guy, than *Rose*? But I didn't ask; something about the way he'd said the last comment left no room for questions. He just got ready to photograph Dale and Patricia once they started undressing the corpse. The doctor had explained to us that we were not to touch the body until he said so, because we could screw up his evidence. Fine with me; I was never in a hurry to touch the messily dead. And the body on the gurney was messy.

The first thing my eyes saw was darkness. The body was dressed in the same dark green SWAT gear that Grimes and his men had been wearing. The blood had soaked into the cloth and turned most of it black, so the body was a dark shape on the tan plastic gurney. His face was a pale blur where they'd removed his helmet, but his hair was as dark as the uniform. His eyebrows were thick and dark, too. But below the eyebrows, the face was destroyed, gone, in a red ruin that my eyes didn't want to make sense of.

I knew why Memphis had thought shapeshifter. I couldn't tell from across the room for sure, but it looked like something had bitten off most of the man's lower face.

Memphis spoke into a small digital recorder. "The examination recommenced at two thirty p.m. Marshals Anita Blake and Otto Jeffries observing." He looked at me from where he stood near the body. "Are you going to do your observation from across the room, Marshals?"

"No," I said, and walked forward. I took a deep breath behind my thin mask and went to stand by the doc and the others.

Olaf came behind me like a scary, plastic-wrapped shadow. I knew he wasn't spooked by the body, so apparently he was going to use the entire thing as an excuse to stay as close to me as possible. Great.

Up close, the ruin of the face was more obvious. I'd seen worse, but sometimes it's not about *worse*. Sometimes it's about *enough*. Lately, I'd begun to feel like I'd had enough. If I'd been on any normal police force, they'd have transferred me off violent crimes after two to four years. I was at six years and counting, and no one was going to offer. There weren't enough marshals in the preternatural branch to trade us around, and I wasn't trained to be a normal marshal.

I stared down at the body, careful to think *body* and not *man*. Everyone copes differently; for me it's very important to think *body*, *thing*. The thing on the gurney was not a person anymore, and for me to do my job, I had to keep believing that.

One of the reasons I didn't do the morgue stakings anymore is that I stopped being able to think of vampires as things. Once a thing becomes a person, it's harder to kill.

"Once you got the plastic off, you stopped because it looked like some really big jaws crunched down on his lower face," I said.

"Exactly what I thought," Memphis said.

There were pale bits of bone showing, but the lower jaw was just ripped away, gone. "Did you find the lower jaw?"

"We did not."

Olaf leaned over me, spooning his much taller body over mine, so that he leaned along me. He was leaning over to look at the wound, but his body was as close to mine as he could get through his protective gown and my clothes. When I put the gown on, I didn't think I'd have to worry about protecting my back. Of course, a second gown wasn't really the kind of protection I wanted from Olaf; guns came to mind.

My pulse was in my throat, and it wasn't the corpse that was bothering me. "Back up, Otto," I said, through gritted teeth.

"I think it could be a tool and not jaws," he said, leaning even closer, pressing himself against me. I was suddenly aware that he was happy to be pressed up against me.

My skin ran hot, and I wasn't sure if I was going to be sick or pass out. I shoved him backward hard and stepped away from him and the body. I must have moved faster than I thought, because Dale and Patricia moved out of my way, and I had the end of the table to myself.

Olaf stared at me, and his eyes were not neutral. Was he thinking of the last time when he'd forced me to help him cut up vampires, and he'd ended the night by masturbating with blood on his hands in front of me? I'd thrown up then, too.

"You fucking bastard," but my voice didn't sound tough. It sounded weak and panicked. Shit!

"There are tools that could crush a man's face like this, Anita." He talked business, but his face wasn't businesslike. A slight smile curled his lips, and his eyes held the kind of heat that didn't match being in an autopsy room.

I wanted to run out of that room and away from him, but I couldn't let him win. I couldn't fail like that in front of strangers. I couldn't give the big bastard the satisfaction. Could I?

I took a few deep breaths through the little mask and got my body under control. *Concentrate, ease the breathing, ease the pulse, control.* It was the same way I had learned to keep the beasts from rising. You had to have that spurt of adrenaline; if you could calm it or keep it from happening, then the rest could not follow.

I finally gave him calm eyes. "You stay on your side of the table, Otto. Do not invade my personal space again, or I will have you up on sexual harassment charges."

"I did nothing wrong," he said.

Memphis cleared his throat, "Marshal Jeffries, if you aren't dating this young lady, then I suggest you do what she says. I've seen men do similar things 'teaching,'"—he made little quotation marks with his fingers—"women baseball, golf, shooting even, but I've never seen anyone try it in autopsy."

"You are a sick motherfucker," Rose said cheerfully.

Olaf turned a look on him that wiped the smile off his face. In fact, Rose went a little pale behind his faceplate. "You do not know me well enough to say such things."

"Hey, man, just agreeing with the doc and Marshal Blake."

"What tool could do this kind of damage?" Memphis asked, trying to get us all back to work.

"There are crushing tools, used in the meat industry. Some to dehorn cattle, others for castration, and some to cut through the neck in a single movement."

"Why would someone carry that kind of stuff with them?" I asked.

Olaf shrugged. "I do not know, but I am saying that there are alternatives to lycanthropes for the injuries."

"Point taken," Memphis said. He looked at me, and his eyes were kinder. "Marshal Blake, are you ready to see the rest of the body, or do you need a minute?"

"If he stays on his side of the table, I'll be fine."

"Duly noted," Memphis said, and he gave a less friendly look to Olaf.

I moved around the gurney, putting it between Olaf and myself. It was the best I could do and stay in the room. But after we finished with this body, I was finding Edward and we were trading dance partners. I could not work with Olaf in the morgue. He saw the whole thing as foreplay, and I just couldn't deal. No, not couldn't, wouldn't.

Bernardo would flirt, but he wouldn't flirt around the bodies. He didn't think freshly slaughtered bodies were sexy; it would be downright refreshing after working with serial killer boy, no matter how outrageous the flirting got.

The doctor started to unfasten the bulletproof vest, then stopped. "Take a few close-ups, Rose." The doc pointed with gloved fingers at places on the vest. Olaf had already leaned in, so if I was to see what had excited the doctor, I had to lean in, too. Shit. Was I so bothered by Olaf that I could not do my job?

I finally leaned closer and saw slash marks in the vest. They could have been from blades or really big claws. It was hard to tell through the cloth. Bare skin would tell me more.

An autopsy for a murder victim is very intimate. It's not just the cutting of the body but the undressing. You don't want to cut or further damage the clothes, in case you mess up clues, so you have to pick the body up, hold it, undress it like some huge doll or sleeping child. At least rigor had come and gone. A body in full rigor is like trying to undress a statue, except it feels unlike any statue you could ever touch.

I've never envied the morgue technicians their job.

Dale and Patricia moved in to raise the body and ease the vest off. I never liked being in the room for this part. I'm not sure why it bothered me to see the corpse undressed, but it did. Maybe it's because it's a part of the process I don't usually get to see. For me, the dead are either fully dressed or naked. Watching them go from one state to the other just seemed like an invasion of their privacy. Did that sound silly? The dead shell on that table didn't give a shit. He was way past embarrassment, but I wasn't. It's always the living that fuck up death; the dead are fine with it.

Olaf was beside me again, but not close enough for me to bitch—yet. "Why does it bother you to see them undress it?"

My shoulders hunched, and I crossed my arms over the green gown, flexing my hands in the gloves. "How do you know I'm bothered?"

"I can see it," he said.

He could only see half my face, and my body was hidden behind the overgown. I knew I'd been controlling how I stood and moved, so how had he noticed? I finally looked at him and let my eyes show that I'd had a horrible thought.

"What did I do now?" he asked, and it was almost that tone that all men use—no, not all men, all boyfriends. Shit.

"Is he bothering you again, Marshal Blake?" Memphis came to stand near us.

I shook my head.

"You say no, but you've gone pale again." Memphis gave Olaf a very unfriendly look.

"I just had a thought, that's all. Let it go, Doc; just let me know when we can come back in and look at the body."

He looked from one to the other of us, but finally went back to join the others. They almost had him naked from the waist up. Even from here, I was almost certain the chest had been clawed up, not cut up.

"I have upset you again, Anita."

"Let it go, Otto," I said.

"What did I do wrong?" he asked, and again it was the boyfriend question.

"Nothing; you didn't do anything creepy or disgusting. You just acted like a guy for a minute."

"I am a guy," he said.

I wanted to say, *But you aren't. You're a serial killer who thinks dead bodies are a turn-on. You're damn near a bad guy, and I'm pretty sure that someday you'll force me to kill you to save my own life. You're male, but you can never be a guy to me.* But I couldn't say any of that out loud.

He was looking at me with those hooded eyes, except there was the faintest glimmer of that look. You know the one. That look that a guy will give you when he likes you and is trying pretty hard to figure out how to please you, and he's not succeeding. That look that says, *What do I do now? How do I win?*

What had my scary thought been? That Olaf was sincere. In some crazy, pathological way, he *like*-liked me. As in *boyfriend*-liked me. Not just for fucking or slaughter, but maybe, just maybe, he actually wanted to date me like one human being to another. He seemed to have no clue how to interact with a woman in a way that wasn't terrifying, but he was trying. Jesus, Mary, and Joseph, he was trying.

17

THE BARE CHEST was sliced and diced, but it wasn't like the others. No one would convince me that this had been done by blades. I knew claw work when I saw it.

"This was no blade or tool," I said. "It's claws."

Olaf leaned on his side of the body, maybe a little closer to both the body and me than he needed, but nothing too noticeable. Maybe I was just being overly sensitive? Naw.

"I know it is not a blade or a tool that I am familiar with," Olaf said.

I looked across the body and found that, yeah, he was looking at me, not at the body. I stood up and moved a step back. Fuck it, he unnerved me and he knew it.

"But what killed him?" Memphis asked.

I looked at the doctor, then back at the body. He was right; none of the wounds so far were fatal. "The jaw bite is terrible, but unless he died of shock, then . . ." I looked at the lower part of the body, which was still covered.

"Yes," Memphis said, "we need to keep looking for the cause of death."

"I'm not a pathologist," I said. "I don't need to know the cause of death, Doc. I'm just here to see if it's something supernatural or not. That's it, all my job."

"Then leave, Marshal Blake, but first can you confirm that it was a lycanthrope attack?"

I had to go back to the body and spread my hands above the wounds. I curled my fingers in the closest imitation I could of the marks. I traced the air above the wounds but was careful not to touch the body. "It was claws and a lycanthrope, and they were in half human, half animal form when the attack took place."

"How can you be sure of that?" Memphis asked.

I held my hand up. "Watch my hand trace over the wounds. The marks were made by a hand, not a paw."

The woman, Patricia, said, "Your hand is too small to make marks like that, even with claws."

"The hands get bigger when the person shapeshifts." I sighed and looked across the table. "May I borrow your hands for a moment, Otto?"

"You may," he said, and held those big hands out.

"Can you place your hands above the wounds like I was doing, and trace the wound track?"

"Show me again," he said.

I traced my right hand over the wounds, and he put his much larger hand over mine, so that we traced the wounds together. I tried to pull away, and he pressed our hands to the wounds, trapping me against the body, our fingers spread. He pushed his fingers into the wound tracks, and the spread of his fingers was big enough to fit the wounds. He pinned my hand to the body, while his gloved fingers dug into the meat of the wounds.

Rose kept taking pictures.

"Stop it, Otto," I said through gritted teeth. I had multiple weapons on me, but nothing he had done here made it okay to shoot him in front of witnesses.

"I am doing what you asked," he said.

I tried to pull my hand out from under, but he pressed harder, pressing our hands into the dead flesh and the fresh wounds. His fingers made wet sounds in the wounds, while he pressed my hand tight under his.

"You're messing up the wound marks, Marshal Jeffries," Memphis said.

Otto didn't seem to hear him. I had choices. I could faint— no. I could throw up on him, but the body was in the way. I could go for a gun left-handed and shoot him. That was appealing, but not practical. Too many witnesses. I thought of one other choice.

I leaned in and spoke low. "If you ever want to date me for real, let me go." I'd rather date an untamed cougar, but I was figuring that he was crazy enough not to understand that.

He looked at me, and there was surprise in his eyes. He raised his hand enough for me to pull away. I cradled my hand against the green gown as if it hurt.

"Are you hurt, Marshal Blake?" Memphis asked.

I shook my head. "I need some air, though. I'm sorry, Doctor." I'd never left an autopsy room early. I'd never bailed on anything before, but it wasn't the body that I bailed on. It was Olaf, standing there, looking at me. The look wasn't serial killer sex now, it was puzzlement. It was that guy look again, as if he truly was trying to figure out what would please me. That was the look I had to get away from. That was the image that made me turn for the door and fight not to run.

18

I STRIPPED OFF the gloves and the gown and threw them away. I was calm until I hit the outer door and the hallway, then I walked away from that room as fast as I could without running. I would not run, but God, I wanted to.

I was more upset than I knew, because I damn near ran into Edward and Bernardo as they came out of another room. Edward grabbed me, or I might have fallen.

"Anita, are you all right?"

I shook my head.

"The bodies are bad," Bernardo said.

I shook my head again. "It wasn't the bodies. The bodies are fine."

Edward's grip on my upper arms tightened. "What did Otto do now?"

I just kept shaking my head and felt the first hard tear begin to trail down my face. Fuck, why was I crying?

"What did he do?" When I didn't answer, he shook me. "Anita! What did he do to you?"

I finally calmed enough to look up at him. I shook my head. "Nothing."

His fingers tightened, almost hurting on my arms. "This doesn't look like nothing." But his voice, his eyes, everything, made me afraid of what he might do if he really thought Olaf had hurt me.

"Honest, Edward, he just did his usual creepy stuff." I calmed enough to be less tense in his arms. When I relaxed, so did he, but his fingers stayed on my arms. He studied my face.

"First, it's Ted, Anita," but his voice still held that anger, and his eyes were Edward at his most dangerous.

I nodded. "I'm sorry, Ted, sorry. Just . . ." I just shook my head. What was I supposed to say, that Olaf had spooked me so badly that I'd forgotten everything else? That would not help calm Edward, or me.

"Second, you don't spook this easy. What did he do?" That last sentence was low and deliberate, and full of carefully contained rage. I understood in that moment that Edward blamed himself for Olaf's interest in me. I guess he had put us together, but I realized that he would blame himself if the worst happened, and neither God nor the devil himself would be able to keep Olaf safe from him. Of course, that would make me dead, and badly, horribly dead, too. I guess I wouldn't really care. Shit.

"We looked at one body that had claw marks on it. Shapeshifters of some kind. The doctor made noises that there might be more bodies like that, but most of it's blades."

Edward and Bernardo looked behind us. I didn't look, because I was pretty sure what I'd see.

"Before he gets to us, I need to know what he did to upset you, Anita," Edward said.

"I don't know if I can explain it, Edward. The pathologists didn't buy that human hands had made the wounds because my hands were too small, so I borrowed Olaf's hands to show the size."

Edward let me go and started for the big man. I grabbed his arm. "No, Edward, Olaf learned things from the wounds on the other bodies. He really did. His expertise with a blade and torture was valuable. Even Dr. Memphis was impressed."

Edward wasn't looking at me but down the hall.

I talked faster. "We didn't learn as much from this body, from him, because it was claws, and that's my area. I let him boss me around, Edward, more than I should have, because he had been smart about the other body. I let him manipulate me until I just broke. It wasn't his fault. He was just being him, and I forgot for a second, Edward."

Edward looked at me then and wrapped his arm around me. It was so unexpected that I tensed. He looked at me, and it was not the least romantic. The look was intense, angry, and down deep in his eyes, a flash of fear. He was afraid for me. Edward was never afraid, almost never.

"Don't ever forget what he is, Anita," he whispered, as he leaned in. "When you forget that they're monsters, they kill you." He kissed me on the cheek. I know he did it for Olaf's benefit. I know he didn't kiss me on the mouth for his and my benefit. It would have been too weird.

I gave startled eyes to Olaf as he came closer to us, pulling off his gown. The gloves had already gone in the trash. He looked from me to Edward, but finally just at Edward. "What has she told you?"

"That it wasn't your fault. That she let you manipulate her because you had been smart with the other bodies. That your expertise with blades and torture had been helpful."

Olaf looked surprised, and his voice matched. "She did not lie."

"Did you think I'd come out here and lie, say you'd been a big, bad man, and ask for help?"

He put those deep-set eyes on me and nodded. "Women lie, and they use men against each other. It's what they do."

I shook my head and pushed away, gently, from Edward. "I don't do shit like that. I let you manipulate me, and that won't happen again, but I knew better. I let you . . . get in my head. And I knew better." I slapped my chest with my hand, hard enough to hurt. "I knew better. I don't ask anyone to protect me from my own stupidity."

"It took you longer than I thought it would to realize that you know more about shapeshifters than I do. You could have just refused me entry to the room."

I nodded. "Yeah, stupid fucking me." I walked away then, shaking my head. I had to get away from Olaf and Edward and Bernardo's interested eyes. I'd had enough testosterone for the day.

Dr. Memphis called from down the hallway. "Marshal Blake, may I speak to you for a moment?"

I looked past the other men to the doctor. He was still in his gown, no gloves, like Olaf. Shit. I'd let Olaf spook me; I wouldn't make the same mistake twice. I walked past them all and pointed a finger at the big guy. "You stay here. The two of you keep an eye on him, so I don't have to." Then I walked past all of them and went for the doctor. I'd put another gown on, another mask, more gloves. I'd look at the damn bodies on my own because Olaf was right—I knew lycanthropes better than any of the rest of them. I would look at these bodies on my own, and God willing, I'd learn something that could help us figure out what the fuck was going on.

"Is Marshal Jeffries coming back in?" Memphis asked.

"No," I said, and walked back through the doors.

19

THEY HAD FINISHED undressing the body when Memphis walked me back inside the room. It lay bare and very unalive. It looked like a body now, without the clothes, and the wounds like bright tears on the skin.

From across the room I could see that the groin was bloody. I couldn't tell how bad the damage was from here. I didn't really want to know how bad it was, but as usual I had to see it all. Crap.

Rose either had taken all the pictures he needed or was too shocked to take them. He stood there, with his camera forgotten in his hands. The other two techs were no better. Dale had busied himself with something at the cabinets. Patricia went to stand by Rose and turned her back.

"Anyone who needs to leave can do so," Memphis said.

Dale went for the door without a word. "They were friends," Rose said, and that was enough.

"Patricia," Memphis said, "do you need to go?"

"No, Doctor, no, I'll stay. I didn't know him as well as Dale did, and there are some of the . . . I did know some of them better. I don't want to work on them, so I'll stay." She turned around, pale, lips thin, but a determined look on her face. She'd do.

"Rose?" Memphis asked.

"I'm okay, Doctor. It's not that I knew him. I'm being all wimpy about the wound. Sorry." He nodded. "Sorry, I'll do better." He raised the camera back up and started snapping.

I walked around the body so I could see the wound closer. Not that I wanted to see it, but it was an odd wound. Of course, once I was on the other side, I could see the inside of the right thigh clearly. Someone had sliced it open from groin to almost knee. The femoral artery would have been toast. You bleed out from that in fifteen, twenty minutes tops. You can save yourself if the wound is low enough for a tourniquet and medical help is coming. But whoever sliced him up didn't want him saving himself with first aid.

Whatever he might have been once as a man, now he was just bloody, but . . . the genitalia were intact, or looked it. The only way to be certain was to touch them and see, and I didn't want to know that badly. I had to peer a lot closer than I wanted to, but I was right, the wounds didn't actually go across the genitalia, more around them. "When are you going to wash the blood away?"

"Yes," Memphis said, "we'll be able to see those wounds more clearly when we've finished cleaning the body, but we wanted you to see it first."

I looked up at him. "Why?"

"You're our shapeshifter expert," he said.

"You have shapeshifters in Vegas," I said.

"We do, but they wouldn't be allowed near a lycanthrope kill."

"Yeah, same at home, so you have to make do with me."

"If half your reputation is real, Marshal Blake, we aren't making do."

I looked away from his too-intense eyes. He wanted me to solve this. He wanted me to help them catch the thing that had killed their people. I wanted to help, but I hated that feeling of pressure. The sensation that if I missed the clue there was no backup. I thought about calling Edward in, but wasn't sure I could call in part of my backup without getting the rest of it back. I was done with Olaf for the day if I could manage it.

I peered as close to the wounds as I could. "It looks like the claws were driven in around the groin, deep, but straight in and out, no tearing." I stood up and gestured at the thigh wound. "Not like that."

"Was it more than one shapeshifter?" Rose asked.

It was a good question. "Could be, but I don't think so. This up close and personal, there just isn't room for two to fight. I'm not discounting it, but all these wounds are so debilitating that once it happened, there wouldn't be any need for two shapeshifters to fight this man."

"His name was Randall Sherman, Randy," Memphis said.

I shook my head. "No names in the morgue. I function because it's a body. I'm sorry that he was your friend, but I can't think of him that way and do my job."

"I thought you had to have a name to raise the dead," Patricia said.

"Yes, but none of these bodies will be able to be raised."

"Why not?" Patricia asked.

"Murder victims tend to go after their murderers, first and foremost. They maim or kill anything that gets in their way, including innocent civilians."

"Oh," she said.

I stared down at what was left of Officer Randall Sherman and cursed Memphis for giving me a name. I don't know why it can make such a difference, but suddenly I looked at him, not at a body. I noticed that he was tall and athletic, and had spent a lot of time staying in shape. He was probably on the other side of thirty, but it had been a good early thirty. All that work, to be strong, to be fast, to be the best, and some monster comes by and is stronger, faster, and better, just because of a disease in its blood. No amount of weight lifting or jogging would ever make a human being the equal of a shapeshifter. So unfair, so true.

"What kind of hair did you find on the body and clothes?"

"We found human hair, but no animal hair," Memphis said.

I looked at him.

"Yes," he said, "you can look surprised. I've seen two other shapeshifter kills, and we found a lot of animal hair at both. You can't get this close to someone and not shed on them, but this shifter cleaned the body of hair so we wouldn't know what it was."

I shook my head. "Not necessarily, Doc. You can police your brass, but not the little bits and pieces of your body. I saw the crime scene. It was a hell of a fight, and there was no time to clean up like that."

"Then what did the creature do? Did he wear a suit?" He touched his own suit.

"I doubt it," I said, "but a really powerful shapeshifter can do a partial shift."

"I know a manwolf or mancat form," Memphis said.

"No, I mean the really powerful ones can shapeshift just the hands into claws, and the feet. I saw a werewolf climb the side of a building like that."

"That was one of your cases?"

"I don't know what you mean by that, but I saw the bastard do it."

"He used claws to shove into the building?" Patricia asked.

"Yes," I said.

"Wow, shades of Spider-Man," Rose said.

"More Wolverine," I said, "but the principle's the same."

"He got away," Memphis said.

"Temporarily," I said.

"How did they catch him?" Patricia asked.

"I got them to approve werewolves to track the rogue werewolf, then I killed him."

"What do you mean you killed him?" she asked.

"I mean, I walked up to him and put a bullet between his baby blues."

Her mouth made a little soundless O. Rose said, "Just one bullet?"

"No," I said.

"Back to the case; you can listen to war stories from the marshal after we've caught our man."

"Sorry, Doctor," Patricia said.

"Sorry, Doc."

"So you think we have a very powerful shapeshifter that did this."

"I'm pretty sure, and that means that it's a very small pool of suspects. There aren't that many shifters in any city that can do it. Maybe five in a large animal group. Maybe one in a small."

"Do you think the shapeshifter cut up the other men?"

"No, it's almost like whatever did it had multiple arms. An arm for every blade."

"Do you know any preternatural creature that has multiple arms, Marshal?"

I thought about it. "There are a lot of mythologies with many-armed creatures, but none native to this country. And frankly, Dr. Memphis, none that I'm sure are real and in existence today."

"So hard to tell fact from fiction when we live in a world where myth is real," he said.

"Some of it's extinct," I said.

"Whatever killed Randy Sherman wasn't extinct," he said.

I felt that unpleasant smile curl my lips and was glad it was hidden behind the half mask. I wouldn't want to scare the civvies. "We'll work on making it extinct."

"You'll need a warrant of execution," Memphis said.

"Four dead police officers. One obviously dead by were-animal attack. Getting the warrant won't be the problem."

"I suppose so," Memphis said, not like he was entirely happy about it.

"Something wrong?" I asked.

"It's just that I signed the petition that they took to Washington to try to get the Domestic Preternatural Endangerment Act repealed. I believe that the warrants for your job are too broad and violate human rights."

"You're not alone."

"Now, all I want is for you to get the bastards that did this; I don't care that the warrant is based on bad law. So that makes me a hypocrite, Marshal Blake, and I'm not used to thinking of myself that way."

"You've seen vampire and shapeshifter victims before," I said.

He nodded. "Not here, though. Vegas has one of the lowest rates of murder by preternatural means of any city in the United States."

I widened my eyes. "I didn't know that." In my head I thought, *Max and Bibiana run a very tight ship.* Out loud I said, "Is this the first person you knew who died like this?"

"No, first friend, though. I guess if I really believed my convictions, that wouldn't make a difference."

"Emotion always makes a difference," I said.

"Even for you?" He looked at me when he asked it.

I nodded.

"I've heard the screams when the executioner has to stake the vampire during the day. They beg for their lives."

"Everyone on death row is innocent, Doctor; you know that."

"It doesn't bother you then?"

I had to look away from that searching gaze. The moment I had to look down, I forced myself to meet his eyes and said the truth. "Sometimes it does."

"Then why do it?"

Was it mean to say the next? I couldn't tell anymore; maybe it was just true. "I'm sorry for your loss, Doctor, I truly am, but this moment is a perfect example of why I do my job. Look at what they did to your friend. Do you want that to happen to someone else's friend, husband, brother?"

His face hardened, and it was back to the original hostile look. "No."

"Then you need me to do my job, Doctor, because once a shapeshifter crosses the line this badly, they almost never go back. They get a taste for letting the beast out. It feels good to them, and they will do it again unless someone stops them."

"You mean kills them," he said.

"Yes, kills them. I want to kill the shapeshifter that killed your friend, before it kills someone else."

It was his turn to look away. "You've made your point, Marshal. If you need it, I'll sign off that a shapeshifter did this, because it's true."

"Thank you, Doctor."

He nodded. "But the way DPEA is written, you don't need me to sign anything, do you? You just need to call Washington, and they'll fax you the warrant."

"Contrary to popular media, we do have to assure them it's preternatural in origin."

"Assure them, but not prove beyond the shadow of a doubt."

"Shadows of doubt are for courts, Doctor."

"This shapeshifter is never going to see the inside of a courtroom, is it?"

"Probably not."

He shook his head. "They offered to let someone else work on Randy, but it's the last thing I can do for him."

"No, it's not, Dr. Memphis. You can help me gather enough evidence to get a warrant and hunt his killer down."

"And see, there you go, Marshal, right back at my moral dilemma."

I didn't know what to say to that; I had my own moral dilemma to work on, and I didn't know Memphis well enough to tell him I was beginning to have doubts about my job, too. I did the only thing I could think of; I went back to work.

"I am sorry for your loss, but can you let me see the personal effects I missed?" In my head, I added, *when I let Olaf run me out of the room,* but I kept that part to myself. It was humiliating enough without sharing. I was thinking better without him in the room. I hadn't realized just how much he was throwing me off my game until he was gone. Division of labor would not leave me alone with him again, I promised myself that.

In a plastic baggie was a silver pentagram. "Was he Wiccan?"

"Yes," Memphis said, "does that matter?"

"It may be why the shifter ate his face off first."

"Explain," Memphis said.

"If I'm right, then Sherman was saying a spell, and the shifter stopped him."

"There's no spell against lycanthropes, is there?" Rose asked.

"No," I said, "but there are spells that impact other preternatural entities. Spells are almost exclusively for noncorporeal beings."

"Like ghosts," Patricia asked. She'd been so quiet in her corner of the autopsy suite that I'd almost forgotten her.

I shook my head. "No, not ghosts. You just ignore them. But spirits, entities, demons, and other things like it."

"You mean like the devil," Patricia said.

"No, my bad, I shouldn't have said *demon*. What I mean is something that is more energy than physical, sort of."

"Whatever wielded the knives was very physical," Memphis said.

"The knives were very physical, but if Sherman thought a spell could help against them, then maybe whatever was using them wasn't."

"I don't understand," Rose said.

"Nor do I," Memphis said.

I hated trying to explain metaphysics. It always came out wrong, or at best confusing. "I'll need to talk to Sherman's coven, or at least his high priestess, but if he was any good at the magic side of his faith, then he wouldn't have wasted breath on something that wouldn't help save them."

"Randy was very devout, and very serious about his faith," Memphis said.

I nodded. "Okay, I'll still want to talk to his priestess, but for right now, I need to see if I can figure out what animal flavor did this."

"There are no nonhuman hairs, Marshal," Memphis said.

I nodded. "I heard."

"It will take time to analyze the claw marks."

"That may not help you that much anyway, not in this modified form. We know we're looking for a smaller person."

"What do you mean, Marshal?"

"When a shapeshifter makes the claws come out, the hand gets bigger than human-normal. Marshal Jeffries was able to palm the marks on the chest. He's a big guy, but his hands aren't as big as a shapeshifter's when it's in half-man form. That means we're looking for someone who isn't that tall, or has smaller hands."

"But you just said that the hands get bigger," Patricia said.

"Yes, but there's a limit to how much bigger. If you take two people who are both the same animal, but one is six feet with large hands, and the other is five feet with small hands, when they both shift, the animal form will be larger than their human form, but the smaller man will still be a smaller shapeshifter than the larger man. It's a mass ratio thing."

"I've read widely on shapeshifters, Marshal, and I've never read where anyone has written that up."

I shrugged. "I know shapeshifters, Doctor."

"All right, then we're looking for a smaller man."

"Or woman," I said.

"You really think a woman did this?" he asked.

"I've seen shapeshifters of both sexes do some pretty amazing things, so yeah, this damage doesn't rule out female."

"You said you're going to try and figure out what animal did this. We've got swabs for DNA, and we may get lucky, but if the lycanthrope was in human form except for the claws and teeth, as you maintain, then the DNA may come back human."

"There should be some of the virus in the DNA," I said.

"Yes, and in a few days we'll have it back."

I shook my head. "We don't have a few days."

"I'm open to suggestions, Marshal."

"I told you, I'm carrying lycanthropy; that means that sometimes I can smell things people can't."

"You're going to try to smell what kind of animal it was."

I nodded.

"But," Patricia said, "if the shapeshifter was in human form, then won't it just smell human?"

"No," I said, "once you know what you're smelling, there's an undertaste." I shook my head. "I can't explain this, but I want to try."

"I would be eager to see you try," Memphis said.

"I'll have to take the mask down."

"That's against protocols."

"I may get my breath, saliva on things, but I can't catch anything from the . . . Sherman."

"If it will catch this creature days early, then do it."

I looked at the objects and tried to decide what would be the piece of clothing or equipment that the lycanthrope had gotten the closest to. I looked at it all in the baggies, and finally settled on the throat/ear microphone getup. It had actually been damaged by the teeth.

"I need one of you to unbag and make sure that the chain of evidence doesn't get fucked up."

"Your smelling something won't be admissible in court, not even with this many officers dead," Memphis said.

"No," I said, "but I'm not looking for court proof. I'm looking for a clue as to where to go to find people to question. That's all we can hope to get from this."

"If you smell a certain animal, then you'll go talk to that local group," he said.

"Yes," I said.

He came over and carefully unbagged the evidence. I took the mask down and leaned forward. I closed my eyes and called on that part of me that wasn't quite human anymore. I could visualize the beasts inside me: wolf, leopard, lioness, white and yellow tiger. They were all lying in the dark shadows of ancient trees that had been the visualization for my inner place since a certain very ancient vampire had messed with me. Marmee Noir, the Queen of All Vampires, had given me the tigers in a bid to control me. So far, I was still ahead; so far.

I called, gently, to the beasts, and felt them stir. I could keep them from trying to physically manifest now. I could call them as energy. I tried that now. I needed to scent something. I called on wolf. She came trotting to my call, white with her black markings. I'd done some research and knew that her markings meant the strain of lycanthropy was probably from the far north, someplace cold. You had more white wolves where you got more snow.

My skin ran in goose bumps, and I lowered my face toward the piece of technology. The first smell was death. The wolf growled, and it trickled out my lips.

Memphis said, "Are you all right, Marshal?"

"I'm all right; please don't talk to me while I do this."

The smell of plastic was sharp, almost bitter. The wolf didn't like it. Underneath that was sweat, fear, and she did like that. Fear and sweat meant food. I pushed the thought back and concentrated. I needed more. I smelled Sherman, the scent of a man, and that he still smelled of the soap and shampoo he'd used that day. It was like peeling the layers off an onion. I think if I'd been a wolf I could have smelled all of it, and interpreted it, but my human brain was slow.

I felt my nose touch the felt piece, and thought, *What animal did this?* I smelled saliva, and it wasn't the same scent as Sherman. Though my mind couldn't interpret how it was different, it just was. I needed the scent of the animal, not the person. I gave myself over to the wolf, to the feel of fur and pads, and . . . there. The faintest whiff of something not human.

I followed that faint scent the way you'd follow a path that you found in the woods. A path that was barely there, lost in weeds and small trees. I pushed my way through that narrow opening, and suddenly the world was full of . . . tiger.

The tigers inside me rushed up, roaring. I stumbled back from the evidence, the scent, Memphis. I fell on my ass on the floor, with the wolf running for cover and the tigers snarling inside my head. Once this would have meant the tigers trying to take over my body, tearing me apart from the inside out, but now I could keep it lower key.

Someone grabbed my arm, and I looked up. What was this plastic man? I looked past the faceplate and found him human, and soft, and knew that all that education, all that determination, was nothing before claw and fang. I had to try twice to speak, "Room, give me room."

He let me go, but just knelt back. I looked at him and the other two. Patricia was afraid, and that made the tigers roil inside me, happy kitties. Fear means food.

I pushed to my feet and stumbled for the door. I had to get away from them. I should never have tried this without Edward here to make sure . . . make sure it didn't get out of hand.

"I need air, that's all. Don't touch me." I made the door and stumbled outside. I ended up on my knees on the floor, leaning against the wall, trying to shove the tigers back into the safety zone. They didn't want to go. They'd smelled another tiger, and it excited them.

Edward spoke from a little distance. "Anita, you all right?"

I shook my head, but held a hand palm out, to say *Stay away*. He did. "Talk to me," he said.

My voice came breathy, but it came. "I called on a little furry energy to try and get a clue."

"What happened?"

"I don't know what killed the others, but we're looking for a weretiger that's probably under six feet in human form, or has abnormally small hands. This one is powerful enough to be able to do claws and teeth only, with no fur and no other outward change."

I felt Olaf and Bernardo close, before I looked up and saw them. Edward kept them back, which was probably just as well.

"Only the most powerful can do that," Edward said.

"Yeah," I said.

"You learned all that from smelling?" Bernardo said.

I looked up, and was pretty sure it wasn't a friendly look by his reaction. "No, I learned most of that from the body, but tiger was smell." I looked past him to Olaf now in his black assassin gear, stripped of the hazmat suit. I pointed a finger at him. "I couldn't think with you in there with me. I didn't know how useless you make me until you weren't there."

"I did not mean to make you work less efficiently."

"You know, I believe that. But from now on you work with someone besides me. No more alone time on the case."

"Why is being alone with me so distracting?" he asked, and his face was neutral enough.

"Because you scare me," I said.

He smiled then, a little curl of lips, but his caveman eyes gleamed with satisfaction.

I stood up then, and Edward was smart enough not to help me. "You know, big guy, most men who really want to date a woman don't want her afraid of them."

His smile faltered a little, but not much. He looked puzzled for a moment, then the smile returned larger and more satisfied. "I am not most men."

I gave a sound that might have been a laugh, if it hadn't been so harsh. "Well, that is the fucking truth." I started stripping off the protective gear.

"Where to?" Edward said.

"We visit the weretigers."

"Aren't they the animal to call of the Master Vampire of Vegas?" he asked.

"Yep."

"So we go visit the Master of the City and his wife."

I nodded. "Yep, Max and his wife, the queen tiger of Las Vegas. Though the actual title is Chang and her name. Chang-Bibiana, in this case."

"Wait," Bernardo said. "Are we walking in there and accusing one of their tigers of killing a police officer and helping massacre three more?"

I looked at Edward; he looked at me. "Something like that," I said.

Bernardo looked unhappy. "Can you please not get me killed until after I've had a date with Deputy Lorenzo?"

I smiled at him. "I will do my best."

"To get us all killed," he said.

"Not true," I said. "I always do my best to keep us alive."

"After you endanger us all," he muttered.

"You whine like a baby," Olaf said.

"I'll whine any way I damn well please."

Memphis came out and asked, "Marshal, are you well?"

I nodded. "I'm fine."

"What animal did you sense?"

Did I lie, or tell the truth? "Tiger."

"Our Master of the City will not like that."

"No, but truth is truth."

"You will need a warrant to enter their home."

"We had this talk already, Memphis. We'll call up and have one faxed to us, but I think I'll try just asking for a visit first."

"You think he'll just let you waltz in and accuse his people of murder?"

"I think Max told Sheriff Shaw to invite me to come play and that I'd sort things out."

Memphis's eyes went wide. "Did he now?"

"So I'm told."

"It doesn't sound like our master."

"No, it doesn't," I said, "but if he invited me, why wouldn't he want to help me sort things out?"

"You won't get in without a warrant. The Master of Vegas is old-time mob; it makes him cautious," Memphis said.

"We'll apply for several," Edward said.

Memphis looked at him. "What do you mean?"

"We have a lycanthrope kill confirmed. Nevada still has varmint laws on the books. We'll be able to get a warrant of execution on the lycanthrope that did this."

"But you don't have a name for the lycanthrope," Memphis said.

Edward smiled, I smiled, even Bernardo smiled. Olaf just looked sinister. "You know we don't need a name. The warrant will read a little vague. I keep forgetting about the varmint laws in the western states; it makes it actually easier to get a vague warrant for a shapeshifter than for a vampire," I said.

"I still believe it's a legal excuse for murder," Memphis said.

I stepped close to the doctor, and he held his ground. "Randall Sherman was your friend, not mine. Don't you want his murderer caught?"

"Yes, but I want to make sure it's the right weretiger, not just the one that pisses you all off."

I grinned at him, but could feel it was more a snarling flash of teeth. The tigers were still a little close. "If you don't like the way I do my job, then file a complaint. But in the dark when the big bad monsters come to get you, you always want us. You see us standing here. You know what we are, what we do, and it makes you feel uncivilized. Even with your friends on gurneys in the morgue, you flinch. Well, we don't flinch, Doctor. We do what the rest of you are afraid to do"—I leaned in close and whispered—"we'll be your vengeance, Doc, so you can keep your lily-white hands clean."

He stepped back as if I'd struck him. "That's not fair."

"Look me in the eye and tell me you don't want vengeance for what it did to your men? Look me in the eye and tell me you don't look forward to weighing their murderer's liver on a scale?"

His eyelids flickered behind his glasses. He opened his mouth, closed it, licked his lips. He finally said, "You are a hard woman, Blake."

I shook my head. "No such thing as a hard woman, Memphis, just soft men." With that, I turned, and the others followed me. We went for the doors, and a phone, and a judge who would give us warrants.

Edward said, "What did the doctor do to piss you off that badly?"

"Nothing, absolutely nothing."

"Then what's with the super bitch act?" Bernardo asked.

I laughed. "Who was acting, Bernardo, who the fuck was acting?" The tigers swirled inside me, happy that I was angry, looking forward to more anger, more emotion. They wanted out. They wanted out so badly.

20

I GOT OUTSIDE in the breath-stealing heat, and Edward grabbed my arm, swinging me around to face him.

I stared up at him.

"Anita, are you all right?"

I started to say *Fine*, but Edward didn't ask questions like that unless something wasn't right.

I looked at his hand on my arm until he let me go. "I'm fine."

He shook his head. "No, you're not."

I opened my mouth to argue, then I forced myself to stop and take a few deep breaths. I tried to think past the feeling of eagerness and anger. I was angry. Why? Memphis had done nothing to piss me off that much. So he was a liberal who didn't approve of DPEA; so what? There were lots of people who felt that way. So why had I pulled him up by the short hairs?

Why was I angry? Okay, scratch that, I was almost always angry. Rage was like fuel for me. It always bubbled just below the surface. It was probably one of the reasons that I could feed on other people's anger. It was my drink of choice. The real question was, why was I being a shit to someone who hadn't earned it? That wasn't like me.

I was about to run off and see the weretigers; a lot of them. The tiger energy inside me was happy about that and just a little too eager. Just because I hadn't shapeshifted for real didn't mean I wouldn't. The only other person I'd met with this many different kinds of lycanthropy in his body had been able to shift to all the forms. He'd also been insane, but that may have been from other things.

What would happen if, with my tigers that close to the surface, I suddenly found myself surrounded by a whole bunch of weretigers? I wasn't sure, and that was reason enough to take it slower.

"Thanks, Ed . . . Ted. I needed that."

"You seem calmer now."

I nodded. "You made me think. First, I'll go back inside and apologize to Dr. Memphis. Second, I'll see if he knows where we can find Officer Randall Sherman's high priestess."

"Why?" he asked.

I told them about the pentagram and my theory that Sherman had been trying a spell when the weretiger killed him.

"Spells don't work against wereanimals," Bernardo said.

"No, they don't," I said.

"A practicing witch would know that," Edward said.

"He would."

"Which means something else besides vampires and weretigers may have been in that warehouse," he said.

"My thoughts exactly."

"If Memphis doesn't know Sherman's high priestess?"

"Then we find someone who does. You call Washington and get started on those warrants. One for a wereanimal that killed Sherman, and the other for searching homes and businesses of the Master of Vegas."

"That second one may be tricky; Max is pretty well connected here and is one of the major funders of the pro-vampire lobby in DC."

I hadn't known that last part. "Then he should want to cooperate with the police."

Edward gave me that smile of his. "He's a vampire, Anita, they always have something to hide."

I smiled back. "Don't we all."

To that, he didn't answer, just got his cell and started working on the warrants. Me, I went for the door back inside.

Olaf followed me, but I stopped him. "You stay with Edward, I mean, Ted."

"The vampire Vittorio made a threat against you. You really shouldn't be alone, not if he has wereanimals on his side."

I couldn't fault his logic. "Bernardo," I called, "you're with me."

Bernardo gave Olaf a speculative look but came to my side. "Anything you say, little lady."

"Don't call me that, ever again," I said, and reached for the door.

"Why him and not me?" Olaf said.

I glanced back at the tall, black-clad man. He'd put the black wraparound sunglasses back on. He stood there, looking like a Hollywood idea of a bad guy. "Because he doesn't creep me out, and you do."

"I am better in a fight than he is."

"I'll let you guys debate that some time, but for right now, I have an apology to make."

"You're really going to apologize to the doctor?"

"Yes."

"An apology is a sign of weakness."

"Not if you're in the wrong, and I was." I actually got to the door before he interrupted again.

"You were short with him, but not wrong."

I finally looked at the big guy. "What's with all the chatter, Otto? Afraid you'll miss me?"

That did it. He turned and walked away. Bernardo came up to stand next to me like a tall, dark, handsome shadow. I pressed the button to let someone know we needed inside.

"Otto isn't better in a fight than I am. He's better with explosives, and he's got me beat all hollow when it comes to interrogation, but he's not better in a fight."

"I didn't say he was."

"I just wanted you to know."

I glanced up at him, that nearly heartbreakingly perfect bone structure. He had his long dark hair pulled back in a braid. With the heat, I was beginning to debate what to do with my hair, too.

"I know you're good in a fight, Bernardo. Edward doesn't hang with people who aren't good."

We had to press the button again and wait to be let inside. "Then why don't you like me?"

I gave him a frowning glance. "I don't dislike you."

"But you don't like either."

The door opened. It was Dale, with his short brown hair and

his glasses. He let us in but wasn't entirely pleasant. I couldn't blame him. "You forget something?" he asked.

"An apology to Dr. Memphis. The case is getting to me more than I thought."

Dale's face softened. "It's getting to all of us." He let us go past and told us where to find Memphis.

I turned to Bernardo. "I don't not like you." I wasn't sure on the grammar, but it said what I meant.

"Okay, then you're neutral. You don't like or dislike me; that's weird."

"Why is it weird?"

He actually stopped walking to spread his hands and do a voilà movement. I realized he was showing himself off. "I've had women not like me because I'm too ethnic for them. I've had women not like what I do for a living. Some chicks hate the violence. But that's not it for you. You don't care about any of that."

"Are you asking why I don't think you're scrumptious?" I couldn't help smiling.

"Don't make fun of me."

I shook my head and fought not to smile more. "I'm not, but I just find this an odd thing in the middle of a murder investigation."

"I know, business first, and I'd have behaved myself if you hadn't started getting all sexual tension around the big guy."

"I am not reacting to Otto," I said.

He held his hands up, like he was surrendering. "No offense meant."

"I do not like him like that."

"I didn't say you liked him; I said you're reacting to him."

"And what's the difference between liking and reacting?"

"You like Ted, but you don't react to him. I know you're getting all cuddly, but it's to get Otto off your back."

I gave him a hard look.

"Hey, I won't spoil it. I agree that it's creepy that Otto likes you the way he docs. I can't even argue with what you and Ted said at the crime scene."

"Then what are you bitching about?"

Two women in the little gowns walked by. One stared

outright, and the other did a more covert checking out as she walked past us. I might as well have been invisible. Bernardo wasted a smile on them both, then turned back to me as if nothing had happened.

I had a clue. "You're used to women reacting to you, and I'm not reacting, and that's bugging you."

"Yeah, I know it's shallow as hell, but it's like you don't see me, Anita. I'm not used to that."

"I'm dating or living with six men, Bernardo."

He gave me raised eyebrows.

"My plate is beyond full, okay? It's nothing personal."

"I don't want to date you, Anita, I just want you to react to me." He smiled, and it was a good smile. "I mean, sex would be great, but I think Ted would kill me, and that takes a lot of the happy out of it for me."

"You really think he'd kill you for sleeping with me?"

"He might, and *might* is good enough from him."

"So, if I just tell you how beautiful you are, then we can go back to work?"

"If you mean it," he said, and sounded offended.

"You know, this is usually a girl problem."

"I'm vain, so sue me."

I smiled, and it was my turn to hold my hands up. I took a deep breath and made myself look at Bernardo. I started at his face. His eyes were that dark solid brown, almost black, darker even than mine. The hair was shiny and black, and I knew it had blue highlights in the right light. The skin was that nice even dark that only certain genetics can give you. But it was the curve of those perfect cheekbones, the line of that nose that plastic surgeons only gave movie stars after lots of money changed hands, the lips full and wide, kissable. His neck was long and smooth, and I could see his pulse in the side of his neck like something that needed kissing. The broad shoulders under his white shirt were nice, and the chest looked like he'd been hitting the gym; so did the arms. My gaze slid to the slimness of his waist, and then the hips. I let myself linger, and had to admit to myself that the bulge in his pants was distractingly bulgy. I knew that the bulge got bigger because I'd seen him nude once. I knew he was actually so well endowed that even I might find it a bit much, and I didn't say that about most men.

I forced myself to keep going down the muscular legs in their jeans, to the boots. I came back up to his eyes.

"You're blushing," he said, but he was smiling.

"I was remembering that time in the bar."

He grinned wider, obviously pleased. "Thinking about seeing me naked."

The blush that had been fading flushed back to life. I nodded and started walking. "Happy now?" I asked.

"Very," he said, in a voice that showed it. He glided beside me, to the stares of every woman we passed, and some of the men. I would have thought they might be looking at me, but Bernardo was a treat both coming and going. I'm used to being the plain Jane when it comes to the men in my life. If it had bothered me to be less pretty than a man, I could never have dated Jean-Claude . . . or Asher . . . or Micah . . . or Richard, or Nathaniel. Hell, Bernardo made me feel right at home.

21

I APOLOGIZED TO Dr. Memphis and got the name of Sherman's high priestess. She was in the phone book. We hit the heat outside, sunglasses sliding over our eyes like some sort of science fiction shield. The gesture was already automatic, and I hadn't been in town a day.

There was music playing, and it took me a few seconds to realize it was my phone. It was playing "I'm Not in Love," by 10cc, but it was not a ring tone I'd chosen. I was really going to have to learn to do my own ring tones. Nathaniel's sense of humor was beginning to get on my nerves.

I hit the button and said, "What's with the choice of songs, Nathaniel?"

"It is not your pussycat, *ma petite*," and just like that, I was standing in the Vegas heat talking to the Master Vampire of St. Louis and my main squeeze. He never called me when I was working with the police unless something really bad had happened.

"What's wrong?" I asked. My pulse was suddenly in my throat.

Bernardo looked at me, and I waved a hand, shaking my head, moving toward Edward and Olaf by the car.

"Why should anything be wrong, *ma petite*?" But his voice held anger, which it didn't usually do. He could say nothing was wrong, but his voice said otherwise, and since he could make his voice as empty of emotion as a blank wall, either he wanted me to know he was angry, or he was so pissed that he couldn't hide it. He was more than four hundred years old; you learned to hide a lot of emotion in that much time. So what had I done to piss him off? Or what had someone else done?

I suddenly wanted privacy for the call. So I got in the SUV and the men stood out in the heat. I offered to do it the other way around, but Edward had insisted, and when he insists there's usually a reason for it. I've learned not to argue when he insists; we all live longer.

I turned on the air-conditioning and got comfortable while the three men seemed to be talking, quietly but intensely. Hmm.

"*Ma petite*, I wake and find you far away."

"I'm not happy about it either," I said. I thought about him, and that was enough to see him lying in our bed, the sheets draped carelessly across his body, one long leg clear of the sheets. One hand held the phone, but the other was playing idly along Asher's back. He would be dead to the world for hours yet, but it never bothered Jean-Claude to touch another vampire when they were still "dead." I found it disturbing. Maybe I'd been at one too many crime scenes.

He looked up into the air, as if he felt me watching him. "Would you like to see more?"

I drew my mind and attention back to the SUV, the Vegas heat pressing against the car. "I think it would distract me."

"There are those who would give all they have to be distracted by me."

"You're angry at me."

"We work so hard to make the vampire community think you are truly my servant and not my master, and then you do this."

"Do what, my job?"

He sighed, and the sound eased over the phone and down my skin like a shiver of anticipation. "Leave without my permission," but he made the last word sound dirty, as if asking permission could have been so much fun.

"Stop that, please. I'm working, or trying to."

"I find that not only are you gone, but you have taken no food."

"I fed this morning."

"But tomorrow will come, *ma petite*."

"Crispin is here."

"Ah, yes, your little tiger." He didn't try to keep the sarcasm out of his voice.

I ignored the sarcasm. "I took your call in the middle of a murder investigation."

"I am so grateful that you could be bothered."

It was way too petty for Jean-Claude, but there it was, his voice, his call. What the hell was going on? But one of the good things about Jean-Claude is I didn't have to protect him from the horrors of my job. He'd seen worse, or close to it, in his centuries of life. So I told the truth. "I've just been to the morgue and seen what's left of some of the Vegas PD's finest. I don't need to fight with you, on top of that."

He sighed. The sound shivered through my mind, down my body as if he were right there, just behind me, whispering, touching.

I threw metaphysical shields in place, though shielding from my master wasn't easy. He had the keys to my shields if he wanted to push it. Today, he let me wrap my shields and my anger around me. "What the fuck was that? I am trying to solve a multiple homicide. I do not need your mind games."

"My apologies, *ma petite*. I think my feelings are hurt."

"What does that mean?" I asked, voice still angry, but the rest of me was calming down. I wasn't sure he'd ever said out loud that his feelings were hurt.

"It means, *ma petite*, that I thought we had made progress in our relationship, and I find that the ground we had gained is not as secure as I had thought."

I said the truth, again. "I have no idea what you just said. I mean, I heard it, and it was English, but I don't understand what you're talking about." I rested my forehead on the steering wheel, closing my eyes, and trying to breathe in the coolness of the air-conditioning. "But I feel sort of vaguely like I should apologize, anyway."

He gave that wonderful laugh. The one that made my body react as if he'd touched way too intimate a part and fed me candy at the same time. His laugh wasn't just about sex; it felt so good, it should have been fattening.

I sighed, but it was just a sigh. I couldn't do his voice tricks. "Please, stop messing with me. God, Jean-Claude, I can't work like this."

He gave a more ordinary chuckle. "I think I needed to hear that you missed me."

"How can you possibly be insecure? That's *my* job."

"You make me insecure, *ma petite*, only you."

I didn't know what to say to that, but I tried. "I'm sorry."

"I know you mean that, and it does help."

How did I get off the phone without hurting his feelings again? I had no clue. Shit. It wasn't like him to call when I was off with the police. I hoped, desperately, that it didn't become a habit.

I realized I was hunching over the steering wheel. I made myself sit up straight and avoid looking in Edward's direction.

Jean-Claude's voice, when it came again, was almost neutral. "When I woke and heard where you had gone, I was not idle. There is a swanmane in Las Vegas. The Swan King, Donovan Reece, has already offered him to be at your disposal for feeding if the need arises."

"Thank Donovan for me, and I do appreciate that you're willing to share me with yet one more man. I know we've talked about not adding any more."

"It's not the feeding, *ma petite*, it's that you seem incapable of sex without emotion. If you could fuck and feed, then I would have no problem with a hundred lovers. Feed, then never see them again, but you collect men, *ma petite*. You can fuck a dozen men, but you cannot date them all."

"I'm sort of aware of that," I said.

"Are you?" There was that edge of anger again.

"I'm just not good at casual sex. I'm sorry."

"No, you are not," and the anger was a little more.

I didn't know what to do with his anger, or this fight, so I ignored it. Men will let you do that sometimes in a relationship because they're not girls. "I may need something not feline that is one of the beasts I carry inside me. I don't carry swan."

"I tell you that I am tired of sharing you with other men, and that you collect them, and you ask for more?"

He was going to be the girl. Great. Fucking great. "I promise when I get back to St. Louis, we can have this fight. I swear. But right now, help me survive this case."

"And how may I do that?"

"The weretigers are a little too much sometimes because of how many different flavors I've got inside me." I'd been attacked by one tiger, but carried five different metaphysical colors of them. No one had been able to explain how that had happened. "Did you happen to find any wolves I could borrow while I'm here?"

"No wolves; the local pack seems to fear that you will be a disrupting influence on them, *ma petite*."

"What does that mean?"

"It means that the news has gotten out that sex with you can be like a vampire's bite. One taste and they belong to you."

"That's not true," I said, but my pulse had sped.

"You lie to yourself, *ma petite*."

"Stop calling me that."

"You have not asked me to give up your pet name in many years."

"It's the way you're saying it, like you're angry and trying not to show it."

"I am angry, because I am afraid for you. Vittorio was vicious in St. Louis, and it has been all over the news that three of their SWAT have been killed. They are not easily killed, your SWAT."

What did I say to that? He was right. "I'm sorry I had to leave without talking to you first."

"I hear true regret in that phrase. What would you have told me, if I had said it was too dangerous? What would you have done if I had said, do not go?"

I thought about that, then finally said, "I would have come anyway."

"You see, you are not my servant. You will never be a servant."

"I thought the idea was to make the vampire community *think* I was a good little human servant. I didn't know you still thought I'd toe the line for you." I had a little heat in my words, again. It was a trickle of anger to warm me. Of course, it was warm enough that anger might not be what I needed.

"That is not what I meant."

"It's what you said."

He made a soft, exasperated sound. "Perhaps I am still fool enough to believe that you will truly be mine."

"And what the hell does that mean?"

He was quiet for so long that it was unnerving. Vampires didn't have to breathe on the phone, and only years of practice made me sure he was still there. I waited, and finally he spoke. "You need some of our people with you. You need your own leopard, and wolf, or lion."

"I don't have a lion of my own, yet."

"Our local Rex would be yours if you would allow it."

"Yeah, and his Regina would hunt me down and kill me. I've met her. She's pissed I'm sleeping with him. If I make him my lion to call, she'll see that as a challenge. I'm good, Jean-Claude, but I'm not good enough to win a fair fight with a werelion of her power."

"Then do not fight fair," he said.

"If I cheat, then by lion law others can gang up on me and kill me for that. I've studied up on it since I met the new Regina of the St. Louis clan. Trust me, Jean-Claude, I have thought about this."

"Do you truly believe she would kill you if you had a stronger claim on her king?"

"Yep," I said, "because she told me that she would share him. That I could be his mistress but not his wife. She was his wife."

"You did not mention this to me."

"It's lions, not wolves. My animal, not yours."

He sighed, and it wasn't his teasing sigh, just tired. "*Ma petite, ma petite*, when will you learn that what is yours is mine. Any danger to you, I need to know."

"I'll tell you all my secrets when you tell me all yours," I said.

"Touché, *ma petite*, a fine deep cut that one." He was back to being angry.

"Why are you angry with me?" I asked.

"You are right, I am being childish, but I don't know how to help you. I don't know how to keep you safe in Vegas. Do you understand that, *ma petite*? I do not know how to keep you safe from Max and his queen. I cannot help you from hundreds of miles away. I cannot send you our guards because you have a badge, and the police will not let our guards guard you. What do you want me to do, *ma petite*? What the hell do you want me to do?" He was yelling now. He almost never yelled. His losing his temper helped me keep mine. I'd never heard him use the word *hell* before. In fact, hearing him that out of control let me know just how scared he was for me. That scared me.

"It's okay, Jean-Claude, I'll think of something. I'm sorry."

"Sorry for what, Anita?" He never used my name; it was a very bad sign.

"I'm sorry that you're afraid for me. I'm sorry that I've made you feel helpless. I'm sorry that I'm here, and you're right, I can't be a marshal and your human servant at the same time. I have to choose, and once the police are involved it means I have to choose the badge. Which may be exactly what Vittorio planned. I'm sorry that Edward may be right, and this is like the ultimate trap for me."

"*Ma petite*, I did not mean to lose my temper, but it is not just Vittorio that you need fear."

"I know that being around the weretigers is going to test my ability to control the beasts inside me."

"I fear so."

"Is there anything you haven't told me about Max or his tigers?"

"Shall I be coy, and say that you know all?"

"The truth would be nice."

"Recently, Max wanted you to visit his city and sleep with more of his tigers. They want, very much, to see if the new psychic powers that Crispin and the red tiger, Alex, gained from you feeding the *ardeur* was a onetime thing or can be shared with others of their clan."

"I'm not sure those were my powers at all. The Queen of All Darkness, Marmee Noir, possessed me for a couple of days. With the help of my inner wolf, I kept from being consumed by her, but I still think any extra powers that the tigers gained came from her, not me."

"That may be, but Max and his queen would like to test the theory."

"I thought they were afraid I'd take over any tiger I fed on and that he was pissed how devoted Crispin is to me?"

"All that is true, but in the last few weeks, Maximillian has asked for a visit, or to send tigers to you for feeding."

"And you were going to tell me all this when?"

"*Ma petite*, I am already sharing you with eight other men, or is it nine? You have enough food here in St. Louis; we do not need more in your bed. I do not really wish to add to your lovers."

Just hearing him say it that way made me feel squeegy. "Do I apologize again?"

"No, for it is my *ardeur* that you carry. I cannot fault you for gaining my hunger."

"Why do you think Max changed his mind about letting me have some more tigers?"

"I believe it is his wife, Bibiana. By the way, *ma petite*, knowing your sense of humor, I will caution you that only Max calls her Bibi. She is Bibiana, or Chang-Bibi."

"You gave me this lecture before Max visited us last time. Chang, depending on pronunciation, is the name of a moon goddess. I won't say it to her face, but it does make me dread meeting her a little to know that it's not enough to be queen; her title has to mean *goddess*."

"It is a traditional title, not one she chose, *ma petite*."

"If you say so."

"I do."

"Okay, I'll do my best not to use her husband's nickname for her, if it's like a serious faux pas."

"It is. She is a very powerful weretiger, and she seeks more power. If she could have other tigers with the new ability that Crispin has, then it would be good for her clan."

"He can call like static electricity, Jean-Claude; it's like a little ouchy, but it's not a weapon. It works best when he has metal to touch, so it's really limited without metal around him."

"Crispin is one of her weaker tigers. The tigers she offered to us recently were not so weak."

"She's hoping that if they're more powerful shapeshifters, then their ability to do the lightning thing will be greater."

"*Oui.*"

"What do you want me to do about it?"

"I do not understand, *ma petite*."

"Do you want me to avoid feeding on her tigers while I'm here?"

"What will you feed on, if not the tigers?"

"I've got the swanmane, thanks to you, and I can feed on anger now."

"If you can avoid feeding on any but Crispin, I think that would be wise."

"I'll do my best."

"Of that, *ma petite*, I have no doubt."

"Thanks."

"It is the truth. I may not always enjoy your choices, and they are certainly not mine, but you always try your hardest and do your best. I do understand that, *ma petite*."

"I'm sorry you don't like the choices, but thanks for noticing that I'm trying."

"You are welcome."

"But if I do have to feed on other tigers, is it okay with you? I mean, will it affect the balance of power among the tiger clans if the white clan suddenly has this uber-version of Crispin's power?"

"A wise question, *ma petite*, but I have a better one."

"Shoot."

"Would you truly sleep with strangers?"

"I don't know, I haven't met the strangers yet."

He laughed then, and it had the first edge of that caressing energy. "So terribly you, that comment, *ma petite*."

"Well, it's the truth. If feeding off a few of his tigers will make Max and his wife happier with me and you, then it's not a fate worse than, whatever."

"You have always been practical, even ruthless, in violence, but this is the first hint I have had that you may be growing practical in the bedroom."

"You aren't here to keep me safe, so I'll have to use what you've taught me to do it for you."

"And what have I taught you, *ma petite*?"

"That sex is just another tool in the arsenal."

"Do you believe that?" he asked.

"No, but you do."

"Not with you, *ma petite*, never."

"Not true; when we first met, you tried to seduce me."

"All men try to seduce the women they want."

"Maybe, but you did teach me that a little sex isn't a fate worse than death."

"Very wise, *ma petite*."

"But cheer up, Jean-Claude, if the weretigers are involved in the murder, then maybe Max and his queen are part of the group that murdered the policemen. If I can prove them guilty, then I can kill them, legally, not as your human servant but as a U.S. Marshal."

"We killed the Master of the City of Charleston and have put our own vampire in his place. If we slay another Master of the City, the vampire council could use it as an excuse to discipline us."

"Discipline how?"

"We have enemies on the council, as you know."

"I remember."

"Also, Max and Bibiana's death would leave a huge vacuum of power in Vegas," he said.

"Is that our problem?" I asked.

"Not if you have no choice, and they have truly murdered all these police officers, but if we could avoid leaving such a vacuum of power, it would be better."

"I'll keep that in mind."

"But do not hesitate, *ma petite*. Do whatever you must to come back to me."

"Count on it," I said.

"I do. Would you, how do you say, frame Max and his queen?"

"No, but I might fudge a bit."

"What does that mean in this context, *ma petite*?"

"It means that we might have enough proof to execute, then find out we were wrong. I'd still be in the clear legally."

"Truly?" he asked.

"Yep."

"Your warrants of execution can be very frightening documents, *ma petite*."

"A license to murder is what one lawyer called it."

"I will trust you to be as practical as you need to be, *ma petite*. I will find others to send to Vegas, for other business reasons."

"What sort of other business?"

"There is always business to do, *ma petite*."

"Like what?"

"Max has asked for some of our dancers to come and guest-star in his show."

"Bear in mind that Vittorio may have had people watching me in St. Louis. He may know who's special to me. Don't give him hostages, Jean-Claude. So whomever you send, make sure they can handle it."

"I will choose carefully, *ma petite*."

"How soon will you get some of them here?"

"Tomorrow, at the latest."

"Okay, but I'm going to push to see the tigers before nightfall. They live in a high-rise, so Max doesn't have the underground to help him wake early like you do. I'm going to try to question the tigers while it's just the queen. She's his animal to call, which means separated by his daytime sleep, she's not as powerful."

"Do remember in chess, *ma petite*, that the queen is far more dangerous to your men than the king."

It was my turn to laugh. "I never forget that a woman can be dangerous, Jean-Claude."

"Sometimes you do forget that you are not the most dangerous woman in a room."

"Are you saying I'm arrogant?"

"I am saying the truth. *Je t'aime, ma petite*."

"I love you, too."

He hung up then, and I guess he was right. We were done, but it still felt like the conversation had gone badly, or like he hadn't said everything he needed to say. I loved Jean-Claude, and Asher, but I missed my house. I missed living with Micah and Nathaniel in our house. I also missed my alone time with Jean-Claude. Asher, or someone, was always with us, because we finally realized we had a spy in our midst. Or maybe that was too harsh; we had gossip. Vampires love to gossip. You'd think living so long would make them great philosophers or scholars, and a few do that, but most are just people with very long lives, and they love a good rumor. So we had to make sure the rumor mill said that Jean-Claude was spending a lot of time with the men. Which meant that suddenly I was never alone with anyone. I liked, or loved, everyone, but a little alone time with them individually would have been nice. But how the hell do you date that many men and have any privacy? No clue. And forget me having alone time with myself; that just didn't happen anymore. It was to the point that the only time I was alone was in the car going from one job to another. Things had to change, but I wasn't sure how.

But for today, all I had to do was find a serial killer. I knew I needed to see a Wiccan priestess, and the queen of all the weretigers in Vegas, or excuse me, Chang of all the tigers. I needed to do the tigers before it got too dark. I had clear-cut goals and a time constraint. When a murder investigation this awful is simpler than my love life, something has gone horribly wrong. The problem was, how did I fix what had gone wrong, and exactly what *was* wrong? I just knew I wasn't entirely happy, and neither were some of the men. I was beginning to realize that unhappiness might include Jean-Claude. Not good.

I got out of the car and watched the three men come toward me, their faces showing that they'd been arguing, too. Great, we could all be grumpy together.

22

EDWARD HAD BASICALLY been telling Olaf to stay the fuck away from me. Olaf had been telling him that unless he was fucking me, it was none of his business. Oddly, if Edward had been doing me, then Olaf would have accepted that I was off limits. Apparently, it had never occurred to Edward to lie about that. I was just as glad because I could never have pretended that. Not to mention that if the rumor got back to Donna, she'd be heartbroken, and their son, Edward's stepson, Peter, would never forgive either Edward or me. It was all too weird and Freudian for me.

The good news was that the warrants would be coming soon. Edward had a fax number for the local police. "You really have worked Vegas before," I said.

He nodded.

Something occurred to me that hadn't before, and I felt stupid for not thinking of it sooner. "Did you know the local executioner?"

"Yes." So Edward, one word, simply yes.

I studied his face and knew that the sunglasses probably didn't hide anything useful in his eyes, but . . . I had to ask. "Did you like him?"

"He was competent."

"Not good, just competent," I said.

"He had more rules than you and I do. It limited him." His voice was utterly cool, no emotion.

"So, you'd met the dead operators, too?"

He shook his head. "Only Wizard."

"Wizard?"

"Randy Sherman."

I studied his face. "You just saw a man in the morgue who you knew, had worked with, and it didn't . . ." I waved my hands, as if trying to grab the right word out of the air. "Didn't it move you?" The question was inadequate, but it would have been too stupid to ask Edward if he cared.

"Only a woman would ask that," Olaf said.

I nodded. "You're absolutely right, but I am a woman, so I get to ask. It would bother me more to have looked at a man who I knew in there. It was bad enough as a stranger. I kept thinking about the SWAT guys I'd met earlier, and knew that all the dead in there had been just as tall, just as professional, just as vital, and now it was all gone."

"You'd have cared more," Edward said, "but it wouldn't have stopped you from doing your job. Sometimes you work better when you're upset."

"Do I say thanks?"

"My reaction bothers you, I get that, Anita, but I've seen a lot of men die who I knew. After a while you either deal with it better or get a desk job. I don't want a desk job."

I wanted to yell at him. Yell that I knew he cared for Donna and the kids. I was pretty sure he even cared for me, but his lack of emotion about the men in the morgue reminded me that Edward was still a mystery to me, and maybe always would be.

"Don't overthink it," Bernardo said.

I turned to him, ready to be mad, because being mad at him would be easier than yelling at Edward. "What's that supposed to mean?"

"It means you're being a girl, and you need to be the guy I know is in there, or you're going to weird yourself out about Ted here. You need to trust him, not doubt him now."

"I do trust him."

"Then let it go, Anita."

I opened my mouth, then closed it, then turned back to Edward. "I'm not going to get this, am I?"

"No," he said.

I did a pushing-away gesture. "Fine, fine, let's do something useful."

"When we serve the warrant, they'll insist that SWAT go

with us. They're very serious about that here in Las Vegas."
His voice was still empty, as if his emotions hadn't caught up
with him.

"We aren't hunting them. We're just gathering information.
You and I both are pretty sure Max is too mainstream to
approve of his people killing policemen."

"One, if we've got a warrant in hand, SWAT goes with us
in Vegas. They mean that. Two, Max is well connected, Anita,
which means the local cops don't want us walking in on his
wife and family with a warrant of execution, and no one watching us."

"Do they really think we'd just go in there and start shooting?" I asked.

Edward looked at me. It was the most emotion I'd seen on
his face in the last few minutes.

"Is my rep that bad?" I asked.

Bernardo said, "Most of the police see us as bounty hunters
with badges. Cops don't like bounty hunters."

"There are going to be things that I need to say that I can't
say in front of Grimes and his men," I said.

"The lieutenant probably won't be coming personally," Edward said.

"You know what I mean, Edward."

"We'll see if we can distract them for you," Edward said.

"If I am not allowed to hurt them," Olaf said, "then I will
not be good at distracting them."

"Fair enough," I said.

Bernardo grinned at me. "I'll do my best, but I'm better at
distracting the ladies."

"I'll see if I can get you some privacy," Edward said, and
frowned at both the other men.

"Hey," Bernardo said, "I'm just being honest, but frankly I
think the SWAT team is going to glue itself to Anita."

"Why me?" I asked.

"Deputy Lorenzo is friends with the woman who works in
the front office for their SWAT. Did you really do a one-arm
curl of two hundred sixty pounds?"

I fought to give him full eye contact. "No."

"Then what did you do?" he asked.

"A two-arm curl," I said.

Edward and Olaf were looking at me now, too. "Why would you draw that much attention to yourself?" Edward asked.

"You've seen them, Edward; if you didn't know me, would you let me serve a warrant with them?"

"You're a U.S. Marshal, Anita. It's our warrant. They're backing us up."

I shook my head. "I needed to prove to them that I could handle myself. The weights were right there. It seemed like the quickest way to settle it."

"How did you explain that you could curl almost three times your own body weight without falling over or busting something?" He sounded disgusted.

"I don't need this from you, Edward, Ted, whatever. You don't know what's it like to be the girl. To always have to prove yourself. You get tired of it."

"What did you tell them?"

"The truth."

He took his glasses off and rubbed his eyes. "What does that mean?"

"That I'm carrying different kinds of lycanthropy. Grimes had read my file, Edward, it's in there now. The Philadelphia police outed me when I ended up surviving and healing after having my skull cracked."

"You don't have a scar," he said.

"No, I don't, just like I don't have a scar from the weretiger attack in St. Louis. You've seen Peter's scars from the same beastie. It gutted me, remember?" I pulled my shirt out of my pants enough to flash my smooth, untouched stomach. "I can't play human anymore, Edward."

23

BERNARDO AND OLAF both moved away a little, as if the emotion were too much for them, or they were leaving the hysterical woman to Edward. There was more than one reason he was the unofficial leader. When you do the hard things, you get to call the shots.

He looked at me for a moment, then asked, "Are you all right?"

It was such a weird thing to ask that I wasn't angry, just puzzled. "What the hell does that mean?"

"It means what I said. You seem on edge."

"Oh, I don't know, I've got a serial killer mailing me body parts. I had Lieutenant Grimes actually ask me if I was Jean-Claude's human servant. My blood test alone should have gotten my badge yanked, but no one's come to talk to me about it. I've been living with Jean-Claude and the guys at the Circus for months, and I miss my house. I miss my stuff. I miss being alone with Nathaniel and Micah. I miss being alone with anybody. There are too many damn men in my life, and I don't know what to do about it."

"You don't want dating advice from me, Anita."

That made me smile, in spite of myself. "I guess not."

"But you aren't the only preternatural branch marshal who's been attacked on the job. I think unless you actually shift and they could prove you a danger in court, they aren't going to bitch. I think they're afraid of getting sued, workman's comp or something like that. They certainly don't want the first of us in court fighting to keep their badge to be you."

"Why not?" I asked.

"You're a woman. You're pretty. You're petite. You'd look like the poster child for being picked on by the big bad government."

I frowned at him. "I'm no one's victim, Edward."

"I know that, and you know that, but the media won't know that."

"So you're saying that if I were a man, they'd have asked for my badge by now?"

"Not necessarily, but being a girl helps you here; don't begrudge that."

I shook my head. "Fine, fine, whatever, fuck it. Do you really think that SWAT will insist on coming with us?"

"If we're serving an active warrant, yes."

"Well, then a trip to the tigers is almost useless. I can't talk freely enough in front of them."

"We can see the priestess first, but you're not going to avoid Grimes and his men."

"Damn it."

"Most of the time it's nice to have that much extra firepower and technology behind us. Just for you, me, Otto, we can do and say things on our own that we don't want SWAT to see or hear. You for all the secrets, and us for practical solutions."

"I'm pretty practical myself, Edward."

"*Ted*, Anita; you need to work on that and use the right name."

"Fine, *Ted*, I do my share of practical solutions." I took a deep breath in and blew it out, slowly. "We can see the priestess while we're waiting for the warrants. It'll give me the illusion we're doing something useful."

Bernardo and Olaf had sidled back over. The fact that I hadn't realized they were within hearing distance said I was a lot more distracted than was good for my job.

"You sound bummed, babe, did your undead boyfriend not come through for you?" Bernardo said.

"Do not call me *babe*, or any other term of endearment, okay?"

Bernardo spread his hands, as if to say, *Fine*.

"Did your vampire lover disappoint you?" Olaf asked, and whereas it had been pure teasing with Bernardo, Olaf made it sound way too serious.

"My relationship with Jean-Claude is none of your business."

He just looked at me, and even through sunglasses I could feel his stare, heavy and uncomfortable.

"What?" I demanded.

Edward stepped between us, literally blocking my view of the other man. "Drop it, Anita. We'll go see Sherman's priestess; by then the warrants will be up. We'll deal with our police escort when the time comes."

I realized that Edward probably needed to know some of the potential problems with the weretigers. But I didn't owe the other two men the explanation. "We need to talk, Edward," I said.

"Talk," he said.

"In private."

"You just had a private discussion," Bernardo said.

"No, I got upset, and both of you bailed on the hysterical woman, and left Ed . . . Ted to deal with me. Now I need to tell him things that really are private."

"We are your backup; don't we need to know what's going on?" Bernardo said.

"I'll tell . . . Ted, and then if he thinks you need to know, I'll tell you."

They didn't like it, but when they got to sit in the car with the air-conditioning, Bernardo liked it better. Olaf went because he had no choice, but he didn't like it.

When we were alone in the pounding, bright heat of the Vegas desert, I told Edward. I told him about Max and his queen wanting me to sleep with their tigers. I told him about accidentally giving powers to Crispin.

Edward took off his hat, wiped the area of the sweat band, and settled the hat back on his head. "You do have the most interesting problems."

"Is that a complaint?"

"Just an observation."

"You know everything I know now; do we need to tell the other two?"

"Some of it."

"I'll let you tell as much, or as little, as you think we need."

"What if I tell them all of it?"

"If you think that's best; I trust your judgment."

He nodded, and started for the car. "Let's get out of the heat, and I'll tell them something while we go see a witch."

"She's a Wiccan high priestess; not all Wiccans like to be called witches."

"I'll remember that."

"You already know that," I said.

He smiled at me. "You know, if we really were sleeping together, Olaf would back off."

I gave him the look the comment deserved. "You aren't serious?"

"About doing it for real, no. Donna would never forgive either of us, and it would destroy Peter. Besides, it would just be . . ." He made a waffling motion with his hand. "Wrong."

"Like doing family," I said.

He nodded. "Something like that. It's not what we are to each other."

"So what do you suggest?"

"How close are you to this tiger Crispin?"

"Biblical," I said.

He smiled and shook his head. "Is he dominant or weak?"

"Weak."

"That won't make Olaf back off. It's got to be someone that Olaf can respect."

"Can't help you there. Wait, he knows I'm doing Jean-Claude and Micah and Nathaniel. Are you saying none of them measure up to his standards, but you would?"

"He doesn't respect any man he thinks might be gay, Anita."

"Yeah, Otto is an all-around prejudiced bastard. But they're all doing me, regardless of who else they're doing; that makes them like girls?"

"Otto is like a lot of people; bisexual is still gay, if you're doing guy-on-guy." He grinned suddenly, and it was pure Ted Forrester. "Of course, girl-on-girl is just one guy away from a fantasy."

"Please, don't tell me you think that's true?"

His grin softened around the edges, and the real Edward leaked into his face, even around the sunglasses. "I have to be Ted while we're here, Anita. We've got too many cops around to be myself." The grin came back, wide and good ol' boy. "And Ted thinks that lesbian means you just haven't met the right man."

"I'd like to introduce Ted to my friend Sylvie and her partner. Trust me, neither one of them thinks they need a man in their life, not in any way."

"We good ol' boys need our illusions, Anita." We were almost to the car.

I spoke low. "You're about as much a good ol' boy as I am . . . Ted."

"I'll have to be Ted if SWAT is with us, Anita."

I stared at him. "Shit."

He nodded. "You aren't the only one who has to be careful with an audience."

"When having police around makes you have to lie all the time, Edward, maybe we aren't the good guys?"

He opened the passenger door for me, which he never did. I let him, for Olaf's sake, but it bugged me. Edward leaned close and whispered in my ear so that Olaf would think he was whispering sweet nothings, but what he actually said, was, "We aren't the good guys, Anita. We're the necessary guys."

I settled into the seat, with Olaf and Bernardo wondering what Edward had said to me. I couldn't make my face match his smiling one. I couldn't play along that he'd whispered something naughty in my ear. I could only sit and let my sunglasses hide my eyes and help me lie to the people who were supposed to be helping me.

I was lying to the police, lying to my backup; the only person I wasn't lying to was Edward. Funny how that was usually the case when we worked together. He explained that the were-tigers' queen might try to fix me up with some of her people in a bid to bind themselves closer to Jean-Claude's power base. True, as far as it went. I just stared ahead and kept the glasses on.

Edward turned in his seat so he could see both men better. He started by explaining to all of us. "I arranged for the warrant to be dropped off here, at the coroner's parking lot. We can chat while we wait."

"Chat?" Olaf said, suspicion plain in his voice.

Then Edward started in with no preamble, just straight to the point. "Anita has a lover among the weretigers. He'll probably be friendly to her, so let him."

"How friendly?" Bernardo asked.

I laughed, I couldn't help it. "Let's just say that Crispin is a little . . . eager."

"How eager?" Olaf asked, and he didn't sound happy at all.

I turned in the seat so I could see them both. "You guys know I need to feed the *ardeur*; well, Crispin will probably be my food either tonight or tomorrow morning."

"Feed, how?" Olaf asked.

"Sex, Olaf, I'll feed during sex."

"So the rumors are true—you really are a succubus, then?" Bernardo said.

"Yeah, I guess I am."

"You don't have to go to the monsters to feed," Olaf said.

"I've fed on Crispin before, so he knows what to expect."

"I would be happy to help," Bernardo said.

"No," Olaf said, "if she feeds on any of us, it will be me."

I shook my head. "I know your idea of sex, Olaf; I don't think I'd survive long enough to feed."

"For you, I would try."

I stared at his sunglass-covered eyes with my own. I tried to see past that impassive face. I understood that he had offered me sex, just sex, not violence, and that for him, that was almost unheard of. It was a positive step for Olaf, but I so did not want to be that step.

I looked at Edward for some help.

"You'd really just have sex with Anita, not tie her up or cut her up?"

Olaf nodded. "I would try."

Edward licked his lips, a sign of nervousness, though in this heat, maybe not. "I didn't think you thought of sex without the violence."

"For her, I would try," he repeated.

"Edward," I said, "help me out here."

"It's a big step for him, Anita. You have no idea how big."

"I have some idea, but . . ."

Edward lowered his glasses enough to give me his eyes, and those eyes told me something. They told me to be careful and not blow this. It took me a second, then I realized he was right. It was a hell of a lot better that Olaf wanted "normal" sex than to go all serial killer on my ass. It was a lesser evil, so I tried to say something that wouldn't crush his attempt at being better.

"I don't know what to say to that Olaf. I'm . . . flattered and entirely creeped all at the same time." Mostly, in truth, I was just freaked, but I didn't want him to think that I rejected his idea that sex could be about something other than death. I mean, maybe if he thought that about me, he might find someone else whom he could actually have a relationship with. Too weird, too entirely weird, that Olaf might be salvageable. But who the hell would I trust in his bed? Who the hell would I risk, on the chance that he might not go apeshit on her? There were no good answers here, just strange ones. I had that feeling of falling down the rabbit hole, except there'd never been serial killers in *Alice in Wonderland*, though I guess you could make a case for the Queen of Hearts. Off with their heads!

24

I FILLED UP the awkward silence by asking Edward questions about his last time in Vegas, and what he knew about the men on SWAT here. It was only minutes later that a big SUV pulled into the parking lot. I caught the green uniforms on broad shoulders before I noticed exactly what faces went with the shoulders.

"Don't uniforms or flunkies deliver warrants in Vegas just like everywhere else?" I asked.

"Did I mention that I vanished on them last time I was here?" Edward asked.

I glared at him. "So this is your fault, not mine."

"Oh, I think we'll share."

Warrants were usually delivered by whomever they could spare. Instead, it was Sergeant Hooper and one of the practitioners. The moment I saw them, I knew Edward had been right; they weren't going to let us serve the warrant on our own. Crap. Hooper was all serious. The practitioner with him seemed more relaxed. This was the one with brown hair so curly that even the short haircut couldn't hide the fact. What was his name? Spider, that was it. If Santa could tell if you were naughty or nice, and Cannibal could eat you, what the hell did Spider do? I wasn't sure I wanted to know.

We all got out of our trucks and walked toward each other. They were both still in their green uniforms, black boots, no concession to the weather. I wondered what it would have to do in Vegas for them to add to or subtract from their wardrobe.

"Sergeant," Edward said, in his Ted voice, managing to put more positive emotion in one word than in most conversations. He walked forward, smiling, hand out.

Hooper took the hand and almost smiled. "Ted."

Edward turned to the other operator. "Spider."

"Ted."

Edward introduced Olaf and Bernardo. Handshakes all around. I joined the ritual, wordlessly, though Spider and Hooper both said, "Anita," as we shook. Edward had explained that not everyone got nicknames; some just used their first names, like Sanchez, whose first name turned out to actually be Arrio.

I hadn't asked Edward what Spider's talent was, but I would when we had some privacy. If we ever had privacy in Vegas again. I was beginning to worry that Bernardo had been right, and SWAT was going to be our new best buddies.

"We thought we'd bring the warrant personally, Ted," Hooper said. He smiled then. "Wouldn't want another misunderstanding."

Ted did an oh-shucks shrug. "It was my first time in Vegas; sorry about the confusion on where we were meeting up, but once the vampire showed up, there wasn't time to call you guys."

"Right," Hooper said, not like he believed it, really.

"All the marshals in your department have a reputation for being the Lone Ranger," Spider said.

"He was a Texas Ranger, not a U.S. Marshal," I said.

Spider frowned at me. "What?"

"The Lone Ranger was a Texas Ranger, not a marshal."

Spider smiled, shaking his head. "Okay, I'll try to be more precise."

That's it, Anita, correct the man's conversation, that'll win him over. I couldn't apologize—one, I hadn't really done anything wrong; two, apologizing would draw attention to the fact that I'd been awkward. In man land, the less said, the better. If Spider had been a woman I'd have needed to say something placating, but one plus to working with men was that they didn't expect, or want, that. I'd been working with so many more men than women for so long, I was actually getting a little rusty on girl talk. I'd had several female clients complain that I was abrupt.

Ted was reading the warrant over. He handed it to me, and I knew that he hadn't liked something in it. Now that the warrants were all federal and run through DPEA, pronounced *Dopa* by our friends and *Dopey* by our not-so-friends, you didn't have to sweat different judges and wording as much, but . . . there were still different people giving them out.

I stood in the heat between the two cars and read. Edward read over my shoulder, waiting for me to get to whatever bothered him. Olaf and Bernardo waited, as if they didn't need to read it.

The warrant was broad in its wording, like usual, then I got to the part I didn't like. "The warrant covers the lycanthrope that killed your operators, but specifically excludes weretigers." I looked up at Hooper and Spider. "I've never had a federal warrant that took into consideration local politics before. Your Master of the City has some serious pull in Washington."

Hooper's face was unreadable. Spider's face was still pleasant in a neutral sort of way, and I realized that was his version of blank cop face.

"Apparently," Hooper said, "but the warrant covers the damage to Wizard. That's proven shapeshifter death. You wanted the weretigers included because you smelled tiger on the body. No one's going to give you a warrant to target the Master Vampire of Vegas's wife and sons just because you said you smelled tiger."

I nodded. "Okay, fair enough. Even if I were a full-blown wereanimal, my sense of smell wouldn't be admissible in court. But it's another thing to exempt the tigers from the search warrant." I folded the warrant up and Edward put it in the pocket of his navy windbreaker that had *U.S. Marshal* in big letters on it. I'd left my windbreaker at home. Vegas was almost too hot for clothes; coats were out, well, until it got dark. Deserts can get cold at night; weird, but true.

"The warrants from DPEA are pretty broad, Anita. I think they were afraid what we might do with it. Your reputation, all of you, is pretty high on the kill count, and we've just lost three of our own. They trust us to back you guys up, and maybe to be a civilizing influence." He took a breath deep enough that it raised all that chest and fluffed out the gray mustache. "I think the powers that be are afraid we might not be so civilized under the circumstances."

"You guys have all been very controlled since I've been here. They should have trusted you."

"Control is what we do, Anita, but trust me, it's not easy on this one."

"It's never easy when you lose your own," Ted said.

We all had a moment of remembering. Not the same losses, or the same dead friends, but we all had names, faces, that would never come through a door again. They talk about moments of silence for the dead, but when you have enough of them behind you, you do it automatically.

"You're taking this well, Anita," Spider said.

"You sound like you expected me not to."

"I did."

"Why?"

"Some people said you had a temper, especially if you didn't get your own way."

"I have a temper, but not about stuff like this. If you got a warrant on the tigers because of the smell, it might not hold up in court later. We don't want to kill upstanding wereanimals of Vegas on a bad-faith warrant, now do we?"

"No, we do not," he said.

I sighed again. "But now you've put me in an awkward situation. I have a badge but no warrant for the tigers, so they can keep me out of their home, badge or no badge."

He nodded. "True."

Then I had an idea, a good idea, an almost happy idea. "Serving this warrant won't get us in to see the tigers."

"No," Hooper said.

"This means I'm going to have to charm my way in and not flash the badge. That means that I'll be going in *not* as a U.S. Marshal."

"What does that mean?" Spider asked.

"It means that as the girlfriend of the Master of the City of St. Louis, I can ask for an audience with Max's wife, and I'll probably get it."

"On what grounds?" Hooper asked.

"On the grounds that Max's wife, Bibiana, would expect me to visit her before I left town. It would be a courtesy that if skipped would be a grave insult. I wouldn't want to insult the Chang of your local weretigers, now would I?"

Hooper was studying my face. "I guess not."

"Without a warrant, all you can do is ask questions," Spider said, "no hunting."

"Trust me, guys, I don't want to throw down the gauntlet to Max and his crew while I'm here. I think if it was one of their tigers, they'd be eager to help solve this; they're mainstream monsters. Killing cops is bad for business."

Hooper was getting his cell phone out. "We'll have everyone else meet us at Max's place," Hooper said.

"Hooper, if we can't go in there as marshals, and I have to make this a girlfriend coffee klatch, then I sure as hell can't take in a tactical assault team. Without a warrant, you guys are not getting in the door. Hell, I'll be lucky to get Ted and me through the door."

"And me," Olaf said.

Bernardo raised his hand and said, "Oh, pick me, pick me." Then he gave me a look so unhappy that I wondered what I'd done wrong now, but I just didn't care enough to ask. Maybe I'd care later, or maybe I wouldn't.

"Ted?" I made it a question.

"I'd feel better if all the marshals went in, but I don't know how the tigers will feel about that."

"I don't know if I'm comfortable going in by myself, to be honest." As soon as I said it, I knew I shouldn't have. One, it sounded weak; two, I wasn't sure how to explain my real reasons for being nervous around the weretigers with Shaw.

The two operators gave me serious faces. Hooper said, "We heard about the weretiger attack in St. Louis."

I realized that he'd take that as a reason why I shook my head. I jumped on it. "Yeah, getting cut up by an animal will make you a little leery of them."

"We'll go in with you, Anita."

"There is no way that Max's security will let me take you guys inside their home on a social visit. I'm sorry, you guys are just too much what you are."

I wasn't sure that made sense, but they accepted it, or understood it.

"I'll still call ahead. We'll wait for you in the parking lot. You give the signal that you're in danger, and we're allowed to go in and save your asses."

"Why, Hooper, you did read the standard clauses in the warrant, didn't you?"

Hooper's mouth gave a tight, unpleasant smile. It was close to the one I had, and Ted had. It was not a good look to have aimed at you, but he didn't mean to aim it at me; he was thinking about the people who killed his friends. "It's Sonny, Anita, and I did read it. You, meaning the marshals, are allowed to use all force up to and including deadly, if you feel that you or a civilian are in imminent and life-threatening danger. It further allows any officers who are with you, or acting in a backup capacity, to use any and all force to protect your lives and the lives of any civilians."

I nodded. "They added that last bit after a pair of vampire hunters got killed, and the police with them defended themselves, saved the human hostages, but ended up on trial. They were acquitted, but it was a mess."

"It's one of the things that led to DPEA," Hooper, I mean Sonny, said.

"Yes, so if we're attacked, then legally we're in the clear because we can make a case for the dead lycanthrope being in league with the rogue on our warrant. Hell, Sonny, it's Nevada, you still have varmint laws on the books."

"I wouldn't want to be quoting varmint laws if we have to shoot Max's entire family."

"Me either, but if they throw down first, legally we won't have broken any laws."

"Is it true that you don't even have to have a hearing after you shoot someone?" Spider asked.

"There's more paperwork now that we're federal officers, officially, but no, no lawyers, no hearings, nothing really. But then if they tied us all up in legalities, who would do all the monster slaying?"

"So, really," he said, "excluding the weretigers from the

warrant doesn't keep them safe if they start the fight with you guys?"

"Not really," I said.

"If they start the fight, we'll help you finish it," Sonny said, "but make damn sure they start it, because you may get out of jail free with your federal badge, but we live here."

"I give you my word, if this all goes up in flames, we won't have started it."

He studied my face—they both did—and then Sonny nodded, as if he'd decided something. He offered me his hand. I took it. "Shake on it."

We shook on it, and Sonny was old enough and guy enough that the handshake meant more than it would have to, say, Spider or Bernardo—or maybe Vegas Metro SWAT was all like this. Your word meant something, and you could still pledge your life to someone's decision with just a handshake. It was like an echo of a time when words like *loyalty* and *honor* really meant something. Since they still meant something to me, that was just dandy.

25

I MADE TWO calls from the car as Edward drove us out of the industrial/business area where the coroner's office was located, through businesses that were Anywhere, USA. One was to Chang-Bibi, to the personal line that Max had made sure Jean-Claude had. A cultured female voice answered on the first ring. I said, "Chang-Bibi, this is Anita Blake . . ."

"Anita Blake, we are glad that you have called, but I am not Chang-Bibi. My name is Ava; I am Chang-Bibi's administrative assistant."

"Sorry, I thought this was the private number."

"It is, but"—she made a small laugh—"a queen does not answer her own phone."

Oh. "Sure," I said, "my mistake. I'm in Vegas, and I was wanting to speak with Bibiana."

"We are aware of the tragedy that has befallen our police. Is this official police business, Marshal Blake?"

"I would like to talk to you all about the murders, yes."

"Is this official police business, Marshal Blake?" she asked again, in a voice that was a little less pleasant.

"I am in Vegas on official police business, yes," I said.

"Do you have a warrant that forces us to let you into our home or business establishments?"

I hated to say it, but . . . "No, I don't."

"Then it's a social call," and her voice was much happier.

"Yes, from one master's . . . mate to another," I said.

"Then Chang-Bibi will be happy to receive you."

"I do need to talk to her about the murders, though, in an unofficial capacity."

"You are extending us the courtesy of speaking off the record to us?" Ava asked.

"I'm trying to."

"I will explain that to Chang-Bibi." The way she said it made it sound like Bibiana might have trouble with the concept.

"Thank you, Ava," I said.

"My pleasure, Anita. Chang-Bibi will prepare a welcome for you. We hoped you would visit us, if you had time in all your crime-fighting."

"What kind of welcome is she preparing?" I asked, and I couldn't keep the suspicion out of my voice. Years of hanging out with shapeshifters had taught me that their society could have some odd ideas on welcoming guests.

Ava laughed again. "Now, now, that would spoil the surprise."

"I don't really like surprises," I said.

"But Chang-Bibi does, and you are visiting her house and asking for her help."

"Maybe I'm offering to help her."

"Are you?"

"I could have come with a warrant, but I'm not," I said.

"You could not get a warrant on the evidence of smelling weretiger, Anita," and there was nothing friendly in the voice now.

"You have a mole in the department, or is your spy more federal?" I said.

"We have our sources."

"Fine, I couldn't get a warrant, but I still need to talk to the weretigers."

"Our clan did not do this."

"Of course not."

"You do not believe we are innocent."

"I believe everyone is guilty of something; it saves time."

She laughed again. "I will go and help prepare. I assume you are coming alone, since this is a social visit of one master's mate to another." There was the slightest edge of humor, as if she knew she was making fun of me.

"Actually I have some other U.S. Marshals with me."

"Now, Anita, that's not very friendly."

"I'm allowed attendants when I visit another Master of the City; in fact, denying my attendants entrance would be a grave insult."

"Oh, good," Ava said, "you do know how to play the game. Some of the younger, human wives don't understand the old rules."

I didn't correct her on the "wives" comment. If they treated me like a wife, I'd have more status, and it wasn't like I could ever "divorce" Jean-Claude. Vampire marks between servant and master were a hell of a lot more binding than any legal document. "Jean-Claude made sure I'd be able to do proper honor if I visit Chang-Bibiana."

"How many of your attendants have guns and badges?"

"By the rules of hospitality, I'm allowed security."

"But only two, on a surprise visit. Beyond that you must have another purpose for them. Are there more than two body-guards with you?" Again, I heard that hint of laughter in her voice. But I'd been laughed at by better and scarier than Ava.

"Jean-Claude is Belle Morte's line, so I'm allowed food."

"Chang-Bibi is eager to supply all your needs." Was it my imagination, or did she sound a little angry about that? Hmm.

"I appreciate the hospitality, and I will avail myself of the Chang's generosity before I leave your fair city, but since I didn't expect to have time in the middle of a murder investigation to visit you today, I brought my own snack."

"So, you have two guards and one *pomme de sang*?"

"Not a *pomme de sang*, just a lover."

"They say your *pomme de sang* is another vampire, is that true?"

She was referring to London, who was a vampire, and one of Belle Morte's sex-oriented line, but his gift was to be the ul-timate snacky-bit for someone with the *ardeur* like me or Jean-Claude. The only upside to it was that London gained power from the feeding and wasn't exhausted by it. I just wish I liked him better. Good lover, bad boyfriend, if you know what I mean. "I haven't given the title to anyone officially yet," I said.

"We heard that you had, but now he seems to be your leop-ard to call. Nathaniel, isn't it?"

I couldn't stop my pulse from racing. I knew all the masters spied on everyone—hell, I knew Jean-Claude had his own network—but it was still unnerving to hear it.

"Yeah." I hoped I wasn't giving away any state secrets. I mean it was pretty well-known, wasn't it? Oh, hell.

"You have how many animals to call now, Anita?"

I really didn't like the way this conversation was going. I wasn't sure how much was general knowledge, how much their spies had discovered, or how much would be really bad to share with them. I had to get off the phone. "I'll play twenty questions with Chang-Bibiana, but not with her assistant." Yeah, it was rude, but it did the trick.

"Then, by all means, come ahead, Anita. Come talk to our queen. I'm sure her questions will be much more interesting than mine." She hung up. Yeah, she was mad.

I couldn't apologize. I guess we just both had to live with it. I hoped I wouldn't regret pissing her off later. I got off the phone to find we were on the edge of not being in Kansas anymore.

The first hint was wedding chapels scattered alongside the more ordinary stores. Most of the chapels looked tired, and more depressing than romantic, but maybe that was just me. I'm not big on weddings.

Then there was Bonanza, the largest gift store in the world. One building that took up most of one block. It's the kind of place you stop on family vacations. There was a huge empty lot, with a sign leaning by it that read *ontier*. I realized they'd demolished the Frontier. That big cowboy that you see in all the movies was no more. The Vegas Hilton sat across the road from another empty lot that was under construction.

Edward said, "Vegas doesn't save its history; it demolishes and builds on top of it."

"How many times have you been here?" I asked.

"Only once as a marshal," he said.

"On other business?" I asked.

"None of your business."

I knew that was all I would get on the subject, so I let it go.

Circus Circus loomed up on the right-hand side; it looked sort of tired in the bright sunlight, like a carnival that's been in one place too long. The Riviera was across the street, then more open space where something else had been torn down. Signs for the Encore were next, but it wasn't there yet. Then something called the Wynn that looked too tall and too modern for the rest of Vegas, though it had a huge billboard where an animated pixie was pushing words on a huge moving screen. It was a commercial for the Wynn. Suddenly there were moving, brilliant billboards every few feet, or so it felt. In daylight they were eye-catching; I wondered what they looked like at night. An odd collection of shapes across the street turned out to be the Fashion Show Mall. The building was ugly; it made me fear for the choice of stores. Then there were casinos in fast profusion: on the left side the Palazzo, the elegance of the Venetian, right across the street from Treasure Island with its huge pirate ship out front; Casino Royale, Harrah's, and then across from that was the Mirage and Caesars Palace. Caesars was huge and took up a big chunk of real estate. The Bellagio looked elegant, too, as we drove past, then across the street was Paris, complete with a smaller version of the Eiffel Tower and a huge fake hot-air balloon, but it was still dwarfed by the tower, even though I knew it was smaller than the real thing. There was huge construction and a sign that read *CityCenter*, then the Monte Carlo, which seemed tired, then New York New York, with a miniature version of the Manhattan skyline rising above little shops and restaurants. There was nothing tired about New York New York. The MGM Grand was across the street, and it looked upbeat, as well. The Tropicana sat beside it, then the Excalibur. Edward got stopped at the stoplight, so I had time to read that the Excalibur boasted three shows: Tournament of Champions, with knights and jousting; the comic Louie Anderson; and Thunder from Down Under, which was male strippers. Apparently, you could take the kids to see the jousting, Dad could see the comic, and Mom could go have beefcake. It was very well-rounded entertainment-wise compared to the mostly girlie-oriented shows that most places were boasting. Though there had been more comics, and Cirque du Soleil seemed to have more different shows at different places than anybody. The Luxor, the big pyramid with a Sphinx out front, was next. Across the street from faux Egypt was faux India. It was the New Taj, which was

Max's casino, hotel, and resort. The building was obviously based on the Taj Mahal, but there were white stone sculptures of animals scattered throughout the lush jungle-like landscaping. There were monkeys and an elephant and birds I couldn't recognize in white, but there were a lot of tigers peeking out and strolling among the rest. The statues were actually almost unnervingly lifelike. Well, I guess they'd had real-life models to work from.

The moving billboard out in front of the Taj boasted a magic act with more of the real-life version of the animals, and two revues. One was beefy-looking men, and I recognized one of the faces, though I was thankful that most of him was hidden behind the other men. The other show was all girls. Max was trying to maximize his resort's appeal as well.

Edward didn't pull into the circular driveway but went past it to a smaller, less landscaped road. I saw signs that promised a parking garage. I guess we weren't going to valet.

"The first time you see it, you either think it's gaudy and awful, or you love it. There's almost no halfway about this town," Edward said.

I realized he'd kept quiet so I could enjoy the view. "It's like Disneyland on crack, for grown-ups," I said.

"You're not going to hate it," he said.

"They don't call it Sin City for nothing," Bernardo said.

I turned and looked at him as Edward slid into the shade of the parking garage. "Have you been here before, too?"

"Yeah, but not on business."

I was debating on asking him what he had come for, and if I'd like the answer, but Edward said, "You sound like you've acted as Jean-Claude's representative before."

"This is the first time doing it without more help from home." The ceilings always seem low to me in parking structures when I'm in an SUV.

"Who will play your lover?" Olaf asked it. I should have known he would.

"You didn't behave yourself well enough at the coroner's. I don't trust you to be able to play the part in the way I need."

"Tell me what you need," he said.

I glanced at Edward, but his eyes were hidden behind his

sunglasses, and he didn't look my way. I wanted to call him a coward, but that wasn't it. I think, for once, he was as confused about how to handle the situation with Olaf as I was. Not good when Edward is out of his depth with his serial killer playmates.

"Hold that thought," I said, and I dialed the only other number in Vegas that I had programmed into my phone. It was the man whose face I'd recognized on the billboard.

26

CRISPIN ANSWERED THE phone on the second ring; his voice still held that edge of sleep, but it was a happy edge. He worked nights, so his sleep pattern was close to mine. "Anita," and that one word was way happier than it should have been.

"How did you know it was me?"

"I programmed a song for you, so I know it's you." I heard the sheets roll as he turned.

Was I the only person who didn't know how to program my own damn phone? "I'm about to park in the garage at the New Taj."

I heard the heavy slither of sheets across skin. Was he sitting up? "Right now?"

"Yes, I should have called you sooner, I'm sorry. I got distracted by the pretty lights."

"Crap, Anita," Crispin said, and I heard other noises on his end of the phone.

"You sound worried," I said. "Why?"

"Chang-Bibi is my queen, but I'm your tiger to call."

"Do I apologize for that again?"

There were more noises, and I realized he was getting dressed. "No, I'd just rather you let me move in with you, or at least move to St. Louis, but we'll have that talk some other time."

"You sound freaked, Crispin. What is wrong?"

Edward pulled into a spot, and Hooper's SUV drove past ours, looking for his own parking spot.

"Let's just say that there are guests here that Chang-Bibi wants you to meet, and you'll want me within touching distance."

"Don't make me ask why again, Crispin."

"Other tigers from other clans, Anita. They want to know if you can bring their powers online, too."

"I'm not coming to feed the *ardeur*, Crispin, just to talk about the murders."

"If Max were awake, that's what you'd talk about. He's business, but Chang-Bibi may think first about the tigers, second about business."

"Are you actually saying that she wants me to . . . do some of the tigers before she'll talk business?"

The phone fell, hit something, and made me take it away from my ear. He came back on. "Dropped the phone, Anita, sorry. I'll meet you downstairs in the casino before you meet anyone else."

"If you do that, won't Bibiana question your loyalties?"

"Maybe, but I don't want you meeting the new tigers without me."

"Jealous?" I asked, and probably shouldn't have.

"Yes," he said, and that was Crispin. He didn't play, really. If he felt something, he told you. It made him very uncomfortable to deal with sometimes.

"Do I apologize for that, too?" I asked, and my voice was less than friendly.

"If you didn't want the truth, you shouldn't have asked," and now he didn't sound happy. When we first met, I'd thought Crispin was uncomplicated, and just about sex and food. I'd learned different. It was like I couldn't be attracted to a man who wasn't difficult in some way.

"You're right; if I didn't want the truth, I shouldn't have asked. I'm sorry."

He was quiet for a few breaths, then said, "Apology accepted."

"Get off the phone, Anita. We need to talk before we get there," Edward said. He'd turned the engine off, and we sat in silence as the air-conditioning died away.

"Crispin, I've got to go," I said into the phone.

"I'll see you downstairs in the casino."

"Will this get you in trouble with your clan?" I asked.

"I don't care," he said, and he hung up. He was twenty-one,

barely, and most of the time he seemed younger. This was one of those times. I knew how harsh some of the wereanimal groups could be if you didn't follow orders. Crispin might not care now, but the weretigers could make him care. They could make him care a lot.

"Crispin will meet us in the casino downstairs. He says Chang-Bibi may try to fix me up with some new tigers before she'll talk about the murders."

"Fix you up, you mean have sex with them?" Bernardo asked from the backseat.

"Feed the *ardeur* on them," I said.

"You mean have sex with them," Olaf said, as if to drive the point home.

"I can feed without intercourse," I said, in a very grumpy voice.

"Good to know," Edward said, and his voice didn't sound much happier than mine.

"You told us that the weretigers might want you to feed on them, but not that you'd have to do it before they'd talk to us," Bernardo said.

"I didn't know," I said.

"Do you mean that we might have to watch you have sex with some of the weretigers?" Olaf asked.

I fought not to squirm in my seat. "Not if I can help it. The tigers are very big on fidelity, marriage, all that. I'm hoping if one of you plays my lover that Bibiana will see it as cheating for me to do one of her tigers. Also, it's a way to get all three of you inside with me. Two as security, and one as food."

I heard a noise and Olaf was suddenly looming over the back of my seat. Height didn't usually intimidate me, but as his arms slid around the sides of the seat, as if to pin me . . . "Back in your own seat, Olaf. No touching."

"If I am to play lover, then I must touch."

"And that is exactly why you aren't doing it," I said.

"I don't understand."

"I believe that, and that's another reason that you are going to be security and not food."

"I've frightened you again, haven't I?" he asked.

"Nervous, you've made me nervous again."

"What do you like to do on a date?"

I turned in my seat so I could see his face. "What?"

"What do you like to do on a date?" He repeated it, looking right at me, his face very neutral. At least he was controlling his face now, though the weirdness factor wasn't lessening for me. No, weird was definitely on the rise.

"Just answer the question, Anita," Edward said in a quiet voice.

"I don't know. See movies, eat dinner, talk."

"What do you do with . . . Edward?"

"We hunt bad guys and kill things."

"Is that all?"

"We go out shooting, and he shows me bigger and scarier weapons."

"And?" he asked.

I frowned. "I don't know what you want me to say . . . Otto."

"What do you do on a date with Ted?"

"I don't date Ted." In my head I thought, *It would be like dating my brother*, but part of what we hoped would make Olaf leave me alone was the idea that Ted felt less brotherly toward me. So, what to say? "He's with Donna, and they've got kids, and I don't date people who are taken. It's against the rules."

"Honorable for a woman," he said.

"What the hell does that mean?" I said. "I know plenty of men who don't obey that rule, either. Bastards come in both sexes."

He looked at me for a long time, then finally blinked and looked away. He nodded. "Bernardo has no such rules."

"I guessed that," I said.

"I am sitting right here," Bernardo said.

Olaf said, "It bothers him that you don't like him better."

"Bernardo and I had this discussion, and we handled it."

"What does that mean?" Olaf asked.

"It means that Anita let me know she thinks I'm cute, so my ego is secure."

Olaf was frowning from one to the other of us. "I don't understand."

"We don't have time for this," Edward said, with a sigh. "Who plays what role?"

"Whoever I pick for a lover may have to do more than hold hands to convince Bibiana that it would be rude to offer up one of her tigers."

"So not Olaf," Edward said.

"And not you," I said.

"I weird you out," Olaf said. "I understand that, but why not Ted?"

"Pretending is too close to doing, and it would make me feel funny the next time I visited his family." That was actually the truth.

Bernardo leaned forward, smiling. "Does that mean that I'm the lucky guy?"

I scowled at him. "I'm giving you another chance to play my boyfriend; don't make me regret it."

"Hey, it wasn't you who ended up being forced to strip half naked at gunpoint last time." He wasn't teasing when he said it.

"Why did they want you to strip?" Olaf asked.

"They asked me a trick question, to see if he really was my lover."

"What question?"

"Whether I was circumcised," Bernardo said, and now he had a touch of amusement in his voice. "They wanted to see if her answer was the right one."

"Was it?" Edward asked.

"Yes."

"How did you know whether he was circumcised?" Olaf asked, and he actually sounded indignant.

I undid my seat belt and turned in my seat. "Stop it, just stop it. You haven't earned the right to sound jealous or hurt."

Olaf scowled at me.

"Sonny and Spider are watching us argue," Edward said.

I'd forgotten that the two policemen were trailing us. That was beyond careless. "Great, fine, but I mean it, Olaf. I'm flattered that you want to try to date me like a normal guy, but a normal guy doesn't get jealous before he's even kissed a girl."

"Not true," Edward and Bernardo said together.

"What?" I asked.

They exchanged a look, then Edward said, "I had a crush on a girl, the first serious one. I never kissed her, or even held her hand, but I was jealous of every boy who got near her."

I tried to picture a young, insecure Edward and couldn't, but it was nice to know that once he'd been a boy. Sometimes it felt like Edward had sprung full grown from the head of some violent deity, like a vicious version of Athena.

"I've been jealous of women who were dating good friends. You don't poach from good friends, but sometimes it cuts you up to watch them be cute together."

"Anita and I thought you would poach," Olaf said.

"Hey, just because I like women doesn't mean I have no scruples. No friends' serious girlfriends, and no wives of people I like."

"Good to know you have scruples." I tried for sarcasm and succeeded.

"Hey," Bernardo said, "what's the old saying about glass houses, Anita?"

"I don't do husbands."

"I don't do vampires," he said.

Point for him. Out loud, I said, "You don't know what you're missing."

"I don't like sleeping with anyone who can bespell me with their eyes. It's too hard to remember not to gaze."

"So it's not morality but practicality."

"That, and sometimes there's a moisture problem."

"What does that mean?"

"It means they're dead, Anita, and dead women need lubricant."

"Stop, just stop, before I get a visual to go with that." Then I added, before I had time to think about it, "That's not true of the female vampires I know." I knew it was true, knew it through Jean-Claude's and Asher's memories that they'd shared with me metaphysically. Knew it through Belle herself visiting my dreams.

"And how do you know that the female vampires you've met don't need lubricant?" he asked.

I tried to think of an answer that wouldn't raise more questions and couldn't come up with one.

"You are blushing." Olaf didn't sound happy.

"Oh, please tell me that the visual I've got in my head is true," Bernardo said, and he sounded very happy. In fact, he was grinning ear to ear.

Edward was looking at me over the lowered rims of his sunglasses. "I haven't heard any rumors about you and the female vampires."

"Maybe you can all just wait outside and I'll talk to the tigers alone." I got out of the car, into the dimness of the parking garage.

Sonny and Spider got out of their SUV, but I didn't want to talk to any more men. I slammed the door and started for the spot marked *Elevator*. I heard the doors opening and shutting. If I got to the elevator first, I was going up to the casino without them. Maybe it wasn't the smart thing to do, but the thought of Edward watching the doors close without him gave me a certain shallow satisfaction. Maybe he understood that I'd had enough teasing, because he hurried to catch up with me in front of the elevator.

"Going up by yourself would be stupid, and that is something you aren't," he said, and sounded angry.

"I'm tired of explaining myself to you or anyone else."

"I've sent Bernardo and Olaf to talk to SWAT, so you can talk to me. Is there something else I should know?"

"No," I said.

"Liar," he said.

I glared at him. "I thought it was just Ted who fantasized about lesbians."

"You're Jean-Claude's human servant; how closely tied are you metaphysically, Anita?"

And just like that, he'd guessed what I didn't want to tell them.

"I've never been to St. Louis," Bernardo said, from just behind us. "What female vamps does Jean-Claude have?"

"They didn't seem to like Anita enough to sleep with her," Olaf said.

The doors opened, and I said, "One more word about this topic and I'm getting in this elevator by myself."

"Touchy," Bernardo said.

"Drop it," Edward said, "both of you."

They dropped it, and we all got in the elevator. Bernardo was smiling all over himself. Olaf was scowling. Edward's face had gone to unreadable. I leaned against the back wall and fought to find an expression that wouldn't make it worse. Was it better that two of them thought I'd been with another woman than that I shared detailed memories with vampires? Yeah, it was. It would have been even better if Edward had believed it.

27

OLAF WAS WILLING to throw his leather over everything, but Edward passed out the dark windbreakers with *U.S. Marshal* on them to all of us. "If this is a social visit, won't this be the wrong message?" Bernardo asked.

"The new law makes it almost impossible for any of us to pass for civilians," Edward said. "We can't enter a casino packing this much firepower without badges showing. The first time they see us on the security cameras, they'll think something bad is happening."

We couldn't argue with that, actually. It took us a few minutes to get jackets over our clothes so that most of the weapons were hidden. I was really going to have to remember to pack my own nifty dark blue windbreaker next time. I always remembered the weapons and the badges, but I did keep forgetting some of the other stuff. Olaf slid everything out of sight in his leather jacket. "It is invisible under this jacket."

"You don't like having a badge, do you, big guy?" Bernardo asked, as he fluffed the jacket over all of his own weapons.

"I like some of it, but I don't like the jacket."

I had to take the backpack off, and just slid the MP5 on its sling so it was under the jacket, and put the backpack on over the jacket. The MP5 was the thing most likely to freak the mundanes and the casino security.

Edward had replaced his own Heckler & Koch MP5 with the new FN P90. It was very science fiction–looking, but he swore once I fired it, I'd trade in my MP5. He'd said the same thing about the mini-Uzi that had been the gun that the MP5 had replaced for me, so I didn't argue. Edward knew more about guns than I ever would.

We stepped out of the elevator and into the casino. It was bright, but oddly elegant in its gaudiness. The Indian theme continued, with more animal statues and painted plants on the walls, with real plants huddled under full-spectrum lights, so it gave the illusion of sunlight coming through a jungle canopy. Then there were the slot machines. Rows and rows of them. There were blackjack tables, and craps being rolled farther in; people were everywhere. The noise was not as much as you'd think, but it was still a room full of movement and that energy people get when they're on vacation and trying to enjoy every minute of it, as if trying to make up for all that work.

Edward shook his head, bending over me, so he could be heard over the noise. "It's too open, and too many places to hide, all at the same time. Casinos suck for bodyguard work."

I looked around the crowd of people, the slot machines, the noise, the color. There was so much to look at that it was hard to actually "see" anything.

Bernardo and Olaf seemed to have picked up some signal from Edward, so that they were suddenly on high alert. I realized, watching us, that any policeman or good security would know we weren't tourists in a heartbeat. It wasn't the guns or the *U.S. Marshal* on the jackets. It was that strange metamorphosis that cops can do. One minute they're joking with you, looking sort of ordinary; the next they're "on"—they are cops, they are alert—and no amount of civilian clothing can hide that they are different from everyone else. We were all doing it. So much for covering the weapons; if I'd been security, I'd have been all over us.

I didn't see anything to be afraid of; what had spooked Edward? I moved back so I could look up into his pale blue eyes. I searched his face. His face was solemn, and his eyes as serious as I'd ever seen them.

I leaned in, and he leaned down, because I couldn't reach his ear without help. "I've never seen you like this, Edward, not without people shooting at us."

"It's just hard security in a place like this."

I put a hand on his arm to steady myself, because we were too close. He slid a hand around me, turning it into something that looked more intimate. It reminded me that we were still trying to work out what to do with Olaf. Great, another problem.

"I'm not your body to guard, Ted. I'm just a fellow vampire hunter." I looked up into his eyes, and we were too close. It was kissing close, but his eyes, this close I could see his eyes, and there was nothing about kissing in them. The look in his eyes scared me.

"There's just too much that can go wrong, Anita, and this is a terrible location for protection."

I couldn't argue with that. I just nodded.

He put his hand on the back of my hair and kissed my forehead. He did it for Olaf's benefit, but it was what we were doing when the weretigers walked up. Perfect.

28

I FELT THEM like a wind on my skin—a tickling breeze of energy that raised goose bumps on my skin and made me shiver in Edward's arms. Most men would have taken credit for that shiver, but Edward looked up and around. He knew I'd sensed something.

His reaction put Olaf and Bernardo on alert. Olaf's hand was actually hovering near the edge of his jacket, where it barely covered one of his sidearms. We were just all back to that "cop" moment.

Edward and I moved apart, enough room to go for weapons if we had to. Enough room that we wouldn't get in each other's way. Bernardo and Olaf did the same thing. Without talking to each other, or even looking at each other, the four of us formed points of a square to watch the room. I made sure my point was watching the coming tigers, but we all knew our jobs. I might have issues with Olaf, and even Bernardo, but it was nice to work with people who knew how to deal. We covered the room, not like cops but more like soldiers. No, we covered the room like people who were used to pulling guns and shooting first. None of us were really cops. Cops save lives; we took them. Four executioners standing in a room; best to be elsewhere.

There were two uniformed and armed security guys at the back of the group, but I didn't give them much of a look. It wasn't guns I was worried about. I trusted Edward to watch the guns. The woman in front had red hair, and that pale skin that goes with it. As she got closer, I saw the dusting of freckles underneath her base makeup. Her eyes were brown and human looking. In fact, she radiated goodwill and humanity. The two men on either side of her didn't waste energy trying to pass for human.

They were both tall, about six feet. The one on her left was the taller by an inch or two; he had white hair cut short and close to his head. His eyes were icy blue but not human. White tigers have blue eyes, and the man in front of me had the eyes he'd have in animal form in his human face. In any other were-animal, it would have been a punishment brought on by being forced into animal form too often, and for too long, but in the tigers it showed purity of bloodline. They were born with the eyes.

The man on her right was just under six feet, with curly hair; some of those curls were black, some white. His eyes were a brilliant orange, like staring into fire.

The woman held her hand out. "I'm Ava, and you must be Anita." She smiled, and you would have thought we were a group of visiting businessmen. I took her hand automatically.

Energy jumped between us like a small electric shock. It made her eyes go round, and her mouth made a little *O* of surprise. I took my hand back and fought not to wipe my palm on my pants to take the insect-crawling sensation away. Mustn't let them see you flinch. We might be on a social call, but it was going to be about power, too. We'd be doing a more dangerous version of what happened when I met the SWAT practitioners. There, the worst that would happen was it might be scary, but no one would have hurt me. Here, I wasn't sure of that.

Ava did wipe her hand on her dress. "I think we might wait until we're upstairs for any more introductions." Her voice was a little breathy.

"I wouldn't suggest anyone pushing power into me, just to test the limits," I said, low.

"I'm just following orders, Anita," she said.

"And what were your orders, exactly?" I asked.

She ignored the question and answered a different one. "This is Domino, and this is Roderic."

Domino had to be a nickname from the hair. He just nodded at me, and I nodded back. White Hair smiled and said, "Rick, I prefer Rick."

I nodded and answered the smile with a small one of my own. I didn't blame him on the name choice. "Rick," I said.

Then I felt something else. Something more. It was Crispin, and he was agitated. I fought to keep my eyes on the security tigers because the two tigers with Ava were so much muscle. Maybe not professional muscle, but they had the feel to them of people you wouldn't want to fight, not if you didn't have to. I'd been the smallest person in violent situations for years now. I knew how to judge potential. They had potential, and not all of it good. But it was an effort not to look away from the danger zone, a real effort not to scan the crowd for Crispin. He was my tiger to call, which meant that sometimes I could feel his emotions. He was upset, scared, nervous, just wrong in his head.

But just as I could feel his agitation, I could also feel him getting closer to us. I fought to keep my attention on the were-tigers in front of me, but they had picked up on my . . . body language, tension, maybe even my scent had changed. I was more tense because try as I might, I was picking up some of Crispin's agitation. Wereanimals with some training are like uber-cops. You can't hide much from them.

Edward spoke low. "What's wrong?"

"Ask them," I said.

Rick was no longer smiling; even Ava wasn't as happy. But it was Domino who said it. "He was ordered to go upstairs and wait for us there."

"He's a little conflicted," I said.

"You can't serve two masters," Ava said, trying for a soothing voice, but her words held an edge of that tension, as if Crispin were leaking over them as well as me.

"Who's conflicted?" Bernardo asked.

"Crispin," I said, and as if his name had conjured him, he was there. Walking through the crowd of humans, moving through them too swiftly, too easily, as if he were made of water and the crowd were rocks to flow and glide around. But *glide* implied grace and ease, and there was nothing easy about his movements. Swift, near dance-like, but too jerky to be graceful. What was wrong with him?

The tigers felt him, too, because Domino turned to watch

him. Were they picking up his scent or his emotion? Rick kept his attention on us, but there was a tension to his shoulders that seemed to scream that he wanted to turn around and face Crispin. Rick assumed that the greatest danger was another wereanimal. Normally, he'd be right.

Crispin was wearing a T-shirt almost as pale a blue as his eyes, jeans, and no shoes. He hadn't bothered with shoes. Most of the wereanimals would leave clothes off if you didn't make them behave.

He held his hand out toward me. I took a step toward him without meaning to. Domino stepped between us. A sound came out of my throat that I hadn't meant to make, either. I growled at him. It rolled up my throat and across my tongue and between my teeth and lips. The growl vibrated on the roof of my mouth like a taste. I saw the white tigress inside me, and we looked at Crispin and he was ours. You do not stand between us and what is ours.

I felt Bernardo and Olaf shift around me, as if they weren't sure what to do. Edward was Edward, and stayed still. I knew he would back my play whatever it was.

Domino looked at me, and there was anger in those orange eyes. "You are not my queen, not yet."

"Get out of our way," I said, and my voice held that note of growl that I'd come to associate with wereanimals. Outwardly, I was human, but the sound in my throat wasn't.

Ava touched Domino's shoulder. "She smells of tiger."

He jerked free of her hand. "You are not my queen, either."

Rick said, "Don't make a scene. Bibiana was clear on that."

"She has no right to order me about." I wasn't sure if he meant me or Ava.

Crispin tried again to move around the other men and come to me. Domino started to grab him, but Crispin simply wasn't there to grab. He might not be professional muscle, but he had the reflexes of a cat. And apparently, he was a quicker cat than Domino.

Domino tried to move forward, with that we're-about-to-have-a-fight energy. Rick grabbed his shoulders, and Ava moved in front of him, facing us. Crispin came to my outstretched left hand, and I moved him behind me, so I'd have both hands free, but he'd be protected. He was quick, and he could fight when he had to, but this was a fight he could not win. The black-and-white tiger had the feel to him of death contained and waiting. I knew that with a certainty that made me want to go for a gun.

"You should have gone upstairs as our queen told you to," Ava said.

"Anita needed me," he said, and his six-foot-plus frame towered over me, just a little. It seemed wrong that so much tall, athletic grace was hiding behind my short, not so athletic, and definitely not so graceful self.

"You're hiding behind her," Domino growled. Rick's pale hands tightened visibly on the other man's shoulders. They both had to look up at Crispin, which should have lessened their tough-guy act but didn't, because it wasn't an act.

"She doesn't need any help with violence," Crispin said.

Edward said, "We're attracting a crowd."

He was right. The tourists were getting a show, or anticipating one. We were drawing them away from the slot machines, and that takes a lot in Vegas. I didn't think we'd done anything that interesting yet. Of course, it could be the three of us in our U.S. Marshal windbreakers and badges, with weapons peeking out all over the place; yeah, that might be enough to attract some attention. Olaf would have looked dangerous anywhere with all the black clothing and leather.

"Let us continue this upstairs," Ava said, and motioned us all farther into the room, in the general direction of the elevators.

I looked at Domino still in Rick's grasp, so angry. Was it a good idea to get in the elevator? Probably not, but nothing scary enough had happened yet to make me willing to back down.

"Fine," I said, "lead the way."

29

DOMINO CALMED DOWN enough to stand beside Rick and Ava in the big elevator. It was one marked *Private*, and seemed to go only to one floor. The penthouse, I was assuming.

"Sorry," Rick said, and sounded like he meant it, "but they can't go into the private chambers with this many weapons on them."

"We can't leave the weapons in the car," I said. "New rules. Once a warrant is in play, we have to be able to do our jobs at full capacity at any minute, and we are not allowed to leave our weapons in a place where civilians could get hold of them."

"You lie," Domino said.

The black and white tigers growled inside me. It was hint enough. The tigresses didn't like me backing down to any of the males. I took a step closer to him, which put Ava between us. Rick put a hand back on the other man's arm, just sort of automatically. "Domino, if you can't smell that I'm telling the truth, then you aren't dominant enough to be this much trouble."

He growled at me, low and rumbling, like close thunder. "I will not answer your call, little queen."

"I haven't called you anywhere."

"You did," he said, "you called us all."

Rick put an arm across the other man's chest, moving smoothly into a more solid hold. "You did, Ms. Blake. A few months back, you did do that."

I sighed, and the anger began to fade, until the tigers inside me swatted at me from the inside out. I flinched, couldn't help it. I was getting used to the sensation of invisible claws cutting me up, but it was almost impossible not to react a little. It wasn't real damage. I knew it was metaphysical pain. It hurt, but it did not bleed me. They'd actually put me through medical tests to make certain of that, at one point. It was just pain. I could ignore it, sort of. When the tigers got this bitchy, I had to pay some attention, or it got worse.

The elevator, which I'd expected to be quick but wasn't, opened. Two more uniformed security guards were there, replacements for the two we'd left downstairs. None of the tigers stepped out; they were all looking at me.

"I didn't mean to put out the welcome mat to everyone, but I won't apologize for it either." The tigers were creeping closer inside me. I said what I hoped they wanted to hear. "If I was queen enough to call you, then it's not up to you if you answer that call."

Ava and Rick sandwiched Domino between them, as he tried to move forward. "You bitch."

There was another swat inside me, as if the white and black tigers were trying to play basketball with my spine. Fuck, it hurt.

Crispin touched my shoulders, and the touch helped. The white tiger eased back. He wasn't as dominant as she wanted, but he was one of hers. The black tiger, and I mean black, like a black leopard, with stripes showing only in bright light, came forward, growling and hissing, flashing those huge canines.

"Please, tell me that Domino here isn't the only black tiger you've got."

"The black clan is nearly extinct," Ava said.

I drew one of Crispin's hands across my face until I could smell the warm scent of his wrist. I rubbed my cheek against the heat of him. The white tiger rose closer to the surface and pushed the black one down. There were other colors of tiger inside me. I had a damn rainbow, impossible colors that had never occurred in any zoo, though I had learned that every tiger inside me had once existed as a real animal. It had just been a few thousand years for some of the subspecies. They were just legends now.

"Maybe if we get out of the elevator and get a little more room," Edward said.

"You do not order us about, human," Domino said.

"He's got a badge; you don't," I said, still being too up close and personal with Crispin's arm and hand. It was hard to be tough as nails when kissing someone's hand, but some days you do the best you can.

"The marshal is right, let's step outside." Rick's voice sounded just a little strained, which meant he was holding on to his friend even tighter than it looked. That wasn't good.

"What will your friend do once we're somewhere without security cameras?" I asked around the sweet smell of Crispin's arm.

"He'll do what Chang-Bibi tells him to do," Ava said.

"And that would be what?" I asked.

"What?" Ava asked.

"What does she want him to do? Obviously he's not happy about it, whatever it is."

"You," Crispin said.

Ava said, "Crispin!"

I said, "What?"

"You," he repeated from behind me, "our queen wants them both to do you."

"Crispin," Ava said, and her face wasn't friendly anymore, almost angry.

Bernardo leaned in and said, "I'd really rather have more room for the fight than the elevator."

I stepped out of the elevator, and everyone followed. I knew why Crispin and the other marshals waited for me, maybe, but I finally realized that at some level the weretigers were treating me like what Domino had said, a little queen. They weren't doing it on purpose, I'd have bet on that. It was all unconscious, which made it both useful and a little scary.

The hallway was white and cream, and much more elegant than the casino or the elevator. I waited until everyone was standing in the cool, wide hallway.

"Look, Domino, this is news to me. I'll make you a deal. You tone it down and I'll promise you won't be on the menu for sex." In my head, I thought, *Food for anger, maybe, but not sex.*

He frowned at me.

Crispin tried to help. "She means she won't do you if you don't want to do her."

"You can't speak for anyone," Ava said.

The uniformed guards were looking at us, with their hands on the butts of their guns. They saw the badges, but they saw the guns, too, and they'd picked up that we might not be getting along with the weretigers. It would be interesting to see where their loyalties would divide.

Edward leaned in. "Either we leave or we go with them. Your call."

I sighed. Leaving was such a good idea. But the bodies in the morgue would still be dead. The head they'd mailed to me would still be waiting to come back to its body for burial. I had smelled tiger on the body in the morgue here. I wasn't wrong, and for clues about weretigers, this was the place to come.

"Anita," Edward said, softly.

"With them, we go with them."

"What about their weapons?" Domino said.

"We have a gun room, if we could lock up some of them?" Rick said.

"We don't give up our weapons," Olaf said.

"Your warrant excludes us, and you don't have other police with you. You do not go before our queen with automatic weapons on you," Rick said, and it was matter-of-fact.

"Would you let someone see your Master of the City armed like this?" Ava asked.

I thought about it, then shook my head. "Probably not."

"Let's get some privacy, and we'll discuss the weapons," Edward said. He'd glanced up at the hallway, near the ceiling. His gaze had found the security cameras. I wondered if it was a law in Vegas, the cameras?

"Sure."

I put Crispin's hand more firmly in my left hand. He squeezed back. I said to Domino, "I'm not into rape; if you don't want me, fine. I'm not crazy about you either."

He almost snarled, and Rick suddenly had a two-armed grip on him. "I must obey my queen," Domino growled. The energy of his beast pushed off him. I braced for it to hit me like a kidney punch thrown from inches away, but it was completely different. No violence, no electric rush. It was like being bathed in a pool of warm, expensive perfume. Except the scent didn't hit my nose. Can something have a scent that hits your brain but not your nose? It was as if the "perfume" hit something deeper inside me. The white tigress and the black paced closer to the surface, opening their mouths in that grimace/growl, so they could taste the scent on the tops of their mouths where the Jacobson organ is located. He smelled . . . good.

I backed up and slid my arm around Crispin. His arm hesitated at the touch of the MP5 on its sling, then just kept moving until he held me close, our bodies touching all the way down side to side. Touching Crispin helped clear my head, but the tigers growled at me. They liked Domino better now.

Domino had gone quiet in Rick's grip. Those orange-fire eyes were looking at me differently now. "You smell . . . like home." He didn't sound angry now, more puzzled.

I needed to leave. It was a bad idea to get closer to any of the tigers. But . . . all that seemed at risk was my virtue; somehow that didn't seem worth another cop's life. If I got a clue here that saved lives, would it be worth it? Hell, yes. Did I want to add another man to my menu? Hell, no. But sometimes a girl's got to do what a man's got to do, or something like that. In that moment, I was angry. Angry that metaphysics would probably help solve the crime, but it was going to fuck me up again. Probably literally.

30

THE ANTECHAMBER HAD white tile and white walls; it was all so pale it was almost disorienting. The only thing that saved it was that the white had more wallpaper on it. The paper had raised designs in silver and gold. It was like standing inside a delicate Christmas ornament. It was almost too elegant for comfort, as if I were afraid I'd break something just by breathing too hard. The chairs were all those delicate, spindly-backed ones that only very small people fit into, if at all, and even if you fit, they won't be comfortable.

We'd come through a big door from the hallway, and there was another set of double doors in the far wall. Behind them, where Ava and Domino had gone, was Bibiana and her inner circle. Ava went to talk to Bibiana, but I think Domino went because they didn't trust him around me and all the guns. Rick was adamant that we weren't going before his queen armed to the teeth.

Crispin was sitting, waiting for us all to finish the debate. He seemed peaceful with all of it, as if it didn't matter to him what we decided. If the delicate chair was uncomfortable, it didn't show. He seemed more at ease than he had in the casino.

"The warrant excludes the weretigers, so you can keep us out of the inner room. But you can't force us to disarm," I said.

"Then you don't get in," Rick said. "But frankly, I thought at least one of you wouldn't be armed. Ava said one of these guys was supposed to be food. We don't arm our food."

"I've been personally threatened by a serial killer here in your town; I thought it was smart to bring food that could take care of itself."

He made a can't-argue-with-that face and said, "Fair enough, but you still don't get inside with all the shit you're carrying."

There were two more uniformed guards by the double doors. The two who had met us at the elevator were still outside in the hallway. Four armed guards, cool, but all human; interesting. If I had a choice of guards, I'd have picked weretigers to guard weretigers. I thought it was an interesting decision to use regular human guards like you'd see at any casino. There were more of them than normal, but still, it was pretty ordinary for the Master Vampire of the City.

"Then we're at an impasse," I said. "You won't let us in without the weapons, and we won't give them up."

"Then you leave," Rick said, "sorry."

Edward said, "What if two of us strip off most of our weapons, while the other two keep the weapons and stand at this door?"

I looked at him.

"You said we needed to come here, Anita. How badly do you want this interview?"

I met his eyes, so blue, so cold, so real. I nodded. "I want it. I want it before dark when the vampires will hunt again."

"Tactical units do this sometimes, when they have to negotiate," he said.

I wanted to say, *But you had a bad feeling downstairs,* but I couldn't say that out loud in front of the guards from the other side. I sighed. "Okay." I took off the windbreaker and lifted the MP5 in its sling over my head. "Who gets to hold for me?"

Edward held out his hand.

I gave him wide eyes. "No, you're going in with me."

"No," he said, "I'm staying out here with all my weapons, so that if you yell for help I'll come through like the cavalry."

We stared at each other for a minute. I thought about what he'd said, tried to be logical, instead of paying attention to my suddenly speeding heart rate. I gave him the MP5.

"Thank you," and I knew he meant not the gun but the level of trust that the gun represented for me.

"You're welcome, but how will you hear me when I yell for help?"

"I've got earbuds and radios."

Of course he did. It was Edward; he always brought the right toys for the play date. I stopped stripping off weapons and said, "Wait, who goes in with me, if you stay here?"

"Shit," Bernardo said, with real feeling to the word. He started taking off the jacket.

"Hold a minute," Edward said. He turned to Rick. "How clean do you want them to be?"

"They can keep the knives and one handgun."

"Thanks for the handgun," I said.

Rick grinned. "You'll do a hideout anyway. This way I know where the gun is."

"You could just search us," I said.

"I waited for you to get out of the elevator. All of us did. I don't think I want to touch you, little queen. In fact, the less I have to do with you physically, the better."

"You aren't on the meal plan?" I asked.

"I was, but I'm going to ask to be reassigned."

"Should I be offended?"

"No, it's a compliment. If you were just good sex, then no problem. I like sex. But you aren't just good sex. You're power. You're things I can't even name. But I know one thing for damn sure: you are dangerous, and it isn't the guns and badge that make you dangerous to me and Domino, and even Crispin." He nodded toward where he was sitting patiently in one of the uncomfortable chairs. "His gaze follows you like he's a devoted dog."

I glanced at Crispin, who gave me a peaceful face, as if the comment didn't faze him. "I didn't do it on purpose," was all I could think to say.

"I believe that. You're like a survivor of an attack by one of us. You don't know what you are yet."

"She's gaining powers as if she were a born tiger," Crispin said, from his chair.

Rick nodded. "I noticed that. Now, whoever is going inside, take off the weapons."

I started taking stuff off and handed it to Edward. Bernardo did the same, handing his gear to Olaf.

Edward handed earbuds and waist radios to the four of us.

Rick never protested the radios. Again, not doing what I thought he'd do.

"I've got it set to broadcast continuously, so Otto and I will hear whatever is going on."

I had a thought. "What's the range on these? I wouldn't want just anyone to overhear."

Edward smiled. "I'd rather not say in front of our host."

Rick said, "Don't mind me."

"But it's small enough that if our local friends are trying to listen in, they'd have to be standing in the room with us to overhear."

"Okay." I understood that he didn't want to tell Rick, and thus all the weretigers, how far they'd have to take Bernardo and me so that we could yell for help and not be heard, but . . . I'd have liked to know the range. But I trusted Edward. I trusted him with my life and my death. I had no higher compliment to pay to another executioner.

I had to readjust my straps on the holsters, to settle the guns again without all the other stuff to get in the way, and with the addition of the radio. Adjustable holsters are a wonderful thing. Bernardo was doing similar things to his guns and knives.

"How did you know Edward was going to pick you to go in with me?" I asked, as I checked the last knife.

Bernardo gave me a look. It wasn't a happy one. In fact, those dark eyes were downright sullen. He straightened up, hands doing one last check on the new location of all his weapons, automatically. "Because if it's the cavalry you want, the heavy hitters stay out here, and neither of you thinks I'm a heavy enough hitter."

I wasn't sure what to say to that. Edward saved me. "If I didn't trust you, Bernardo, I wouldn't send her in with only you as backup."

Bernardo and he exchanged a long look, and then finally the other man nodded. "Fine, but we both know you'd send Olaf if you didn't think he'd eat her."

"I thought we were the only ones who ate people," Rick said, with his hand on the door.

I gave the weretiger the look the comment deserved. He smiled at me.

Crispin had moved up beside me, just waiting for us to finish the weapons. Apparently, he had no qualms about following me anywhere. He'd already done enough to get him in trouble in most of the wereanimal groups that I was familiar with. Insubordination isn't tolerated among the furry.

Rick touched Crispin's arm. "You must either wait here with her other friends, or go ahead alone."

"I want to stay with Anita."

"You have already refused one direct order from your queen and master. Do not make it two, Crispin." Rick's face softened. "Please, stay here, or go ahead."

I didn't argue for Crispin to stay with me because Rick was right. Crispin had already gotten himself in potential trouble. I didn't want to make it worse.

He turned to me. "What do you want me to do?"

I blinked at him. What I really wanted him to do was not to have asked that. I really wanted him to make the decision on his own in case it came back and bit him. But either you're the dominant or you aren't. Fuck.

If he stayed here, he'd be safer. If he went ahead, they might punish him, but I might also be able to get him back at my side and help me control the tigers.

"If he goes ahead, what happens to him?"

"He has earned discipline, but since he is your white tiger to call, he falls under vampire rules."

"You can't hurt him because he's mine."

Rick nodded. "As long as you're in Vegas, yes."

We looked at each other. I didn't know Rick well enough to know that look this well, but I did. The look said, plainly, that if I left Crispin in Vegas, bad things might happen to him. Jean-Claude was not going to like me coming home with extra baggage, but I couldn't leave him to be hurt, could I?

"Go ahead, Crispin. We'll be right behind you."

Crispin looked from me to Rick, then finally nodded. He went through the far, whooshy doors, and we were one man down.

Olaf finally spoke. "Do you wonder why I did not protest Bernardo going with you?"

I turned and looked back at him. His face was its old mask

of anger and arrogance, and things I could not read. "I thought you might argue about Bernardo, yes."

"If you are Ted's woman, then it's his choice who goes in with you. It's his job to protect you, not mine."

I let the "Ted's woman" comment go, and concentrated on something I could understand. "I don't need anyone to protect me, Otto. I do a fine job on my own."

"All women need protection, Anita."

Bernardo touched my arm. "We don't have time for you to win this argument."

I took a deep breath, let it out, then turned back to the big guy. "You might ask Edward which of the three of us he'd trust most to protect his back." Then I nodded at Rick. He swung the door open. Bernardo gave me a sideways glance. I stepped forward, and he followed me. Or maybe he just didn't want to be the first person through the door.

31

WE STEPPED FROM the waiting room into a box. Okay, maybe it was a room, but it was smaller than the elevator we'd come up in, and the walls were solid and gray. I knew metal when I saw it, and something about it felt wrong. As the doors were sliding closed, I said, "I think you'll lose the signal for a few minutes."

"Why?"

"I think it's a quiet room." Then the doors closed, and there was static in my ear. I tried anyway. "Edward, Edward, say something if you can hear me."

"He can't," Bernardo said, and he sounded disgusted. He looked at Rick. "That's why you didn't protest the radios; you knew they wouldn't do us a damn bit of good."

Rick shrugged, smiling like he was enjoying our discomfort. "The radios will work once we get into the room beyond. Promise." He even made the Boy Scout salute.

"Were you really a Boy Scout?" I asked.

His eyes widened a little, and then he nodded. "Max wanted us to have the all-American experience, so he started a troop just for us, so we wouldn't scare the humans."

I tried to picture an entire troop of little weretigers, and was both amused and impressed. "Is the troop still active?" I asked.

"You're looking at the current scout leader."

Bernardo said, "Muscle by night, scout leader by day; who are you, Clark Kent?"

Rick just grinned, and said, "Now what else is different about this room?"

"It's a test, isn't it?" I said.

"What kind of test?" Bernardo asked.

"The walls are reinforced metal of some kind. I'm betting they'll stand up to wereanimal and vampire strength, so no one can batter their way through."

He nodded and looked pleased. "Very good."

Bernardo took the next part. "That's why you wouldn't let us have the heavy artillery, because that might get through the far door."

"Another point for you."

"Are we going to be graded on this pop quiz?" I asked.

He nodded, and the smile faded. "Oh, yes, you'll get a grade."

"But you aren't the teacher, are you?"

He was solemn now. "No."

"Have we passed?" Bernardo asked.

"I'd hate for our backup to get too jumpy with the radio silence," I said.

"Good point," Rick said. "What else do you sense in here, Marshal Blake?"

"It's a metal box. It's proof against electronics. It's strong enough to stop most preternaturals, or at least slow them down."

"What else?" he asked.

I glared at him. "What do you want from me?"

"I want the energy that made us all wait for you to get off the elevator first."

"You want me to use the tigers to sense something."

"Yes, please."

"That's why you didn't want me to have Crispin with me, because as a vampire I could use the abilities of my animal to call, and you wouldn't be able to tell how much was me and how much was Crispin."

"Exactly," he said.

I sighed. I couldn't say out loud that I didn't want to call tiger energy when we were about to step through into a room full of them, but there were other things inside me. I reached down into that dark, quiet place and called wolf.

She came padding up through that dark, tree-filled place that was what my mind had made of where the beasts waited.

It wasn't really where they waited inside me, but my human mind needed something concrete for them to stand on, and this was it. The she-wolf was white and cream, with black markings. She was huge and beautiful, and seeing her always made me remember where huskies and malamutes and a dozen other breeds had come from. You could see it in her, but once you looked past the beauty of the fur and saw her eyes, the illusion of dog was gone. Those eyes were wild and had nothing in them that would curl up by your fire at night.

"You smell like wolf," Rick said, and he grimaced, either trying to get a better scent or not enjoying what he was smelling. On a tiger face, it was tasting the scent; on a human face, it was disgust. He looked human, but I had no way of knowing how much like a tiger he thought in this form.

I started to walk close to the walls, but I didn't have to scent them. With the wolf so close to the surface, it had peeled down some of the shields I kept up automatically. Some of my metaphysical shields had become like a bulletproof vest for most cops. You put it on every day before you went out the door. You put it on so automatically that you forgot sometimes that you needed to take it off to do certain things. I could now shield so tight that magic I should have sensed easily didn't get through. I was shielding too tight if I had stepped into this space and not felt this. Which proved just how nervous I truly was about being surrounded by this many weretigers, with no other physical animal to back me up.

The magic in the walls crawled over my skin. I broke out in goose bumps from it. "What the fuck is in the walls?" I asked.

"Can't you tell?"

I shook my head and guessed. "Magic to keep magic out."

"Very good."

"Seriously," Bernardo said, "if we keep radio silence much longer you're going to find out how well that door stands up to heavy artillery."

"Are you making a threat?" Rick asked, and was very serious again.

"Not me," Bernardo said, spreading his hands wide, "but I know my friends outside. They aren't patient men."

Rick looked at me.

I shrugged, and nodded. "Ted will want to know what's happening to us."

"You, he wants to know what's happening to you," Bernardo said.

"You're part of his team, too."

"Yeah, but I'm not his 'woman,'" and he made little quotation marks around the word with his fingers. Was Bernardo starting to believe the lie that we were feeding Olaf?

I didn't know what to say to that, so I kept my mouth shut. When in doubt, shut the fuck up.

Rick was looking from one of us to the other. It was way too thoughtful an expression for muscle. But then, I hadn't believed that Rick was just muscle. If he had been, I didn't think his queen would have wanted him on the feeding list.

"Have we passed your tests?" I asked.

"One last question," he said.

"Shoot."

"Why do you smell like wolf?"

I realized that the she-wolf was still just below the surface. I had called her energy, but had not had to put her back in her box. She seemed content to be ready to manifest more, but not to make a nuisance of herself. I had a spurt of pure happiness. I'd been working really hard with the beasts inside me, to be able to work with them and not fight them.

The wolf looked at me, as if she were standing in front of me. I had a moment of staring into her dark amber eyes, then I wanted her gone, and she just vanished. I didn't have to watch her walk down the path inside my head. She just went. For a second, I thought she was truly gone, but a moment's thought found her pale and distant in that not-so-real forest. She was still there, but I could bring her out and send her back with that little fuss.

I fought to control my emotions and not be as happy as I felt, or not show it. Bernardo was too observant, and wereanimals were way too observant.

"You don't smell like wolf anymore," Rick said. "How can you smell of tiger one moment and wolf the next?"

"Your Master of the City knows the answer to that question. If he didn't share with you, not my problem."

He nodded, as if that made perfect sense.

I didn't hear Edward bang on the door, I felt the vibration of it. Rick glanced at the doors, then pressed his hand on a panel he'd been standing in front of; it was a fingerprint scanner. The doors leading farther into the penthouse whooshed open.

32

EDWARD WAS YELLING in our ears. "Anita, Bernardo! Damn it!"

"We're here," I said.

"We're cool," Bernardo said.

"What happened?" Edward asked.

"The first room is a box that's soundproof and electronics proof. We had to play twenty questions before they let us in." I was looking around us as I spoke. It was a living room, just a living room. It was white and elegant, with windows that gave an amazing view of the Las Vegas Strip. There were huge white couches with cream and silver cushions. There were even a few touches of shiny gold in small cushions. The coffee table in the middle of the couches was glass and silver. I realized that it looked like a bigger version of Jean-Claude's living room. It didn't make me feel at home. It actually kind of creeped me.

"Talk to me, people," Edward said in my ear.

"We're in the living room," I said.

"Nice view of the Strip," Bernardo said.

"Thank you," Rick said. He walked back to a hallway that was on the other side of the room. But before he got there, Ava walked out. They spoke low together, then she came on into the room, and Rick walked back until he vanished through the door at the end of the short hallway. It was like a changing of the guard.

I called after Rick and to Ava. "Where's Crispin?"

"He's safe," Ava said, "I promise. We just want to talk to you without him for a few moments."

"More tests?" Bernardo said.

"Not exactly."

"Ava," I said, partially so Edward would know she was here, "when do we get to talk to Chang-Bibiana?"

"Rick will tell her what you said in the outer room. Then either she will come out to meet you, or we will take you in to meet her."

"What decides who goes where?" I asked.

"Chang-Bibi does."

"When does Crispin join us?"

"When Chang-Bibi wishes him to."

"She is the queen," I said, and fought to keep the sarcasm out of my voice. I probably failed.

"She is," Ava replied. "Would you like to sit down?"

Bernardo and I exchanged glances. He shrugged. "Sure," I said.

We took opposite corners of the couch. It put neither of our backs to a door, and it gave us the maximum view of the surroundings. We did it without asking each other. Bernardo looked at me as we settled into the overstuffed couch, and I looked back. He gave a small smile, not his flirting smile, but I think a smile at how we'd divided the room up.

"Would you like coffee, tea, water perhaps?" she asked.

"Coffee would be great," I said.

"Water for me, if it's bottled."

"Of course."

She left us alone in the huge, pale room, with the Vegas sun beating against the nearly solid wall of windows. Even with the air-conditioning blasting, you could feel the heat pressing in against the room, like something almost alive and with malevolent intent.

"Why bottled water?" I asked.

"Because if you travel, the new water is the thing most likely to make you sick. Stick to bottled and you can eat almost anything."

"Makes sense, I guess."

Bernardo began to report the room through the headset. Which direction the windows were, the lay of the land, including doors and all exits.

Edward spoke in my ear. "You want to add anything, Anita?"

"Nope. He covered everything I see."

"Thank you," Bernardo said.

"You're welcome," I said.

A disgusted sound came through the earbud. "I wish you were in here with us, big guy," Bernardo said.

"Yes," was all that deep voice said, but it was enough to make me shiver, and not in a good, happy way.

"How do you really feel about Otto?" Bernardo asked.

I gave him a disgusted look. "Oh, right, like I'm going to discuss my personal feelings about team members over an open radio."

He grinned at me. "I had to try."

"Why?"

Whatever his answer was, I never heard it, because Ava came back from the hallway. Rick was with her, and Domino was back. Bernardo and I both stood up.

Ava spoke in a clear, ringing voice. "Chang-Bibi of the White Tiger Clan!"

The doors at the end of the short hallway behind the tigers opened. Chang-Bibi strode through the door, with Crispin on her arm. She was taller than me, because her head was a little above his shoulder, and then I had to revise that, because I saw her heels. Four-inch spike heels, and I was back to being unsure of her height. But other things were very sure.

White hair fell to her waist in perfect waves. She was wearing makeup that emphasized the pale, perfect blue of her tiger eyes in that human face. Her eyes tilted up at the edges, and there was something in the bone structure. It was as if her face held some genetic link to the long-ago Chinese origins of her ancestors. But, as I'd learned a few months back, the weretigers had been forced to flee China many centuries ago, in the time of the Emperor Qin Shi Huang. He'd seen all the preternatural races as a danger to his authority and had them slaughtered on sight. The weretigers had fled to other countries and been forced to marry outside the purity of their race, so most of them looked like the country they'd fled to.

There was something very exotic about Bibiana, and though they had similar hair and eyes, Crispin came off looking more ordinary. If you could have changed the eyes to human, he would have looked at home at any bar or club on a Saturday night. Chang-Bibi would have stood out anywhere, as if the aura of her difference was something that couldn't be hidden.

She wore a white dress with long silky sleeves, and a V-neck so it showed off the spill of white breasts. The belt at the waist emphasized how tiny her waist, how curvy the body. She came from a time when being too thin was not in, and she looked voluptuous. That was the only word I had for it. She was voluptuous.

Someone touched my arm, and it was Bernardo. I looked at him, startled. "You okay?" he asked.

I nodded, but had to take a shaky breath. Fuck, she had bespelled me like some kind of vampire, but it hadn't been eye contact. It was as if her very being attracted me. Fuck, again.

I called wolf again, but the white tiger snarled in front of the wolf. I didn't want the beasts to fight inside me. One, it hurt—a lot. Two, I didn't want the weretigers to know that I didn't have perfect control of my beasts.

I let the wolf slide back inside. I was left with white tiger pacing inside me, and she was going to be no help against the fascination of the white queen.

"I am Bibiana, wife of Maximillian, Master Vampire of the City of Las Vegas, Nevada."

Bernardo touched my arm again, and I nodded. "I am Anita Blake"—I hesitated—"girlfriend of Jean-Claude, Master Vampire of the City of St. Louis, Missouri, and U.S. Marshal."

"Ava said you come on a social visit."

"I do, but I would ask questions about the crime we are here to investigate. Solving it helps both your people and the humans."

"Have you come here to visit with me, Anita, or to interrogate me, as a marshal?"

I licked suddenly dry lips. Why was I having such trouble concentrating? What was she doing to me? I'd never had this kind of trouble around a wereanimal that wasn't one of the men in my life.

"I . . ." Why couldn't I think?

Bernardo touched me again. That helped. I moved around

so that I could take his right hand in my left one. It left both our gun hands free. He raised eyebrows at me, but didn't take his hand back. I was just glad it was Bernardo; anyone else on our little team, and one of us would have had to compromise their gun hand. The moment his hand was warm and real in mine, I could think a little more clearly. Interesting. I hadn't even had to call up the *ardeur*, just another human hand to touch, and Chang-Bibi's fascination was less.

"I am honored that you agreed to see me, but would you honor me with answering some questions that are more my job than social? I beg your indulgence, but it is a most . . . frightening crime."

"It is most sad that our good policemen have been so slaughtered." Her face showed distress, and she hugged Crispin's arm a little tighter to her. She moved first, and he escorted her to the couch opposite us. She sat down, smoothing her skirt out.

Crispin took a step toward me. I let go of Bernardo and held out my hand. Crispin started for me with a smile.

"Crispin," she said, "sit by me."

His face looked less happy, but he did what she told him. He sat beside her, and the moment she laid her hand on his thigh, I was fascinated again. I could almost feel the weight of her hand on my own thigh.

"Shit," I whispered, and took Bernardo's hand again. The touch helped steady me, but I was beginning to realize what was wrong.

"What's wrong?" Bernardo asked.

"I think she's using Crispin to get to me."

"Very good, Anita. I am his queen, and though he is your tiger to call, I am still his queen. Through your tie to him, I am your queen, too, so it seems."

I shook my head. "I need your help to solve these crimes. Your husband, Max, told the police here that I'd help sort things out."

"Max wanted you here, and so did I," she said. She began to trace small circles on Crispin's thigh. I could feel it on my leg. Fuck, fuck, fuck.

"She's not going to help us," I said, and turned for the far door, Bernardo still hand in hand with me.

"I have every intention of helping you, Anita," she said.

I turned back, putting my other hand higher on Bernardo's arm. The reality of his muscled warmth helped me think. I wasn't sure why, but it was almost as if anyone and anything that wasn't tiger was useful. Then I had a thought: was it tiger, or was it white tiger?

"Then stop the mind games."

"I needed to know if Crispin was more yours than mine. But not only can he not resist my touch, but through him, I also have a door into you. Very nice."

"Why do you want a door into me?" I asked.

"Because it is there," she said, and looking into her face, there was nothing there to talk to. It was a human face, but the expression in it gave me the feeling I'd gotten a couple of times when I stared into the face of a wild animal. There was that same neutrality. Bibiana didn't want to hurt me, but she didn't not want to hurt me either. It didn't move her either way. It's not the same thing as being a sociopath, but it's close. It meant that she wouldn't think like a human being. She'd think more like a tiger with a human brain. It changed everything about this interview. It meant that I couldn't reason with her the way I could have with Max. It might mean I couldn't reason with her at all.

"What's happening, Anita?" Edward said in my ear. It startled me, made me jump.

"If your friends wish to join us, by all means bring them in. Listening devices are so impersonal," she said.

I licked my lips again and tried to fight down my rising heartbeat. "The other marshals are holding our weapons for us. Rick didn't want us to bring in an arsenal."

She glanced back at Rick. "Are they that dangerous?"

"Yes, Chang-Bibi, I believe they are."

She nodded, and turned back to us. "I trust Roderic's judgment on such things." She touched Crispin's bare hand, and the power jumped like an electric charge through me.

Bernardo jumped, too. "What was that?"

"Power," I said, "her power."

"She sent it through the kid, to you?"

I didn't argue with Crispin being "the kid"; it wasn't just his age but the feel of him. "Yeah," I said.

"Will you stop the power games long enough to answer some questions?" I asked.

"I will, if you do one thing first," she said.

I knew it was a bad idea, but . . . "What do you want me to do?"

"Call Crispin to your side. If you can call him away from me, then I will answer your questions with no more games." She smiled as she said it, but it was like watching the tiger in the zoo smile. You knew it didn't mean it.

I squeezed Bernardo's hand, then let go. He leaned in and whispered, "Are you sure this is a good idea?"

"I'm pretty sure it's not," I said.

"Then why do it?"

"Because she'll keep her word. If I can call Crispin to me, away from her, she'll answer our questions."

"It's still a bad idea," he said.

I nodded. I took the Browning BDM out of its holster and handed it to him. "Bibiana seems to fascinate me like a master vampire, sort of. Just in case she decides to try to see how much control she has over me, I'd rather you have all the guns."

"You think she's going to mind-fuck you that badly?" he asked.

"I think she's going to try."

Edward was in my ear. "Just get out of there, Anita. We can find this information out somewhere else."

I said, "Excuse me" to our hosts, and turned my back to talk out loud to Edward. "Night is going to come, Edward. Whatever killed these cops was deadly in the daylight. When you add their vampire masters to the mix, it's going to be even worse. There is nowhere else to go for weretigers in Vegas."

"Can she roll you, completely?"

"I don't know."

"Bernardo," Edward said.

"Yeah, boss," he said.

"If she goes, don't be a hero, yell for us."

"Don't worry, Ted, I'm no hero."

"Fine, we'll be listening. Be careful, Anita."

"As a virgin on my wedding night."

There was a sound, I think it was Olaf. Maybe I had amused him, or maybe he just thought I was being stupid. He might be right on that second part.

33

I DIDN'T USUALLY try to call the wereanimals that were tied to me metaphysically. It just sort of happened. My psychic mentor, Marianne, told me that my natural abilities were so strong that I did most things without thinking about it first. That could be good and powerful, or bad and a weakness. But I'd been learning how to be a grown-up psychic and do stuff on purpose. It was the difference between driving really fast on a public street, or driving really fast on a track with professional drivers. One was for kids; the other was for grown-ups.

I tried simple first. "Crispin, come to me." I held my hand out.

He stood up. Bibiana's hand fell away. He actually took a step my way before her power breathed through the room. It stopped my breath in my throat, made me taste my pulse on my tongue. Crispin's face was almost pained. His eyes looked at me with such longing, but he didn't move closer.

But the white tiger inside me did move. She began to pad eagerly up along that well-worn path inside me. She began to trot, and I knew once she started running, when she hit the "surface" of my body, it would feel like getting hit by a truck from the inside out. I hadn't had it happen in months, and I had seconds to stop it, if I could.

I tried to call wolf, but tiger was too close. The tigress was running full-out, a white blur, streaking toward me.

"Fuck," I said.

Rick and Domino had moved closer to us, as if they couldn't help themselves. Only Ava seemed able to resist, but then she wasn't the same . . . color.

I called black tiger, I called it with a scream and a roar inside

my head. The black form smashed into the white inside me and
sent me spinning across the room. I ended up on the floor near
the windows, with the two tigers snarling inside me, trying to
tear each other apart, but my body was their battlefield.

I cried out. I couldn't help it.

Crispin yelled, "Anita!"

Bernardo was beside me, kneeling. I heard Edward yelling
in my ear. "Anita, talk to me, or we're coming in."

"Don't . . . don't come. Not yet." My voice held the pain I
was feeling. There was nothing I could do about that.

Crispin was halfway across the room, but she was beside
him. I could not force him to me with the white queen be-
sidehim. Domino was walking toward me with a scowl on his
face. The black tiger and the white hesitated in their battle. They looked up and used my eyes to see him. They both
liked him.

I said, "Domino, come to me."

He shook his head, but the black tigress broke free of the
fight, and the white tigress let her. The black began to stalk
closer to me. I put that energy into the man I could see. I called
him with images of dark fur and eyes like fire in the night.

He came to me as if each step hurt. He came to me with a
look on his face that mirrored Crispin's when Bibiana kept him
from me. But I didn't have time to care or think it through. I
had to satisfy the tigers or risk becoming one for real. That
was the real danger of what I was, that I might finally pick an
animal that wasn't Jean-Claude's animal to call. If I did, then
I might end up controlled by someone else, like Bibiana and
her Max. To keep that from happening, I would mind-fuck
Domino. Was it evil to think it all the way through and still do
it? Maybe. Was I still going to do it, if it would keep the white
queen from mind-fucking me? Oh, hell, yes.

34

BIBIANA TRIED TO call his white side, but the black tiger
was so hungry. So hungry to find another black-furred side to
rub up against. So lonely, so terribly lonely. The black tiger
didn't try to burst out the way the white was trying to with
Bibiana's urging. The black was sniffing the air and making
low eager noises as Domino came to us.

He dropped to his knees beside me, as if someone had cut
his strings. He just fell to his knees beside me on the white tiled
floor. His face was a mask of anger and fear and longing.

His voice came out strangled. "You are a black queen. You
really are."

I held my hand out to him. He reached out to me. Bibiana
yelled, "Roderic, stop him!"

But it was too late. Our fingers touched, and the black tiger
made a sound that spilled out of my throat. Domino let me pull
him in against my body. He stared down at me, and those fire-
colored eyes were still afraid, and still angry, but underneath
that was a glimpse of something that felt better.

He whispered, "You smell like home." He lowered his face,
not to kiss me but to rub his cheeks, his mouth, his nose, against
my skin. He drew in the scent of the black tiger inside me, like
a cat trying to roll in catnip. Except that this catnip was me, my
body.

I felt the black tiger want to take him. There was sex in
there, but also to force him into his tiger form, but the black
tiger was content, happy even, just from his closeness. I think
I could have calmed things down. It would have been all right,
but then the power of the white queen breathed through the
room like the wind from the open door of hell. Bibiana's

energy hit us both. It made the white tiger snarl and begin to creep forward.

"No," and I yelled it. The white tiger hesitated. I stared up into Domino's face. "Give me permission to feed on you."

"What?" he asked.

The white tiger leapt onto the black, and they started trying to tear me apart again. I writhed and struggled not to scream in Domino's arms. I knew if I screamed, Edward and Olaf would come through those doors.

Domino said, "My Queen, if by my flesh or my seed I can feed you, then feed."

I didn't understand everything he said, but the tigers stopped fighting. They panted and stared up at him, through my eyes. The black tiger growled low and soft, and it spilled from between my teeth.

I had a few moments to realize that among the tigers, when they said *feed*, they meant either flesh or sex, or both. Domino had given me permission to take his life. The black tiger understood that, but she and I were in agreement. It had been so long since we'd found another of us. We didn't want to eat him. We wanted to save him. We wanted to keep him.

Bibiana sent another wave of power over us, but this time the black and I were ready. We were both angry with her. Angry that she interfered in this. She had no right. He was ours. Ours!

The anger became rage, the rage became my beast, but I had other uses for anger now. It didn't translate into shapeshifting for me. I called that part of me that was vampire powers, that was the *ardeur*, and there was a moment where it could have spilled to sex, but it wasn't sex I wanted. I was pissed, and now I could feed that anger. I'd tasted Domino's anger earlier in the casino. I knew it was in there. All I had to do was throw my anger into him.

I let my rage spill into him. He screamed, head back, and the rage was so great, so long inside him. His beast began to rise with that anger. I drew him down into a kiss, and I fed through the touch of his mouth on mine, through the bruising grip of his hands on my arms, through the struggling of his

body against mine. I held him and I breathed in his rage
through his lips, his skin, his body. I breathed in his anger and
let it join that seething mass of rage inside me.

I fed on Domino's anger, and with that anger came knowledge. I got glimpses of what had filled him with such rage. I
saw him as a child, alone in a foster home, crying. I saw the
other children making fun of the eyes and the hair. I saw him
saved by Bibiana, but even here, he wasn't white enough. He
belonged, and he didn't. He was like the others, but he wasn't.
Always, he was not quite home.

He stopped struggling, and by the end of it, he was crying
in my arms. I held him, and the black tigress snuggled close,
so that we both held him.

I saw Bernardo standing over us, uncertain, as if he wasn't
sure if I was all right or not. I spoke to the uncertainty on his
face. "I'm all right, Bernardo."

"Your eyes," he said, "they're all brown and black light, like
a vampire."

I kissed Domino's forehead and tested the truth of his
words. I could taste Domino's pulse like candy on my tongue.
I had that urge to plunge teeth into flesh and see if the candy
squirted red. You can't be a living vampire, but whatever I was
becoming was close.

But I didn't just taste blood and food. I felt the other tigers.
Not just the one lying in my arms. I felt them all. I turned my
head, and the moment Bibiana saw my eyes, she was afraid. Her
fear appealed to both the vampire part of me and the beast. Fear
means food. If something is afraid of you, you can control it,
or kill it.

I called Crispin to me. Not by using tiger powers, but the
way a vampire calls its animal to call. "Crispin, come to me."

Bibiana tried to hold him by the hand. I said, "Let him go,
or I'll see how many tigers I can call today."

"You would not dare try to steal the animal of another master vampire."

"You mean, like you didn't try to steal away the human
servant of another master vampire." I sat up, and Domino
curled around me, utterly passive, utterly content.

She didn't let go, so I reached out to her as a vampire would. A vampire that could call tigers. She let go of Crispin, and held her hand as if his skin had burned her.

Bibiana's power reached out, but not to us. Rick came to her hand, and the far door opened, and more of the white tigers came to stand with their queen. But I didn't care. Crispin had taken my hand. I sat there with his hand in mine, and Domino curled around my waist, and it was nearly perfect, like being wrapped in your favorite blanket at the end of a long day's work. I'd learned that the *ardeur* could be about friendship and not just romance. In that moment, it was even more than that. It was about that feeling of belonging, of being home.

Then I felt a different energy, in all that sea of white tiger power. I felt a thread of something new. Something unique. I didn't know what it was until the blue tiger inside me stepped from the shadows and started to pace forward.

She was truly blue with black stripes, a deep cobalt color, almost a black, but it wasn't. She was true blue, and she'd smelled something that belonged to her.

He stepped out from the rest, a puzzled look on his young face, because he was young. Young enough to make me start to swim up to the surface of myself. Young enough for me to know that whatever I had just done to Domino might destroy him.

I stared at the short dark blue hair, a perfect match to the tiger inside me. I stared into his eyes that were two shades of blue, as if Crispin's eyes had married with Jean-Claude's, and knew he was mine to call.

I asked, "How old are you?"

"Sixteen," he said.

"Shit," I said.

35

EDWARD'S VOICE IN my ear said, "We've got Max's son, Victor, out here with bodyguards. We're letting Victor through, but we're keeping the bodyguards."

"We've got another half-dozen tigers in here with us. They came out of the far rooms," Bernardo said.

"This just keeps getting better," Edward said, and the sarcasm came through the earpiece loud and clear.

The blue tiger inside me pressed closer to the surface of me. I had an image of her face against mine, trying to get closer so she could sniff the air.

The doors opened and a tall, broad-shouldered man in an expensive tailored suit strode through. His white hair was cut very short, and in one of those cuts that looked like it had been done one hair at a time. He actually wore those pale yellow sunglasses over his eyes. The glasses weren't dark enough to do a damn thing against the Vegas sun. Was he trying to pass for human? If that was the idea, then he needed to tone down the energy that boiled off him.

That wash of energy turned the blue tiger snarling toward him. I would have fallen forward if Domino and Crispin hadn't caught me.

"You're going to bring her beast, Mother," he said, and he kept coming toward us. The blue tiger didn't like that. The white one did. Black was just content to cuddle Domino. The blue tiger tried to turn me toward the boy. The white liked Victor. The black was fine. It was like having three different roommates inside me, and all of them liked different guys.

"You have no right to interfere," Bibiana said.

"Father warned you against this," he said, and he was at our side. He knelt in the dark suit, his eyes hidden behind the glasses, but no amount of colored glass could hide the power spilling off him. The power was enough that the white tiger knew what we'd find behind the glasses.

I came to my knees. Crispin had to let go of my hand, but he touched my shoulder. Domino slipped lower down my body like a reluctant piece of clothing. My hands went to those glasses.

Victor caught my hands in his. He stared into my face as if he were trying to see through me. He raised my hands to his face and sniffed my skin. "Impossible."

"I told you, Victor, she carries them all," Bibiana said.

He rose up from my skin. I could see his eyes clearly, but the pale yellow lenses stole what I needed to see. My voice sounded like a stranger in my head when I said, "Take them off."

He blinked at me. "What?"

I repeated it. "Take them off."

"Why?" he asked, and let go of my hands.

I shook my head because I wasn't sure, and then the answer came, "I have to see your eyes."

"Why?" he said, again.

I reached upward, and this time he didn't stop me. I touched the thin wire frames of his glasses and pulled them gently down, until I was looking into pale blue tiger eyes. They were a deeper blue than Crispin's eyes, but still a color and a shape that you wouldn't mistake for human unless you wanted not to see what was there.

I knelt in front of him, with his glasses in my hands, and stared up into those eyes. But it wasn't just the eyes; they were only a sign of what my tigress needed. It was the power in him. I hadn't understood until that moment how weak every other weretiger I'd touched had been.

Victor stared down at me with those perfect eyes. He swallowed hard enough that I heard it. His voice was a little shaky as he said, "You really are another queen, aren't you?"

I leaned in toward him. I wasn't aiming for a kiss. It was more as if there were gravity to his power, and it drew me in.

He stood up, stumbling a little. I reached for him, and it was Crispin who drew me back. He and Domino pulled me back into their arms, but it was like I could hear music in my head that I'd never heard before. Victor's power drowned out their touch.

Victor put the glasses back on and turned to his mother. "Father expressly forbade you from calling her power until he had met with her."

"I am Chang here, not you," she said.

"You rule the clan of the white tiger. I have never disputed that, but Father has put me in charge of other parts of his domain. When you put the tigers' power above the good of this city and the other citizens, then you have broken your master, my father's, rules."

"Would you deny Domino and Cynric the only queen of their clan they may ever meet?"

"I would never stand in the way of another clan's destiny, Mother, but you cannot feed Cynric to her. Look at what she has already done to Crispin and Domino."

Something about the way he said it made me look at the two weretigers still beside me. Crispin had looked at me with that devotion before, but to see it in Domino's face was just wrong. A look of puppyish devotion in that angry, arrogant face; it hurt my heart to see it. Not because I cared for him, because you can't care for someone you've just met, but because no adult should look at anyone like that. It was a look I'd seen before, on the faces of vampires. I was a true necromancer and called to all the dead, but I wasn't supposed to call to the wereanimals like this, not like this.

"Oh, God," I said, and tried to stand up. Domino clung to me, and I fought the urge to slap at him in a kind of panic. "I fed on your anger, damn it. I fed on your anger so you wouldn't look at me like that!"

He gave me calm eyes, and he shouldn't have.

"Fuck," I said.

"Talk to me, Anita, Bernardo. What's happening?" Edward asked.

"Wait, Edward, just wait." I turned to Victor. "Can you fix this?"

Bernardo said, "Anita has it under control." The look on his face didn't match the surety of his words, but he was giving me the benefit of the doubt.

Victor looked where I was pointing, at Domino. "You mean undo your possession of him?"

"Yes," I said.

"You are queen," Bibiana said, "you do not ask any male for such help."

"Fine, can you undo it?" I asked.

Victor studied me some more. "You said you fed on his anger. I thought the *ardeur* was all about sex."

"I can feed on anger, too. I thought if I didn't feed on lust, or love, for your people that I wouldn't bind them to me. I don't want any more men, damn it."

"Jean-Claude can't feed on anger, can he?" Victor asked.

That was a little too close to truths we didn't want to share with anyone. That I had powers that my master didn't share. I tried to be cool about it, but my pulse had sped. Weretigers are like living lie detectors. They can sense, smell, all those little involuntary body functions.

"Can either of you make it so he isn't"—I waved a hand at Domino—"like this?"

"It may pass on its own," Victor said.

"Are you sure?"

He smiled. "No, but what you've done seems to be a combination of vampire and Chang tiger. You've rolled him. If you leave him alone, he may recover. If it's more vampire than were-animal, then you know that you'll be able to repossess him anytime you want."

I licked my lips and said the only truth I had. "I don't want to possess anybody."

"I felt your power. I felt you shove it into my mother. I felt it blocks away."

"Would it sound childish to say she started it?"

He gave a quick smile. "It's a little childish, but I know my mother."

"Victor," Bibiana said.

"You know you tried to raise her tigers, Mother. You know you provoked her power. Don't deny it."

"I would never deny it," she said.

Bernardo said, "Chang-Bibiana promised that if Marshal Blake could call Crispin away from her, she would answer our questions."

Bibiana wouldn't look at anyone in the room.

"Did you promise the marshals that, Mother?"

She gave a little nod, still not looking at anyone.

"Then answer her questions, like you promised."

I did my best not to glance at the blue boy. "I think a little privacy would be good before we start discussing an ongoing police investigation."

"I don't want to leave," he said.

Ava tugged on him. "Come on, Cynric."

"No," he said, and pulled away from her. "You're not pure. You don't know how it feels to be part of a clan."

"Cynric," Bibiana said, and her anger cracked like a hot whip through the room, "you will show Ava the respect she deserves. One of our brethren attacked her. He broke the most sacred rule among the clans. She is not one who sought this life."

He looked sullen for a moment, then guilty. "I'm sorry, Ava. I didn't mean it."

She smiled, but it didn't quite reach her eyes. "It's all right, Cynric, but let's leave the marshals to talk to Bibiana and Victor." He let her lead him through the far door, but he looked back as the doors closed, and the disturbing thing was that I was there to meet his eyes.

Bernardo touched my arm, made me look at him. "You all right?"

Was I all right? That was an excellent question. What I needed was an excellent answer. I said the only thing I could think of. "We have work to do, Marshal Spotted Horse."

He gave me a look that raised one eyebrow, then nodded. "Yes, we do, Marshal Blake."

"Ask your questions, then get the fuck out of there," Edward said, "I do not want Anita in that room when Max joins his wife." Edward was absolutely right. Bibiana had almost rolled me on her own, without her master at her side. There were so many reasons to want this thing cleared up before the vampires rose for the night.

The fact that there was no way on God's green earth to solve this crime before dark was not only disappointing but getting more dangerous every minute.

36

ONE OF THE white female tigers with hair the color of pale buttermilk, and eyes like a spring sky, came and took Domino deeper into the penthouse. He didn't want to leave me, but between me and Victor, he did what we wanted. If he got out of my physical presence and started breaking free of the fascination, then I could leave him here to his life. If it didn't start to wear off at all, then I'd have to take him with me. What I'd do with him after that, I had no bloody idea. Other people pick up stray puppies; I kept collecting men. Crap.

The rest of us settled down on the overstuffed couches. Bernardo and I sat far enough away from each other on our couch that we wouldn't get in each other's way if things went south. Crispin sat as close to me as any boyfriend, an arm across the back of the couch touching my shoulders, one hand on my leg. I could have told him to back off because I was working, but it would have hurt his feelings, and I knew enough about lycanthrope society to know that touching was just what they did.

Bibiana sat across from us, with her son and Rick. No one touched her much. Maybe tigers were different from the other animal groups I was familiar with? I'd ask later.

"What do you know about what happened to the police here?" I asked.

"Only what we heard on the news," Victor said.

Bibiana simply looked at me with those uptilted blue eyes. Her silent scrutiny might have been unnerving, but between the morgue, Olaf, and what had just happened with my inner tigers, her stare just didn't have enough weight to move me.

If this had been a normal interrogation, there would be rules, methods. I should have volunteered little and asked repetitive

questions. But we were burning daylight. Once the vampires
rose for the night, and Vittorio added his power to his daytime
servants . . . I had no idea what he would do. Slaughtering the
SWAT team like that and mailing me the head was throwing
down a serious gauntlet. I thought that if it was Vittorio and not
someone framing him, or even if it were, then when darkness
fell, all hell was going to break loose. We didn't have time for
hours of questions.

Crispin began to move his hand on my thigh in small circles. He'd picked up my tension and was trying to soothe me.
It didn't really work, but I appreciated the effort.

"Anita?" Bernardo said, making a question of my name. He
looked at me, trying for blank, and failing to hide some concern
around the edges. He'd seen some seriously weird shit from me
in the last hour. In fact, he'd been a damn good sport about all
of it. Did I owe him, like, flowers? What did you get a coworker
for not freaking when you went all metaphysical on him? A
card? Did Hallmark make a card for that?

Crispin leaned over me, his breath warm against my hair.
"Anita, are you all right?"

"Anita," Bernardo said again, and this time he didn't try to
keep the worry out of his voice.

Edward joined in my ear. "Bernardo, what's wrong with
Anita?"

"I'm fine," I said, "I'm just thinking." I turned back to the
weretigers on the other couch. "We're running out of daylight,
so I'm going to talk to you like one master's lady to another."

Bibiana gave a regal nod. "I am honored."

"One, I need you to listen to Victor and Max, and not screw
with my inner tigers until after this investigation is over."

"You could tell her just to leave your inner tigers alone,"
Victor said. He smiled, but his eyes were just visible behind
the yellow glasses. Part of me was really bugged by the glasses,
but I was trying to be human here, not all tigerish, so he could
keep the glasses.

In the interest of being a little more human, I leaned away
from Crispin, putting myself on the edge of the couch. All I had
to do was lean back and he'd be there, but I needed to think,

and something about a man you've had sex with doing little circles on your thigh isn't always conducive to clear thinking.

"I'm trying to negotiate in good faith here. I'm not going to start by asking Bibiana to promise something she won't deliver. I don't understand everything that she wants from my inner beasts, but I heard her say that I may be the only queen of their clan that Domino and the blue boy, Cynric, will ever see. Bibiana isn't going to let me walk out of Vegas without wanting to explore that again, are you?" I looked at her when I said the last.

She smiled and dipped her head, very demure. "No," she said, simply.

I smiled. "Good, no denials. I like that. Two, do we all agree that these murders are bad for business for both the vampire and lycanthrope communities?"

They all agreed.

"Then I need to know, honestly, if you know anything about the animal that helped this vampire kill these police officers."

"You say *animal*, but you come to us," Victor said.

Bibiana said, "You think it is one of our tigers." There was something about the way she said it that made me say the next.

"You think so, too," I said.

"I did not say so," she said.

I licked my lips, but not because they were dry this time. "You taste like the edge of a lie," I said.

"What does that mean?" Olaf asked in my ear.

Edward told him, "Let her work."

Bibiana smiled up at me. It was almost a flirtatious look. "I am not lying," she said.

I smiled at her. "Okay, then answer this: Do you suspect that one of your weretigers was involved with these killings in any way?"

She wouldn't look at me now, but concentrated on her small, neat hands that were clasped so ladylike in her lap. Her ankles were crossed. She was so prim and proper, but I knew it was a lie. She was one of those people that no matter how buttoned up they are, you can simply feel that if you scratch them hard enough, get them in the right place at the wrong time, there would be absolutely nothing proper about them. Women tend to give off that vibe more than men, but I've seen men do it, too. Some of them don't even know how much heat they're hiding behind the mask of civility. But Bibiana knew; she knew that human and prim was not really what she was at all.

"Do you want me to answer the question, Mother?"

She gave him a look so fierce, so vicious, that it turned that pretty face into something frightening. There, the masks were coming down. "I am still queen here, or do I have to remind you of it more forcefully?"

"Father told us that if asked, we were to answer Marshal Blake honestly and completely."

"Until he rises for the night, I rule here," she said.

I fought not to glimpse back at Crispin. He wasn't good at hiding his face. Instead, I glanced at Rick and found him visibly uncomfortable. I got the impression that this squabbling was common, maybe even growing worse. I knew enough about weretiger society to know that they were all run by queens. It was one of the few wereanimal groups that was always female run. Some groups had women that got to be top dog, or cat, but it was the exception, not the rule. So Victor, no matter how powerful, couldn't rule the White Tiger Clan. But he was certainly acting as if he wanted to be in charge.

"Bernardo reminded you of your promise, Chang-Bibiana. Now I remind you again that I have called Crispin to me from your side. You said if I could do that, that you would answer my questions. Is the word of the Chang of the White Tiger Clan to be depended on, or is there no honor in Vegas?"

I felt the couch move before Crispin put a hand on my back. It was a careful touch, not too sexual, but it was a physical reminder to be careful. I didn't resent it. If I didn't take Crispin back with me to St. Louis, this was his pond I was shitting in, and he'd be left alone to swim in it.

Bibiana turned those angry eyes to me. Her power started to pour toward me, in a nearly visible roil of heat. Victor stood up. He moved between that power, her, and me.

It hit him, and his head went back, his arms to the sides, as if it felt good. His breath came out in a long sigh. He shuddered and said, "Your Master of the City gave you express orders not to bring her beasts. I obey his orders, even if you do not."

She made a snarling sound. Crispin tucked himself up closer to me, as if afraid. Or was he afraid of what I'd do? I fought not to stiffen at his touch or look too nervous. I tried for calm, though I felt anything but at ease.

Bernardo had moved forward to the edge of his piece of couch, too. Rick was still sitting back, but the tension showed in every muscle.

"You are your father's tool and nothing more."

"I am my father's instrument in the daylight. I am his right hand, and I will not betray him."

"It is not betrayal to seek power for our clan and our people." I couldn't see her because Victor was still standing between us.

"You can seek power after the marshals have killed the traitor and his master."

"What traitor?" I asked.

Victor turned, giving his mother his back. I'm not sure I would have done that, but then she wasn't my mom. "The first murders were strippers, just like the ones in your city. But the last one had claw marks and vampire bites."

I cursed the Vegas PD for not mentioning this little fact to me. It would have been nice to know that the last victim had shown claw marks. That was a change from all the other cities that Vittorio had hunted in. It proved that some part of the Vegas force didn't trust me. That was going to make solving crime, any crime, harder here. Crispin picked up my anxiety again. His hand on my back began to make those soothing circles.

"What makes you think it's a weretiger?" I asked.

"Mother," Victor said, and stepped aside to let us see each other again.

She gave him a not entirely happy look, but spoke. "I have felt another vampire's pull on my tigers. As you tried today to call me to you, and ended by calling some of my children, so this other vampire was seeking. I thought I had prevented it, but now I believe that he managed to steal away one of mine. Or perhaps a different clan, but tiger, he was calling tiger."

"Do you know for certain that the vampire was a he?" I asked.

She nodded. "The energy was male."

"Ask her how she knows that for certain," Edward asked in my ear.

I held my hand out to the weretigers. I moved a little away from Crispin's hand, too. He took the hint and let his hand drop away from me. "Excuse me, she knows it was male, Marshal Forrester, because the energy tasted or smelled male to her."

"You can tell from energy if a vampire is male or female?" Bernardo asked.

I nodded. "Sometimes."

Bibiana smiled at me, as if I'd said a smart thing. "Yes, he tasted of men, but . . ." She frowned.

"But what?" I asked.

"You are of the line of Belle Morte?"

"Jean-Claude is," I said.

She waved it away as if I were quibbling. "Most vampire lines are cold things, but not hers. You are closer to the warmth of the wereanimal, I think. Can you taste someone's sexual energy from a distance?"

I thought about that. "Sometimes."

Again, she smiled like I'd said the right thing. "There was something wrong with this vampire's energy. Something stunted, or thwarted in some way. It was as if his sex had become rage."

"Have you ever felt something similar from anyone else?" I asked.

"We had a weretiger that came to us. We tried to discipline him, save him, but in the end he had to be destroyed for everyone's sake."

To his mother's explanation, Victor added, "He was a serial rapist. The attacks became more violent." He sighed.

"Ava's attacker?" I asked.

He gave me a startled look. "Did you look at her case file?"

I shook my head. "Just a guess."

"It was not a guess," Bibiana said. "You read his body posture. You smelled his scent."

I shrugged because I didn't want to argue, and wasn't entirely sure I could. "But you're saying that this vampire's energy felt similar to the serial rapist that you'd sensed before?"

"Yes, but . . ." She shivered, and this time I could taste her fear.

"He scared you," I said.

She nodded.

"My mother does not frighten easily," Victor said.

"I got that impression," I said.

He smiled at me. "We have answered your questions. Now, would you answer one of ours?"

"Sorry, but one more. Do you know who the traitor is?"

They exchanged a look.

"I swear that I do not. If this vampire has stolen one of our people, he has done it so completely that I did not suspect until the first claw marks showed on the bodies."

"If I could help you narrow down the field, would you gather them for me, and let us question them at the police station?"

They exchanged another look that included Rick. Finally, Victor nodded, and Bibiana said, "We would."

"How can you help us narrow it down?" Victor asked. "Are you hinting that you're a more powerful weretiger than we are?"

"No, absolutely not, but I've seen the bodies."

Olaf came on the earpiece. "Do not share this information with them."

I ignored him. "I know we're looking for someone under six feet in human form, or with abnormally small hands for his or her size."

"Anita," Olaf said.

Edward said, "She knows what's she doing, Otto."

"You measured the claw marks," Victor said.

I nodded.

"I do not trust the tigers," Olaf said.

"Let her work," Edward said.

I did my best to ignore it all, as Victor said, "That narrows it a little."

"Here's the real narrowing," I said. "This tiger is able to shift just his or her hands into claws, and teeth into fangs, without changing into half human completely."

I'd shocked them, all of them. They weren't vampires, so they didn't try to hide it. "That would explain it," Victor said.

"Explain what?" I asked.

"Why my mother and I couldn't find the truth from our traitor. If he's powerful enough to do that, then he may be powerful enough to lie to us."

"That would have to be pretty damn powerful," I said.

"Yes," he said.

I stared at him, and then at Bibiana's stricken face. "You think you know who it is."

"No, but it is a very short list of possibilities. Some of our most trusted people are on that list," Victor said.

Bibiana gave me a look of such pain. "Whoever it is, it will hurt us as a clan. It will undermine our authority, and make us have to discipline our people."

"You mean, if they find out you missed this guy hiding in plain sight, some of them will challenge you for leadership."

"They will try," she said, and there was something so calm, so sure, so confident. I wouldn't have wanted to go up against her, and with Victor at her side, you'd have to be pretty confident—or nuts.

Then I had a thought, a bad one. "If Vittorio's animal to call is tiger, and he's master enough to do all this, then he's master enough to challenge Max for the city."

"The vampire council has forbidden Masters of the City to war against one another in America," Bibiana said.

"Yeah, and they frown on that whole serial-killer-slaughtering-cops thing, too. I don't think Vittorio sweats the rules much."

"You think he'll try for my father?" Victor asked.

"I think it's a possibility. I'd take extra security measures until we get him."

"I'll see that it's done," he said.

"He has more than just one weretiger at his daytime beck and call," I said.

"What else?"

"I'm not sure, but if I were you, I'd call that extra security in now. Because it would be a bitch to miss saving Max by a few minutes."

Victor and I had one of those looks, and then he simply reached into his pocket for a cell phone and started calling in more help. He walked to the far side of the room so I couldn't hear exactly what he was saying. I was okay with that.

Bibiana looked at me. "You are the first true queen with no clan that we have found since Victor showed himself worthy."

"Worthy of what?" I asked.

"Starting his own clan. We have not had a male king among the tigers in centuries. The little queens will hive off, but it is only because we do not wish to kill our daughters. It is not because there is enough power to make another clan. Victor has that power, but he needs a queen."

I stared at her. "Are you hinting that you want me to, what, be your son's queen?"

"I'm saying that if you were not already wedded so tightly to Jean-Claude, I would ask you to marry my son."

I stared at her. "Gosh, I don't know what to say, Bibiana."

Victor came back from his side of the room, clipping the phone back into his pocket. "I've got extra men around Father, and I'll up the security on our clubs, just in case." He looked from one of us to the other, frowning. "Did I miss something?"

Bernardo laughed.

Crispin said, "Chang-Bibi offered you to Anita in marriage."

"Mother!"

"You may never meet another queen of her power, Victor."

"She belongs to another master vampire. It is against every rule to interfere in that."

"I am your mother and your queen. It's my job to interfere."

"Leave Marshal Blake alone, Mother."

Bibiana smiled at us both, and it was that smile you never want to see on anyone's mother's face. That look that says they'd welcome you to the family in a hot second, if only their son would cooperate.

Bernardo saved me. "When can you bring the weretigers to the station for questioning?"

"We need to do it carefully." He looked at us. "I will admit this here, but never publicly. It would go better if the police in full gear went with us from weretiger to weretiger. If they are good enough to lie to us like this, then I won't be able to lie to them about why we want them to go to the police."

"I'll talk to the Vegas police." But I wondered how hard it was going to be to keep them from being a little trigger-happy as we hunted the weretiger that had killed one of their own? Everyone had been calm, almost unusually calm, about it all. It was almost like the pause between storms.

"You look worried," Victor said.

"How many weretigers on this list?"

"Five," he said.

"Six," she said.

"Mother . . ."

"You would leave the woman out, but she is powerful, and she is under six feet."

He nodded. "You're right, I would have left her off. I'm sorry. You get a team of your people ready, and I'll try to have them gathered in one place. I can't lie well enough to take them to the station for you, but I think I can arrange something."

"It might be better to take them in their homes," I said.

"Take them, you mean kill them."

"No, I really need this guy, or girl, alive. We need to question them about Vittorio, to find out his daytime resting place. If we get this weretiger and make him or her talk, then we could execute Vittorio before nightfall."

"We will give you the addresses, but if you want to question them, you will need Victor or me present."

"Why?" Bernardo asked.

"Because we can do things to make them talk that you cannot," she said.

"If it's illegal, I don't think . . ."

"He killed, or helped kill, police officers. Tell me that you can't get everyone to look the other way for just a few minutes?"

I looked at Victor and met his eyes in their gold glasses. I would have liked to defend my fellow officers, but frankly, if roughing up this guy would find us Vittorio before dark, I'd disable the cameras in the interrogation room personally. Was it wrong to admit that? Only on record. Which was another reason I was still more assassin than cop.

37

WE WERE IN the parking lot of an elementary school. It was long enough after hours that the school was empty, no children to peer out of the windows at the show outside. Because when I say *we*, I mean Las Vegas Metro SWAT, Edward, Olaf, Bernardo, Undersheriff Shaw, a bevy of homicide detectives, and some uniforms and cars that would eventually close off the streets so no one drove by at the wrong moment. Victor was in one of the cars because Shaw had kicked a fit about him being in on the planning. The powers that be had insisted he be nearby to maybe talk the weretiger down, like getting the wife on the phone to talk to someone who's taken hostages. At least Victor was sitting in air-conditioning unlike the rest of us. But it wasn't just people that made for the show. It was every SWAT operator's SUV or truck. It was the huge white RV that would be the command center. The big, black shape of the B.E.A.R., which I would have called huge if the RV hadn't been sitting near it. There was a BearCat, like a smaller brother of the B.E.A.R. It was Sergeant Hooper, who had the biggest sticky notes I'd ever seen laid out on the hood of his truck. The huge sticky notes held notes incorporating everyone's information. Notes from the small laptop that was hooked directly to the huge white RV, where Lieutenant Grimes and his tech team were shooting them all the information they could find on Gregory Minns, the first weretiger on our list.

Part of that info was the layout of his house. In St. Louis they have to scout the actual house, but in Vegas, because of the huge number of cookie-cutter housing developments, the two operators had found out which model Minns's house was, and scouted an identical one blocks away. They'd gotten the information without any chance of alerting the weretiger, which was a lot harder to do than it sounded.

"We know that wereanimals can smell our scent, which is why we're paying attention to the prevailing winds," Hooper said.

"You mean you're sneaking up on the house as if Gregory Minns were big game, and you were in the jungle," I said.

Hooper seemed to think about it, then nodded. "Not a hunt in the traditional sense, because we're hoping to take the suspect alive, but yes."

I looked at Edward. He said, "They've done this before, Anita."

"Sorry, Sergeant, just not used to working with this many people who actually seem to understand that lycanthropes aren't human, but still have the same rights as regular humans."

"We know our job," Hooper said.

"I know that, Sergeant. I'll just shut up now."

He almost smiled, then went back to his notes.

"How do you get around the fact that they can hear your heartbeat from yards away?" Edward asked, and I knew by his tone that he was actually wondering if they'd figured out a solution. When Edward asks someone else a question like that, there is no higher praise.

"No one can be quiet enough to stop their heartbeat," Hooper said.

I thought, *Vampires can*, but I didn't say it out loud. It wouldn't have helped anything. No police force in the United States allowed vampires to join up. If you were a cop and "survived" an attack and became a vampire, you were fired. I had a friend back in St. Louis, Dave, who'd been a cop until he became a vampire in the line of duty, but instead of a fancy cop funeral, he got kicked out. The police honor their dead, as long as they aren't still able to walk around.

Bernardo said, "They can't all hear a heartbeat from yards away, and they hear better in animal form than human."

I looked at him and couldn't keep the surprise off my face. He grinned at me. "You look surprised, so I must be right."

I nodded. "Sorry, but sometimes the flirt act makes me forget that there's actually a pretty good mind in there."

He shrugged those broad shoulders but looked pleased.

Harry, who was the assistant team leader (ATL), was younger than Hooper, but older than most of the others. SWAT was a young man's game, and the fact that the team had this many people over forty was impressive, because I knew they kept up or they got out. He said, "The last visual we had of the subject was human form, so the hearing, sense of smell, all of it isn't that much above human-normal from a distance, and once we're in the room with him, he can smell us all he wants, we'll be on top of him."

"What's your policy if he's shifted?" I asked.

Hooper answered, with no glance at anyone, "With an active warrant of execution, if they shift, it's a kill."

We all nodded.

"It is easier to kill them in human form," Olaf said.

The operators looked up at him, and he was the only one of us that they had to look up to, by even an inch. "We're hoping to get the location of the serial killer's daytime lair, Jeffries, which means we need Minns alive."

It was nice to have someone else in charge who could lecture Olaf. I had to turn away both to hide my pleased expression and not to make eye contact with Edward or Bernardo; I was afraid it would have turned from a smile to giggles. The tension was growing thicker around all of us, anticipation and adrenaline in the very air. I realized that was something that lycanthropes could sense, too. But again, what could we do about it? If they'd truly been animals, we could have used things to disguise our scent, but if we smelled strongly of something weird, they'd know it was all wrong. They were people with the senses of animals; it made them hard to kill, dangerous to hunt. I looked up at the sky and the sun that was moving, inexorably, toward the horizon.

"We want to do this before dark, too, Blake," Harry said.

"Sorry, but when you spend most of your life hunting vampires, you get very aware of where the sun is in the sky."

He looked very serious. "I wouldn't want to do your job every day."

I smiled, not sure it was amused. "Some days neither do I."

Undersheriff Shaw moved closer. I'd hoped he was just

going to observe. "You know more than you're telling about the local tigers, Blake."

"You questioned all of us for hours apiece, Shaw. We could have been ahead of this, and maybe, just maybe, done before dark. Now there's no way. We'll do our best, but dark will catch us, and this situation will go from bad to worse."

"I heard you came out of Max's place with a new friend. Hand in hand with one of his weretigers. You really have a thing for strippers, don't you, Blake?"

That let me know that we'd been watched, or Max was being watched. More than that, Edward hadn't picked up on it, either, so they were good, whoever it had been.

I lowered my sunglasses enough to give him my eyes. "I find your overly intense interest in my personal life disturbing, Shaw."

He actually blushed a little for me. That was interesting. I wasn't the only one who noticed that, because Hooper said, "You better suit up, Sheriff Shaw."

"What?" he asked.

"You're going in with us, right?"

"You know I'm not."

"Marshal Blake is going in with us. Please don't distract her."

"You're defending her, Hooper?" He glared at me. "I thought you didn't do cops, Blake."

"What's that supposed to mean?"

"It means you visit SWAT for a couple of hours, and suddenly they're willing to trust you at their backs, and talk back to their superiors. You must be as good as they say."

You don't get to see men like this—shocked—often, but I saw it now. That open-mouthed moment when you can't believe that slipped from someone's mouth. They moved around us, and there was that sense of the pack tightening around someone they didn't like.

Hooper spoke low, but clear, not yelling, but the emotion was there. "This woman is about to put her shoulder next to ours and go into that house, while you stay outside where it's nice and safe."

"I don't have the training anymore," Shaw said. His face

couldn't seem to decide if it wanted to be pale or red, so it tried for both.

"But you did once, and you know better than to mess with our heads this close to go time."

It was Cannibal who sidled up through the green uniforms and spoke low, near Shaw. "Getting up in Anita's face isn't going to make your wife come home."

"That is none of your business."

"You made it our business when you accused us of fucking a federal officer rather than doing our jobs."

Lieutenant Grimes was suddenly working his way through the group, but he wasn't going to get there in time to stop the next few moments.

"You stay away from me, Rocco," Shaw said.

"Yeah, that's right, you're afraid of psychics, too, but you don't hate us like you do shapeshifters, because your wife didn't run off with one of us."

And just like that, the clue to why Shaw hated my ass was there. Cannibal shouldn't have said it to his boss's boss, but . . . I appreciated him defending my honor, or maybe he was defending his; either way, it was nice not to be alone.

38

GREGORY MINNS'S PROFESSION was listed as bouncer, but Victor had just flat-out told us that he was an enforcer for their clan and, by hint, maybe some not-so-legal activities for Victor's dad. Most of the wererats that guarded Jean-Claude's businesses had police records, or just hadn't been caught, so I really couldn't bitch. Lately, when I didn't have room to bitch, I didn't. Maturity, at last.

We had the guy on the metal shield with its little window leading the way. We even had one guy with the little battering ram, and the rest of the team in full gear, weapons at the ready. Each of us—Edward, Olaf, Bernardo, and I—were assigned to one of the team members. We would follow their lead and go where they went. The suburbs are not great for finding spots to put a sniper, but we had them in place, some in evacuated houses near Minns's house. He had to know we were out here, but with this many people and this much procedure, it was the best we could do. Good thing about this many people, though, was we had eyes on the back of the house the whole time, and he didn't run. They'd seen him in there, and no one had seen him leave, so he was still in there. Getting everyone in place took more time. That was the thing we had the least of, and I was having trouble staying calm about it. I wasn't bitching, but I wanted to start pacing and knew I couldn't. It was one of those moments when smoking seemed like an interesting idea, or just anything to do while we waited to do this. I watched the sun get lower in the sky and had to fight my pulse from speeding up. I did not want to tackle Vittorio and his people in full darkness. I admitted to myself, if to no one else, that the feel-

ing in the pit of my stomach was fear. One serial killer sends
me a human head in a box, and I get all spooked; go figure.

I tried one more time to explain how precious our time was,
as we waited for yet another team member to get into some
distant place. I was actually assigned to Hooper, which meant
that I'd be in the front of the line. I don't know how they decided who went where.

"Hooper, they killed your men in daylight; once darkness
falls, the vampires will be able to help them, and it will be
worse, much worse."

"How much worse?" he asked.

"If we keep dicking around, we're going to find out."

"I can't go against orders, Blake."

I nodded. "I know it's not your fault, but it will be you and
your men who are going to be at risk."

"My men and yours," he said.

I nodded. "I'm not sure they're exactly my men, but yeah.
Your men and us."

"I'd heard that the preternatural marshals didn't have a
strict command structure."

I laughed. "That's one way of putting it."

That earned me a smile. "Then how do you decide who
does what?"

"Ted has the most experience, and I let him take the lead a
lot. Sometimes he gives it to me. I've worked with Otto and
Bernardo before, so we sort of know what our strengths and
weaknesses are." I shrugged. "Mostly, we work by ourselves,
and we end up being shoved into the command structure of
whatever police force we're working with, but mostly it's just
us, alone."

"Like the Lone Ranger," he said, and he held up his hand.
"I remember what you told Spider, that the Lone Ranger was
a Texas Ranger."

I smiled. "Yeah, but the whole lone-gunman mentality is
pretty high in the preternatural branch. We worked alone for so
many years that we just don't play well with others."

A boy who looked too young to be doing this, even to me,
with huge blue eyes and his hair hidden completely under his

helmet, as if he'd hoped a shorter haircut would make him look legal, said, "Rumor says you play real well with others."

"Georgie," Hooper said.

He looked embarrassed.

I said, "It's not just Shaw's personal issues, is it?"

Hooper managed to shrug under all the equipment. Maybe it was the tension of waiting, knowing that once this tension was over there was a whole new set of it coming down the road. "And what did you hear, exactly, Georgie?" I asked.

He looked uncomfortable then; apparently, it was one thing to hint, but another to tell me to my face in detail.

"Come on, Georgie Porgie, you have something to say to me, then say it. If you don't have anything to say to me, then shut the fuck up."

The other men were listening, watching us, waiting to see what happened. Cannibal was with the perimeter team, so he wasn't here to defend my honor, and apparently Hooper would only defend me against outsiders. Edward was quiet nearby, letting me fight my own battles. He knew I was a big girl.

Georgie's face hardened, and I realized he was going to tell me. I probably shouldn't have made fun of his name. Oh well. "I heard you're shacking up with your Master of the City."

"And," I said.

His angry face tried to frown and still be angry. "And what?" he asked.

"Exactly," I said.

It was Bernardo who said, "She means, Georgie, that, yeah, she's shacking up with her Master of the City, so what?"

"I heard she was doing you, too," he said.

Bernardo laughed. "Man, I've been trying to get into her pants since the first time I worked with her."

All I could do was shake my head. Olaf was scowling at him. Edward was trying for a neutral face and making it. Bernardo had the attention of all the guys, though.

It was Sanchez who said, "And?"

"Ask her, she's right there," Bernardo said.

They all looked at me. I smiled, not exactly amused. "No."

"No," Bernardo said, in a dramatic voice. "She said no, and

she's been saying no. I've tried for over two years, and it's been no." He did a voilà gesture, as if to say, *Look at all of this*. "Guys, if I can't get a piece of the action, how many of the bastards that said they hit the mark do you really think hit it?"

"I'm not an it," I said.

Bernardo gestured at me. "See, Anita is not easy, not in any sense of the word."

That made them laugh. In that moment, Bernardo came closer to getting a kiss from me than he ever had before. But, weirdly, for his defense of my honor to work, I couldn't even say thank you. I just had to shake my head in disgust and call him a horndog.

The radios crackled to life, and Hooper said, "We're up." Everyone gathered the equipment they'd put down and settled it in place. Hooper looked at me. "Anita, you're with me." You could taste the tension level rise hotter than the heat.

Sanchez said, "Try not to shoot any of us by accident, Anita." He said my first name with only the syllables it's supposed to have.

"If I shoot you, Sanchez, it won't be by accident."

The other men made noises of either encouragement or disparagement. Then the second order came down, and there was no more time for teasing. I'd been told how Hooper wanted me to enter behind him, because I was the only one of the four marshals who didn't have official tactical training. I did what I was told. I put my left hand on the back of Hooper's vest so that as he moved, I'd move. I kept my other hand on the MP5 on its tactical sling so that it wouldn't accidentally point at anyone, and away we went.

39

THE LAST TIME I'd been with SWAT, we'd come through the door with flash-bang grenades and a green light to shoot everything inside the condo but the victim we were trying to save. This time, we knocked.

Sergeant Hooper called out from behind the shield guy, who turned out to be Hitch, who was almost as broad through the shoulders as I was tall. "Vegas Police, search warrant. Open the door!" He had a nice loud voice, a drill sergeant voice. Even being prepared, it made me jump a little. He repeated it twice more.

Victor's energy poured across the heat from behind us, well behind us. Since he wasn't close enough to yell, he'd compromised by sending his energy ahead of him. In some ways it was better than his voice. People might imitate a voice, but no one could imitate that roll of power. In some ways it was not better than his voice. His voice wouldn't have pressed against my throat, like a hand that wanted inside. I had to up my metaphysical shields to get the energy to back off enough for me not to almost taste it. It was like pushing against some huge weight, to move his power away from me. I'd never felt any lycanthrope with this kind of power.

Gregory Minns would feel all that energy coming from his clan's "king," and if he was a good guy, he'd open the door. If he was a bad guy, he'd run, or he'd fight.

I tightened my grip on Hooper's vest and fought to keep my pulse even. I could feel the adrenaline coming off the other men, and my own tension; so much could go wrong. Victor's power just made it worse for me. If I hadn't fought it off, maybe it would have been soothing, but I couldn't afford to embrace it. The tigers inside me liked it too much. I got a glimpse behind my eyes of them putting their heads up and roaring in that coughing, harsh sound that tigers do. My body vibrated with it, and all I could do was fight to keep my pulse even and my breathing slow, because until I lost control of my body, my beasts could not hurt me. Much.

I really wished that Victor had been allowed to talk through the door.

Sanchez said, "What the hell is that? Is it the tiger inside?"

"Quiet," Hooper said.

Sanchez could feel Victor's energy and maybe my tigers. I'd have to remember that he could feel the energy. It might change what I did when we got inside.

Hooper yelled again, "Minns, open up!"

I felt energy moving in the house, almost like one of those infrared pictures, except it was a feeling, not a visual. I almost said, *He's at the door,* but all I knew for certain was that it was a weretiger. It didn't have to be Minns. I was debating on whether I should say that I could "feel" a tiger on the other side of the door when the weretiger called out.

A man's voice called from behind the door. "I'm opening the door now. Don't shoot me, okay?" The door started to open, but the SWAT never gave him a chance to finish the gesture. They poured in, and I poured with them, dragged along by my hand on Hooper.

There was a lot of yelling. "Hands on your head! Get on your knees!" Minns did what he was told and was in a circle of weapons and officers. He looked calm enough. Calmer, frankly, than he should have been at the center of that circle. The calm bothered me.

His hair was actually pale blond, not white. I caught glimpses of his eyes through the legs and bodies of the officers. The eyes were that pale, perfect tiger blue, and he seemed to have no other goal than to look at me. I didn't like that either.

The white tigress did, though. She paced closer to my surface. I kept controlling my breathing, counting my pulse down, but I could feel Minns's power. Again, like Victor it was more, different, somehow. Something about the dominants of this clan gave them more . . . crunchy goodness, as if I should have been able to eat the power, and it would have been something with texture and caramel in the middle. Something you had to chew and swallow hard to get down, but it would be sweet, and you'd want another bite.

He stared at me while they cuffed him and put ankle cuffs on, too. They were taking no chances. He let them do whatever they wanted and just kept staring at me, and I seemed unable to move from the weight of that stare.

"I would have opened the door for you, little queen, all you had to do was ask," he said, in a voice that held weight and had too much intensity to it.

Hooper glanced up at me. "Is he talking to you, Anita?"

I just nodded.

Edward touched my arm, and it helped, but I kept staring into those pale eyes. Bernardo actually stepped between me and Minns. He broke the gaze line, and I could suddenly step back. What the fuck was wrong with me?

I stepped away from Minns and the other SWAT and went to stand near the door. Edward asked, low, "What's wrong?"

I shook my head. "I'm not sure."

"You acted like he had vampire gaze and had rolled you."

"I know." I tried to shove the tigers deeper into me, but Victor's energy just rolled over and around me. It was like the air was alive with it. The energy was keeping the tigers closer to the surface of me. Damn it.

Hooper joined us. "What just happened between you and Minns over there?"

I hate explaining metaphysics to the nonpsychic. It's like explaining daylight to someone who's been raised in a cave. You know that fire is light, but how do you explain that the fire that cooks your food can be so bright that it takes up the whole sky? You can't, but you still try.

"I think he likes me."

Hooper gave me a hard look, and it was a good one. His gray eyes were as cold as Edward's could get; almost. "No one makes friends that quick, Blake. You know him, and he knows you."

"I swear to you that I have never met this man before."

"He has a pet name for you, Blake. Little queen; cute. You don't give pet names to people you don't know."

I was debating on how much to try to explain to Hooper when I felt Victor getting closer. I knew he was walking toward the house. Shit.

I shook my head. "I need Victor to tone down his energy or I'm going to drown."

"What?"

Sanchez said, "The weretiger outside is pushing his power like some freaking river at the house. I know it calmed the weretiger on the floor, but my skin is crawling with it, Sonny."

Hooper looked from one to the other of us. He toned down his anger with a visible effort. "So you and Sanchez are picking up on Victor's power?"

"Yes," I said.

"Fine, that explains why you're pale. It doesn't explain how Minns, who you say you've never met, has a pet name for you, and said he'd have opened his door for you if you'd just asked. I'm sorry, that kind of talk says serious girlfriend."

"Or good lay." This from Bernardo.

We all frowned at him. He raised his hands as if to say sorry. "I'm just saying that some women have that effect on you."

"Don't help me," I said.

He grinned at me and wandered back toward the center of the room and our waiting "suspect." Hooper gave me that cold look again. "He's right, though."

"Look, *little queen* is what the tigers call me, apparently."

"Why, and how would Minns know that, since you just got to town today?"

Sanchez and I both looked toward the door because we could feel all that power about to walk in. Sanchez actually raised his M4 up but didn't point it; I fought to just caress mine. Victor came through the door, like we'd known he would.

Sanchez said, "Sarge, can you tell the leading citizen over there to tone the power down? I'm going to get a power headache."

"You tell him, Sanchez, the marshal and I aren't through talking yet."

Sanchez gave me a look, almost of sympathy, then went for the door and Victor with his police escort. Hooper turned back to me. Edward had stepped up beside me, sort of protective, maybe. Olaf had drifted over, but was keeping his eye mostly on the weretiger. Nice to know he didn't let his interest in me interfere with business. I couldn't tell if Edward was supporting my cause with Hooper, or if he was closer to me for Olaf's benefit.

"Shaw said you knew more than you were saying, but I was willing to believe that he was letting personal issues cloud his judgment." Hooper shook his head. "But now your little friend over there has outed you, Blake. When did you meet him?"

The air seemed less heavy suddenly, as if I'd been struggling to breathe but hadn't realized it until the moment there was more air. I looked over at the door and found Victor inside the room and Sanchez giving me a thumbs-up. I returned the gesture. It was actually kind of nice not to be the only one bothered by the psychic shit. Freakiness likes company.

"I met Gregory Minns just minutes ago. You've seen all the interaction I've ever had with him."

"You are lying," Hooper said.

"She's not lying," Edward said.

"I don't need to hear from her boyfriend."

"Would it do any good to say that he's not my boyfriend?" I said.

"No," Hooper said, "the minute that weretiger called you sweet nicknames, you lost credibility with me, Blake."

"I am sorry that my attempt to calm Gregory spread to you and Officer Sanchez, Marshal Blake," Victor said as he walked toward us. His power was tight like a drum. I could feel the vibration of it, but that was all. He'd locked it down tight.

"As long as it wasn't on purpose, we're cool."

"You've felt what my mother can do; trust me, on purpose would be worse."

I nodded. I believed him.

"When did you first meet Marshal Blake, Mr. Belleci?" Hooper asked.

"This afternoon," he said.

"When did Gregory Minns first meet her?"

Victor frowned at him. "I don't believe they have met."

"He called her his little queen. That's pretty personal for strangers."

Victor smiled, then fought not to. "*Little queen* is our nickname for Marshal Blake."

"You met her this afternoon, and she already has a nickname; right. And Minns, who just met her, knew the nickname enough to use it. Don't yank my chain. One of you, or all of you, are lying."

"I swear to you that we just met Marshal Blake. Her rather unusual psychic abilities hit the radar for the tigers as a little queen. It's not a personal nickname but more a title."

"And she earned this title how?"

"By the feel of her psychic energy."

"Sanchez," Hooper said.

"She is a powerful psychic, Sarge."

"I know what Cannibal said, but I need to know if her power would do what Victor here says, or whether they're all lying."

"She shields good. I'd have to read her on purpose to answer that question, and that's against psychic protocol without permission of the other psychic, or except in an emergency situation where lives are in danger."

"You sound like you're quoting regs," I said.

He nodded. "I am."

"Cannibal is just outside with the doc. He could read you again," Hooper said.

I shook my head. "I won't give permission for him to be in my head again."

"Then I want Sanchez to read you. I want to know if you are powerful enough to set off the weretigers like this."

"It may not be as powerful for him, since he's human," Victor said.

"He's my practitioner, and I want him to read her, and you, stay the fuck away from my team."

I sighed and turned to Sanchez. "What do you need from me to make this work?"

"Drop your shields," Sanchez said.

I shook my head. "I can't drop them all."

"Ease down, then," he said.

"Can Victor be farther away?"

"Why?" Hooper asked.

"I seem to have trouble shielding against his clan. I don't know why, but their power seems to fuck with me."

Hooper said, "Georgie, escort Mr. Belleci outside the building."

Georgie came and did it, without a question. It was one of the things that most of the cops were better at than those of us in the preternatural marshal program: following orders without debate.

Victor let himself be led out. Then the others moved back a little, as if we'd asked, though we hadn't. Sanchez and I stood in the middle of Minns's living room, with its dark brown carpet and nondescript living room set. People always want the houses of the preternatural to be unusual, but in truth, most of them look like everyone else's. Going furry once a month doesn't make you that different.

Sanchez slipped off more of his headgear, his black hair wet with sweat. "Ready?"

I took a deep breath and eased down my shields. This far from Jean-Claude and all my people, I wasn't dropping all of it. No way. It was more like cracking a window on a car to let the breeze inside.

Sanchez took his glove off one hand and held it near me, as if he could feel heat. "God, your aura crackles with energy. It's like if you let all your shields down, you'd burn." Then his eyes rolled back into his head, behind fluttering eyelids. "But it would burn black, as if the night could catch fire and eat the world."

He stumbled, and I reached for him automatically. His hand convulsed on mine, and suddenly my shields came down. We were both on our knees, as if we'd been hit. The psychic hammer had hit us both, and there was nothing we could do but ride the power. I hadn't thought that they might have another practitioner that would scare me. I was so used to being the biggest bugbear in the room psychically that it had never occurred to me that Sanchez might be one, too. Now, it was too late, and the bear was going to eat us both.

40

SANCHEZ HAD TRIED to peek behind my partially raised shields, and he was too powerful, or it was like when we shook hands and he alone of all of the practitioners spiked me. I had a pure human mind-fuck me for the second time in one day. It was a record.

I felt his power, but it was like looking at calm water; you don't always see the rocks just below that will tear the bottom out of your boat and sink you.

One minute we were calm; the next he'd ripped my shields open like a wound. His power poured into that wound, but other things had been waiting, and they followed on the tail of his energy like a mugger coming in behind your key.

I felt vampire first, powerful, but just vampire. It breathed in on Sanchez's coattails. I didn't fight it, because I hoped it was Vittorio. I drew the taste of his power into me like wine that you hold in your mouth, warming it until the bouquet of it fills your mouth, your nose, your senses. If this was him, I wanted the scent of him to stay with me, because there was a chance that I might be able to track him through his own power, if he would just give me a little more of it.

Sanchez said, "What is that?"

"Bad guy," I whispered.

I felt him try to push at the power, too. "Don't help me," I said.

"I'm pretty good."

"Don't . . . ," but I didn't have time to finish the sentence because something else found us. Marmee Noir was the Queen of All Vampires. But that didn't quite prepare you for the wave of living darkness that poured over us both. It drowned out the subtle energy of Vittorio's daytime power, if it had even been him. She drowned everything else.

I was left kneeling on cold stone, in a cavern lit by torches. Sanchez knelt with me, his hand still in mine. He looked up. "What is this?" I knew our bodies were still in the house in Vegas, but our minds, not so much.

Something moved in the shadows between the torches. She was cloaked in blackness, and I couldn't tell if it was a black cloak or if she had formed herself from the darkness and it only looked like clothes. Her delicate foot stepped into the light, and tiny seed pearls caught the light, with bits of shiny black jet embroidered between them. I'd seen those shoes once before when she almost manifested physically in St. Louis.

Her body should have been upstairs in a room where she'd been hidden away for over a thousand years, but there she stood. Was it a dream? Was she really awake?

She answered my thought. "My body sleeps, but I am no longer trapped by flesh."

"What is she?" Sanchez asked.

"Shall we show him, necromancer?"

"No," I said.

"Let us see if his mind survives."

"NO!" I screamed it, and tried to bring us back out, but she flung her arms wide, and the cloak was darkness, because it stretched out and out, up and up, until we knelt staring into the perfect blackness of a starless night. The scent of jasmine choked me. I couldn't taste anything else.

Sanchez clung to my hand. "Anita, Anita, are you all right?"

I couldn't talk, couldn't speak, couldn't breathe. I clung to him because he was all I had to cling to, but she was pouring herself down my throat. Once I'd thought she meant to kill me that way, but now I saw her thoughts too clearly. She didn't want to kill me, she wanted to possess me. Her body upstairs had lain too long unused, and she could not mend it. She wanted a new one. She wanted me.

There was a light in the dark, suddenly, like a bright hot star. The light came like the rising of the sun, and she screamed as she fell back. I came to myself in the living room in Sanchez's and Edward's arms. The room was full of crosses, glowing bright like stars. Everyone's cross was glowing as I fought to breathe. Edward turned me over so I could cough out onto the carpet. I spat out something clear and too thick for water. It smelled like flowers.

Edward held me until I was done and too weak to move.

"Was that our killer?" Hooper asked at last. "Was that our vampire?"

"It was a vampire," Sanchez said, "but I don't think it's here in Vegas."

I shook my head. My voice came out hoarse. "It's nothing to do with Vegas."

Sanchez said, "The Darkness wants to eat you."

"Yeah, she does. I have my shields for a reason, Sanchez. Don't fuck with them again."

"I'm sorry," he said. "What the fuck is she?"

I shook my head. "Nightmares."

"Fuck," he said.

"Sanchez, talk to me," Hooper said.

"Marshal Blake is powerful enough, Sarge. She's powerful enough, if you see through her shields, she's powerful enough to make the tigers call her Annie Fucking Oakley, if they have a title for it."

"What did you see, Sanchez?" Hooper said.

He looked at me, and we had a moment of understanding. He said, "Nightmares, Sarge. She fights nightmares, and they fight back."

"What the hell does that mean?"

Sanchez shook his head and clung to his sergeant's arm as he helped him stand. "It means I want to feel the sun on my face, and I never, ever want to make Blake drop her shields again. I really didn't mean to do that, by the way, Marshal. I'm sorry."

I tried to sit up and found that I could, though Edward's hand was a good thing to steady against. "I would say it's okay, but it's not. You almost got me hurt, Sanchez, bad hurt."

"I know"—Sanchez gave a little laugh that sounded wrong—"I saw what wanted to hurt you, Blake. I wish I hadn't seen it. How the fuck do you sleep at night?"

Edward helped me stand, and I almost fell. It was Olaf who

took my other arm, but I wasn't steady enough to pull away. In that moment, help was okay. "I sleep fine," I said.

"Then you are an iron-willed motherfucking bastard." He started toward the door, so shaky that Hooper called another officer over to help him to the door.

When he was outside, Hooper turned to me. "Sanchez is solid. What the fuck did he see to shake him that bad?"

"You don't want to know," I said.

"Our holy items lit up like the freaking Fourth of July; what kind of vampire can cause that from a distance?"

"Pray that you never find out, Sergeant." I took a deep breath and let go of both men. When Edward let go, so did Olaf.

Hooper looked from me to Edward. "Do you know what it is, Forrester?"

Edward just said, "Yes."

"What is it?"

"The ultimate vampire," he said.

"What the hell does that mean?"

"She's the queen of them," I said, "and she's more powerful than anything I've ever felt. She's still in Europe somewhere. Pray that she never comes to America."

"She did all that from Europe?" Hooper sounded skeptical.

I glared at him. "Yeah, she did. Your man stripped my shields, like taking away your vest just before shooting a gun at your chest. You saw what happened to me."

"I didn't mean for Sanchez to fuck you up today, Blake."

"Sure," I said.

He frowned at me. "I fucking hate the psychic shit, but I didn't mean for you to get hurt." With that, he walked toward the door.

Edward leaned over me. "Are you all right?"

I shook my head, then said, "Sure."

"Liar," Bernardo said. But I noticed he'd been standing farther away than either Edward or Olaf. There were a lot of reasons that I didn't count on him.

"Fuck you," I said.

He grinned. "Hopefully."

I rolled my eyes at him, but it helped put things in perspective. The Mother of All Darkness was apparently just waiting outside my shields for a chance to eat me. I was so scared my skin was cold. I'd go out into the desert heat. I'd warm up. It would be all right. I tried to believe that, but I stared down at what I'd spit up on the carpet.

I asked, "What is that shit?"

Edward said the one thing I hate to hear him say. "I don't know." When Edward doesn't know the answers, we are so fucked.

41

I CALLED JEAN-CLAUDE from the car while Edward drove. I was way past caring what Olaf and Bernardo heard. The Mother of All Darkness was waiting just outside my shields to eat me. I could still feel some of her emotions. The primary one was fear. What the fuck could she be afraid of?

Jean-Claude answered a little breathlessly. "*Ma petite*, I felt something reach out to you. Something dark and terrible. If it is Vittorio, you must leave Las Vegas now, right now, before nightfall."

"It wasn't him," I said.

"Then who?" he asked.

I clung to the cell phone and the sound of his voice like a lifeline. I was still so scared I could taste metal on my tongue. "Marmee Noir."

"What I felt was different than ever before. It was smaller, more . . ." He seemed to search for the right word. "Human."

I nodded, even though he couldn't see it. "She was small like in the church in St. Louis. She had those damned little slippers with the pearls on them."

"Perhaps they are what is on her real body up in the room where she rests."

"She wasn't in the room, Jean-Claude. You need to call Belle Morte, or whomever, and tell them she was walking around in the bottom room of the cavern. The part of the cave where her windows overlook. She was down there."

He cursed long and elegantly in French. In English he said, "I will call the others. I will call you back as soon as I can. I would tell you to hide in a church with holy items until this is done."

"I've got a murderer to catch."

"*Ma petite*, please."

"I'll think about it," I said. "Okay?"

"That is something. I love you, Anita; do not let her take you from me."

"I love you, too, and I won't. I'm shielding like a son of a bitch. I had to drop the shield for her to get through."

"*Ma petite*, Anita . . . *Merde*, I will call you back as soon as I have reached someone in Europe." He hung up with more French, too rapid for me to catch.

The SUV went around the corner a little rapidly, keeping up with the police car in front of us. They hadn't turned on sirens or lights, but we were breaking several speeding laws. Apparently, we weren't the only ones spooked by what had happened back in the house. I wondered what Sanchez had told them. I wondered what the cops who saw it all had told everyone? Had they, like Jean-Claude, blamed it all on Vittorio? Had it spurred them on to get this done before the vampires in Vegas rose for the night?

"What did Count Dracula say?" Edward asked.

"Don't call him that, Edward."

"Sorry, what did he say?"

"He's going to call some of the vamps in Europe."

Olaf spoke from the backseat. "Did you say that the Queen of All Vampires, who we saw in spirit in St. Louis, is walking around in the flesh somewhere?"

"I saw her in a vision. It may just be a vision, but I've had visions with her before, and she's always been in the room where she's trapped. I've never seen her walking outside it."

"Fuck," Edward said.

I looked at him because he didn't cuss that often. That was usually my job. "What?" I asked him.

"I was approached about fulfilling a contract on her."

I turned in the seat and stared at him. I studied his profile, but between the sunglasses and his usual blank face, there was nothing to see. My own face had fallen into open-mouthed astonishment. "Are you saying that someone approached you to assassinate the Queen of All Vampires?"

He gave a nod.

Olaf and Bernardo both leaned up in their seats—which meant they hadn't put their seat belts on, but strangely, for once, I hadn't thought to tell them to put them on.

"You got a contract to kill Marmee Noir, and you didn't mention it to me?"

"I said I was offered a contract. I didn't say I took it."

That made me turn as far as the seat belt that I was wearing would let me. "You turned it down? Was it not enough money?"

"The money was good," he said, his hands still careful on the wheel, his face still blank and unreadable. You'd never know at a glance that we were talking about anything remotely interesting. It was the rest of us who were showing the interest.

"Then why didn't you take the contract?" I asked.

He gave me the smallest glance as he slid the truck around the corner, almost on two wheels. We all had to grab parts of the car, though Olaf and Bernardo had to grab harder without seat belts to help them. We barreled after the other police cars. They'd hit lights, but were still siren free.

"You know why," he said.

I started to say, *No I don't*, and then I stopped. I got my grip on the dashboard and the seat tighter and thought about it. Finally, I said, "You were afraid that Marmee Noir would kill you. You were afraid that this one would finally be too tough."

He said nothing, which was all the yes I would probably get.

Olaf said, "But all the years I have known you, Edward, you have sought to test yourself against the biggest and baddest monsters. You seek to be tested. This would have been the ultimate test."

"Probably," he said, in a low, careful voice.

"I never thought I'd live to see it," Bernardo said. "The great Edward's nerve finally fails."

Olaf and I both glared at him, but it was the big guy who said, "His nerve did not fail him."

"Then what?" Bernardo said.

"He didn't want to chance dying on Donna and the kids," I said.

"What?" Bernardo said.

"They make you fearful," Olaf said, quietly.

"I said his nerve had failed, and you yelled at me," Bernardo protested.

Olaf gave him the full weight of that flat, dark gaze. Bernardo wiggled a little in his seat, as if he fought not to back off from the inches-away gaze, but he held his ground. Point for him.

"Edward's nerve will never fail him. But you can still be afraid of something."

Bernardo looked to me. "Did that make sense to you?"

I thought about it, let it roll around in my head. "Yeah, actually it did."

"Explain it to me, then."

"If Marmee Noir comes here and attacks us, then Edward will fight. He won't run away. He won't give up. He'll fight, even if it means dying. But he's chosen not to hunt down the biggest and baddest anymore because they're more likely to kill him, and he doesn't want to leave his family behind. He's stopped courting death, but if it comes looking for him, he'll fight."

"If you fear nothing," Olaf said, "then you are not brave; you are merely too foolish to be afraid."

Bernardo and I looked at the big man. Even Edward took enough time to glance back at him. "What scares you, big guy?" Bernardo asked.

Olaf shook his head. "Fears are not meant to be shared; they are meant to be conquered."

Part of me wanted to know what could scare one of the scariest men I'd ever met. Part of me didn't want to know at all. I was afraid it would either be another nightmare for me, too, or make me feel sorry for Olaf. I couldn't afford to feel sorry for him. Pity will make you hesitate, and one day I would need to not hesitate with him. A lot of serial killers have pitiful childhoods, hideous stories where they were the victims—most of them are even true. But none of it matters. It does not matter how horrible their childhoods were, or whether they were victims themselves. It does not matter when you are at their mercy, because one thing that all the serials have in common is that for their victims, there is no mercy.

When you forget that, they kill you.

42

EDWARD SPILLED OUT into the line of flashing police vehicles to find that the show was almost over. The second weretiger was on her knees in the yard with guns pointed at her, and Hooper and his men were piling on top of her. I got only a glimpse of white hair, cut short, and a flash of tiger-blue eyes before they bundled her into the truck.

"You start without us?" Edward called out to Hooper, in his best good-ol'-boy Ted voice. Good that he had a nice voice because I was ready to be pissed.

Hooper answered as they closed the doors on the truck. "She was kneeling in the yard, waiting for us."

"Shit," I said.

He looked at me. "Why shit? This was easy and quick."

"They know, Hooper. The other tigers know."

I watched his face get it. "Our bad guy may run."

I nodded.

"Alert your surveillance on them," Edward said.

"What surveillance?" I asked.

Edward and Hooper got a glance between them, and then Hooper was on his radio. Edward explained, "The moment we put their name in the hat, there was surveillance on them. It's standard ops."

"Fuck, no wonder they know."

Edward shrugged. "It's a way to follow them if they run."

"It's a way to spook them and get them to run. And no one mentioned this to me because . . . ?"

"Hooper either didn't want you to know, or figured you'd realize it was standard ops."

I took a deep breath in and let it out slow, or tried to. "Fuck standard ops, the idea was surprise."

It was Shaw who came up. "We don't have to pass everything by you, Marshal. If a dangerous suspect runs, we want to know where."

"You don't get it," I said. "These guys can hear your blood in your veins. They can smell you, though admittedly a tiger's sense of smell is a lot less than, say, a wolf's, but still, they will know the cops are out there."

"My men are good at their jobs, Blake."

"Shaw, it's not about being good. It's about being human and hunting things that aren't human. Don't you get that yet?"

"They'll do their jobs," he said, and gave me those persistently unfriendly eyes.

"Yeah, I know they will. I just hope that it doesn't get them killed."

I don't know what Shaw would have said to that, because Hooper came back. "We've got radio confirmation on three of the other houses, but no answer on one."

"Shit," Shaw said.

I kept my mouth shut; an *I told you so* wouldn't go over well.

Shaw glared at me, almost as if he'd heard me thinking too hard. "Radios break, Blake. It doesn't have to be bad."

Edward touched my arm lightly. I understood the gesture. I kept my voice even. "You're a cop, Shaw; you know always to assume the worst. Then if it's not true, great, but if it is, you have a plan."

"Officers are already on the way to check on the men," Hooper said.

"Take us there, Hooper," I said.

"I think my men can take it from here," Shaw said.

"This is a preternatural case," I said, "we don't need your permission to be here."

Officers came out of the mob surrounding us, as if Shaw had already tapped them for the duty. He probably had. They were almost all in uniform, except for Ed Morgan. He nodded at me, smiling. It made the little crinkles at his eyes look pleasant and smiley, too. I wondered if the eyes behind the glasses were actually smiling, or if his face just went through the motions?

"Morgan here is chief of detectives at homicide," Bernardo said, smiling. His face looked just as pleasant as Morgan's had a moment ago. The announcement of his real title made the chief detective's smile falter a little around the edges. I wondered how Bernardo had found out Morgan's actual rank. I'd ask him later, when it wouldn't make us look less smart.

"Just because I'm chief of detectives doesn't mean we can't be friends," he said, recovering himself.

Hooper came up. "We've heard back. The car's empty. Blood, but no bodies."

"Shit," Shaw said.

"Let us help you," Edward said.

"You weren't any help with Minns; in fact, you slowed the operation down."

Edward looked at Hooper. "Is that how you see it, Sergeant?"

Hooper gave him his blank face. "No, but he outranks me."

"Nice of you to remember that," Shaw said.

"Which weretiger went rogue?" I asked.

"Martin Bendez," Hooper said.

"Sergeant," Shaw said, "we don't need to share with the marshals anymore."

"Is it your team going after him?" I asked Hooper.

"Henderson's team has point."

"Sergeant Hooper," Shaw said, "I gave you a direct order not to share with the marshals."

"Now it's a direct order," Hooper said, and he walked away to gather his men and his equipment and leave. He never looked back, but I knew that whatever he had told Shaw and his other "superiors," it hadn't been that we slowed them down. But he had to report that I'd gone all weird on them. They might have hired psychics for their force, but I wasn't one of their practitioners. They might be open-minded, but the fact that something had happened that their own practitioner didn't understand would count against me. I had an idea.

"Can the other marshals go to the next scene?"

"I told you, you slowed us down," Shaw said. He started to walk away.

"You mean I went all metaphysical on you and creeped everyone out. Fine, punish me, keep me out of it, but no one is better at tracking these guys than Marshal Forrester. Let the other marshals go on to the next scene. I'll sit it out."

Edward was looking at me. Not saying anything, just looking at me.

"No," Shaw said.

Morgan said, "Why not, Sheriff? It'll keep the Marshals Service from getting pissy, and I've heard nothing but good about the others."

Shaw looked at him, and again there was that feeling that Morgan carried more weight than he should have, even as chief of detectives.

Shaw came to stand over me, trying to intimidate me, like I cared. "Why do you want the other marshals to go?"

"Because I don't want another crime scene in Vegas like the warehouse."

"You think we can't handle it?" Shaw asked, already getting angry.

"I think that I'd trust Ted to lead me into hell itself and get me out the other side. Marshals Spotted Horse and Jeffries are both good men in a fight. If the shit hits the fan, you couldn't do better. Let them help you, and I will stand down, Shaw."

"What could it hurt?" Morgan asked.

"Fine," Shaw said, reluctance so strong in the one word it sounded like cussing.

Edward leaned in and spoke soft and fast. "I don't like leaving you alone."

"I'm surrounded by uniforms, so I'm not alone," I said.

I knew the look I was getting even behind his sunglasses. "If I help the locals but Vittorio finds a way to get to you, that won't make either of us happy."

"Nice way to put it, but it's daylight, and if I keep my shields in place, then I'm vampire-proof."

"And once darkness falls?"

"One disaster at a time." I gave him a little push. "Go find

Martin Bendez. If we can get information from him, best, but just help keep our police friends alive."

"Why?" he whispered.

I realized he meant that. Sometimes I forget that when I first met Edward, he scared me almost as much as Olaf. Then he'll say something like this, and I'll remember that he's still a predator. He's my friend, and he likes me, but most other people are just things to him. Tools to use or obstacles to overcome.

"If I said it's the right thing to do, would you laugh at me?"

He smiled. "No."

"You coming, Forrester, or is chatting up your girlfriend more important?" Shaw called.

We let it go, and Edward moved away with the officers still left on the scene. Most of them had vanished when the *officer down* call came through.

Bernardo followed Edward, but Olaf hung back and said, "I would stay with you."

I yelled, "Ted?"

He looked back, saw the big guy, and called, "Jeffries, catch up."

Olaf hesitated, then turned and started at a march/trot to catch up. Training will tell, and he'd fallen back into that fast march without thinking about it.

I watched them get into the SUV. Edward never looked back. I trusted him to take care of himself and wished I were going along. There was also that small part of me that felt if I were there he'd be safer; everyone would be. God complex, me? Surely not. Paranoia? Maybe. All I knew was that more than almost anything else in the world, I did not want to explain to Donna and the kids why Edward would never come home to them.

Another uniform led Victor over to stand with me and Morgan and the handful of officers still with us.

I looked at Victor in his designer suit. He looked so much more elegant than the rest of us, but it didn't matter. No matter what we looked like on the outside, the police had labeled us freaks, and they were done playing with us for the day. Now it was left to the humans to chase the monster down and kill it, if they could. The fact that I was standing here with Victor said, clearly, that at least some of the Vegas PD considered me one of the monsters. You don't let monsters hunt monsters. Why? Because there's a part of every human being that believes that the monster's sympathy lies with its fellow freaks. Because that's where their sympathy would lie. In the end, it's not us they don't trust; it's themselves.

43

VICTOR WENT TO stand in front of Morgan. "Detective Morgan, without Marshal Blake and me, you have no hope of taking Martin alive."

I said, "We have two officers missing, presumed injured or dead. It's not about taking him alive anymore, Victor."

"But if he dies, we lose the chance to find Vittorio's daytime lair," Victor said.

I shook my head. "It doesn't matter. We could pretend that it does, but your tiger gave up his safety when he touched the officers."

"You won't even try to get them to bring him in alive?"

"They don't trust me anymore, Victor. I went too weird on them."

"Your friend Forrester, then."

"Until they find the missing officers, it doesn't matter."

"What if killing Martin means you never find the officers' bodies?"

I turned to Morgan. "What about that? That Martin Bendez may know where your officers are?"

"I'll radio it in, but you called it, Blake. The moment he touched our officers, we're not going to be able to contain this."

"He is a very powerful weretiger," Victor said. "He will not be easy to kill."

"That a threat?" Morgan asked.

"No, honestly. If Martin has gone rogue, and you won't allow us to try to use metaphysics to contain him, then killing him from a distance is your only hope."

"So you're telling me to try to get our men to take him

alive, and to shoot him from a safe distance." Morgan smiled and shook his head, and I knew the smile for what it was now, his version of blank face. "You can't have both, Victor."

"I know that, Detective. I'm telling you I'd rather bring him in alive for the information he holds, but without the marshal and me, you have no hope of taking him alive. So if we are truly to be sidelined, then you must get a sniper in place with silver ammunition and take him out."

"I'll give your advice to my superiors." Morgan was still smiling, but his tone made it clear he either wouldn't do what Victor asked or thought the advice was amusing.

I didn't find him amusing; I found him honest. Morgan walked away, maybe even to do what Victor wanted done, but I doubted it.

I looked around at the other officers. "Sorry you're missing out on the tiger hunt babysitting us."

"My wife won't be sorry," one man said. His name tag read *Cox*. He was older, maybe late thirties.

"I'm sorry," one of the other officers said, "I mean a real hunt for a weretiger. How often does that happen?" I turned to find that this officer, Shelby by his name tag, looked bright and eager. I fought the urge to sniff the air and go, *Hmm, rookie*.

"When you've been on the job long enough," Cox said, "you'll know that going home alive is win enough."

"Getting married made you a wussy," Shelby said.

Other officers joined in the good-natured ribbing. Cox took it like the ten-year veteran he probably was; I knew what he meant. I didn't even have my ten years in, but getting home alive to the people I loved had become more important to me than catching the bad guy. It's a grown-up attitude, but sometimes it means it's time to change jobs. Or ride a desk. I'd suck at desk work.

It made me feel less wussy that Edward had turned down a contract to hunt Marmee Noir. When Death himself, his nickname among the vamps, starts turning down hunts so he can get home alive to his family, the world has become a different place. Or maybe the world is the same, and it was Edward and I who had changed.

Everyone's radios went off at the same time: handheld,

shoulder mic, all of it. I caught the dispatcher's words. Some-one had hit the emergency button on their handheld. The next thing we heard was a full-out *officer down* call.

Everyone ran for their cars. I stuck at Cox's heels. Shelby, too; apparently they were riding together. "Take me with you, Cox."

He hesitated at the door of his car while car after car squealed away, sirens and lights roaring. "Orders say you stay here."

"Forrester is my partner."

"You guys don't run in pairs," Cox said.

"He's my rabbi."

"I heard he was more your Svengali," Shelby said.

Cox said, "Shut up, Shelby."

Shelby did.

Cox and I had one of those long stares, and then he nodded. "Get in."

Victor glided up beside me.

"Not him," Cox said as he opened the door.

"If one of my tigers has attacked officers, I might be able to stop him."

I wasn't sure it was a good idea, but . . . "Let him ride; if we leave him behind and he gets hurt, we'll get shit for that, too."

Cox cursed softly.

"I know," I said, "some days you just choose which ass-chewing you're gonna get."

"Ain't that the truth." He got in, and Shelby got in with him. Since he hadn't said no, Victor and I got in the back. Lights and sirens went, and we were screaming out after the other cars. I was still hunting for the seat belt when we went around a corner fast enough to throw me into Victor.

He put an arm around me, held me close, and I was left with another problem. How do you make someone who can bench-press a small car let go of you, short of bleeding him? Answer: you don't.

44

I SPOKE OVER the noise of the sirens. "Let go of me."

He leaned his mouth in closer and spoke next to my ear. "We have little time, and there are things you need to know."

I fought my muscles not to tense and keep trying to push him away. I tried to relax into him, but finally had to settle for just nodding. "Talk."

"I felt your power in Gregory's house."

"That wasn't just my power. Sanchez had messed with me."

"I do not mean when the energy changed and was not you." So he had felt Marmee Noir. I wondered if he knew what it had been, if he'd sensed Her. "I felt your energy, Anita. Together we might be able to force Bendez out into the open."

"How?" The car careened around another corner, and only Victor's death grip on the door and me kept us still. I wondered, if we wrecked, would he be able to hold me? I needed my seat belt, but he kept whispering in my ear, kept holding me close, and I kept not moving away.

"I can sense him, and combined, you and I might force him into the open."

"How do we combine?"

"I read the article you wrote for *The Animator* about combining powers between yourself and your two fellow animators for raising more and older dead. It is not dissimilar to that."

I wanted to turn, to see his face, because he'd read the business journal for my profession. The only reason to do that was to research me. But turning my head would have put those whispering lips from ear to mouth, and that didn't feel like an improvement. The car was going about a hundred miles an hour, and Cox drove like a maniac in a line of maniacs. The speed, the driving, put my pulse in my throat and scared the hell out of me, but still I let Victor hold me, still I hadn't pushed away and gone for a seat belt. I wore a seat belt like a religion, but it was like I couldn't move. I could only listen to that soft, masculine voice in my ear. It all sounded so reasonable, and in that moment, I was no longer certain if it was really reasonable or if Victor was rolling me like some sort of vampire. I couldn't tell anymore. That couldn't be good, could it?

The car slid to a screeching stop. Cox opened all the doors, and Victor let me slide away from him, though his hand slid down to hold mine. But just the hand was better. I could think without him wrapped around me. Fuck.

Cox put a hand on Victor's shoulder, shaking his head. "Civilian, stay in the car."

I kept pulling on Victor's hand. He kept trying to hold on. Officer Cox said, "Let go of Marshal Blake, Mr. Belleci."

Victor's fingers fell away from me, and I pulled to make it happen sooner. Something was wrong when he touched me. Something that had never happened with any other wereanimal, not even the ones that were my animals to call.

The moment Victor wasn't touching me, it was as if I could draw a deeper breath. Surrounded by sirens, lights, police officers, guns, and not yet knowing what officer was down and how deep the shit; and it was already better. I moved the MP5 on its tactical sling to my hands, ready to go, and followed at Cox's heels. He was tall enough that his back was my view, but that was okay. He was letting me come along, and eventually I'd find Edward.

Then something flew over our heads. We all ducked instinctively, and it took a moment for my mind to catch up to what my eyes had seen. Someone in a Vegas PD uniform had just been thrown completely over our heads, to hit on the far side of a second line of cars.

"Fuck!" Shelby said.

Couldn't have said it better myself.

45

THE NEXT SOUND was gunfire, a lot of it. But the moment I saw the airborne officer, I knew there would be. Martin Bendez was about to die, and there was no way to save him. Whatever information he had was gone. The real kicker was that if I'd been near the front of the line, I'd have helped kill him. When a wereanimal goes a certain level of apeshit, you run out of options fast.

Cox eased forward, and I followed. Shelby brought up the rear. It looked like almost every other officer in Vegas was already clustered at the front area. They'd made a mass around some point I couldn't see. I wasn't tall enough to spot Edward or even Olaf from the back of the crowd, but somehow I knew that Edward, at least, would be near the front.

He was like one of those antitank missiles. Point front toward the enemy, and make sure you know where to stand.

I didn't try to push; Cox did it for me. He just eased us through the crowd. I followed in his wake. Shelby got a little separated, but then he took up more room than I did, so people were more likely to not let him push through. Sometimes smaller is better.

We wormed our way close enough to the front that I glimpsed Olaf towering over everyone. I knew that Edward had to be close to him. I left Cox behind and continued to work my way closer to the big guy. I actually saw Bernardo first, then Edward, all with their guns still out. All still pointed at something I couldn't see on the ground. Most of the rest of the police had eased up; some had even holstered.

"It's dead." I recognized Sergeant Hooper's voice but couldn't see him yet.

"It's not dead until it shifts back to human form," Edward said.

"What are you talking about, Marshal?" another man asked.

I eased up until I was just behind them. I could glimpse a white-and-black-furred body on the ground. "As long as it's furry," I said, "it's still alive. Dead, they turn back to their original shape."

Edward almost looked back at me, but kept his eyes and his gun on the downed tiger. "Better late than never," he said.

I shouldered my way between him and Bernardo, and aimed my gun with theirs. "Sorry I missed it."

"No," Bernardo said, "you're not." Something in the way he said it made me wonder what else I'd missed besides the body on the ground.

"It isn't shifting, just like the tiger in St. Louis," Olaf said.

I settled the MP5 tighter in my arms, but not too tight, and sighted down at the still form. I couldn't see any movement, or sense anything but stillness, but the one in St. Louis had done that, too. That one had nearly killed me and Edward's stepson, Peter. It had killed one of our people.

"I know," I said, and felt my body go still, sinking away into that silence where I went if I had time in a fight. It was a good quiet place to kill things from, the static narrowing inside my head.

Then the body moved. Someone actually shot into it, but it wasn't that kind of movement. The skin receded like the ocean drawing back from the shore. What was left was a pale, nude man lying on his side. I couldn't tell if he'd been handsome or ugly, because there wasn't enough of his face left to answer the question. There was daylight showing through his chest now because the wounds remained the same, but the weretiger's body was so much bigger, bulkier, that once they changed to human shape, the wounds all looked nastier. Less mass, more damage taken, as if once dead the lycanthropy stopped protecting the human host.

It took me a few seconds to draw myself back from that silent place. Almost everyone else in the circle of guns had let go of their tension by the time I shook it off and dropped my own shoulders.

I found Olaf staring at me when I finally looked around. "What?" I asked, and I didn't try to keep the hostility out of my voice.

Those cave-dark eyes gave me a look that held too much weight, and there was nothing sexual about it. I'd thought his attempts at dating me had been creepy enough, but there was something about this look that bothered me almost as much, even though I couldn't have told you what the look meant.

"You reacted like Ed . . . Ted and me."

"What, am I invisible?" Bernardo asked.

I don't know what I would have said to Olaf's comment, since I didn't understand it, but Sergeant Hooper was at our side, and there were other things to talk about. Thank God.

"I guess we won't be finding out the location of the vampire's lair from this one," he said.

We all stood in the breath-stealing heat and too-bright sunshine and looked down at the body. "I guess not," I said.

I heard someone yell my name. "Blake, what the fuck are you doing here?" It was Shaw striding toward me through the crowd. Great.

"Did you find the missing officers?" I asked.

"Dead," Edward said. He wasn't looking at the body, but outward. He wasn't looking at anything in particular. It was as if he were scanning the horizon for more trouble. It made me look where he was looking, but all I saw was a thin line of small houses and desert beyond, stretching out and out to brown mountains that seemed just as dry and lifeless as everything else outside the city limits. Desert is desert unless you add water. I tried to picture it with the rains and the flowers of the cacti like rainbows scattered across all that brown, but I couldn't. I couldn't see the color that might have been, only the desolation that was, and that was the cop in me. You don't look for what might be in a situation; you take the truth of it and deal. Pretty flowers could wait for the rain, and us catching Vittorio.

I felt Shaw's anger almost like something touchable. It made me turn away from a hand that I hadn't even seen yet. He had reached for me, totally inappropriate, but I'd moved just out of reach without ever having seen his hand.

My moving like that, like magic, put my pulse into my throat, so when I spoke it sounded hoarse and not like me. "No touching."

"Everyone else but me, I guess," and he said it with as much nasty inflection as he could muster.

"Wow," Bernardo said, "what is your problem with Marshal Blake, or do you just not like girls? That the real reason the wife left?" He lowered his sunglasses enough to give me a wink as he faced Shaw. He'd done it on purpose to get Shaw away from me. If I hadn't thought he'd take it totally wrong, I would have hugged him.

Edward started moving away from Shaw's one-sided yelling match with Bernardo. Olaf trailed us like an oversized shadow. Hooper caught up to Edward and me. None of us said a word. It was like we all knew where we were going and what we'd find. I guess the three of them did.

The first body was SWAT, still in gear. He still had his helmet on, so the body was almost anonymous except for general height. On television they take the headgear off so you can see the pretty actors and watch them act, but in real life most of the men are covered pretty much head to toe. It meant that I couldn't see the wounds that were making the spreading pool of blood underneath him. It's supposed to be safer covered head to foot in gear. The man at our feet probably didn't think so anymore. Of course, he wasn't really thinking anything anymore. Dead is dead.

The moment I thought it, I wished I hadn't, because I felt it. The soul, the essence, whatever you want to call it, hovering. I didn't look up. I didn't want to try to see the invisible, because even to me there'd be nothing to see. I knew it was floating there. I could probably have traced its outline in the air, but there was nothing to truly see. Souls don't look like anything to me. Ghosts, those I can see sometimes, but not souls. Most of the time I didn't see the souls at the crime scene. I'd gotten better at shielding because souls aren't helpful. They just hang around for three days, or less, and then they go on. I don't know why some souls hang around longer than others. Most of the time really violent deaths send the soul packing quicker, as if they don't want to wait around for more trauma.

Oddly, you will get more ghosts out of violent deaths. Fewer souls, more ghosts; I'd always thought that was interesting, but it did me no damn good as I stood there staring down at our fallen operator. His soul was watching us. It might even follow his body to the morgue before it moved on. I did not share this information with Hooper. He didn't need or, honestly, want to know.

It had been a while since a soul had been this loud psychically. But sometimes violence will be so loud psychically to the victim that it gives them *oomph*. It makes them so loud to my abilities that I can't not notice them.

I stood in the heat, sweat trickling down my neck, the equipment smothering in the beating weight of the sunlight. People always think you only see spirits at night, or twilight, or shit like that, but spirits don't care. They'll show up any time they can manage to find someone able to see them. Lucky fucking me.

"Not one of your men?" I made it a question. My voice sounded normal, as if I weren't working at not seeing someone's soul floating above us.

"No, it's Glick. He was one of the first psychics we hired."

"That might explain it," I said.

"Explain what?" Hooper asked.

Edward actually brushed my arm with his fingertips, like a warning. "Marshal Blake sometimes picks up impressions from the dead."

"I'm not a psychic like one you'd bring in to help solve a case through visions," I added, "but I feel the dead sometimes, all kinds of dead."

"You can feel Glick?"

"Something like that."

"Talking in your head?"

"No, the dead don't talk that clearly to me. Call it more emotions."

"What kind of emotions? Fear?"

"No," I said.

"Then what?"

I cursed myself for saying that first little comment out loud. I told part of the truth. "Puzzlement. He's puzzled."

"Puzzled about what?"

"About being dead," I said.

Hooper stared at the body. "You mean he's in there thinking?"

"No, not at all," I said.

Edward shook his head. "Tell him; what he's imagining is worse."

"Please don't share with anyone else that I can do this, but sometimes I can sense the souls of the freshly dead."

"Souls; you mean ghosts," Hooper said.

"No, I mean souls. Ghosts come later, and most of the time feel really different."

"So Glick's soul is floating around here?"

"It happens. He'll watch for a while, and then he'll go on."

"You mean to heaven?"

I said the only thing I could. "Yes, that's what I mean."

Olaf, who had been so quiet throughout, said, "Could it not go to hell?"

Shit.

Hooper glanced at Olaf, then back to me. "Well, Blake? Glick was Jewish; does that mean he burns?"

"Was he a good man?"

"Yes. He loved his wife and kids, and he was a good man."

"I believe that good is good, so you go to heaven."

He motioned off toward some scrubby bushes. "Matchett was a bastard. He cheated on his wife. He had a gambling problem and was about to get kicked off the team. Is he in hell?"

I wanted to say, *Why ask me?* How did I end up having a philosophical discussion over the bodies? "I'm Christian, but if God is truly a God of love, then why would he have a private torture chamber where he put people that he was supposed to love and forgive to be punished forever? If you actually read the Bible, the idea of hell like in the movies and most books was invented by a writer. Dante's *Inferno* was ripped off by the Church to give people something to be afraid of, to literally scare people into being Christian."

"So, you don't believe in hell."

Philosophically, no. Truthfully, once a Catholic, always a Catholic, but out loud, because it was the answer he needed while staring down at his dead friend, I said, "No, I don't." No lightning bolt struck me. Maybe if you lie for a good reason, you get a pass.

46

THE TWO OFFICERS who had been on surveillance were crumpled in the scrub bushes like broken dolls. So much damage that my eyes couldn't make sense of it in one glance. It's always bad when the brain goes, *Nope, I'm not letting you see that.* It's the mind's last warning for you to close your eyes and not to add to the nightmares. But I had a badge, and that meant that I didn't get to close my eyes and wish the bad things away.

All of us with our various flavors of badges stood around and looked at what was left of the two men. One was dark haired; the other's head was so covered in blood that I wasn't sure. The bodies had been torn apart, as if something very big, and very strong, had used the bodies for a wishbone and pulled. There were a lot of internal organs mixed in with the blood, but the organs weren't recognizable, as if someone, or something, had trampled them into mush.

"Did they pull them apart first," I asked, "then walk in the internal organs?"

"That would explain it," Edward said.

Bernardo had trailed up behind us. Shaw was nowhere to be seen. Maybe Bernardo had distracted him enough for him to forget that he didn't want me here, or maybe it was all the newly dead officers. Shaw had other things to worry about than little ol' me.

Bernardo joined us at the bodies, but he looked away first; he usually did. And yes, it was a point against him in my book. Though, frankly, on this one, I sort of sympathized.

"I've seen a lot of lycanthrope kills," Bernardo said, "but nothing like this, not from just one of the things."

"Well, it was only one of them. We got him," Hooper said.

The faint, hot wind gusted and brought the scent of bowels and bile, too strong. I felt my last meal start to climb up my throat, and had to step away enough to make certain that if I did lose control, I wouldn't contaminate the crime scene.

"Are you all right, Anita?" It was Olaf. Edward knew better. Bernardo didn't care enough. Hooper didn't know me well enough to feel either way.

"I'm fine," I said. I hadn't thrown up at a crime scene in years. What was wrong with me?

Hooper pointed, "That's Michaels, because of the dark hair, and that's . . ."

"Stop," I said, "don't tell me names yet. Let me look at it without emotion first."

"Can you really look at this and not feel anything?" he asked.

The first flare of anger came. It chased back the nausea. I gave him an unfriendly look, but part of me was grateful for the distraction. "I'm trying to do my job, Hooper, and it helps me to think of them as bodies first. They are dead, and they are not people. They are *it*, *the body*, no personal pronouns, no humanizing them. Because if I think too hard about it, about them, then I can't function as well. If I feel too much, I will miss something. Maybe I'll miss the clue that will help us stop this from happening again."

"We killed the animal that did this," Hooper said, pointing back in the direction of the weretiger's body, though it was all out of sight through the crowd now.

"Did we? Are you a hundred percent sure of that?"

"Yes," he said.

Edward was watching us like it was a show. Olaf was back to staring at the body. Bernardo was looking away from all of us.

"Did anyone personally see the weretiger we just killed do this?"

Something passed through his eyes—it might have been surprise—but he was too much cop to show it. "No witnesses yet."

"Then think like a cop, not someone's friend. We think we

got the only weretiger involved, but we don't know that for sure." I pointed at the bodies. "That is a lot of damage for one weretiger in a really limited space of time. The blood hasn't even begun to clot or dry much. In this heat, that means they haven't been dead long at all."

"I am thinking like a cop. You're the one who's complicating things, Blake. When a wife turns up dead, it's usually the husband. When the kid disappears, look at the parents. When a girl disappears on a college road trip, look at the boyfriend, and then the professor who was supposed to keep her safe."

"Yeah, most police work is very Occam's razor."

"Yeah, the simplest solution is the right one."

"Until you add the monsters," I said.

"The fact that our bad guy was a weretiger doesn't change how we do our jobs, Blake."

"You want to jump in anytime, Ted?" I let him hear the irritation in my voice. He could help more.

"What Marshal Blake is trying to say," he said, in his oh-so-reasonable Ted voice, "is that maybe we're looking for more than one wereanimal. And that if it helped Bendez do this to your officers, then we need to find the son of a bitch."

I sighed. Hooper had been right; I was complicating things. I pointed a thumb at Edward. "What he said, and I apologize for explaining way more than I needed to."

"You were shaken at the sight of the bodies," Olaf said.

"What does that mean?"

"You overexplain when you are nervous or frightened. It is one of the few times you act like a girl."

I had no idea what to say to that, so I ignored it. I rarely got in trouble doing that with men, unless I was dating them. Then there was a limited amount of ignoring that they would let you get away with.

"The bodies were pulled apart, Hooper; either it was something bigger than the weretiger that I saw dead, or it was two of them working together."

"There are no bite marks on the bodies," Olaf said.

"I'm not even sure these are claw marks," Edward said, and he did what I didn't want to do. He hunkered down beside the bodies, just out of reach of the blood pattern.

I so did not want to get closer, but I breathed shallowly through my mouth and hunkered down with him. When working with Edward, it was always a little bit of a pissing match. He knew I'd gotten nauseous, so he'd make me get closer to it all. Bastard.

I looked past the carnage and really tried to see claw marks. I had assumed they were there, like my mind had filled them in, but were they really there?

Olaf knelt beside me; hunkered down, he still towered over me. But it wasn't the towering, it was the fact that he'd chosen to be close enough that our legs were almost touching. I couldn't move away from him without standing first, for fear I'd hit the edge of the blood and mess. Standing up seemed to be admitting too much discomfort. Then I had a thought.

"You know how I said that I couldn't think as well in the morgue with you close to me?"

"Yes," he said, in his deep voice.

"Would you please go kneel on the other side of Ted instead of next to me?"

"Are you saying I am disturbing?"

"Yes," I said.

His lips twitched, but if it was a smile, he stood and hid it from me. He went to the other side of Edward. With him not beside me, I could think. Frankly, not as big an improvement as it might have been.

I forced myself to really stare at the torn edges of the bodies. "Shit," I said, and stood, not because I wanted to be farther away, but I have a bad knee, and you can't hunker forever without it beginning to complain. I stood, but kept looking down at the bodies. I wasn't sick anymore, or scared, I was working. It was always like that; if I could push past the ick factor and the emotions, I could see and think and find out things.

"I think you're right. I can't see claw marks. It looks like they were simply pulled apart, like by some giant."

Edward stood smoothly. "Like a boy pulls wings off a fly."

"What is that supposed to mean?" Hooper asked.

"I can see no weapon marks," Olaf said, then stood.

Bernardo said, "Lycanthropes don't just pull people apart

with their human hands. They aren't as strong in human form, right?"

"I don't think so, but there's some debate on it. It's one of the reasons some lycanthropes are fighting in the courts to be allowed to do professional athletics. If they can prove that the lycanthropy only gives them a little edge in human form, then maybe," I said.

"The reason no one knows is that when it comes to a fight, they're like anyone. They use everything they've got," Bernardo said. "If a wereanimal could make claws appear at the ends of his hands, he'd do that, at least, to take out two cops."

"That would make sense," I said.

"But just because it makes sense to us," Edward said, "doesn't mean it's what the bastard did."

"So you are honestly saying we have another rogue lycanthrope in Vegas?" Hooper asked.

"You have something in Vegas, and it's not just Bendez," I said.

"How sure are you?" he asked.

"Let the medical examiner look at it all," Edward said. "Maybe we just can't see the claw marks. Maybe once the bodies are cleaned up . . ." He shrugged.

"You don't believe that," Hooper said.

Edward looked at me. I shook my head. "No, we don't."

"So, was Bendez our guy, or did he just go apeshit for some other reason? Do we still need to question the other weretigers? Did our only lead to the bastard that offed our team die with Bendez?"

"Those are excellent questions," I said.

"But you don't have excellent answers to go with them, do you?"

I took a deep breath, a mistake so near the recently dead. I fought my stomach one more time, then said, calmly, "No, Sergeant Hooper, I do not."

47

I WAS BACK in one of the Vegas interrogation rooms, but this time I was on the other side of the table. Paula Chu was on the wrong side of the table this time. She was the weretiger who had so obligingly knelt in her front yard, waiting for the police to take her into custody. She had also been the serious girlfriend of Martin Bendez. Coincidence? Police don't believe in it. Coincidence is just a crime you haven't figured out yet, unless it's not. Just because you don't believe in something doesn't make it not true.

Paula Chu wasn't much taller than me, maybe five-five or five-six. Her white-blond hair was cut short, but she had enough little tufts of hair artfully sticking out here and there that I was betting she'd have wavy hair if she let it grow out. Her eyebrows matched the hair, and her eyes were the palest blue I'd ever seen, almost white. She wore makeup that complemented the paleness of her skin and accented her eyes, dragging what color she could out of them. She was so overall pale that without eye makeup she'd have looked unfinished, like dough that needed baking. With the makeup she was lovely and delicate as the first blush of spring.

The lovely eyes with their uptilted edges had nothing delicate in them when she glared at me across the table. Why wasn't she mourning her dead boyfriend? Easy: she didn't know he was dead yet. She'd gone into this room before the fireworks. I sat across from her and knew that the man she loved was dead, and I didn't tell her. I was saving it for when I thought it might gain me something in the questioning. Did that make me a bastard? Probably, but after the crime scene I'd just seen, I could live with that.

"Are you just going to sit there and stare at me?" she asked at last. Her voice dripped with hostility.

"We're waiting for someone," I said, and even managed a smile, though I wasn't able to push it all the way up into my eyes.

Edward was leaning against the far wall. He smiled wonderfully at her. "Sorry for the inconvenience, Ms. Chu, but you know how it is."

"No," she said, "I don't know how it is. I know that the police put surveillance on my house, and came and dragged me away. Apparently, I'm a suspect in the slaughter of the SWAT officers and our local executioner."

I reacted to it, just a tightening of the shoulders, but she felt it, saw it. My pulse went up just a notch. "Who told you that?"

She smiled at me. Her smile didn't reach her eyes, either. "So that *is* why I'm here."

"We didn't say that, Ms. Chu," Edward said, in his happy Ted voice.

"You didn't have to; she reacted to it." She gave me the full weight of those pale eyes.

I stared into those pale tiger eyes in the human face and felt a thrill of fear, or adrenaline? She meant to spook me, but adrenaline isn't good for you when you carry beasts inside you like furry hitchhikers.

I'd been shielding as hard as I could. Hard enough that she hadn't picked up on the fact that I wasn't completely human. Interesting to know that I could shield well enough to pass for prey to Paula Chu. But that tiny spurt of adrenaline was enough to make the white tigress get to her feet and gaze up the long distance of that interior landscape.

It was Chu's turn to tense. My turn to see it and give her a satisfied smile. Her voice was even a little shaky around the edges. "You can't be one of us."

"Why not?" I asked.

She touched her white hair. "You aren't pure."

"I survived an attack," I said. Which was true; if she thought that meant I was a full-blown weretiger, not my bad that she misunderstood.

Her face was instantly scornful. "Then you don't understand. It's not your fault, but you can't understand."

"Help me understand," I said.

Her eyes narrowed. "I thought that if you became a shapeshifter, they took away your badge."

"I'm with the preternatural branch of the Marshals Service. The rules are a little more lax."

She kept giving me that suspicious look. Her dainty nose flared as she sniffed the air. "You don't just smell of tiger; you smell of our clan. You smell like white tiger. That is not possible."

I shrugged. "Why isn't it possible?"

"You should smell like tiger, but only regular, orange. One of us could attack you and make you a tiger, but you'd still not be clan."

"You mean I wouldn't turn into a white tiger, even if a white tiger were my attacker."

She nodded, and she was puzzling over me. "Exactly."

The white tigress had risen to her feet and was beginning to trot up that long, dark path through the forest that was not, in a place that only dreams should have been real. I had concentrated and gotten her to slow, then stop. She began to pace around the path, like something caged. But she had stopped, and that was all I cared about.

Chu leaned a little closer over the table. "I smell white tiger. You smell like clan. Are you hiding from us? Did you dye your hair and put contacts in? Your skin is white enough to pass."

"Sorry, but I'm all natural." I wanted to glance back and see Edward in his corner, but didn't dare. I knew he was there and would help if I needed it, but he was mostly there in case Paula Chu tried to go all tiger on our asses. We had been told to wait for Detective Ed Morgan before questioning her about the crimes. So far, we hadn't broken that rule. Just two shapeshifters talking shop.

She half-rose from her chair. The manacles kept her hands from rising and kept all of her from standing completely, but Edward still said, "Sit down, Ms. Chu, you'll be more comfortable that way."

She gave a sound that might have been a laugh, but was all bitter. She let herself fall back into the chair. "Yeah, I guess it is more comfortable." She stared at me, and I felt the first trickle of her energy like a hand searching in the dark for another hand to hold.

"Don't try to read my energy with yours," I said, and I tried to shut the shields back as tight as when I'd started the interview. But the white tigress was still pacing on the path. She couldn't get past my orders to stay where she was, but I didn't have enough control to shut her down completely. That knowledge made my heart speed just a little. It let the tigress inside me start moving down the path again. It made Paula Chu take in a great, noisy breath of air. Her eyes actually fluttered closed, and she shivered in her chair.

The white tigress inside me began to hurry along the path. I could try to tough it out, or I could leave the room. Normally, I'd have toughed it out, but I couldn't afford to fall to the ground and start twitching. I'd had a near-change cause blood to flow from under my fingernails. If I did that where the Vegas police could see me, being kicked off this case was the least that would happen.

I stood up. The tigress was running now, so fast that the black stripes vanished into the white blur of her.

"Anita, are you all right?" Edward asked, moving a little away from the wall.

I shook my head. "Need some air," I said.

The woman on the other side of the table opened her eyes and said, "You're powerful, but you're new. You don't have the control yet."

I went to the door and banged on it. "Hit the buzzer," Edward said. He'd moved closer to me and to the suspect.

I fumbled for the buzzer. I heard it sound. Nothing happened. Someone had to let us out. Until this moment, I'd been okay with that. I pictured a brick wall across the path of the tiger in my head. She stopped running and snarled at the wall.

My pulse was still thudding in my throat, but there was relief under the taste of my own heartbeat. I could do this; I'd been practicing for months so I could control my beasts and

travel out of town without a posse of wereanimals to help me
control all that internal strife. What was it about these tigers that
made the control so much harder? Or was it simply being too
far away from Jean-Claude and our power base? That thought
sped my pulse up again. What if I couldn't control my powers
if I was too far away from . . . my master? I really wished I
hadn't thought of that.

The tiger in my head hunkered down, pushing her body
against the ground of that impossible place. I felt her body tense
for the spring and realized my mistake too late. Tigers can jump
eighteen to twenty feet vertically. My brick wall hadn't been
tall enough. She was over the wall in one muscular bound, and
running full-out down the path. If she hit the end of it, she'd hit
me. It was like being hit by a small truck from the inside out.

It was Paula Chu who said, "You are in control, not the
beast. That must always be so."

"It's your energy that's fucking with me." I put another wall
in the tiger's path. This one was metal, tall and shiny, so tall
that it lifted through the trees. She wouldn't jump this one.

"I am not doing enough to cause this much trouble, even
among the newly found."

I shook my head, still not looking at her. "I don't know
what it is about your clan, but your energy fucks with me. It
just does."

"That would only be true if you were a born member of our
clan, lost and now found, but if your coloring is real, then you
cannot be pure born."

The white tiger in my head snarled and paced before the steel
wall. She bared those glistening fangs and roared at me. The
sound reverberated along my spine as if she'd turned me into
some human-sized tuning fork.

"I hear your call," she said, and her voice was strained.

"I'm not doing it," I said. I hit the buzzer again, but I knew
now. Shaw, or someone, was watching. They wanted to see
what would happen to me if I stayed in here long enough. If I
changed shape for real, I'd lose my badge. The only thing that
had saved it was that I had too many types of lycanthropy, and
they couldn't prove that I was a real shapeshifter. Shaw would

love proving that. I wouldn't just be off this case—I'd be off every case, forever.

"You are calling for aid. It is a distress call, but only our queens can make the call that loud."

I tried to make the roaring tiger inside me be quiet, but she wouldn't. She just kept calling for help. Shit.

"What do I do to stop it?" I asked.

"I can help you calm it, but I would have to touch you to do it."

"Bad idea," Edward said, and took a step closer to me.

I shook my head and looked at him. "If she can help me?"

"And if she makes it worse?" he said.

We looked at each other. The intercom that fed into the room came on. "What the fuck are you doing in there, Blake? The other tigers are going apeshit."

"Let me out," I said, "and it'll get better."

"You cannot stop it on your own," Paula said.

"Fuck you," I said.

"Let me quiet you. It is the way of tigers to calm the young and the inexperienced."

I'd had Crispin do it for me once, when things were much worse than this. But . . . I did not know her, and she was the dead bad guy's main squeeze. Would she help me, or hurt me?

"Let me help you, Marshal. One of our people attacked you, and for that our entire clan owes you a debt."

"It wasn't a white tiger," I said, but I'd moved away from the door and was closer to the table.

"Anita," Edward said, and he reached out, then let his hand drop. "Are you sure this is a good idea?"

"No," I said, but I kept moving toward her.

"If it wasn't a white tiger, then who attacked you?" she asked.

"Yellow," I said, and I was standing beside her, staring down into those blue eyes. Just that made the tiger inside me stop screaming. It was as if just being closer to another white tiger soothed my beast.

"Yellow tiger," she said, and frowned.

I nodded.

"The yellow clan has been dead for centuries. They do not exist."

"She was an animal to call for a really old vampire."

"What happened to her?" Paula asked.

"She's dead."

"You had to kill her."

I nodded.

"But a yellow tiger attacked you," she said.

"You say it like that makes a difference. What difference does it make what color tiger attacked me?"

"The yellow, or golden, clan was supreme to all the other clans. They ruled the earth and all the energies on it, including the rest of the clans."

"News to me," I said.

She shrugged as much as the chains would let her. "What good does it do to talk about something that is lost? But if a yellow tiger attacked you, then it might explain why you seem to have so much power."

"She was yellow," I said. I turned to Edward.

He knew what I wanted without my having to say anything. "She was pale yellow with darker stripes."

"You were there?"

"Yes," he said.

"Was anyone else attacked?" she asked.

"Yes, but he tests clean for lycanthropy. I'm the only one that got lucky." Just standing next to her made it easier to breathe. Maybe the idea that I could travel without my own cadre of wereanimals was just not true. Maybe I'd never be able to travel alone. Shit. If that were true, I might have to give up the federal badge anyway. What good was an executioner who couldn't travel to where the bad guys were committing their crimes?

The intercom sounded again. "The other tigers are calm again. What are you doing in there, Blake?" It was Shaw, just like I'd known it would be. I was sorry his wife had run off and shacked up with a shapeshifter, but it wasn't my fault.

Edward went to the intercom on our side and spoke. "We got the tiger energy toned down, that's all."

"What's Blake doing?" Shaw asked.

"Her job," Edward said, and let go of the button.

I looked into those strangely soothing tiger eyes in the woman's face. "Did you know what Martin was involved in?"

She blinked up at me. Her face told me nothing, but her lips parted, her breath a little faster. Was that because she knew something, or because I mentioned her boyfriend? Or was it just being in cuffs from top to bottom and being questioned by the police? That tends to make people nervous, even overreact. It's one of the reasons I prefer to question people at home or some place more casual. But it was too late for casual today. Too late for so many things.

I was staring into her eyes as she said, "No." I didn't believe her. I wasn't sure why, but looking into those pale blue kitty-cat eyes, I knew she was lying. It wasn't metaphysical powers. It was the same gut reaction that any cop gets after a while. You just begin to know. Now, maybe she wasn't lying to hide something. Maybe she was lying because she was scared, or just because she could. People lie for the stupidest reasons. But I went with her lying to hide something. She was lying because she had information we needed. That was helpful. That gave us somewhere to go and someone to question. That gave us something useful for all the new deaths I'd seen today. If Paula Chu knew something, then maybe the officers who'd died, and the SWAT who was in critical condition in the hospital . . . Maybe it all wouldn't have been for nothing.

I realized, staring down into her lying eyes, that I no longer believed that. Even if she knew everything, the fucking secret to the secret sauce, and would tell us all of it, it didn't matter. It didn't matter to the families of the slain officers. It didn't matter to the member of SWAT who might never walk again, if he even woke up. That it mattered was a lie that we told ourselves so we could keep moving and not want to eat our gun.

Closure was a word therapists used to make you believe that the pain would stop, and that punishing the bad guy, or finding out why, would bring you peace. It was the biggest lie of all.

"Anita," Edward said, "you all right?" He was closer to me

than he had been, all the way on the side of the table with Paula and me. I hadn't heard, felt, or seen him move.

I shook my head. "No, I'm not all right." In my head I thought, *I am off my game.* What was wrong with me?

Edward took my arm and moved me back from the woman. The farther away, the clearer my head, but the tiger inside me was still there, crouched on the other side of the metal wall in my head. But she was lying down; only the end of that black-tipped tail twitching let me know how irritated she was with me.

The door opened and Chief Detective Ed Morgan came through smiling. He was playing those big brown eyes and those nice-guy good looks for all he was worth. He just radiated charm. Oh, right, we'd been waiting for him. Hadn't Shaw warned us not to ask any questions directly related to the case until Morgan arrived? Guess he had. Fuck it.

"Good afternoon, Paula, may I call you Paula? I'm Ed." He set files down on the table between them, took the chair I'd been sitting in, and smiled at her. You'd have thought Edward and I didn't exist.

"I can take it from here, Marshals. Undersheriff Shaw would like to speak with you." Morgan smiled, broad enough to flash dimples, but in the depths of those brown eyes was an unfriendly spark. I thought we were going to get yelled at. Great.

Edward kept his grip on my arm, as if he didn't trust what I'd do. If there'd been a mirror to look into, I'd have checked what my expression was, but there was nothing but walls. They didn't have enough interrogation rooms with those big shiny two-way mirrored windows, so they'd put the woman in one where they couldn't watch her as well. There was a camera on her, but she didn't rate the window. She was the only one with a real connection to the dead weretiger, and she hadn't rated the best room, though she now had one of their best interrogators. I smelled office politics.

Edward led me toward the still-open door. Whatever he saw or felt from me, or in me, was making him nervous. I didn't feel that scary. I didn't feel much of anything. Again, there was that little thought, *What is wrong with me?*

He eased me out the open door. I glanced back and found

Paula Chu staring at me. The moment I met her eyes, the tigress in me stood up. She roared again, but this time the metal wall trembled with the sound, as if her roar had hit it like some huge gong. I staggered, and Edward had to steady me.

He leaned in and whispered, "What is wrong?"

"Not sure, but I need to get away from these tigers."

Morgan said, "Close the door on your way out. Paula and I will get along just fine, won't we?" He was turned away from us, but I knew he was wasting that brilliant smile on her. She didn't even look at him. Her eyes were all for me.

I pushed through the door, and only Edward's grip on my arm kept me from starting to run. My breathing was trying to speed up. My pulse was already racing. I could feel the other tigers inside the interrogation rooms. I could *feel* them. The only were-animals I should have been able to feel like that were ones that I was metaphysically bound to, or that Jean-Claude was bound to. I was not close enough in any way to the white tigers of Vegas to sense them this strongly. Something was wrong.

Edward's fingers dug into my arm. Dug in enough that I would have protested the pain, but it helped clear my head. A few bruises were worth it, and the moment the pain helped, I knew something else.

I whispered to him, "I'm being messed with."

"Vampire?" He made it a question.

"Unless the white tiger queen can do shit that I've only seen vampires do before, yes."

"Vamp or tiger?" he asked, voice low.

We were getting a few glances from the police officers we passed. Did they see the bruising grip, or the whispering? Or were the rumors so good that we'd just become a curiosity?

I glared at a couple of uniforms who were staring. "Like what you see?"

"Leave it, Anita." Edward just kept us moving past them. He loosened his grip on my arm a little, and instantly I could feel the tigers behind us in the rooms. I could almost see them looking up and trying to see me.

I leaned in, and whispered, "Tighten the grip."

"What?"

"The pain helps keep my head clear."

He went back to bruising my arm, and we kept walking toward the doors. I could see the press of the hot, white sunlight against the doors.

"If the sunlight helps . . ." he said.

I said, "Then it's vampire."

"If it doesn't . . ." he said.

"Tiger," I said.

He didn't even bother to say yes. We both knew what we were doing, and why. Bernardo called from behind us, "Where's the fire?"

Edward looked behind, but I didn't. I had my eyes on the goal of the doors. I concentrated on the pressure of Edward's fingers on my arm and the sunlight just ahead. He called back, "We need some air." Bernardo, and Olaf if he was with him, would know that we weren't moving that fast for a little air. It was the shorthand of people that knew each other. They knew Edward better than they knew me, but shorthand for him in that moment worked just dandy for all of us.

Bernardo and Olaf caught up with us as we got to the outer lobby area. Victor stood up from where he'd been sitting. The moment I saw him, the tigress in me roared again, and this time the metal shield that I'd built in her path wavered like metal water. It didn't break, but it bent.

Edward didn't even slow, but waved Victor off, and kept us heading for the door. Bernardo had the door open and waiting for us, as if he'd picked up on the urgency. Olaf trailed after all of us, not helping but not hindering, either. Right now, I'd take not hindering.

The tigress inside me leapt onto the warped metal and began to try to climb. "Hurry," I said.

Edward pulled me through the doors. The heat hit me first, breath-stealing, like walking into an oven. The tiger didn't hesitate. She wanted out.

Then the light hit me, and it was like some hot, white searchlight. It slashed through a darkness that I hadn't been able to see. A darkness that held Her. She stood in the dark and shrieked at me. But the sunlight cut her off, and all I had to fight now was the weretiger that had managed to climb my shields and was running full tilt toward the surface of me. I didn't know why Marmee Noir liked tigers so much, but she had done something to weaken my defenses.

I tried to put up another shield, and I couldn't. Marmee Noir was gone for now, thrust out by the sun, but what she'd done inside me was still there. It was still crippling me.

Edward still had a light grip on my arm. "Anita, are you all right?"

"The vampire's gone, but she's done something to me." The tiger was running full-out, a blur of white and black; if she hit the surface of me, the least bad thing that was about to happen was I'd fall on the ground and almost change. Worst case, whatever Marmee had done to me would make me tiger for real.

"What has happened?" Olaf asked.

"I've got a better question, what *is* happening?" Bernardo asked.

If I'd had a wereleopard or a werewolf, or even a werelion, I could have distracted the tiger inside me, turned the beasts against each other, or even a tiger of a different color. I stood in the heat and the light, and I needed things that I couldn't explain to the others.

"I can help you calm your tiger." Victor's voice came from behind us. He'd followed us into the light.

"I don't think so," Edward said.

"No," I said. "I mean, yes."

Edward looked at me. "Anita, he almost brought your beast earlier."

"That was an accident," Victor said, "but I am trained to help the females of my clan keep their human form."

Edward drew me closer to himself. But we were out of time; the tiger was about to hit the surface of me. "Let him try, Edward, or I could be tiger for real."

I reached for Victor, and Edward let me go, reluctantly. Victor put his hands on either side of my face, the way that Crispin had done when I'd first met him in North Carolina. Victor threw his colored glasses away, so that I gazed into those pale blue eyes, naked to the light. I fell into those eyes, and the tiger slowed inside me. It didn't stop, but it slowed.

He lowered his face toward mine.

I sensed movement to the side and caught the tall, dark presence of Olaf. Edward stopped him from touching us. "Let him," Edward said.

Victor kissed me. He pressed his mouth over mine. With Crispin I had forced my beast into him and brought his own tiger, but now Victor breathed his power into me. Not his beast, but his power. That skin-tingling, breath-stealing power, like nothing I'd ever felt from any lycanthrope except his own mother.

The tiger inside me paused, then started trotting again, so close, so close to being out.

Victor drew back enough to say, "You must accept my power willingly. You are too strong for me to force your beast into stillness."

The tigress was at the surface of me, like she was gazing up from the bottom of some pool, and I was that pool. Always before the beasts had slammed into me, as if I were a solid object to tear through, but now I was water, and the tigress hesitated.

"Look at me, not your beast, Anita." He drew my attention back to his eyes, his face.

The tigress scraped a claw down the underneath of the water that was me, and only Victor's hands kept me standing. Always before it had hurt more, but now I knew, absolutely knew, that this new watery barrier would not hold the beast. Whatever Marmee Noir had done, she wanted me to shift. She wanted me to be tiger. I didn't know what was happening, but I knew that anything she wanted, I shouldn't give her.

The tiger took another pass, and I swear I felt my skin move with it. "Save me," I whispered.

"Let me in," he whispered back, as he pressed his mouth on mine one more time.

I wasn't sure how to do it, so I dropped the shields to my beasts. The tigress let out a roar of triumph, in the same instant that Victor's power smashed into her. She screamed at its touch, but the power drove her back. Victor's power was a warm, living wind that chased her back, gently but inexorably.

Then, suddenly, she was gone, and I was alone in my skin. Alone in my skin, but still wrapped in Victor's arms.

He drew away from the kiss, but kept his arms on me, as if he wasn't sure I could stand. Me either.

"You're bleeding," Bernardo said, softly.

I looked down and couldn't see anything under the vest, but Victor had blood on the lower part of his body. "I don't think it's mine," he said.

Edward moved up to block the view. "We need to get out of here."

"You make friends too damn fast for comfort." Hooper was there, with some of his team.

Victor whispered, "Can you stand?"

I thought about it, then nodded.

Victor stepped away from me, standing so that the cops might not see the blood on his front. I said, "Sorry you don't like how I make friends, Sergeant." I meant that, actually. I liked Hooper and would have liked to keep his good opinion, but . . . The most important thing was to get the hell away from all the other cops and see how badly I was hurt.

"I'll be your friend." This from Georgie.

"Sorry, my dance card is a little full."

"No fucking joke." He gave me that look that you never want to see from a man who is supposed to be a coworker and has never been your boyfriend. His too-young face didn't carry the look well.

But Hooper was giving me a look I wanted even less. He'd narrowed his eyes and was trying to see around the blocking bodies of the other men. He started toward us. Edward started us toward the car. Victor came with us. We did our best to keep the blood out of sight. It didn't show on my black-on-black, but Victor's pale shirt showed the blood scarlet.

Hooper sent the other men inside, then kept walking toward us. Sanchez caught up with him, kept him talking. It looked like they were arguing, but it gave us enough time to get me in the back of the car. Victor rode shotgun so he could direct Bernardo to the doctor. Edward rode in back with me, and Olaf, too. We tried to get Olaf to drive, but he simply would not agree to driving. Hooper had broken away from Sanchez and was moving our way again. We were out of time to argue.

"Drive," Edward said.

Bernardo drove.

48

"TAKE OFF THE vest, Anita. We may need to put pressure on the wound."

If it had just been Edward and me in the backseat, I'd have been okay with that, but Olaf sat beside me like some looming shadow. I gave one glance up at his face, and there was nothing in his face that made me want to undress in front of him.

"Stop being a girl," Edward said, "just do it."

"That's not fair," I said.

"No, and I know why you don't want to do it, but bleeding to death because you don't want Olaf to see you bloody and half naked is a stupid reason to die."

Put that way . . . "Fine," I said, and let that one word hold as much anger as it could. I helped him get me out of the holsters and weapons. I gave them to Edward, as I'd given them to him at Bibiana's place, because who else would I trust with my weapons? But that left Edward's hands full, and Olaf to help me unfasten the side of the vest. I expected him to dwell on each movement, the way he had in the morgue, but he was strangely businesslike. He simply unfastened the Velcro on the sides and lifted it off me. The blue of my T-shirt had streaks of purple on the stomach area, where blood had soaked through. Not good.

Olaf just suddenly had a knife in his hand. I said, "No! You don't have to cut the shirt off me!" I started pulling the shirt out of my jeans. I admit that I was tensed, ready for it to catch and hurt on the wounds. Cutting it off would actually have been more practical, and the shirt was ruined anyway, but the sight of the big man looming over me with the huge serrated blade . . . No way was I giving him an excuse to bring the blade closer to my skin.

I must have made some small involuntary pain sound, because Edward put my weapons on the floor and had his own knife in his hand. "We need to see, Anita."

I opened my mouth to protest, but he'd picked up the slack of the shirt and was already cutting. I could have stopped him, but he was right, and I wasn't afraid of Edward. He cut up the middle of the shirt, his blade sharp enough that it made a straight, almost surgical line up the center. He cut it until the collar of the T-shirt stopped the blade. I might have protested that I really was half naked now, but I could see my stomach, and the fact that everyone could see my bra just didn't seem important.

"Crap," I said.

There were bloody claw marks on my stomach. I'd bled before when I almost changed, but I'd never had wounds from it before. Blood had seeped out from under my nails, but never this.

Olaf's fingers hovered over one ragged-edged wound. I started to tell him, *Don't touch me*, but he said, "The edges of the wounds are wrong."

"They go out, not in," Edward said.

I stared down at the wounds, but the angle wasn't as good for me, or maybe it's just harder to look at your own body when it's cut open and analyze the wounds. I tried to be positive. "Well, at least it's not as bad as the last stomach wound."

"True," Edward said.

"Yes, your intestines are not bulging out this time," Olaf said. He said it so calmly, as if it hadn't mattered then and didn't matter now. I guess, what can you expect from a sociopath?

He put those big fingers just over the wounds. There was a faint shudder in his hand, and he had to raise it higher to flex the hand, and then he put it back over the wounds and traced his hand over the wounds. "It looks as if something has tried to get out, not slashed from a distance." He spread his hand over the marks. I started to protest, but realized his hand could almost cover it all; a dainty claw as claws went. Dainty as the wounds we'd found on the victims.

"They are the same size," he said. He laid his hand on the wounds. The pain was sharp and immediate, and I know I made some small sound, because two things happened at once. Edward said, "Olaf," with that warning in the word; and Olaf let his breath out in a sigh that was totally inappropriate for blood and wounds. Okay, inappropriate if you weren't a serial killer.

"Stop touching me," I said, and made every word as hard and firm as I'd ever made them. I don't know why, but for the first time this kind of behavior from him didn't scare me. It just pissed me off. Let's hear it for anger.

He moved his hand and gazed down at me with those cave-dark eyes. Whatever he saw in my face didn't please him, because he said, "You aren't afraid."

"Of you, not right now. I just had something try to tear its way out of me. Sorry, but on the horrible scale, that's got my attention. Now stop using my pain as your foreplay and fucking help me."

He took his leather jacket off, folded it, and put it against my stomach. "It will hurt, but if I apply pressure to the wounds you will not lose as much blood."

"Do it," I said.

He pressed, and it hurt, but sometimes things need to hurt some now, so they don't hurt a lot more later. I must have made a small sound because Edward asked, "Is he hurting you?"

"No more than he needs to," I said, and was proud that my voice was almost steady. Let's hear it for the tough-as-nails vampire hunter. Not fazed by overgrown serial killers or the beasts inside her. Shit.

"Victor," I said.

He turned in his seat to look at me. His glasses had apparently been left on the sidewalk because I was gazing into the bare blue eyes of his tiger. No, of him. The weretigers, like Victor, were born, not made. "Yes, little queen."

"First, stop calling me that. Second, are the claw marks on me what my tiger would be sizewise, if it could get out?"

He thought about that for a second or two. Bernardo had to ask, "I made the last turn; what now?"

He gave him more directions, then turned back to me. "You are a very different kind of . . . case. But, I believe, yes. It is the size you would be."

"Shit," I said.

Edward said, "Martin Bendez had bigger hands than Anita, even human."

"Our killer is a woman," I said.

"No, some men have hands as small as yours," Olaf said.

"Any of your male weretigers have hands this small?" I asked, and held up one hand for Victor to judge. He reached through the seats and held his own larger hand up next to mine.

"Only Paula Chu."

"Wait," Bernardo said, "if Bendez wasn't the weretiger we were looking for, then why did he attack the police?"

"Good question," Edward said.

Victor gave us an answer. "He had an ex-wife who was charging him with abuse. He had not been one of our successes, and if the charges were served, then he was either going to jail for life, or . . ."

Bernardo finished for him. "Or have a warrant of execution on his ass."

"Yes. In other states, they might offer him a permanent place in one of the government areas for shapeshifters, but Nevada, like most of the western states, still has varmint laws on the books. Three strikes for us in this part of the country usually means death."

"It might have been useful to know that going in," Edward said, and not like he was happy with ol' Victor.

Bernardo took a corner a little sharp, making Olaf have to struggle for balance. He pressed harder on me, and I fought not to make pain noises. He put one long leg out to wedge himself in place. "That pain was accidental," he said.

I'd been doing a good job of ignoring him, which, considering he was like six foot six and leaning over me, with his hands and jacket in my blood, was a testament either to shock or to my powers of concentration. I was betting on shock. But now I looked up at him, *saw* him. I saw the flicker of him deep down in those eyes of his. I saw him looking at me. I saw him fighting not to show everything he was feeling in his face, and failing.

He moved his face so that the only person who could see

directly into his was me. He gazed down at me, with his big hands in the leather, pressing on the wounds in my body, and he let his lips part, his eyes go soft. His own pulse beat thick and heavy against the side of his neck.

I tried to think of what to say, or do, that wouldn't make things worse, and finally tried to concentrate on the job. "They would have run him for priors, just routine." I looked at Victor as I said it, because I couldn't bear to look at Olaf anymore. I wanted him to stop touching me, but he'd enjoy fear, or even revulsion. I didn't know a reaction that would lessen his pleasure except ignoring him.

"But Marshal Forrester is right, I should have mentioned it."

"The claw marks prove that it's someone else, most likely Paula Chu," I said.

"But we can't explain to the police how we know that without explaining your wounds," Edward said. "They might yank your badge. We get a lot more leeway in the preternatural branch, but if they think you might turn furry for real on the job, they'll want you out."

"I know."

"So," Bernardo said, "we know something they need to know, but we aren't sharing."

"Would they understand and believe us even if we shared?" I asked.

Everyone was silent. Finally, Edward said, "Sanchez might, but I don't know about the rest. If Anita is going to lose her badge, I'd rather it be for something that the cops would take seriously, not something that they'd blow off."

"They have their bad guy," Bernardo said. "They aren't going to want to believe they killed the wrong guy."

"But if it is Paula, then we could get the daytime retreat from her," I said.

Olaf surprised most of us in the car by saying, "Ted, can you take over?"

Edward didn't argue, just moved up on his knees to put pressure to the wounds. But he gave me wide eyes, as if to say, *What the hell?* I agreed. Olaf had voluntarily given up a chance to touch me bleeding and hurt. What was wrong?

Olaf was staring at his hands. They were bloody. "Do you

remember, Anita, how you could not do your job in the morgue
with me there?"

"Yes," I said.

He licked his lips, closed his eyes, and let a shudder go
through him from that bald head to the tips of his boots. He
opened his eyes and let out a breath that shook. "I cannot do
my job, touching you like that. I cannot think of anything but
you, and the blood, and the wounds." He closed his eyes again,
and I think he was counting, or doing whatever he did to regain
control.

We were all staring at him except Bernardo, who had to
drive. "Is this it?" he asked Victor.

"Yes," he said.

Olaf opened his eyes. "Some of us need to go back and
watch over the woman, Paula Chu."

"Agreed," Edward and I said, together.

"Bernardo and I can go back," he said.

"Thanks for volunteering me, big guy."

"You are welcome," Olaf said, as if he didn't get the sarcasm at all.

We were in a part of town that was more downscale than the
Strip, but beyond that, I couldn't tell much more from where I
was half-reclined on the seat.

Bernardo and Victor got out; Bernardo opened the door behind Edward. I started to try to scoot out, but the pain grabbed
me like a sharp hand and made me stop in midmotion. "Just let
me do it, Anita," Edward said. He started to pull me out, as
gently as he could.

Victor peered in and said, "We're being watched. Maybe
even photographed."

"Then why bring us here?" Edward asked.

"It was closer, and you can legitimately say you're here to
question Paula Chu's coworkers, but we need Anita to walk in
on her own power, if possible."

"Can you walk?" Edward asked.

"How far?"

"Ten yards." Just like that, he knew exactly the distance to
the door. I'd have never been able to be that precise.

"Let me lean on someone's arm and be all girly, and I'll do it."

I got upright, and the leather jacket fell to the floor. Olaf crawled over the seat and picked it up, as Edward let me take his arm and begin to try to get out of the truck on my own power.

Olaf reached out and helped arrange my shirt over the wounds. Though red and blue made a lot of purple on my shirt. We tucked the ends into my pants to hide the slice.

I got standing, though my grip on Edward's arm was as serious a hold on any man's arm that I'd ever had. It hurt just to stand, and I could feel the blood begin to trickle down my stomach. Not good, and if it hurt to stand, it was going to hurt more to walk. Perfect.

Edward had tucked some of my weapons in and around his body, but a lot of them and my vest were on the floor. "Weapons," I said, in a voice that was a little strained.

"Leave them," Victor said.

"No," I said.

Olaf simply started gathering them up and tucking what he could into his waistband. Edward had already added my backpack to his load. He picked up the leather jacket. "To hide my hands," he said.

I realized that his hands were spattered with my blood. I'd seen it moments before, but something about the sight of it, and standing at the same time, made the desert heat swim around me.

"Inside," I whispered, "need inside soon."

Edward didn't ask any questions, just helped me turn for the walk. Things in my stomach pulled wrong when I turned. My inside stomach rolled threateningly. I prayed that I would not throw up while my outside stomach was cut up. That would be very painful. I took shallow breaths through my mouth of the hot, still air, and concentrated on each step. Concentrated on making the movement as natural as possible for the cameras, and not moving so fast that I ripped the wounds open more. It was one of the most careful walks I could remember. I was concentrating so hard that I wasn't really aware of the building until Victor was holding the door for us. Then I looked up, and saw the sign that said *Trixie's*, which had a neon-formed seminude woman sitting in a huge martini glass. The sign was enough, but they'd felt compelled to put more neon in the window by the door that simply said, *Girls, girls, girls— all nude, all the time.*

I gave Victor a look as we walked slowly past him. He whispered, "The doctor is waiting inside, and this is where Paula Chu works. You can find a clue that lets you tell them to keep holding her without giving away your secret."

I couldn't argue with his logic, and the air inside the door was cool. At this point if I could lie down and have air-conditioning, I didn't care where we did it. I swallowed past the nausea one more time and let Edward help me into the cool twilight of Trixie's; all nude, all the time. At least hell was cool.

49

THE MUSIC WAS loud, though not the ear-jarring loud of some clubs. The music sounded tired, or maybe that was just me. My eyes adjusted and saw small tables scattered around a surprisingly large room. There was a main stage and smaller table/stages with seats around them. It was before seven o'clock, and men were already sitting in the darkened room. Women crawled around on the table/stages, as nude as the sign promised. I averted my eyes, because some views should be seen by only your gynecologist or a lover.

The main stage was empty, but huge. It had a small runway and a circular area with seats around it. I'd never seen a stage like it in any strip club, outside an old movie.

Victor led us through the tables, and we followed, because having me carried in front of the customers would not help our cover story.

Edward didn't try to comfort me; he just kept his arm flexed and solid under my double-handed grip and walked slowly. Olaf and Bernardo were still behind us. Victor got to a small door to one side of the main stage long before I managed to get there. The pain had gone past just pain and was dizziness. My vision was beginning to spot, and that was not good. How much blood had I lost, and how much was I losing?

The world narrowed down to concentrating on moving my feet. The pain in my stomach was growing distant, as my vision started to blur and run in light and dark streamers around me. I had a death grip on Edward's arm and trusted him to keep me from running into anything.

Edward's voice. "Anita, we're through. Anita, you can stop walking." He had to grab my shoulder, make me look at him.

I just stared at him, seeing his face but not understanding why the lights were brighter.

A hand touched my forehead. "Her skin is cool to the touch," Olaf said.

Edward picked me up, and that hurt, too, enough that I cried out, and the world swam in bright streamers. I concentrated on not throwing up, and that helped me through the pain. Then we were in a room that was dim again, but not as dark as the club. They laid me on a table underneath a light. There was cloth underneath me, and the crinkle of plastic underneath that.

Someone was fumbling at my left arm. I saw a man I didn't know, and said, "Edward."

"I'm here," and he came to stand by my head.

Victor's voice. "This is our doctor. He really is a doctor, and he's patched a lot of my people up. He's very good at sewing us up so we don't scar."

"This will sting a little," the doctor said. He put an IV in me and started fluids. I was in shock. I had only an impression of dark hair and dark skin, and that he was more ethnic than either Bernardo or me. Beyond that, he was sort of blurry.

"How much blood did she lose?" he asked.

"It didn't look like that much in the car," Edward said.

There was movement, and I started to try to look at it, but Edward caught my face between his hands. "Look at me, Anita." It was the way a parent would try to keep you from seeing the big bad doctor.

"Oh," I said, "that's not good."

He smiled. "What, I'm not interesting enough? I can get Bernardo for you to gaze up at. He's prettier."

"You're teasing me, trying to distract me. Shit, what's about to happen?"

"He doesn't want to give you painkillers, between the blood loss and the shock. If we were in a hospital with more equipment, he'd chance it, but without it, he doesn't want to take that risk."

I swallowed hard, and this time it wasn't nausea, but fear. "There are four claw marks," I said.

"Yes."

I closed my eyes and tried to slow my pulse, and fought off

the urge to get off the table and run for it. "I don't want to do this."

"I know," he said, but he kept his hands on my face, not exactly holding me but keeping me looking at him.

Olaf said, from somewhere off to the right, "Anita has healed worse than this. They did not have to sew her wounds in St. Louis."

"That's because she was healing too fast to need it," Edward said.

"Why can't she do that now?" he asked.

I'd fed off the swan king, and through him every swanmane in all of America. It had been an amazing rush of power. Enough to save my life, and Richard's, and Jean-Claude's. We'd all been terribly hurt. So much energy that even later when I'd been cut up much worse than this, I healed it scar free in record time, almost like a real lycanthrope. But I didn't want to explain that to strangers, so out loud I said, "Don't have the energy."

"She'd need a really big feed," Edward said.

"Ah," Olaf said, "the swans."

"Do you mean the *ardeur*?" Victor asked.

"Yeah," I said.

"How big a feed would you need?" he asked.

"She fed before she was hurt. I don't think sex in this condition would be that fun."

I seconded that.

Hands raised my shirt back, away from the wound.

I tried to see, and said, "What's happening? What is he doing?"

The doctor's voice. "I'm just cleaning the wound. Okay?"

"No, but yes."

"Just look at me, Anita." Edward's pale blue eyes were staring at me upside down. I'd never have said his face was kind, but now there was sympathy where I'd never thought to see it.

Hands began to clean the wound with something cold and stingy. "Crap," I said.

"I was told that she isn't to be scarred. If she moves this much, I can't promise that."

"Who made you promise that?" Victor asked.

"You know who," he said, and sounded frightened enough for me to catch it.

Edward pressed my face a little harder, "Anita, you need to hold still."

"I know," I said.

"Can you do it?" he asked.

"Who?" Victor asked the doctor.

"Bibiana."

"We need to hurry," Victor said, "my mother knows. Someone has talked to her. I'd rather not have Anita here when she arrives."

"Hold still," Edward said.

The doctor cleaned a little too deep, and I moved again, my hands convulsing on the table. "I can't not move," I finally admitted.

"Bernardo, Olaf," he said.

"Shit," I said. I did not want to be held down, but . . . there was no way I wasn't going to fight some. I couldn't not.

It was funny how none of us argued that we didn't want to be here when Victor's mom arrived. She'd almost rolled me under her power when I was well; this weak, this hurt . . . I didn't know if I could keep her out of my head.

Bernardo took my right arm and held it in two places. Victor took my other arm with the IV drip still in it. When I felt a hand on either of my thighs, I knew whose hands were left to touch me: Olaf.

"Shit," I said.

"Just look at me, Anita. Talk to me."

"You talk to me," I said.

I felt hands on my stomach.

"What are you doing?" And I hated how high and frightened my voice sounded.

"I'm going to start stitching. I am sorry to cause you pain." Then I felt the prick of the first needle pass, but it would not be the last. To avoid scars they'd use a finer needle, a finer thread. It would take more time, more stitches all together. I wasn't sure my vanity was worth it.

Edward talked to me, while the others tried to hold me still.

He talked about Donna and the kids. He whispered about missions in South America where I'd never gone with him, and he'd killed things I'd never seen outside books. It was more personal details than he'd ever given me. If I could just lie still, he'd keep whispering his secrets.

I kept waiting for the pain to dull, but some pain doesn't. This stayed sharp and nauseating, and the sensation of my skin being pulled together was more than my stomach could take.

"Going to be sick," I managed to say.

"She's going to be sick," Edward said, and the hands moved away. I tried to roll too fast onto my side, and lost the food I'd tried to keep down at the last murder scene. Vegas was turning out to be a real fun town.

The pain in my stomach was fresh and cutting somewhere in the middle of vomiting. The doctor wiped my mouth for me, then laid me back on my back. "She's pulled some of the stitches out."

"Sorry," I managed.

The doc sounded angry now. "I need her held down; she's still moving, and if she keeps throwing up from the pain, the stitches may not hold."

"What do you want us to do?" Victor asked.

I was just happy that he wasn't sewing me up. They could talk forever if he just didn't start again. I realized it wasn't just the pain, but the sensations.

"Hold her," the doctor said.

The fluids had helped clear my mind and my vision, so that I could see him clearly now. He was African American, hair cut close to his head, medium build, small sure hands. He was wearing a green surgical gown over his clothes, along with the gloves to match.

Edward's hands went from my face to pressing my shoulders to the table. Victor took my legs and let Olaf have the arm he'd been holding; when the man protested, Victor had said, "I am a weretiger; no human, no matter how strong, can match me."

Olaf didn't like it, but he put a hand on my arm, above the elbow, and Victor climbed onto the table to pin my lower body.

He was strong. They were all strong, but thanks to Jean-Claude's vampire marks, so was I.

Edward pressed down hard enough to hold my shoulders still, but I couldn't help but move as the needle began to move through my skin again.

"Scream," he said.

"What?"

"Scream, Anita, you have to let it out one way or another. If you scream, maybe you won't keep moving."

"If I start screaming, I won't stop."

"We won't tell," Bernardo said from the arm he was pressing, sort of desperately, into the table.

The needle bit into my skin, and tugged. I opened my mouth and screamed. I put all the fear, all the fight-or-flight into that sound. I screamed as fast as I could draw breath. I screamed loud, long, and let myself sink into it. I screamed and wept and cursed, but I stopped moving so much.

When the doctor was finished, I was shaking and sweat covered, and nauseous, unable to focus my eyes, and my throat hurt, but we were done.

The doctor switched out the empty bag of clear fluid with a fresh one. "She's in shock again. I don't like that."

Someone brought a blanket and covered me with it. I managed to say, in a voice that sounded so rough it wasn't mine, "We need to go. Bibi will be here, and Paula Chu needs looking at."

"You aren't going anywhere until you have another bag of fluids in you," the doctor said.

Edward was back at my head, smoothing down the edge of my hair, where the curls had stuck to the side of my face. "He's right. You can't go out like this."

"We will go and make sure Paula Chu does not get away," Olaf said.

"Yeah," Bernardo said, "we can do that."

They left, and another blanket went over me because my teeth had started to chatter. Edward touched my face again. "Rest, I'll be here."

I didn't mean to sleep, but once I stopped shaking, it just seemed so hard to keep my eyes open. Bibiana was coming, but there wasn't a damn thing I could do about it. I slept and let my body start to heal. The last thing I saw was Edward pulling up a chair so he'd be beside me and able to see all the doors at the same time. It made me smile, and then I was gone to the warmth of the blankets and the tiredness of my body.

50

I DREAMED, AND in the dream I walked down a white hall-way with doors on either side. I knew there was something behind the doors, but I didn't know what. One of the door-knobs rattled, and it frightened me. I started to move faster down the hallway and realized I was wearing some long, white dress. It was heavy and hard to move in. I'd never owned any-thing like it. Mirrors showed between the doors, and I caught glimpses of myself in them. Pale oval face, black hair piled high on top of my head, curls artfully around my shoulders. There was a feather in my hair, and jewels around my throat. This was not my dream.

The next mirror showed a second figure keeping pace with me. She wore red, the color of crushed velvet and rose petals. Gold flashed here and there as she moved. She'd put me in white and silver, with the flash of diamonds. She wore gold and rubies.

I forced myself to stop running down the hallway that never seemed to get any shorter. I faced one of the mirrors, and there she was looking back at me, standing just over the shoulder of my reflection.

"Belle Morte," I whispered, and it was as if her name con-jured her, because I felt her hand slide around my shoulders, draw my back against her front. She was a touch shorter than I was, but heels gave her height. Our hair was nearly the same shade of black, but where my eyes were deepest brown, hers were almost amber.

"*Ma petite*, you have been a very busy girl." She whispered it, and laid crimson lips against the white of my neck.

"No," I said.

She left only a perfect print of her lipstick on my skin. She smiled at me over my shoulder, putting our faces together. "Didn't you enjoy our time together, *ma petite*?"

I wanted to say no, but her ego was too large, and too strangely fragile for truths. If it was a truth. She'd come to me when I was unconscious, near death, and we'd had sex. She'd fed me enough energy to come to, and feed in the real world and save myself and Jean-Claude and Richard, though I wasn't sure how much she cared about our wolf king. But she had wanted to save me and Jean-Claude. I still wasn't entirely certain why she'd done it. Belle never did anything without a gain for herself.

Her hand slid down the white front of my dress until her fingers started to slide into the bodice. I grabbed her wrist to stop the movement. "If you'd wanted sex, you'd have put us in a bed. What's behind the doors?"

She pouted at me, that soft mouth, bowed and petulant. Through Jean-Claude's memories I remembered loving that pout. I remembered thinking that she had the most kissable mouth in the world.

"Open a door and see."

"I'm afraid."

"They are parts of yourself, Anita. Why be afraid of them?"

They were my beasts. "I just got sewed back together from one of them. I'd rather not repeat it."

She wrapped her arms tight around my waist; at least she wasn't trying to grope me. "You know why you couldn't heal it, don't you?"

"I didn't have enough energy."

"You have been feeding the *ardeur* barely, just enough to keep it sated but not enough to grow it stronger."

"I don't want it stronger."

"But I do, *ma petite*."

"I am not your *ma petite*."

"You are anything I say you are," and her eyes were drowning in amber fire.

I closed my eyes like a child hiding under the covers from a monster, but vampire gaze really can be avoided by just not looking.

Her voice whispered in my ear. "The Mother of All Darkness is trying to turn you into her instrument by raising your tigers. I don't know why that is so important to her, but I've felt what she's been doing to you. You must embrace the *ardeur* because it is a power she does not understand. You must grow strong in the parts of your power that are my bloodline, *ma petite*, or the Darkness will win you from me and from Jean-Claude."

"Why do you care?"

"Because She is trying to use your body as her vessel. I want her dead here and now, not escaped into you. She must die here, so you must be strong enough to keep her out. Embrace the *ardeur*, Anita, and you will have power such as you have never dreamt. I will help you."

"I don't want . . ."

She breathed in my ear. "I hear you thinking. You don't want to feed on your friend. I don't understand that; he's handsome enough. I think he would be skilled."

The thought made me open my eyes. "No"—my anger flared, and it felt good—"he's family; you don't do family."

"So prudish, but very well, the tigers will do."

"No," and I could look her in the sparkling eyes because my anger helped push that soft, insistent power back.

"You really can feed on anger, how interesting. It does not come from my bloodline."

The first spurt of fear washed through me and drowned the anger. That was something we hadn't wanted anyone else to know.

"It is dark, and the vampires rise where your body sleeps, *ma petite*."

"Stop calling me that."

"The tiger queen was kept away from you by your friend and her son, but now the vampires rise, and they will be naughty. If they are as naughty as I think they will try to be, I will give you the ability to fight back."

"What are you going to do?" I asked, and the fear was real. I needed to break the dream before she finished whatever she had planned.

"You cannot slip away unless I allow it, Anita, please. You are powerful, but you have not had even a lifetime to practice your skills. You cannot win against me, and without my help, you cannot hope to win against the Mother of All Vampires."

"What are you going to do?" I asked again.

"You don't trust me."

"No," I said.

"After I saved you and my Jean-Claude, still you doubt me?"

"I'm afraid of you."

She was suddenly in front of me, pressing us together, coming for her kiss. "Good, that's good. I would rather you love me, but if not love, fear will do."

"Machiavelli," I said.

"Where do you think he got it from?" she laughed, as she pressed her mouth to mine. Her voice eased through my head, or maybe it echoed in the hallway. "If they do not attack you, then my gift lies dormant. I can be no more fair than that, *ma petite*."

It was a kiss, but it was also heat. Vampires are supposed to be a cold thing, but she was not. She burned with all the life she had fed on for centuries, and she pushed that fire inside my mouth, into my body. One minute I was kissing Belle Morte, the next I was awake, gasping, staring up at a ceiling I didn't know, and had an arm across my shoulders. For a moment the dream and reality met, and then I saw the muscles and that it was male. It wasn't Belle, but what the fuck?

Edward was standing over me and whoever belonged to the arm. "You started to go into shock, and they said being close to the aura of another wereanimal like yourself would help."

I turned my head to find Victor blinking at me, as if he, too, had slept. From the feel of things, I wasn't sure he was wearing any clothes. "And this seemed like a good idea to you, Ed . . . Ted?"

"It helped, Anita. The moment he touched you, like this, it helped."

"See, you are one of us, Anita." It was Bibiana's voice.

Edward handed me the Browning BDM before he took the blankets off me, which let me know that things were not good.

Victor tightened his body around me, where he'd curled into place. The sudden tension let me know that he might not have known his mom was there either. Me in a drugged sleep was one thing, but why had Victor slept through it all?

Edward helped me sit up. "How does it feel?"

I waited for it to hurt. "Not bad." It felt way too good, actually. "What time is it? How long?"

"It's been four hours."

Victor's arm wrapped around my waist, and I had to admit that it felt solid and real and not bad. But then when I was channeling my beasts, touch was always good.

I could see more of the room now. Bibiana sat on a little couch that was to one side of the room. This was the first time I'd really seen the room. It was a little apartment complete with a round bed that would have looked fine in a red velvet whorehouse. The couch was the same red velvet. There were chairs and cushions and a small kitchenette. The table I was lying on was the dining table, with carved chairs pulled back from it to make room for the doctor and everyone else.

The doctor was still there. He came forward to check me out, and Edward let him check my pulse. I was shirtless, so checking the stitches was easy enough. He had to move Victor's arm to move bandages aside. "It's almost healed." He looked at me. "I saw that the claw marks had come from inside you, like it was clawing its way out; you're not human, are you?"

"I shared my energy with her," Victor said. He sat up on his side of the table, drawing the blanket around the bareness of him.

"But if she had not had her own white tiger for you to share with, it would not have worked," Bibiana said.

"Whatever," I said. I let Edward help me stand. I could stand. Yea!

Edward looked at me, then moved his hand away. I stood on my own. "Good, we're out of here then." He put my backpack over his shoulder. He'd already added some of my weapons to his visible arsenal. We started for the door.

Then I felt it, like a cold breeze down my back. I said, "Vampire."

Edward grabbed my arm and hustled us for the door, where Rick and some of the other white tigers blocked the way. We aimed our guns at them in unison. "We'll just say you jumped us," I said. "With all the dead cops in this town, they'll buy it."

"Anita Blake, so good of you to visit my little family."

I didn't even turn around. "Hi, Max. Thanks for the hospitality." Then I screamed at the men blocking the door. "Move, or bleed!"

Max's voice. "Move out of the marshals' way. She's a federal cop; you don't mess with the Feds. It's bad for business."

The tigers at the door looked to another part of the room. They were looking at Bibiana.

"I am master of this city, and I say get the fuck out of the marshals' way." His voice had gone ugly with rage.

The weretigers moved, a little.

"Keep going," I said, and we waited for them to move well away from the door. As they moved, I moved sort of with them, so I had my back to Edward and my empty hand on his back, so I could feel his movement and still watch the room. Edward would know that left him the door and the room beyond.

He opened the door with an audible click, and we eased through it. I looked away from the weretigers long enough to see Max in a doorway on the other side of the big bed. He was dressed in 1940s gangster chic, mostly bald, tall, but solid. If you didn't know what you were looking at, you'd say *fat*, but it was all hard and muscled. Bibiana was glaring at him.

"Thanks, Max," I said.

"Tell Jean-Claude that I know the rules."

"I'll do that." And Edward was through the door, and my hand on him took me with him. We were into the other room; all we had to do was get the door shut.

Bibiana had to have the last word. "You have slept with my son. Tell me, what did you dream?"

The question was so odd that it made me stumble at the doorway. "Anita," Edward said.

"It's okay," I said. I concentrated on the gun in my hand and watching the room. I kicked the door shut behind us, and we were suddenly in the dimness and noise of the club beyond.

Edward moved up beside me, both putting his arm around me and lowering my gun hand down to my side. He leaned over and whisper-shouted into my ear, "Ease down."

The club was crowded, mostly with men at the tables and stages. The only women were the waitresses and the dancers.

Edward started leading me through the crowd. He slipped into that half-drunk-boyfriend-who-brought-my-girlfriend-to-the-strip-club act like someone had turned a switch. He was suddenly a good ol' boy who was having a good ol' time. The best I could do was not look too uncomfortable under his arm and try not to let anyone bump the gun in my hand. Though no one noticed the guns once we were away from the door, or they pretended they didn't. I'd noticed that a black gun against black jeans in a dark club was pretty invisible.

I was still trying to keep the door in my peripheral vision, though I was pretty sure that neither Max nor Bibiana would want to mess up the front of the club. They'd hide the dirty laundry.

What had she meant about my dreams? I pushed the thought away and tried to push that itchy feeling between my shoulder blades away, too. I wanted to sprint for the far door, but we were pretending, and that means you blend in, so I pretended to help my drunk boyfriend through the crowd. Though I knew that Edward was watching everything and would go from this act to action in the blink of an eye.

A hand came out of nowhere and tried to grope my breasts. I had grabbed his wrist and twisted before I'd had time to think.

"Hey," he said, and his face had that soft, confused look of the very drunk.

Edward leaned over my head, leering drunkenly, "Mine," he yelled.

"Sure, man, sure," the drunk said, as if it had been Edward who'd protected my honor and not me. Maybe if I shot the drunk he'd look at me as if I were a real person, but that would probably be overkill for one attempted grope. It wasn't the grope, though, it was the attitude that the women weren't real; none of us in the club were truly people to most of this crowd.

I'd seen it with the female customers at Guilty Pleasures and how they treated the male strippers. Dancers weren't quite the same as real people, or you'd never be able to act like you do at a club. It was probably one of the reasons I had never been comfortable at one of them; even before I was dating a stripper, I never forgot that everyone was real.

We stopped at the little bar/gift shop area and bought me a T-shirt. It was white and had *Trixie's* in swirling script right across the breasts, but it was better than the black one with the nude girl in the martini glass on the front.

"Nice fit." This from one of the dancers who was wearing a short robe and, since it was open, proving that it was all she was wearing. She had short brown hair and an open, pretty face, like the high school sweetheart that everyone's supposed to have but never does.

"Thanks," I said. If the T-shirt had fit any tighter across my chest it would have ripped like the Incredible Hulk's pants.

She moved closer, stroking her hand down my side, not exactly touching my chest, but the edge of it all. "Come to the stage, I'll give you a lap dance for free." She gave a smile that managed to contain both innocent friendliness and the promise of something evil, hidden in the quirk of that one dimple and deep in those hazel eyes.

Edward drew me into his body with a slightly sloppy movement and grinned at the woman. "Sorry, but we gotta go. But next time, I'd love to watch."

She smiled at him, bright, lovely, and empty as a lightbulb. I had a smile like that for difficult customers. She switched to flirting with him, putting an arm as far as she could with the backpack in her way. "Promise."

"Oh, yeah," and he laughed.

The dancer leaned in and whispered, "Ask for Brianna. I'm here six nights a week after six."

I nodded. "I'll remember."

Her hand lingered down my arm until we actually held fingertips, as Edward pulled me toward the outer door. We got outside, and Edward kept up his drunk act for half a block; then he straightened and we could walk normally. "I know you attract wereanimals and the undead, but now human women. What was that all about?"

"Let's find a dark alley and you give me all my weapons. I'll re-arm and explain."

We did what I suggested. It was the part of town that had a lot of dark alleys. He handed me the first layer of holster, and the re-arming began. "If you can get a female customer to shed some clothes while you're playing with her, the men love it. You can make a lot of money."

"The old lesbian fantasy," he said.

"Yep." I had the Browning's holster with its extra ammo, and the big knife down the spine settled in place. My backpack next, tightened enough so it didn't move around.

"She seemed to like you better than she liked me," he said.

"You noticed that, too." I had the MP5 dug out of the backpack, where it didn't quite fit, and on the tactical sling around me. "I've seen it with some male dancers; even the straightest of them can get pretty disgusted with the way the female customers act. I imagine it's the same for the women with the male customers. If your experiences are bad enough, it can turn you a little bisexual."

"Interesting; does that go for some of the men in your life?"

"I think the sexuality of the men in my life was set before anyone of them started working as strippers. Besides, only Nathaniel and Jason actually strip, and Jason is just our friend in bed."

"What about Jean-Claude?"

"He doesn't strip anymore."

"He does get onstage, Anita. I've seen him offering kisses for money."

That was a fairly recent act of his, and the question made me look at Edward. "When were you in the club to see his act?"

He stepped out into just enough light that I could see that smile. The one he used when he knew something I wanted to know, but he wasn't going to tell me.

"Are you spying on us?"

"Not exactly."

"What exactly?" and my voice was just a little grumpy.

"I don't trust him, and just in case one day you decide you don't trust him either, I just want to know what's happening in St. Louis."

"Don't treat Jean-Claude like a mark, Edward." I had all my weapons in place and had stepped away from him, given myself a little room.

"Is that a threat?" he asked.

"You're the one spying on one of the loves of my life. I'm not coming into Donna's shop and pretending to be a customer."

He nodded. "Fair enough." But his voice was careful, cold.

I heard a car stop before the light hit the mouth of the alley. I shielded my eyes. Edward stepped back farther into the shadows. If it had been an ambush, I'd have died, and he wouldn't. There are still moments when his more standard training and my learn-as-you-go method show the holes in my education. I tried to fade out of the light and into the shadows, but the light followed me.

"Hands where I can see them, right now!" A male voice, very serious. Then belatedly, "Police."

Other way around would have been better, but I had already done what he wanted before he added it. I was pretty sure about the police part before he said it. I clasped my hands on top of my head without being told, then moved, slowly, so that the badge on its lanyard would catch the light, or that was the plan. I was carrying some serious, visible firepower. If I didn't know me, I'd be nervous, too.

Edward stayed where he was, invisible in the shadows. Hell, I knew he was there and had to stare to see him. How did he do that? But I had other things to worry about, like the nervous cop.

"Come out, slow."

I did what he said, hands still firm on my head. I did try to identify myself. "U.S. Marshal. I'm a U.S. Marshal." He didn't seem to have heard me the first time.

"On your knees, now!"

Either he couldn't see the badge, or the amount of weapons he could see made him blind to anything else. I guess I couldn't blame him. It was probably the MP5, or maybe the visible tac vest, or maybe the two handguns, or shit, all of it. I was loaded for monster, which meant I was way overloaded for human.

I dropped to my knees, trying not to hit too heavy; no need to bruise. I did keep trying to talk to him. "I am U.S. Marshal Anita Blake; I am serving an active warrant of execution."

"On the ground, now!"

I'd caught a glimpse of the gun silhouette aimed at me. I got on the ground, wondering what Edward was planning on doing. Of course, if he stepped out of the alley now, he might get shot. The cop was well and truly into making me safe to be around. Another person armed this heavily and, well, accidents happen.

The sidewalk was not as clean as I would have liked it to be against my cheek. I wasn't scared, and probably should have been. A good guy's bullet would kill me just as soon as a bad guy's. This was one of those moments when I wondered if the people who wrote the laws understood how it looked to be walking around with this much firepower on us. We were going to need badges on our tac vests or somewhere more prominent than normal, or some vampire executioner was going to get shot by the police.

I stayed passive under his knee, while he handcuffed me. He started patting me down and found the second badge next to the gun on my waist. He unclipped it and brought it out into the light.

"Shit," he said, with real feeling.

I did not say *I told you so*. I was still handcuffed, and he was still armed. I did try, one more time, to say, "I'm U.S. Marshal Anita Blake, I am with the preternatural branch, and I am serving on an active warrant of execution."

"You're hunting vampires down here?" he asked.

"That is my job, officer." I was really wanting to raise my cheek off the concrete to talk, but wasn't sure if he'd take that for me trying to get up. I did not want another misunderstanding.

He knelt again, but this time his knee wasn't in my back. "I saw all the weapons, and then you tried to hide." He uncuffed me, then stepped back from me.

"Can I get up?" I asked.

"Yeah."

I got up, carefully. There is always that urge after one of these misunderstandings to do something startling to the guy who just cuffed you and made you eat pavement. I fought off the urge because it can lead nowhere good.

He handed me my badge back. I took it and clipped it back next to the Browning. "My partner is down the alley. Marshal Forrester, can you come out where the officer can see you?" I wasn't sure this was what Edward would want, but we had badges, and when you have badges you have to play by at least some of the rules.

Edward came out with his hands very visible to his side and a little up, so they showed empty. He'd fastened his windbreaker with the big *U.S. Marshal* written across it. I didn't even know what had happened to the windbreaker he'd loaned me.

"Officer," Edward said in his Ted voice, and even managed a smile.

"Marshal," the uniform said. He'd put his gun up, but the holster was unclipped. "I'm going to check on the radio. Nothing personal."

"If I saw people with this much firepower, I'd check, too," Edward said, still easy and smiling. He so would not have checked; he'd have taken care of it himself, or ignored it as not his problem.

Officer Thomas, according to his nameplate, walked just a little away from us, without turning his back on us. He hit his shoulder mic and spoke quietly into it. He was far enough away that we couldn't quite hear him, which was fine. He was trying to get someone to vouch for us. As long as he didn't talk to Undersheriff Shaw, we'd be safe enough.

He made *uh-huh* noises; just from a distance you could tell he was simply agreeing. He took his hand off his mic and walked toward us. "You check out. Sorry about the misunderstanding."

"Don't worry about it," I said, and meant it. I was going to have to find someone to give a memo to about the thought that the new law on carrying a small arsenal on our person was going to get us vampire executioners shot.

Edward put his hands down and, still looking pleasant, said, "We could use a ride back to the station, though."

"No problem," Thomas said. He took a breath as if he was going to ask something, then stopped himself. I was betting he wanted to ask where our car was, but he didn't. It's both a cop and a guy thing to not ask too many questions. Besides, he'd already made me kiss pavement; he probably was going to try for best behavior.

"I call shotgun," Edward said.

"Fine," I said.

Something in that one word had let him know I wasn't happy. We just knew each other too well to hide much of anything. He looked at me, his face half in shadow and half in the light from a distant streetlight.

He called to Thomas, "Give us a minute." Then it was our turn to step far enough away from the officer to not be overheard.

I wanted to tell Edward about at least part of my dream, and ask what he thought about Bibiana asking about it. How had she known? What did she know? Had Belle Morte changed the dream, or was she in touch with the Vegas tigers? Cats were her animals to call, just like Marmee Noir. But metaphysics like this wasn't really Edward's forte. He wouldn't know more about this than I did. I needed to talk to someone who might. I needed to talk to Jean-Claude, alone.

"You all right?" he asked quietly, his back to Officer Thomas.

"Not sure. I need to ask Jean-Claude some stuff in private, soon."

"She asked you about your dreams."

I looked at him and realized that he had caught it and understood more than most. "I had a dream, and it was a doozy."

He smiled, "A doozy, okay. Can you wait to talk to Jean-Claude, or do you need me to entertain Thomas?"

I thought about that. "Let's get back to Olaf and Bernardo.

Let's see what's happening with Paula Chu and the case. I'll try to put the metaphysics on the back burner for a while."

"Okay, if you're sure."

"Am I sure? Not really, but I'm here with a badge; let's act like I'm a real marshal and not some freak."

He touched my shoulder. "Anita, this isn't like you."

"Yeah, it is, Edward. I'm wondering if I can do my job, or if the metaphysics is getting too deep for a badge."

"The metaphysics helps you be better at the job."

"Sometimes, but we've just spent four hours with me in a healing sleep wrapped around a naked weretiger, so that the other cops couldn't see that my own internal beast had cut me from the inside out. We had to take both you and me off the case while we did it. That's not good, Edward. Now it's full dark, and Vittorio is out there. We lost important time because we were trying to hide what I am."

"Then let's stop arguing about it and go to the station. Bernardo will catch us up."

"Don't you see, Edward, Ted, whatever, that for you and me for the last four hours, healing me, hiding me, was more important than the case. That's not how cops think."

"We think just fine, Anita."

I don't know what showed on my face, but he grabbed my arm. "Don't do this to yourself. Don't tear yourself down."

"It's the truth."

"It's only the truth if you buy into it. Yeah, we lost four hours, but you're healed, and we know that Max doesn't agree with what Bibiana is doing. We know that Victor isn't happy with his mother and sides with his father. Knowing the politics of a city's monsters is valuable, Anita."

I wanted to argue, and might have, but Thomas said, "Sorry to interrupt, but if I'm leaving patrol, I need to get you guys to the station, then get back."

"We're coming," Edward called. He still had my arm. "Do you need to call Jean-Claude now?"

I shook my head. "It can wait. We've lost enough time."

He looked at me a moment longer; I met his eyes clear and straight. He let go of my arm and stepped back, then turned back to Thomas all smiles. "Sorry, Thomas, didn't mean to keep you."

"It's okay, but I gotta answer to my supervisor, you know?"

"We know," I said. Actually, we didn't. One of the reasons the U.S. Marshals Service didn't like having us on their team was that we'd be grafted on without any extra support staff. Basically, we were marshals, but we didn't have to answer to their hierarchy much. The preternatural branch was almost a law unto itself. While the other marshals were filling out tons of paperwork every time they fired their guns in the line of duty, we were blowing people away with no paperwork required. Our warrants of execution were the only paperwork. They'd experimented with having some of us do reports, but the details were so grim, so disturbing, that some suit up the line decided the Marshals Service wasn't sure it wanted the preternatural branch's exploits immortalized on paper. In normal police work, reports are supposed to cover your ass, but sometimes when it's really bad, they can be used against you later. We'd never had to do reports before, and so far still didn't. That might change, but for now, it was a sort of don't ask, don't tell policy.

I sat in the back of the squad car musing on what it meant to have a badge when your job description hadn't changed. We were assassins. Legal, government-sanctioned assassins. Some of us tried to be good marshals, but in the end, the other marshals saved lives, and all we did was take them. In the end, all the badges in the world didn't change what we were and what we did. I rode through the darkened city until light hit and I saw the Strip rising over the buildings like some force of nature glowing against the night. We weren't headed that way, but I knew it was there, like being able to feel the ocean even though you can't see it.

Thomas drove us away from the bright lights, and that was about how I felt tonight, like I was getting pushed further from the light, further from what it meant to be human, further from who I thought I was and who I thought I'd be. I sat in the back letting Edward's and Thomas's soft voices wash over me. They were talking shop; all cops do it. Talk about crime or women, and with me in the car, they wouldn't do that.

Edward would see to it, and Thomas would still be on his best behavior.

I sat there and let my confusion wash over me until it was a kind of depression. I didn't know how to be a good cop and a good monster at the same time. My two worlds were beginning to clash, and I had no idea how to stop it.

51

EDWARD AND I got to flash badges and go down the corridor that held the interrogation rooms, but we heard the argument from around the corner. I recognized Bernardo's voice and that of another man. I caught words: "How do you know . . . You can't let her go . . . Why not?"

We came around the corner to find Detective Ed Morgan arguing with Bernardo. I hadn't realized that Morgan was a little under six feet until I saw him next to the very six feet of Bernardo. Always harder to get up in someone's face if you have to look up at them, but Morgan was trying. Olaf was leaning against the wall, slouching so he didn't tower over everyone, looking bored.

Morgan turned on us like a storm looking for somewhere to fall. He pointed a finger at us. "You know something that you're not telling us about Paula Chu."

"We just got here," I said. "We don't even know what the fight's about."

Olaf pushed himself upright and said, "They want to let the weretigers go, and Bernardo is trying to hold Paula Chu."

Bernardo looked at us, his eyes black with anger. The bones of his face tight with it.

"But he won't tell me why he wants to hold Chu," Morgan said, striding down the hall toward us. Edward and I kept walking, so we sort of met in the middle. He waved a finger in Edward's face, then mine. "And one of you told him to keep her here, but not why. Why? What are you holding back?"

The anger vibrated off him in waves. I had the thought, *I could feed on that anger. I'd feel better, and the fight would be over. No, bad, Anita, bad idea.* I tried to put my hands in my pockets, but had too many weapons in the way.

"Maybe it's the fact that she was the live-in girlfriend of the weretiger that went apeshit this afternoon," Bernardo said, coming up behind us all. Olaf trailed behind him.

"That's not enough to hold her," Morgan said.

"I know you can hold her for longer than this, Morgan," Edward said.

I had an idea. "What if we make a cast of the claws on all these tigers, match them to the wounds. We can let them go after that, if you want."

"We are not encouraging these people to shapeshift inside the police station, Blake. No way."

"They don't need to shift all the way, just the claws," I said.

He frowned at me. "What?"

"I told the ME that the claw marks were those made by the very powerful shapeshifters that can just put claws out and then back down, sort of like switchblades."

"We had the lecture on lycanthropes," Morgan said. "The powerful have two shapes: full animal and man-animal. And once they shift, they can be overcome by a desire for fresh meat and killing. They can't shift back for at least six to eight hours, and once they shift back, they are comatose for hours after that. I'm not setting weretigers loose in our station, when we can't guarantee that they'd even be thinking enough like people to let us take a cast of their claws."

"Trust me, if they can do the instant claws, then they're thinking just fine, and only the very new lycanthropes have the overpowering need to feed right after they shift."

"And I'm just supposed to believe you instead of our own experts," Morgan said, disdain thick in his voice.

"She's who I call when I'm stumped," Edward said.

I looked at him and tried to see behind that pleasant Ted face. "Thanks, Ted."

"It's the truth."

"I don't care that you trust her. *I* don't trust her. I don't trust any of you."

I said, trying for patience, "Your expert either hunts them or studies them academically, right?"

Morgan frowned, thought about it, then nodded. "Yeah."

"I live with two of them. Trust me when I say that I know shapeshifters better than your expert."

"So because you're fucking some shapeshifters, I should just trust you?"

I smiled, but it wasn't my happy smile, it was the one I did when I was trying not to get mad. "Yeah, actually, I know shapeshifters in ways that your expert couldn't imagine."

"I don't need to hear about your kinks, Blake."

I took that last step, invading his personal space. I stepped until either he had to back up or we'd touch. He stood his ground, so that we were a hairsbreadth apart. From any distance at all, you'd think we were touching.

Morgan blinked down at me. That blink was a nervous gesture; his tell, like in poker. He didn't like me this close, or . . .

I spoke carefully, letting the anger seep into my voice. "My kinks are none of your business, Morgan. Catching this bastard is. Do you want to help me catch him, or her, or do you want to piss and moan and criticize my sex life?"

"What am I supposed to think when you tell me you're living with two of them?"

"You're supposed to think that I am a valuable resource of information about a little-known minority in this country, and that my insight might be invaluable to this investigation." I spoke lower and lower, and watched him lean in to hear.

His face was almost touching mine when I finished. He had an odd expression on his face as he said, softly, "Invaluable."

I didn't kiss him, didn't touch him at all, but in that moment he surrendered to me, and I fed on his anger. One breath, it was inside him; the next, it was on my skin like a warm rush of air. I closed my eyes and breathed it in, and it was good, and I hadn't meant it.

Edward touched my shoulder and eased me back from the detective. Morgan stayed standing, staring at where I'd been, as if I hadn't moved.

Bernardo whispered, "Your eyes."

We heard someone behind us. Edward got his sunglasses

out of his pocket and handed them to me. I didn't ask why; the look on all their faces was enough. My eyes had gone all vampiry. I'd had it happen a time or two, but I'd always been able to feel it happen. I slipped the glasses on and realized that I hadn't done it on purpose, but Morgan was still standing there, staring at nothing. Not knowing what I'd done to him, or how, I didn't know how to bring him out of it. Feeding on someone's anger had never done this before. Shit.

Bernardo started walking down the hall. "Sheriff Shaw, how you doing tonight?"

Of course, it would be Shaw. Double shit.

"Bring him out of this, Anita," Edward whispered.

"I don't know how."

"Do something," Olaf said under his breath as he moved not down the hall but to block Shaw's view of Morgan and me. With his broad back in the way, I moved closer to the detective.

I said, "Morgan, Morgan, you in there?"

"Hurry," Edward said.

I snapped my fingers in front of his face. Nothing. In desperation I shook his shoulder, enough to bob his head, and said, harshly, "Morgan!"

He blinked and raised his head. He looked around as if he didn't expect to be standing in the hallway. I waited for him to accuse me of using magic on him, a serious breach of so many laws, but he just looked around us. "I'll get to work on those subpoenas."

"Subpoenas?" I said.

"Yeah, so we can get claw mark casts from the weretigers. Either that'll clear them, or we'll know we have our bad guy, or girl." He smiled at me, a real smile. Then he moved past us toward Shaw, who was finally getting past Bernardo.

"What the hell is going on here?" Shaw asked.

Morgan, still smiling, explained about the subpoenas and all of it.

"It's not possible for them to shift just claws," Shaw said.

Morgan corrected him and parroted back almost word for word what I'd told him.

Shaw looked past Morgan to me as he said, "And who told you all this?"

"Marshal Blake."

"She did, did she?"

Morgan nodded and went off to do what I'd wanted him to do, and what minutes before he would never have done at all. Mother of God, what had I done? And was it a good thing or a bad thing?

52

SHAW CAME DOWN the hallway, so angry it bordered on rage, and that little voice in my head said, *Food.* I could siphon off his anger and feed. Anger wasn't as complete a feed as lust and romance for the *ardeur.* It was having a snack but not a meal. It had been nearly twelve hours since I'd last fed the *ardeur.* It took energy to heal wounds, and though I'd slept in the shadow of Victor's energy, I hadn't fed off him. Shit, shit, shit, I needed to be away from the other cops, and soon.

"You did something to Morgan. I don't know what, or how, but you did something."

I moved a little behind Edward so there'd be no chance of Shaw getting too close to me. I didn't trust myself around all that rage.

"You can't hide behind Forrester forever, Blake."

"Think of it as more for your protection than mine," I said, smiling sweetly. Which was the wrong thing to say, and the wrong thing to do. Why had I done either? What was wrong with me?

His face began to mottle with his anger. His big hands folded into fists. "Are you threatening me?"

"No," I said, and tried to make that one word inoffensive.

His cell phone went off, and he stepped away, sort of sideways to us, as if he didn't want to give us his back, to bark into the phone, "Shaw, what?" He was quiet for a few minutes listening, then nodded and said, "We'll be there."

He walked back to us, the anger level lower, and his face edged with lines that hadn't been there a moment before. I was almost a hundred percent sure what the news would be.

"We have another dead stripper. It looks like it's this Vittorio again."

I didn't chastise him for not giving us the files on the earlier stripper deaths. The tiredness in his face showed just how much this case was taking out of him. "We'll follow you," Edward said.

"Fine." He turned and went back the way we'd come. We trailed behind him.

Edward dropped back and whispered, "Are you all right?"

"I don't know," I said.

He lowered his voice even more, "You fed on him somehow."

"His anger," I said.

"I've never seen you do that."

"It's new."

"What else is new?" he asked, and the look in his eyes wasn't one I liked seeing from Edward. He was my friend, my good friend, but there was still part of him that wondered which of us was better. I knew who was better—him—but he wasn't a hundred percent sure of that. There was a part of him that was no longer certain he'd win, and a bigger part of him wanted the question answered. Now he looked at me, not like a friend but like he was wondering how much more powerful I'd grown, and what that might mean if we ever hunted each other.

"Don't go there . . . Ted," I said.

He gave me eyes as cold as a winter sky. "You need to tell me about the new stuff."

"No," I said, "not with that look on your face, I don't."

He smiled then, and it was a smile to match the eyes. It wasn't that different from the way a shapeshifter looked at you when they were wondering what you'd taste like, except Edward's smile wasn't as warm.

We were out in the neon-lit dark, but it was still too dark for the glasses . . . had my eyes turned back? I waited until we'd followed Olaf and Bernardo to the SUV. When we were all in our seats, I lowered the glasses enough so I could flash them at Edward. "How do I look?"

"Normal," he said, and his voice was crawling back out of that Edward cold, to something that wouldn't frighten small children if they heard it.

I handed the glasses back to him.

He shook his head. "Keep them, just in case."

"What happened to mine?"

"Smashed." He started the engine and followed the line of police cars that were trailing out, lights and sirens filling the night, as if we were trying to wake everyone up.

"How did my glasses get smashed, and what happened to the windbreaker you loaned me?"

"Bibiana and her tigers wanted to put another weretiger in the bed with you and Victor. I didn't agree."

Bernardo leaned forward over the backseat, holding on to the seat as Edward took a corner a little fast. "What happened in the hallway, Anita?"

"She did something to the detective," Olaf said.

I glanced back at the big man, almost lost in the shadows of the car. "How do you know what I did?"

"I don't know what you did to him, but I know you did something. I saw your eyes change."

"You didn't say anything," Bernardo said.

"I didn't think we wanted the other policeman to know."

"Sorry that I blurted that out," Bernardo said, giving Olaf a look, then back to me. "But what did you do to Morgan?"

I glanced at Edward.

"Tell them, if you want to."

"You saw what I did."

"You made him agree with you," Olaf said.

"Yeah."

"How did you do it?" Bernardo asked.

"If I said *I don't know*, would you believe me?"

Bernardo said no, and Olaf said yes.

Bernardo frowned at him again. "Why do you believe that?"

"The look on her face when she realized what she had done. It frightened her."

Bernardo seemed to think about it, then frowned again. "She didn't look scared; nervous, maybe."

"It was fear."

"And you're sure of that?" Bernardo asked.

"Yes," Olaf said.

"Because you know Anita so well."

"No, because I know the look of fear on someone's face, Bernardo, man or woman. I know fear when I see it."

"Fine." Bernardo turned back to me. "Are you a vampire?"

"No." Then I thought about it. "Not in the traditional sense."

"What does that mean?"

"I don't feed on blood. I'm not dead. Holy objects and sunshine don't bother me. I go to church most Sundays and nothing bursts into flame." I couldn't keep the bitterness out of my voice on that last part.

"But you can cloud men's minds and make them do what you want, like a vamp."

"This was the first time for that."

The cars had stopped ahead, smearing the bubble lights into the mix of neon from the buildings. We were just off the main Strip, so that the brighter lights of it peeked over the buildings around us like some artificial dawn pressing against the night.

"We're here," Edward said.

"Which is your way of saying, *Stop asking questions*," Bernardo said.

"It is," Edward said.

"I think we have a right to ask questions when we're helping her cover up whatever she's doing."

I couldn't really argue that.

"You've both volunteered to feed her with sex," Edward said. "You might want to understand what you're volunteering for before you open your mouth." With that, Edward opened his door and got out. I didn't wait for an invitation. I got out, too, and left our backseat drivers to scramble out and follow us. Okay, Bernardo scrambled. Olaf just seemed to pour himself out of the car and be walking behind us. Funny that Bernardo was all spooked, but Olaf seemed fine with it. Of course, if he wanted me to overlook the whole serial killer thing, he'd have to be a little more understanding with me. Living vampire, serial killer; po-tay-to, po-tah-to.

53

THE BODY LAY in a broken heap in an alley behind the club she worked at, as if when they dumped the body they'd brought her home. The last body dump in St. Louis had been just outside the club where the dancer worked, too. But that one had been clean compared to this, just vampire bites. Death by exsanguination. This woman hadn't had time to bleed to death.

I realized that this one, like most of the body dumps in St. Louis, was in a place where shadows would hide some of the damage. Almost as if even the killer couldn't face what he'd done in bright light.

The woman's neck was at an angle so sharp that I could see spine poking against the skin of the neck, not quite through the skin, but close. The neck was ugly and wrong, but that was nothing compared to what he, or they, had done to the rest of the . . . body.

There were burns on half her face, and going down one side of the body. The skin was red and angry and blackened and peeling, and the other half of her body was perfect. Pale and young and beautiful, paired with the blackened ruin of the other half of her.

Bernardo took a sharp breath in and walked a little way down the alley. I forced myself to stay squatted by the body, and tried not to smell anything. The alley didn't smell that good to begin with, but usually burned flesh overpowers everything else. This didn't. The burns weren't that fresh, or they would've smelled more.

I swallowed hard and stood up, letting myself look at the people around me instead of the body. I had to keep thinking of it, really hard, as the body, because to humanize it at all would be too much. It wouldn't help me solve this crime to think about what this woman had gone through. Honest, it wouldn't.

Shaw stood there, staring down at the body, with a look on his face that I could only describe as lost. Morgan had rejoined us, telling us that he had the subpoenas in the works. He now seemed to think it was his idea, and was back to not being all that friendly with me. I was actually relieved. Whatever I'd done to him seemed to be short acting. Detective Thurgood had joined us in her ill-fitting skirt suit, sensible high heels, and bad attitude. But no one's attitude was particularly rosy, so it was okay.

I asked them, "Have the other bodies looked like this?"

"Not like this," Shaw said.

"No," Morgan said.

Thurgood just shook her head, lips in a line so thin that her mouth was almost invisible in her face. From the lips and the lack of talking, I was betting she was fighting off nausea.

"Were the other bodies burned?" I asked.

"The last two, but not nearly this bad," Shaw said.

"Are you even sure it's the same guy from St. Louis? He never did anything like this in your city," Morgan said.

"How do you know what he did in my city?" I asked.

"We talked to Lieutenant Storr, and he filled us in," Shaw said.

I didn't want to tell them that Dolph had not told me about the inquiry from Vegas. I didn't want to admit that someone who I was supposed to be working with had cut me out of the loop completely. So I pretended like this wasn't news and went back to trying to pretend that half the cops I worked with weren't treating me like a perp.

"Vittorio and his people didn't burn any of the bodies, but yeah, I'm pretty sure it's him."

"How can you be sure, if this wasn't his MO in St. Louis or any of the other towns?" Morgan asked.

Edward had moved up beside me, not too close, but close enough to let me know that he had understood that Dolph hadn't told me. That he understood how much that might bother me.

"Because this is what the Church used to do to vampires they could capture alive. They used holy water, which burns like acid. It was supposed to burn the devil out of them. But the only two I know of personally that were treated like this were both beautiful, very beautiful. It's a lot about the dark side of the Church; they say they did it to save the soul, but they usually pick victims that satisfy some need in them."

"Are you saying the Church was like a serial?" Thurgood finally spoke in a voice that was a little choked but still nicely angry.

"I guess; I just find it interesting that the only two men I know who were treated like this were very fair of face and body, and they were burned like this. I've never heard of a vamp that started life as plain that they did this to. I'd be interested to know if it was the same priest, or group of priests."

Thurgood again. "Are you saying that beautiful men were some priest's victim profile?"

"I guess two isn't a pattern, maybe a coincidence, but if I find a third, than yeah, that's what I'd be saying."

"That's a monstrous lie," she said.

"Hey, I'm Christian, too, but there are bad guys in every profession."

"What does it matter what some priest that has been dead for hundreds of years did or didn't do?" Bernardo said. He'd walked back to join us at the body. "We can't catch him; he's already dead. We need to catch Vittorio."

"The marshal's right," Shaw said. For a minute it was a little unclear which marshal he meant; then he said, "We need to catch the live ones."

"Are you saying that this vampire is trying to duplicate his own injuries?" Morgan asked. It was almost like he was ignoring them both.

"Looks like," I said.

"The others died of blood loss; there was no broken neck," Shaw said.

"Maybe they took pity on her," Bernardo said.

We all looked at him.

He nodded toward the body. "Maybe one of Vittorio's people put her out of her misery."

"Or maybe they got tired of her screaming," Olaf said.

We looked at him then; I think anything was better than looking at the body. Olaf was still staring at the body. If it bothered him, it didn't show.

"Or maybe she passed out from the pain, and it wasn't fun anymore," Shaw said.

"You don't pass out from this," Bernardo said. "You don't sleep. You don't rest. You don't do anything but hurt unless they can get enough drugs in you, and even then, sometimes the pain overrides it."

"You talk like you know," Shaw said.

"I had a friend that got burned bad." He looked away so that he wasn't looking at any of us. Whatever expression was on his face, he wanted to keep it to himself.

"What happened?" Shaw asked.

"He died." Then Bernardo walked away from us. This time he walked farther, pushing his way through the crowd, until he found a piece of alley to lean against. It put him closer to the reporters, who started shouting out questions when they saw his badge and the gloves on his hands. He ignored them all, just closing his eyes and leaning back. Whatever he was seeing, or trying not to see, cut out anything they could shout at him.

"Is he right," I asked Olaf, "you never stop screaming or pass out?"

"I do not know," Olaf said. "I do not like fire."

I realized that though it didn't seem to bother him to look at the body, he wasn't enjoying it the way he had the bodies in the morgue. He liked blades and blood, but not fire. Good to know, I guess.

I turned to Shaw. "We need to see the other photos, the other victims. Especially the last two."

He looked at me, frowning. I was getting a lot of that in Vegas. "There's nothing in the reports from St. Louis that you guys actually saw Vittorio. How do you know he's burned?"

I fought to keep my face even, empty, not to widen even my eyes, because I had forgotten. I knew Vittorio's fate from a letter from his lady love, who had left him after St. Louis, afraid for her life and her new lover's life. She hadn't been able to deal with his madness anymore. She'd even helped us in St. Louis, putting the bodies where we'd find them sooner, trying to leave clues. The letter had come to Jean-Claude, as Master of the City. It had never occurred to me to share it with the cops.

Jean-Claude had checked with the vampire council about Vittorio and had it confirmed. But again, I hadn't shared it with the police. It hadn't seemed important then.

I thought about what to say now. "I asked some of my vampire informants if they had any background on him." Even to me it sounded lame.

"What else did your vampires tell you?" Shaw said, and disbelief was firm in his voice.

"Just that the holy water burns are bad enough that he's probably unable to perform sex, so he puts all that energy into this."

"The vampires told you that?" This from Thurgood. She gave good disdain. The alley's shadows couldn't hide the scorn, or maybe it was just that with the short hair you could see it clear and hard. Or maybe I was just being overly sensitive.

"No, they told me the burns are bad enough he can't function. I made the logical leap about what that kind of anger might do to someone who was going to have to live forever in a body that damaged."

"You should leave the profiling to the professionals, Blake," Shaw said.

"Fine, but I've told you what I know."

"Why isn't it in the notes on the case?"

"Because I didn't find it out while the case was going on. In fact, for a while they said the case was closed."

"You told me why you were the only one who believed you hadn't killed Vittorio in that condo in St. Louis."

"No one we killed was powerful enough to be him," I said.

Shaw stepped close, looming over me. "You know what I think, Blake? I think you saw Vittorio. I think you saw him face-to-face. I don't think you learned any of this from your vampire friends. I think you learned it in person."

"Then why isn't he dead?"

"You're so sure you could kill him?"

"Fine, then why aren't I dead? Because I promise you this, Shaw, if we met face-to-face, it would be one or the other."

"Maybe he was one of your vampire lovers."

I looked down at the ground, trying not to get angry.

"You aren't going to deny it, then?"

I finally looked up and didn't try to hide that I was pissed. "I've tried to be a good sport here, but I've already told you, if reports are accurate, then he's not capable of sex. And trust me, if I'd seen him, I'd have tried to whack his ass."

"Intercourse isn't possible, but a girl as busy as you are should know there are other things you can do."

Thurgood and Morgan came up by Shaw. Thurgood said, "Sir, why don't we step back a little."

Edward touched my shoulder, which meant I'd probably made some involuntary movement toward him. Edward leaned over and whispered, "File a complaint."

I nodded. "Do you want me to file an official complaint for sexual harassment? Is that what you want?"

"File and be damned, but you know more than you're sharing with the humans, Blake."

"Even if that's true, Sheriff," Morgan said, now actually standing between us, "this isn't the way. We have reporters watching us."

Shaw glanced back, then forward. "I was willing to believe the rumors weren't true until I saw you hand in hand with one of Max's weretigers and then kissing his son, also a weretiger. You claim that you just met him, and just met Gregory Minns, but no one, no one, makes friends that fast. You managed to convince some of my best men that you're telling the truth. But I know"—he hit his big chest hard—"you fucked at least one of Bibiana's guards, maybe more. I know that you're no more human than the things that tortured that girl." He pointed dramatically at the body.

What he'd just said was wrong, odd. "Which guard did I fuck?" I asked, watching his face.

He seemed to hear himself and shook his head. "How do I know, all cats are gray in the dark," he said.

"How do you know I fucked anyone when I went to visit Bibiana?" I asked.

He fought to put his cop face back on, but it was shaky around the edges. "You came out holding hands with one of her tigers."

"Crispin's a stripper, like you said, not a guard. If you're going to accuse me in front of the other policemen, you need more proof than just me holding hands with someone."

"Maybe your reputation precedes you, Blake." He made it mean, but it lacked a certain edge.

I was pretty sure I knew now why Shaw had gone from distrustful to hostile, and it wasn't just issues with his wife. He'd heard tapes from our visit to Bibiana, which meant that someone had the apartments bugged. It had to be federal of some flavor, and they'd let Shaw hear just enough to smear my reputation to hell.

I tried to hear what it might have sounded like if all you had was the sound with Domino and Crispin and the rest. Would it sound like sex? Maybe. It would if that's the interpretation you wanted to put on it. You often find what you're looking for if that's all you look for; expectation becomes truth.

Bernardo had come up behind us all when it looked like it was going to get interesting. He'd heard, so he got to say, "What flavor of Fed are you friends with, Shaw?"

Morgan and Thurgood had moved back from him, as if he were suddenly contagious, and maybe he was. Some Fed had let him listen in to an ongoing investigation, and he'd just spilled the fact that they had successfully bugged Max's home to people that Shaw thought had fucked their people and were maybe more on their side than the cops.

"Shaw," Morgan said.

Thurgood just stood there, hands at her sides, not quite looking at him, as if that would make it better. If you don't see it, then it didn't happen, maybe.

He knew he'd fucked up; it was there in his eyes, caught in a line of light in all the shadows. He talked to us then. "I don't know what you're talking about, Marshals. With Blake's rep, why wouldn't I think she'd fucked every tiger in the place?"

He'd tried for mean, but I smiled sweetly at him.

"What's so funny?"

"You can still save this," I said, "just ask."

"I don't know what you're talking about."

He was going to pretend that he hadn't said too much. Thurgood and Morgan would probably back him on it. Did he trust that I'd play ball just because I had a badge?

"Ironic," I said, "you've just finished telling me I'm more on the side of the monsters, but you're counting on me being a good cop. You've accused me of fucking multiple weretigers, but you're depending on me honoring the badge above my supposed lovers. Or is it just that you'll pretend you didn't say it, and it will go away? I didn't think cops did that. I thought cops looked things in the face."

"You said it yourself, Blake; you're an assassin, not a cop."

I smiled, but this one wasn't sweet. "Perfect, Shaw, perfect."

Edward moved me back with a hand on my shoulder, so he was facing Shaw. "Bernardo, take Anita for a walk, that direction." He pointed away from the reporters.

Bernardo started walking, and I fell in step beside him. I half-expected Olaf to protest that he wanted to go on the walk, but he moved up to be at Edward's back. Good to know that we were there to back each other up. I wasn't sure about some of the Vegas cops anymore.

Bernardo led me past the body, and as if we'd agreed, we didn't look at it much. We just walked until the alley was a little darker without the lights they'd set up at the far end. Though what got me to stop was that the smell was less sour here, and a few more feet and we'd run into another group of cops holding the other end of the alley.

"That was interesting," he said.

I nodded. "Yeah."

"They've got the place bugged."

I nodded again. I tried to think of everything I'd said in the apartment. I couldn't remember all of it, but it had been enough.

"You're trying to remember everything you said, aren't you?"

"Yes."

"If all I had was the sound, I might think sex, and I'd so believe that you could shapeshift for real."

"Which will cost me my badge."

"Not until they're willing to admit how they got the recording," he said.

"With Shaw blabbing, who knows?"

"Do you feel conflicted?"

I looked up at him, studying his face in the dim light for what little it did me. "Do you mean, am I going to go tattle to the tigers?"

He shrugged.

"No," I said.

"You wouldn't want Jean-Claude's place bugged."

"No, but we sweep for listening devices on a regular basis. Max should, too."

"So you won't tell because it's sloppy business practices on Max's part?" He started to lean against the wall, then thought better of it and stopped in midmotion.

"Partly, but I am a federal officer. I do have a badge. Max is into criminal activities. How can I blow an operation that may save lives?"

"So, badge first," he said, softly.

I glared up at him, not sure he could see it in the dimness. "What, you believe what Shaw was saying, that I'm more loyal to the monsters than the police?"

He held up his hands as if holding me off. "That's not what I meant. It's just that if I had all your issues, I might feel conflicted."

I sighed. "Sorry, but I'm tired, Bernardo. I'm tired of having the other police think I'm one of the freaks." I shook my head. "Hell, I'm not sure they're wrong. I've begun to wonder if I can serve the badge and my other master at the same time."

He leaned forward. "Are you thinking of hanging it up?"

It was my turn to shrug. "I don't know, maybe."

"I can't see you not doing this, Anita."

"Neither can I, but . . . Shaw isn't the first cop to think my loyalties are divided. He won't be the last. I'm a walking sexual harassment suit lately. It's like sleeping with vampires and shapeshifters offends the police at some really basic level."

"Oh, I know that one."

I looked up at him. "What do you mean?"

He grinned, and I could see the flash of it even in the shadows. "It's the idea that if you prefer the monsters, then the rumor that they're better in bed than us mere mortals may be true. That would squick a lot of men, and a badge doesn't change that. In fact, maybe cops are more guy than most guys, so it bothers them more."

"That sounds . . . childish for a cop."

"I didn't say they were thinking it in the front of their heads, but somewhere in the back, where all those Neanderthal urges still live, they are wondering if just being human makes them less in every way than the monsters."

I tried to look past that flash of smile and see what was underneath, but it was too much shadow. I finally said, "Is that how you feel?"

He shook his head. "I had a lady leave her wereanimal lover for me."

I smiled; I couldn't help it. "That must have happened in the last two years because when we first met, you were a little insecure about my werewolf lover."

He shrugged and spread his hands. "What can I say, I am as good as I think I am."

That made me laugh. "Oh, nobody's that good."

"Are you saying I'm conceited?"

"Yep."

He laughed, then his face sobered, and he turned so that some stray patch of light caught his face. He was suddenly serious, painted in shadows and light like some abstract photo. "No brag, Anita, just fact. I'd love to prove that to you someday."

"I do not need to have the other cops hear that kind of shit from another man right now."

"I'm still willing to help you feed."

"I thought you were creeped by what happened with Morgan."

He frowned, thinking about it. "I was."

"I thought that would make you take the offer to feed the *ardeur* off the table."

He frowned harder, making creases between those big, dark eyes. "Yeah, actually I thought it had changed my mind."

"So, why the renewed offer?"

"Habit, maybe." But the frown stayed.

I had an idea, and not a good one. I did need to feed soon. In fact, I should have felt more energized, less "hungry," because Victor was supposed to have helped share his energy with me. But maybe all he'd been able to do was help me heal. I'd used up a lot of energy healing and fighting, and Belle Morte had been right about me feeding only the minimum to get by lately. We were also past the twelve-hour mark, when food was usually a good thing. Then I realized that I hadn't eaten any solid food, either. Shit, I knew better than that. One hunger did feed the other, and if I didn't eat enough real food, both my beasts and the *ardeur* rose faster and stronger. I knew this, but in the middle of a case, it was hard to find time to be human. Was I accidentally shopping for food now? Was I trying to bespell Bernardo without knowing it? It was the not knowing that creeped me the most.

"I need to get some food."

"You can eat after seeing that?" He didn't motion at the body; it was just implied really loudly.

"No, I'm not hungry."

"Then I . . ."

"If I don't eat solid food often enough, it makes it harder to control all the other hungers," I said.

"Ah," he said, then frowned. "I'm thinking something really inappropriate, even for me."

"Do I want to know?" I asked.

He shook his head. "You'd be pissed."

If it was bad enough that Bernardo wouldn't say it out loud, then it was bad. That he'd thought of it, then thought better of it, was a sign that something was wrong. I was betting that I was what was wrong. Was the *ardeur* calling to Bernardo? I didn't even know how to tell.

"Okay, let's get back to . . . Ted, and see if we can get the files we need from the locals."

"If you want to eat tonight, it has to be before we see more crime photos."

"Agreed," I said.

We turned and started walking back toward the knot of men and the remains of Vittorio's latest victim.

54

MORGAN WAS SAYING, "You'll have everything you need in a couple of hours, but we have to finish up here."

"Call someone," Edward said.

Shaw was a little bit down the alley talking to some of the crime scene techs. It was just Thurgood and Morgan to watch us come closer and frown. Morgan just seemed generally cranky, but Thurgood had passed to hostile.

"We'll get you the information, but you'll have to wait until one of us gets back to the station."

"Why?" Edward asked.

"Because you're going to have to borrow one of our computers, and someone's going to have to babysit you."

"You don't trust us with paper copies?" I asked.

"We don't trust you," Thurgood said.

"So much for my sisterhood."

"I am not your sister," she said. "Women like you make it harder for the rest of us to do our jobs. Women like you make it harder for us to be taken seriously by the other cops."

"Women like me," I said. "What does that mean?" I knew, but I wanted to see if she'd say it out loud.

"Anita," Edward said.

I said, "What?"

"You know what you are," she said.

Morgan said, "Thurgood."

"I know what you think I am," I said.

"That's enough," Edward said. "Both of you."

"You aren't my superior," Thurgood said.

"We'll see how our superiors like knowing that the Vegas PD is preventing us from doing our jobs," Edward said. His voice was low and cold, with an edge of warmth to it. He didn't lose control that much normally. Apparently, Edward hadn't been able to soothe things.

"We just don't want her and her lovers going through our files."

"Geez," Bernardo said, "because you're a slut, we're sluts, too."

"Shut up, Bernardo," Edward said. He started walking down the alley away from them and toward the reporters. It was where our car was parked, unfortunately. The rest of us trailed after him. We all pulled our gloves off at the entry to the alley and put them in the trash bin someone had set up for it. There was a uniform guarding the can to make sure no one tried to take a souvenir. You think I'm kidding, but people go nuts on serial cases. The glove would be on eBay that night, if they listed it right and it didn't get pulled before purchase; eBay tried to police itself, but people put weird shit up.

Another uniform held the tape up, and we were suddenly blinded by camera flashes and the lights from handheld shoulder cams. They'd moved all the bigger equipment back, but the mobile stuff had crept forward.

We ignored all questions. It wasn't our town, and one of the fastest ways to piss off the locals was to talk to reporters. Some of the uniforms had to actually wade into the crowd and make a hole.

The questions were about the murders at first, and then someone in the crowd recognized me. You'd think that a serial killer vampire would be more interesting than my love life with a different vampire, or maybe they just thought I might actually answer those questions.

"Anita, Anita, what does Jean-Claude think about you hunting and killing other vampires?"

I ignored it, like I had all the rest. Because I'd learned that no matter what I said, it would go worse than if I said nothing. No matter what questions I answered, the locals would see it and think I was talking about the case. They were already pissed at me; I didn't need to help them hate me.

Olaf moved to one side of me, blocking the microphones and the reaching hands. Edward moved in front of me, and

Bernardo took the back. They were protecting me from the press, the crowd. That wasn't right. I was either a real U.S. Marshal and an equal of the team, or I was just some stupid girl who needed protecting. Fuck.

The uniforms had to escort us to the cars. The press trailed us. Jean-Claude had recently appeared in some of the major celebrity magazines. Not on the cover or anything, but inside in the little tidbits. Pictures of what you're doing, profiled in one of the hottest vampire clubs in the country. I'd been caught twice by his side in pictures. Worse yet, he'd admitted that I was his girlfriend in an interview. The press seemed fascinated that a vampire hunter was dating a vampire. I'd turned down more interviews for that little factoid than most murders.

Why hadn't I warned Edward? Honestly, I thought a serial killer case would make the press ignore the stupid shit. Some were still yelling questions about the murder, but in among it, like raisins in a piece of toast, were questions about dating and vampires. That would really make the Vegas PD take me seriously. Oh, yeah.

We got in the car and started easing out through the snarl of official cars. Beyond that were news vans with huge science-fiction antennas. The cops had made a corridor between it all, for anyone who was trying to leave the scene. I think we were the first.

"If Randy Sherman's high priestess is home, let's go see her," Edward said.

"Yeah, but first food," I said.

"Food would be good," Olaf said.

"Fast or sit-down?" Edward asked.

"Fast will do," I said, "as long as there's meat involved." I'd learned that protein helped keep the beast at bay, more than veggies.

"Am I the only one who doesn't want to eat after what we just saw?" Bernardo asked from the backseat.

"Yes," Olaf said.

"I told you, Bernardo, I have to eat."

"When did you eat last?" Edward asked, as he moved into the bright and shiny of the Strip.

"About eight, for breakfast and the *ardeur*."

"More than thirteen hours," he said. "How are you feeling?"

"Like I need some protein," I said.

He handed me his cell phone with the screen already lit up. "Call the number, see if she'll see us, while I find someplace."

I hit the button and waited for the dialing to go through.

Edward didn't ask preference, just pulled into the first fast-food place he found. Burger King was fine with me; I like Whoppers.

I thought I was going to get a machine, but after seven rings a woman answered. "Yes," she said. Her voice sounded cautious.

"This is U.S. Marshal Anita Blake. I'm investigating the murder of one of your coven members, Randall Sherman."

"And all the others who died with him," she said, voice still soft.

"Yes," I said, "but I thought you might be able to help us with some questions."

"I know little about vampires and shapeshifters."

"It's more a question of magic, and what Randall Sherman would have done in a given situation."

"That is a different question from the ones the other police have asked me."

"Let me guess: they thought you might be involved just because you're Wiccan."

"Some of them are fine men, but some do not trust a witch."

"I'm getting a lot of that myself," I said, "and I've got a badge."

That made her laugh, just a little.

Edward got my attention, and motioned that I needed to know what I was ordering. I held up a finger.

"Do you know how to get here?"

"We've got the address."

"Then come, and we will talk about magic and Randall Sherman."

"Thank you, Phoebe Billings."

"You are welcome, Anita Blake." There was something to the way she said it that had a ring to it, almost of power.

I hung up before I could worry about it. One problem at a time. Edward handed the food around. Bernardo had gotten over his issues enough to get French fries and a fish sandwich, no sauce. I guess he didn't want the whole dripping thing after the murder scene.

I ate my sandwich, with its drippy sauce, and wasn't fazed. Once upon a time, I couldn't have eaten a messy sandwich after a scene like that. But that had been a while ago. Either you get over it, or you don't. I guess I'd gotten over it.

"You remember the address for the priestess?" I asked.

Edward just glanced at me, and the look was enough. Of course he remembered the address. And he'd been to the city before, and he was Edward, which meant he remembered his way around. He ate his very messy sandwich, one-handed, while he drove. He made it look neat, easy, while I fought not to dribble sauce down my vest with two hands and a bunch of napkins. The Coke was good, though, and it didn't drip on me.

My cell phone rang. I actually jumped, spilling just a little Coke. So much for being calm. I fumbled the drink into the cup holder, and the phone out of my pocket.

"Yeah."

"Anita, this is Wicked; we're on the ground in Vegas. Where are you?"

I tried picturing him on the other end of the phone. He'd be dressed in something designer and well fitted and very modern. His blond hair cut long, but neat. He was one of those utterly masculine men who also managed to be pretty, though handsome would probably have made him happier.

"Other than Truth, who else is with you?" I didn't ask if Truth was with Wicked. They had been the Wicked Truth for centuries. Two brothers, two mercenaries, two vampires, who were some of the best warriors I'd ever seen; but more impressive, they were some of the best warriors that Jean-Claude knew of in all of vampire land. Now they were our muscle, but they weren't food. I had crossed that line only once to save Truth's life, but other than that, I didn't touch them.

"Requiem, London, Graham, Haven, a few other werelions, and some werehyenas."

"Are the lions and hyenas muscle or food?" I asked.

"Muscle."

"Good," I said.

"Fill me in."

"Are you point man on this?"

"Jean-Claude put me in charge of the muscle."

"How did Haven take that?"

"Eventually the lion's Rex and I are going to have to have a talk, but not tonight." Translation: Haven had wanted to be in charge, but he'd bowed to Jean-Claude's authority, reluctantly.

"Wait, you said you're in charge of the muscle. What else is there to be in charge of?"

"Well," he said, "technically, I'm chief bodyguard on this operation, but Requiem is third in the power structure in St. Louis, so he's the boss."

"That makes sense, I guess." I wasn't sure how I felt about Requiem being in charge, or even in Vegas. He was a master vamp, but he was also moody as hell, and he and I weren't getting along exceptionally well lately. I'd tried to take him off the feeding list, and now here he was in Vegas when I was far from home and my usual men.

"You're thinking too hard, Anita," Wicked said. "Why aren't you happy that Requiem is here?"

I didn't owe Wicked the explanation about Requiem and me, so I said, "I told Jean-Claude not to send anyone who couldn't handle themselves in a fight. I've never seen Requiem fight."

"He does okay, but honestly, Jean-Claude didn't want to send us into another vamp's territory without someone who could be more diplomatic than the rest of us. Requiem's here just in case we need to negotiate with Max and his people."

"Like I said, Wicked, it makes sense."

"Now, ask me how Requiem likes his cover for this assignment."

"Cover, he's here to represent Jean-Claude's interests, right?"

"He is, but that's only if things go wrong with Max. He saw it as an insult to send this many people for him, but Jean-Claude explained we were worried about your safety with the serial killer."

"Makes sense," I said, not like I was happy.

"Max wanted to put his guards around you, Anita."

"No," I said.

"This is the compromise."

"What is?" I asked, and couldn't keep the impatience out of my voice.

"Requiem is being loaned out as a dancer to Max's revue."

"He hates stripping."

"Yeah, and I hate torturing people, but I'm really, really good at it."

I didn't know what to say to that, so I ignored it. "Couldn't we just tell Max that everyone's food for me?"

"We can explain bodyguards for you. We can explain a *pomme de sang* for you, that's London. But we can't tell Max that you need this much food, Anita. It would be too close to admitting you don't have control of the *ardeur*. Requiem is going to look over Max's club for a possible guest role, and if it works out for him, then Jean-Claude has agreed to the possibility of loaning other dancers occasionally."

"Max has been wanting that for a while," I said.

"Which is how we explained Requiem."

"Why are you telling me all this and not Requiem?"

"He's soothing hurt feelings among our little group."

"How pissy is everyone being?" I asked.

"You told Jean-Claude to pick people who could handle themselves in a fight, Anita. That means you've got a lot of big dogs in one room, fighting for the same bone. Requiem and I can handle it, but I thought you should know before you walk into it."

"Thanks," I said.

"Now, where are you?"

"On the way to the outskirts of town. We're going to interview a witness."

"Have you fed?"

"Solid food just a few minutes ago."

"But no wet food?" *Wet food* was slang among the vamps for blood, and lately I'd noticed some of them referring to my feeding on sex, or emotion, the same way. I couldn't argue with it, I guess, though part of me wanted to.

"No," I said.

"You're approaching fourteen hours between feeds, Anita. You got anyone with you, in case?"

I licked my lips. "I've got absolute-emergency volunteers, but no, not really."

"How far out are you, and what road?" he asked.

I asked Edward, who told me. I repeated it to Wicked. "This time of night, it will be quicker if one of us flies to you."

"Which of you can fly that well? And if it's Requiem, he can't come by himself. He may be okay in a fight, but okay isn't enough. I don't want any of our people alone until we get this bastard."

"You really think Vittorio will make a grab for your people?"

"Humor me. Who can fly well enough to come to me?"

"I can; Truth can. I'll ask the others." He put the phone on mute while I waited. Knowing Wicked, he'd simply ask London and Requiem which of them flew the best. I had no idea.

"We can't have Jean-Claude's men meet us at a witness's house, Anita. That'll just confirm what the PD thinks," Edward said.

"I know that, Edward. I'm hoping he'll catch up to us afterward."

"Are you planning on feeding before we drive back?" Olaf asked.

"No, but it's been fourteen hours, and I had to heal a lot of damage. That takes energy. He'll meet us, but it's just a precaution."

"I said I would feed you," Olaf said.

"Thanks, Olaf, I mean that, but . . ." I thought about what to say next. "I don't think we want our first time together to be in the back of a truck."

He seemed to think about it for a minute or two, then said, "More time and room would be welcome."

I had not agreed to have sex with Olaf, but I had managed not to crush his good intentions of sex that didn't involve killing his partner. Edward had asked me to try, and I was trying.

The phone came back to life in my hand. "I'll meet you."

"Wicked, I just finished saying, nobody travels alone."

"If they can take me on my own, then they're going to kill us all, so if I don't make it, you get out of town, and take our people with you."

"Are you setting yourself up as bait?"

"No; are you sure you're worried about my safety, or about the fact that you might have to have sex with me?"

"That's not fair, Wicked. You know why I'm trying to cut down."

"I know, I'm not on the meal plan. Turns out neither of the other two vamps are really that good at flying. And you scare my brother."

"I don't scare him; he just doesn't want to be food."

"You're right, he doesn't, but I'm right, too. You scare him, and Truth isn't scared by much."

"And you're not afraid I'll possess you, or something?"

"I'll take my chances. Besides, you said it yourself, you're in control right now. I'm just in case." He sounded bitter.

"Wicked."

"Yes."

"I don't need attitude from you, too."

"You can order me around, and I have to take it, but you can't dictate how I feel."

He had a point, but . . . What I wanted to say was that I didn't understand why all the men wanted to be on the feeding list. I had a mirror; I knew what I was seeing, and though I was pretty, and maybe even beautiful given the right outfit, it wasn't the same level of gorgeous of the men that were chasing me. But every time I tried to say it out loud, they accused me of being humble, or lying. I didn't think it was humility, just honesty.

"I will not apologize for trying to keep my list of feeds from growing, Wicked. Jean-Claude made noises that he didn't want to share me with any new men, and now he sends me nothing but, almost. What's with that?"

"He'd rather see you and all his people back home in St. Louis, alive, then save his ego."

"What's that mean?"

"It means that he agreed with your assessment of Vittorio.

If he sent anyone who could be used as a hostage and couldn't handle themselves in a fight, it might be too tempting. Especially considering that his choice of victims is mostly strippers, and most of your closest lovers are also strippers."

That made my stomach clench tight.

"I feel your fear, Anita. He thought you'd reasoned that out."

"I had, just not that bluntly."

"I'm surprised; usually you're the more blunt of the two of you."

"Yeah, yeah," I said, "but I don't feel like I'm about to lose control right now."

"Then I will ride back with you and the nice executioners. But when you get back to a hotel, you are going to have to feed on someone." His careful vampire voice held self-mockery, and I knew that wasn't how he felt. It was his tone when he was hiding what he felt. "But if you feed on vampire tonight, then in the morning you are going to have to pick one of the wereanimals, because vampire only works after dark when we're aboveground."

"I know that."

"I'm just saying, be thinking about your menu choices, because I do not want you losing control of the *ardeur* because you've gone squeamish."

"I am not squeamish."

"If you weren't, then you'd have already slept with Haven."

I let that go because he was probably more right than I wanted to admit. "How many other people with you are ones I've never slept with?"

"Most of the wereanimals."

I made an exasperated sound.

"Anita, you said not to send anyone that you'd care about too much, and only to send people that could fight. That cuts out most of your regulars. Either they mean too much to you, or they can't fight worth a farthing." For a moment there was an echo of an accent, mostly lost long ago. "Fight off the *ardeur*, and you don't have to touch us."

"It's not that, damn it. It's just that I'm trying to trim down the list of men, not add to it."

"I understand that, too, but that you not only can resist my charms, but are actively disturbed by the thought of sex with me, now that does hurt an old vampire's heart."

"Damn it, Wicked, don't make this about hurt feelings."

"I'll do my best."

"Wicked . . ."

"I will wait by the car, outside the house, so I don't compromise your investigation." He hung up.

"I didn't know Wicked was on the menu for you," Edward said.

"He's not."

Edward gave me a look, one pale eyebrow raised.

"Don't you start, too." I curled into the corner of my seat, crossed my arms, and let myself pout. Yes, it was childish, but every time I thought I was getting control of my powers, I was wrong. I did not want to add to the men I was sleeping with, honest. Why didn't I want to sleep with gorgeous men who were usually pretty good in bed? Because though I'd found I could have sex with this many men, I couldn't "date" them. I couldn't be their emotional rock. I was trying, and failing, but I seemed incapable of just fucking and feeding. Jean-Claude was right; I had to either stop needing so much, or stop trying for emotion with my sex. I just didn't have a clue how to do that. If it didn't matter emotionally, why have sex at all? Oh, because you are a succubus, and would die and drain the life out of people you loved, so they died first. Yeah, that was reason enough. I guess Wicked was right; I was still trying to pretend that it wasn't my reality.

"So a vampire is going to meet us at the witness's house?" Bernardo asked.

"Yes. He'll be waiting by the car when we get out."

"Won't his car be there, too?" Bernardo asked.

"He's going to fly," I said.

"Fly . . . oh, you mean *fly*." Bernardo actually flapped his arms a little.

"Yeah, but they don't actually flap their arms. It's more levitation than actually flying."

"Like Superman," Olaf said.

I glanced back at him in the darkened car. "Yeah, I guess so, like Superman."

"Are you feeling shaky enough to need them to meet us out here?" Edward asked.

"No, but he's right, it's going on fourteen hours. Let's just say I love you like a brother; I'd rather not have to explain that whole incest taboo to Donna and the kids."

"So, if you lose control . . ." He didn't finish the sentence.

"It could go badly," I said. I made myself sit up straighter. I would not pout in the corner, damn it.

"You mean, you could just lose control of this *ardeur*?" Bernardo asked.

"Yes," I said, and let the first hint of anger into that word.

"How much loss of control?" Olaf asked.

"Let's hope none of you find out."

"We're at the house," Edward said.

"Let's put on our cop faces," I said brightly, "and pretend that one of us isn't a living vampire that feeds on sex."

"Don't let the other cops make you feel bad about it, Anita."

"Edward, it *is* bad."

"Everything that has happened to you happened because you were trying to save someone else. The vampire powers are the same as a gunshot wound, Anita. You got both in the line of duty."

I looked into his face, studied it. "Do you really believe that?"

"I don't say things I don't mean, Anita."

"You lie like butter wouldn't melt in your mouth, Edward."

He smiled. "I don't lie to you."

"Really," I said.

The smile became a grin. "Okay, not most of the time, anymore." His face sobered. "I'm not lying now."

I nodded. "I'll take that."

"I feel like a voyeur," Bernardo said.

We both frowned at him, together. He raised his hands. "Sorry to ruin the touching moment, but honestly, if you want to have the heart-to-heart talks, let us get out of the car first. I'm not kidding on the voyeur part."

"Get out," Edward said.

He opened the door and did, without asking another thing. Olaf's face showed clearly in the sudden overhead light. He was studying us both, as if he'd never seen us before.

"What?" I asked.

He just shook his head and got out, too. We were left alone in the car. Edward patted my leg. "I meant what I said, Anita. It's like an injury, or a disease that you got on duty. Don't let the rest of them get to you."

"Edward, I've never touched Wicked intimately, and now he's speeding his way through the night to offer himself up for sex and maybe more."

He frowned at me. "What do you mean, maybe more than sex?"

"It's like when I feed off the preternatural men, they're under my power, or something. It's why his brother, Truth, doesn't want to sleep with me. He's afraid I'll possess him."

"Would you?"

"Not on purpose."

"How much of this can you control?"

"Not enough," I said.

We looked at each other as the overhead light dimmed and went out. "I'm sorry, Anita."

"Me, too. You know, Edward, if I can't travel without needing to feed, then I can't travel."

"We'll work it out."

"It's getting in the way of my doing the marshal stuff."

"We'll work it out, Anita."

"What if we can't?"

"We will," and he sounded very firm when he said it. I knew that tone; arguing wouldn't help me. It was the tone he used when he simply expected you to listen and do what he said.

I'd listen, but even the great Edward couldn't solve everything. I'd like to think he'd be able to help me keep working as a marshal while I had to feed the *ardeur*, but some things aren't fixable.

"Let's go question the witch."

"Most of them don't like to be called that."

He flashed me a smile as he opened the door, and the light

went on again. "I'll let you take the lead. You're our magic expert."

I realized he would let me take the lead not just because I was the magic expert but because he wanted me to feel in control of something. For a control freak like me, I didn't feel in control of very much lately. But I got out; we closed the doors, locked it, and walked through the Nevada dark to the house of Phoebe Billings, high priestess and witch.

55

WE STOOD IN front of a modest suburban house in a street full of other modest suburban houses. There were enough streetlights that we had a good view even in the dark. People forget that Las Vegas's famous Strip with its casinos, shows, and bright lights is only a small part of the city. Other than the fact that the house was set in a yard that ran high to rocks, sand, and native desert plants, it could have been one of a million housing developments anywhere in the country.

Most of the other houses had grass and flowers, as if they were trying to pretend they didn't live in the desert. The day's heat was browning the grass and flowers nicely. They must have a limit on how much they can water, because I've seen yards in deserts as green as a golf course. These yards looked sad and tired in the cooling dark. It was still hot, but had the promise that as the night wore on it would get cooler.

"A high priestess lives here?" Bernardo said.

"According to the phone book," I said.

He came around the car to stand on the sidewalk beside us. "It looks so . . . ordinary."

"What did you expect, Halloween decorations in August?"

He had the grace to look embarrassed. "I guess I did."

Edward walked to the back of the car and opened it. He reached into his own bag of tricks and got out one of the U.S. Marshal windbreakers.

"It's too hot for that," I said.

He looked at me. "We're armed to the teeth, and it's all visible. Would you let us in your house if you weren't sure we were cops? But I *am* running low on them. Someone keeps getting them all bloody."

"Sorry about that."

I tapped my badge on its lanyard around my neck. It was what I wore in St. Louis when the heat was too hot for a jacket. "See?" I said. "I'm legal."

"You look more harmless than we do," Edward said, and started handing out jackets to the other men.

Bernardo took his without comment and just slipped it on, pulling his braid out of the back with a practiced flip. Some gestures are not about being a girl or a boy, but just how long your hair is.

Olaf had his badge on a lanyard around his neck, too. It bugged me that we'd both done it, but where else are you gonna put a badge when you're wearing a T-shirt? I did have one of the clips and had put the badge on my backpack a couple of times, but I'd run into situations where I took off the backpack, and got separated from it and my badge. I had the badge on my belt by the Browning, because you always want to flash a badge when you flash a gun. Just good survival skills, and saves the other cops from being called by some panicked civilian who spotted it. You want your badge in the middle of a fight with police and bad guys. It helps the police not shoot you. Yeah, being a girl and looking so uncop helped the good guys know what I looked like, but accidents happen when you're drowning in adrenaline. Badge visible, at least the accident wouldn't be my fault.

Edward clipped his badge to his clothes so that he'd be doubly visible, and Bernardo followed suit. There were still moments when Edward could make me feel like the rookie. I wondered if there'd ever come a time when I truly believed we were equal. Probably not.

I wasn't really a fan of desert landscaping, but someone with an eye for it had arranged the cacti, grass, and rocks so that everything flowed. It gave the illusion of water, dry water, flowing in the shape and color of stone and plant.

"Nice," Bernardo said.

"What?" I asked.

"The garden, the patterns—nice."

I looked up at him and had to give him a point for noticing.

"It's just rocks and plants," Olaf said.

I took a breath to say something, but Edward interrupted. "We're not here to admire her gardening. We're here to talk to her about a murdered parishioner of hers."

"I don't think they call them parishioners," Bernardo said.

Edward gave him a look, and Bernardo spread his hands as if to say, *Sorry*. Why was Edward being so tense all of a sudden?

I took a step toward him, and suddenly I felt it, too. It was a faint hum up the skin, down the nerves. I looked around the door and finally found it on the porch. It was a mosaic pentagram in pretty colored stone, set in the concrete of the porch itself. It was charged, as in spell charged.

I touched Edward's arm. "You might want to step off the welcome mat."

He glanced at me, then where I was pointing. He didn't argue, just stepped a little to one side. A visible tension lifted in the set of his shoulders. Maybe Edward only thought he couldn't sense things. Being a little psychic would explain how he'd managed to stay alive all these years while hunting preternatural creepy-crawlies.

"I didn't see it," he said, "and I was looking."

"I didn't see it until you acted too tense," I said.

"She's good," he said, as he rang the doorbell.

I nodded.

Olaf was looking at both of us, as if he didn't know what the hell had just happened. Bernardo said, "A hex sign on the porch. Step around it."

"It's not a hex sign," I had time to say before the door opened.

A tall man answered the door. His dark hair was shaved close, and his eyes were dark and not happy to see us. "What do you want?"

Edward slid instantly into Ted's good-ol'-boy persona. You'd think I'd get used to how easily he became someone else, but it still creeped me.

"U.S. Marshal Ted Forrester; we called ahead to make sure Ms. Billings would be home. Or, rather, Marshal Anita Blake called ahead." He grinned as he said it and just exuded charm. Not that slimy charm that some men do, but that hail-fellow-well-met kind of energy. I knew some people who did it naturally, but Edward was the first person I'd known who could turn it on and off like a switch. It always made me wonder if long before the army got hold of him, he'd been more like Ted. Which sounded weird, since Ted *was* him, but the question still seemed worth poking at.

The man glanced at Edward's ID, then looked past him at us. "Who are they?"

I held up my badge on its lanyard so it was even more visible. "Marshal Anita Blake; I did call and talk to Ms. Billings."

Bernardo said, in a voice as cheerful and well meaning as Ted's, "U.S. Marshal Bernardo Spotted Horse."

Olaf sort of growled behind us all. "Otto Jeffries, U.S. Marshal." He held up his badge so the man could see it over everyone's shoulders. Bernardo did the same.

A woman's voice called from deeper in the house, "Michael, let them in."

The man, Michael presumably, scowled at us but unlatched the screen door. But before he let us cross the threshold, he spoke in a low voice. "Don't upset her."

"We'll do our best not to, sir," Edward said in his Ted voice. We went in through the door, but there was something about Michael at my back that made me turn so I could keep him in my peripheral vision. With everyone inside, I could put him at a little over six feet, which put him taller than Bernardo but shorter than Olaf. I had a moment as we all bunched into the foyer to see just how much smaller Edward was than the other men. It was always hard to remember that Edward wasn't that tall, at five foot eight. He was just one of those people who seemed taller than he was; sometimes physical height isn't what *tall* is about.

The living room was probably as big a disappointment to Bernardo as the outside had been because it was a typical room. It had a couch and a couple of chairs and was painted in a light and cheerful blue, with hints of a pinkish orange in the cushions and some of the knickknacks. There was tea set out on the long coffee table, with enough cups for everyone. I hadn't told her how many of us were coming, but there they sat, four cups. Psychics, ya gotta love 'em.

Phoebe Billings sat there, her eyes a little red from crying, but her smile serene and sort of knowing. My mentor Marianne had a smile like that. It meant she knew something I needed to know, or was watching me work through a lesson that I needed to learn very badly, but I was being stubborn. Witches who are also counselors are very big on you coming to your realizations in your own time, just in case rushing you would somehow damage your karmic lesson. Yes, Marianne drove me nuts sometimes with the lack of direction, but since one of the things she thought I needed to work on was patience, it was all good for me. Irritating, but good, or so she said. I found it mostly irritating.

"Won't you sit down. The tea is hot."

Edward sat down on the couch beside her, still smiling his Ted smile, but it was more sympathetic now. "I'm sorry for your loss, Ms. Billings."

"Phoebe, please."

"Phoebe, and I'm Ted; this is Anita, Bernardo, and Otto."

Michael had taken up a post near her, one hand on the other wrist. I knew a bodyguard pose when I saw it. He was either her priest or her black dog—though most covens didn't have one of the latter anymore. The covens that still had it as an office usually had two. They were bodyguards and did protection detail magically when the coven did work. Most of their work was of a spiritually protective nature, but once upon a time, the black dogs had hunted bogeys that were more flesh and less spirit. Michael had the feel of someone who could do both.

Phoebe looked from one to the other of us, then finally came back to Ted. "What do you want to know, Marshals?" There was the slightest of hesitation before she called us by our titles.

She poured tea into our cups. She put sugar in two, and left two plain. Then she handed them to Michael and directed where they should go.

Edward took his tea, as did the others. I got mine last. Neither she nor Michael got cups. I had absolutely no reason to mistrust Phoebe Billings, but unless she drank the tea, I wasn't touching it. Just because you're a witch doesn't mean you're a good witch.

She smiled at us all as we sat with our untouched cups, as if we'd done exactly what she'd known we would do. "Randy wouldn't have taken the tea, either," she said. "Police, you're all so suspicious." She dabbed at her eyes and gave a ladylike sniff.

"Then why did you give us the tea if you knew we wouldn't drink it?" I said.

"Call it a test."

"A test of what?" I asked, and I must have sounded a little more unfriendly than was called for, because Edward touched my leg, just a nudge to let me know to bring the tone down. Edward was one of the few people I'd take the hint from.

"Ask me again in a few days, and I'll answer your question," she said.

"You know, just because you're Wiccan and psychic doesn't mean you have to be mysterious," I said.

"Ask me your questions," she said, and her voice was sad and too somber to match the bright room we sat in, but then grief comes to every room, no matter what color it's painted.

Edward sat back a little more on the couch, giving me the best view of her he could give without changing seats. It let me know he was letting me take the lead, like he'd said in the car. Fine.

"How good at magic was Randall, Randy, Sherman?"

"He was as competent at magic as he was at everything he did," she said. A woman appeared from farther into the house. She carried a tray with another cup and saucer on it. She had the priestess's long brown hair, but the body was slender and younger. I wasn't surprised when Phoebe introduced her as her daughter, Kate.

"Then if Sherman started to say a spell in the middle of a firefight, he'd have a reason to think it would help?"

The woman poured tea for her mother from the pot and handed it to her. "Randy never wasted things, neither ammo, nor physical effort, nor a spell."

She drank from the cup. Bernardo followed suit and did a pretty good job of not leering at the daughter as she walked back toward the kitchen with the empty tray. Edward sipped his tea, too.

Phoebe glanced from Olaf to me. "Still don't trust me?"

"Sorry, but I'm a coffee drinker."

"I do not like tea," Olaf said.

"Kate could fix you some coffee."

"I'd rather just ask our questions, if that's all right." I meant that, but it's also been my experience that tea drinkers make bad coffee.

"Why do you think that Randy was saying a spell during a shooting?"

I glanced at Edward, and he took over. I just wasn't sure how much to tell her. "We can't really share too much information on an ongoing investigation, Phoebe. But we have good reason to think that Randy was saying a spell in the middle of a fight."

"Saying?" she asked.

"Yes."

"Randy was very good; he could have simply thought a blessing in the middle of a fight."

"What kind of spell would he have had to say out loud?" I asked.

She frowned. "Some witches need to speak aloud to help focus; Randy didn't. So if he was chanting aloud, then it was something ritualistic and old. Something he'd memorized, like an old charm. I don't know how much any of you know about our faith, but most ritual is created for the purpose of an individual event. It's a very creative, and fluid, process. When you're talking about set words, then it's more ceremonial magicians then Wiccans."

"But Randy was Wiccan, not a ceremonial magician," I said.

"Correct."

"What would he have known, or thought, to say in the middle of a fight? What would have prompted him to think of an old chant, a memorized piece?"

"If you have a recording of what he said, then I can help, or even some of the words, and I can give you some hint."

I looked at Edward.

"We don't have anything we can let you listen to, Phoebe;

I'm sorry." It was neatly done, not that we didn't have a recording but that we couldn't let her listen to it. I'd have just told her we didn't have one, which is why I'd let Edward answer.

She looked away from all of us and spoke in a voice that was shaky. "Is it that awful?"

Shit. But Edward moved in smoothly, even touching her hand. "It's not that, Phoebe. It's just that it's an ongoing investigation, and we have to be cautious what information we let out."

She looked at him from inches away. "You think someone in my coven could be involved?"

"Do you?" he asked, in a voice that was not the least surprised, as if to say, yes, we had suspected it, but we'd let her tell us the truth. I'd have sounded surprised and spooked her.

She looked into his eyes from inches away, and his hand on hers was suddenly more important. I felt the prickle of energy, and knew it had nothing to do with wereanimals or vampires.

He smiled, and pulled back his hand. "Trying to psychically read a police officer without permission is illegal, Phoebe."

"I need to know more than you're telling me to answer your questions."

"How can you be sure of that?" he asked, with a smile.

She smiled and put her teacup on the coffee table beside the rest. "I'm psychic, remember. I have information that you need, but I don't know what it is. I only *know* that if you ask the right question, I'll tell you something important."

I jumped in, "You know psychically."

"Yes."

I turned to the men with me and tried to explain. "Most psychic ability is pretty vague. Phoebe knows she has information that will be important, but there's a question we need to ask to spark that knowledge in her."

"And she knows this, how?" Bernardo asked.

I shrugged. "She couldn't tell you how, and I couldn't either. I've just worked with enough psychics to know that this is as good as the explanation gets sometimes."

Olaf scowled. "That is not an explanation."

I shrugged again. "The best we've got." I turned back to the priestess. "Let's go back to Marshal Forrester's question. Could anyone in your coven be involved?"

She shook her head. "No." It was a very firm no.

I tried again. "Could anyone here in the magical community be involved?"

"How can I answer that? I don't know what spells were used, or why you believe that Randy was trying to say something. Of course, there are bad people in every community, but without more information, I can't tell you whose talents this could have been." She sounded impatient, and I guess I couldn't blame her.

I looked at Edward.

"Do you have a priest's seal of the confessional?"

She smiled. "Yes, the Supreme Court upheld that we are truly priests, so what you tell me is covered under the law."

He looked at Michael's looming figure. "Is he a priest?"

"We are all priests and priestesses if we are called by Goddess," she said. It was a very priestess answer.

I answered for her. "He's her black dog."

Both Phoebe and Michael looked at me, as if I'd done something interesting. "They come here pretending not to know anything about us, but they've checked us out. They're lying."

"Now, Michael, you should know not to jump to conclusions." She turned those gentle brown eyes to me. "Have you checked us out?"

I shook my head. "I swear to you that other than finding out you are Randy Sherman's priestess, no."

"Then how did you know Michael was not my priest?"

I licked my lips and thought about it. How had I known? "There's a bond between most of the priests and priestesses I've met. Either they are a couple, or the magical working as a team just forms a bond. There's no feel of that between you and him. Also, he just screams muscle. The only job in a coven that is all about muscle, either spiritual or physical, is the black dog."

"Most covens don't have them anymore," she said.

I shrugged. "My mentor is into the history of her craft."

"I see the cross, but is it your sign of faith, or merely what the police make you wear?"

"I'm Christian," I said.

She smiled, and it was a little too knowledgeable. "But you find some precepts of the Church limiting."

I fought not to squirm. "I find the Church's attitude toward my own flavor of psychic ability limiting, yes."

"And what is your flavor?"

I started to answer, but Edward made a motion and I stopped. "It doesn't matter what Marshal Blake's gifts are."

I didn't know why Edward didn't want me to share with her, but I trusted his judgment.

Phoebe looked from one to the other of us. "You are very much a partnership."

"We've worked together for years," he said.

She shook her head. "It's more than that." She shook her head as if shaking the thought away. Then she looked back at me, and the eyes were no longer gentle. "Ask your questions, Marshal Blake."

"If Michael leaves the room, then we'll talk more freely," Edward said.

"I will not leave you with them," the big man said.

"They are policemen, like Randy was."

"They have badges," he said, "but they are not policemen like Randy."

"Does my grief make me blind?" she asked him.

His face softened. "I think, it does, my priestess."

"Then tell me what you see, Michael."

He turned dark eyes on us. He pointed at Olaf. "That one's aura is dark, stained by violence and evil things. If you could not feel him at your door, then you are head-blind with grief, Phoebe."

"Then be my eyes, Michael," she said.

He turned to Bernardo. "I don't see any harm in that one, though I wouldn't trust him with my sister."

She smiled. "Handsome men are seldom trustworthy with people's sisters."

He skipped me and went to Edward next. "That one's aura is dark, too, but dark the way Randy's was dark. Dark the way some people that have seen combat are dark. I would not want him at my back, but he means no harm here."

I have to admit that my pulse was up. Michael looked at me, and I fought not to look down but to meet those too-perceptive eyes.

"She is a problem. She is shielding, very tightly. I cannot read much past those shields. But she is powerful, and there is a feel of death to her. I don't know if she brings death, or if death follows her, but it's there, like a scent."

"Destiny lies heavy on some," Phoebe said.

He shook his head. "It's not that." He stared at me, and I felt him pushing at my shields. After what had happened with Sanchez, I did not want my shields down again.

"Stop pushing at my shields, Michael, or we're going to have words."

"Sorry," and he looked embarrassed, "but I don't find many who aren't Wiccan who can shield from me."

"I've been trained by the best," I said.

He glanced at the men with me. "Not by them."

"Never said I learned psychic shielding from the other cops."

"They aren't cops; there's something unfinished, or wilder, about you all. The only other cop I've met who felt close to you was one who had been undercover so long he'd almost become one of the bad guys. He got out, he got the job done, but it changed him. It made him less cop and more criminal."

"You know what they say," I said, "one of the things that makes us good at getting bad guys is that we can think like one."

"Most cops can, but there's a big difference between thinking like one and being one." He studied us all. "The badges are real, but it's like putting a leash on a tiger. It never stops being a tiger."

And that was a little too close to home.

56

MICHAEL WOULDN'T LEAVE. He thought we were too dangerous. We asked questions, but Edward didn't want to tell about the crushed jaw, and other things, so it was like walking in a pitch-black room. You knew what you wanted was in there somewhere, but without a little light, you might never find it.

I believed that Phoebe knew something, but we needed the right question to unlock it. She couldn't tell us what she didn't know we needed to know, or something like that. It was one of the most frustrating interrogations I'd ever done, though I let Edward take over before I completely lost patience. If I'd been alone, would I have told her everything I thought she needed to know? Maybe. I'd almost certainly have told her things that the other police wouldn't want a civilian to know. Did that make me a bad cop? Maybe. Did that make Edward a better cop? Probably.

I was actually pacing the far side of the room. She was a magical practitioner; for all we knew, she or Michael there could be involved. It wasn't likely, but . . . and yet I would have spilled the beans to her. I was second-guessing myself about everything. It wasn't like me, so if it wasn't like me, then who was it like?

Then I felt it: vampire. I just knew one was out there; I could feel it. "There's a vampire outside," I said.

I heard the guns clear the holsters. I had my hand on my Browning out, too, but . . .

"Is it a good vampire, or a bad vampire?" Bernardo asked.

Edward came close to me, where I stood next to the big picture window and its pulled drapes. He whispered, "Can you tell who it is?"

I put my left hand against the drape, hard enough to press it into the glass behind it. I concentrated, just a little, and thought at that push of energy. I had a choice of pushing back or simply opening enough to taste it. I was pretty sure it was Wicked, because whoever it was hadn't tried to hide his presence from me. Vittorio was able to hide not just from me but from Max, and if he could hide his energy signature from the Master of the City, then he sure as hell could avoid my radar.

But it was better to be sure, so I reached out a little more to that cool, wind-from-the-grave power. I touched that energy, found a taste of Jean-Claude's power. All the vampires bound to him had a flavor of him, like a spice that had touched all their skins. Then my power touched Wicked, and him I could feel, like the word should be in bold letters. I felt him look into the air, as if he should be able to see me hovering. If it had been Jean-Claude, I could have used his eyes to look where he was looking; with Wicked it was just a feeling.

"It's him," I said, low to Edward. I started to say, louder, "It's okay, he's on our side," but stopped in midbreath, because a different power had pushed through the opening in my shields. The opening I'd had to make to sense the vampire. I'd forgotten about Michael. I'd forgotten that he was a psychic and that his priestess had ordered him to sense my abilities.

There was a moment where I was caught between sensing the vampire outside and trying to push the witch out of my shields. It should have been simply a matter of closing the door that I'd opened, but something about Michael's power made the door wider. It was like I'd opened a door, and he turned it into a tunnel mouth big enough to drive a semi through. The door I could guard, but the other opening was too large. And all tunnels are dark.

Darkness boiled toward me. I could see her in my mind's eye like a cloud of night, ready to pour into that opening. Michael stood in that vision with me, if *vision* was the word for it. He could see it, too. He didn't waste time asking, *What is it?* He acted. He was the black dog, the black man, and he did his job. It is an old, old custom that no guest be harmed in your house.

A golden glow appeared in his hand and grew like lightning

to form a sword. He faced the coming dark with that burning sword in his hand. There was a second shadow over him, if a shadow could glow with light; it was larger than the man, and as the blackness framed him, rising up and up to eat the room I knew we had to be standing in, the glowing figure was more clear, and I saw for a moment the shadow of great, burning wings.

My first thought was demon; then I knew that was just the front of my brain. I knew what the demonic felt like, and this was not it. It was power, raw and real, and destruction was in that fire, but it was holy fire, and only the unholy need fear it. But it takes faith to stand that close to the flame and not be afraid. How strong was my faith? What did I believe in as the darkness swept upward and Michael stood there with his sword and the shadow of angels at his back? I had a heartbeat to think, *Oh, Michael, I get it.*

The man stood there between me and the dark, and I could not let him stand alone. I moved to stand with the man, Michael, and that glowing shadow, reciting as I moved, "Saint Michael the Archangel, defend us in battle"—the fire burned brighter against the dark—"be our protection against the wickedness and snares of the devil." It was like the fire in holy objects that came when faith was all you had against the vampires. "May God rebuke him, we humbly pray: and do thou, O Prince of the heavenly host . . ." It was as if I were seeing the source of every glowing holy object I had ever seen, burning before me. "By the power of God, cast into hell Satan . . ." I was at the edge of those burning wings, and for a moment I hesitated. The darkness swept up and over the man and the glow, and I knew that I had seconds to decide. What was I; whose side was I on? Was I holy enough to step into that light?

Marmee Noir's voice spoke in my head, or maybe the darkness all around us spoke. "A piece of me is inside you, necromancer; if you step into the fire of God, you will be destroyed like any vampire."

Was she right?

Then Michael the man stepped back, to put himself in harm's way again. He faced that overwhelming ocean of darkness, when it had given him the chance to be left out of it. It wasn't even thought; I moved forward, because he was trying to take my harm, my blow, my fate, and I couldn't let him do that. I stepped into that fire and expected to be blinded by the light, but it wasn't like that. It was as if the world were light, and I could only see the light, flickering and real around me. The man in front of me was real, and the fire was real, but . . .

"Necromancer, help me!"

I didn't understand what she meant, but it didn't matter. Evil always lies. I finished the prayer: "And all other evil spirits who wander through the world seeking the ruin of souls. Amen."

It was as if the power around us took a breath, the way you'd do before blowing out a candle. The power took a breath, then let it out, but this breath was like standing at ground zero of a nuclear bomb. Reality blew outward, then re-formed. I half-expected the house to be destroyed around us, but we were left blinking in the living room of Phoebe Billings's house. Not so much as a teacup had moved.

Edward was standing very close to us, but Phoebe was holding him back. Telling him, "Wait, Michael knows what he's doing."

I was standing behind Michael, as I had been in the "vision"; there was no burning sword in his hand, but somehow I knew, if he needed it, it would be there.

He turned around and looked at me with dark brown eyes, but there was a glimmer in them, a hint of fire, down in their depths. Not the light of vampires but of something else.

"Anita, talk to me," Edward said.

"I'm okay, Edward, thanks to Michael." And I meant the double entendre. I'd find a church and burn a candle for the Archangel Michael. It was the least I could do.

"Someone explain what just happened," he said, and he sounded angry.

"What did you see?" I asked.

"You looked up and saw something, something that scared the hell out of you. Then he"—and he shoved a thumb in Michael's direction—"went to stand by you. I tried to go to you, but she told me it wasn't a matter of guns."

"She was right," I said.

"Then every holy object in the room burst into flame."

"You mean they glowed," I said.

"No, flame, they burned."

"Bernardo panicked," Olaf said, "and threw off his cross."

I looked at the big man. I almost asked him how he justified faith in God with being a serial killer, but didn't. Maybe later if I wanted to piss him off.

"Once I lost the cross," Bernardo said, and I realized that he was the only one not standing close to us, "I saw . . . things."

"What?" I asked.

"Light, darkness." He stared at me from the edge of the couch. "I saw . . . something." He looked pale and shaken.

I started to ask *What?* again, but Michael touched my arm. I looked at him. He shook his head. I nodded. Okay, let Bernardo's vision alone. It had scared the shit out of him, and that made it private. He'd tell, or he'd get drunk and try to forget it. It's not every day you see demons and angels. Marmee Noir wasn't technically a demon, but she was an evil spirit.

"What is it that hunts you?" Michael asked.

"You saw it," I said.

"I did, but I've never seen anything like it before."

I stared up at him. "You stepped in her way, twice, and you didn't know what she was, or what she could have done to you?" I couldn't keep the astonishment out of my voice.

He nodded. "I am the black dog, the circle guardian. You are our guest, and no harm shall befall anyone in my care."

"You have no idea what she could have done to you."

He smiled, and it was the smile of a true believer. "It could not have touched me."

"Is he talking about . . . ," and Edward hesitated.

"Marmee Noir."

"Mother Dark," Phoebe said.

I nodded.

"The dark goddess is not always fearful; sometimes she is restful."

"She isn't a goddess, or if she is, there's no good side to her; trust me on that."

"This was not goddess energy," Michael said.

"Couldn't you see it?" I asked.

"I could feel it, but I concentrated on repairing the damage to our wards so that more would not follow her. I trusted Michael to chase out that which had crossed our borders and to keep you safe."

"That's a lot to trust someone with," I said.

"You've seen him armed for battle, Marshal; do you believe my trust is misplaced?"

I flashed back on the image of Michael with the burning sword and that shadow of wings over him. I shook my head. "No, it's not misplaced."

"Someone talk to me," Edward said, "now."

"I lowered my shields to see if the vampire was ours, and Michael here tried to taste my power by making the opening a little bigger."

"You mean like what happened with Sanchez earlier," Edward said.

I nodded.

"I did not damage your shields deliberately," he said.

"I believe you," I said. "And the Mother of All Darkness tried to eat me again. But Michael stopped her, cast her out."

"To hell?" Bernardo asked, still looking haunted.

I shook my head. "I don't think so, just out of here."

"How did it get through our wards?" Michael asked.

"I think I carry a piece of her inside me all the time now," I said. "Once you let me inside your wards, she had an in."

"You don't taste evil, Marshal."

"She did something to me earlier today. It's messed with my psychic abilities, opened me up, somehow."

"I think we can help there, and I would love to hear more about what she is and how you came to her attention."

"We don't have time for this, Anita," Edward said.

"I know," I said.

"The Darkness has tried to eat her twice in the same day," Olaf said. "Eventually, if Anita doesn't learn how to guard herself better, she will lose."

Edward and I stared at the big man. "How much did you see or feel?" I asked.

"Not much," he said.

"Then why are you the one encouraging me to get all meta-physical?"

"Marmee Noir wants you, Anita. I understand obsession." He stared at me with those cave-dark eyes, and I fought not to look away. I couldn't decide which was more unsettling, the intensity in his gaze or the lack of any other emotion. It was as if, in that moment, he was simply pared down to the need in his eyes. "She's chosen you for her victim, and she will have you unless you can fix what she damaged inside you, protect yourself better, or kill her first."

I gave a harsh laugh. "Kill the Mother of All Vampires? Not likely."

"Why not?" Olaf asked.

I frowned at him. "If she can do all this to me from thousands of miles away, then I do not want to see what she's capable of if I'm physically closer. All vampire powers grow with proximity."

"A bomb would do it, something with high heat yield."

I searched his face, trying to read something in it that I could really get a handle on and understand, but it was almost as bad as staring into the faces of the shapeshifters in their half-human forms. I just couldn't decipher him.

"I'd still have to get to the city she's in, and that would be too close. Besides, I don't know anything about bombs."

"I do," he said.

I finally got a clue. "Are you offering to go with me?"

He just nodded.

"Damn it," Edward said.

I looked at him. I shook my head. "I won't ask you to go."

"I can't let you go off alone with him to hunt her." He said it as if it were a done deal, a given.

I shook my head, and waved my hands as if erasing something in the air. "I'm not going either. None of us is getting any nearer to her."

"If you do not kill her first, she will surely kill you," Olaf said.

"Should we be talking about this in front of witnesses?" Bernardo asked. He had finally moved closer to us.

We looked at Phoebe and Michael as if we'd forgotten

them. I almost had. Edward never forgot anything, but as he looked at me, I realized that there was guilt in his eyes. I'd never seen that for anyone but Donna and the kids.

I reached out and laid fingers on his arm, a gentle touch. "You dying trying to kill Marmee Noir would not have helped me now. You'd be dead, and I'd be alone with these two."

That almost earned me a smile. "Or she'd be dead, and you'd be safe."

I gripped his arm, tight. "Don't second-guess yourself, Edward, you're not good at it. Certainty is all we have on shit like this."

He did smile, then. "Look who's talking, Ms. Doubting-All-My-Choices."

"Are you saying that thing has a physical body, on this plane, right now?" Michael asked.

I thought about the question, then nodded. "I've seen where her body lies, so yeah."

"I thought you'd never been physically close to her."

"Only in dreams and nightmares," I said.

Music started—"Wild Boys" by Duran Duran—and it still took me a minute to realize it was my cell phone. I fumbled it out of my pocket, vowing to pick a different song for Nathaniel to put into the phone so I could get rid of this one.

"Anita," Wicked said, "are you all right?"

"I'm fine."

"Are you being coerced?"

"No, no, I'm fine, really."

"I cannot get inside. I cannot even step on the doorstep." Wicked's voice sounded afraid; other than for his brother's life, I'd never heard him afraid.

"You don't have to, Wicked, just wait outside. I'll come to you in a little bit."

"I felt the Mother of All Darkness, and then I felt . . ." He seemed at a loss for words.

I almost helped him out, but he was a vampire, and it had been angels. I wanted to know what he'd sensed.

He finally spoke again, "When I first arrived, I could have entered the house with an invitation, but now I wouldn't dare. It glows like something holy."

"The priestess had to redo the shields," I said, "to keep out Marmee Noir."

"If anything goes wrong in there, I cannot help you."

"It's covered, Wicked, honest."

"I know you have Edward with you, but I am your bodyguard, Anita. Jean-Claude charged me with your safety. If I let you die here, Jean-Claude would kill me and my brother. He'd probably kill Truth first and make me watch, and then he'd kill me. And right this second, I can't reach you. Shit."

"Isn't that usually my line?" I said.

"Don't make a joke of this, Anita."

"Look, I'm sorry you can't enter past the wards, but we are all right, and you couldn't have kept me safe from Marmee Noir even if you'd been with me."

"And that is another problem. I could see her like some black storm towering over the house. She ignored me as if I didn't exist, but I felt her power, Anita. All the weapons training in the world won't stop her."

"Apparently, magic does," I said.

"Would the wards you are behind keep her out?"

"Maybe."

"But they would also keep out every other vampire, and Vittorio has wereanimals to send for you, so Jean-Claude tells me."

"I'm pretty sure of that, yeah."

"Then we need to be with you," he said.

"Agreed."

"But we need to keep the Mother of All Darkness from you, too. How do we do both?"

That he was asking me was not a good sign. "Wolves," I said, finally.

"What?"

"Wolf, she can't control wolf, only cats."

"What about the werehyenas?"

"I don't know, I've only made wolf work for me."

"We have Graham."

"Any other wolves would be helpful," I said.

"I'll call Requiem and see what we can find." Then he hung up. I was left to turn back to the room and say, "Um, nope, no idea how to explain it, so I'm not going to try."

Phoebe said, "You are wearing something that was supposed to help you against the Darkness."

I almost touched the medallion on its chain with the cross, but stopped myself in midmotion.

She smiled.

"Fine," I said, "but it doesn't matter, since it seems to have stopped working."

"If you will permit me to look at it, I believe it only needs to be cleansed and recharged." There must have been a look on my face because she added, "Surely whoever taught you to shield well enough to keep Michael outside taught you this as well."

"She tried, but I don't put a lot of stock in jewelry."

She smiled again. "Yet you believed in the piece of metal around your neck."

I wasn't sure if she was talking about the cross or the medallion, but either way, she had a point. "You're right, my teacher has talked to me about stones and stuff. I just don't believe in it."

"Some things don't require your belief to make them work, Marshal."

"I've got stuff on me," Bernardo said, "that just works, Anita."

"Stones?" I made it a question.

He nodded.

Phoebe said, "It is supposed to help you see your prey, but when you removed your cross, you had only things that made you see more into the spirit world and nothing to protect you from it."

He shrugged. "I got exactly what I asked for; maybe I just didn't know what I needed."

I looked at him. He'd put his cross back on, but there was still a tightness around the eyes. Whatever he had seen of Marmee Noir had spooked him. "I didn't see you for the mumbo-jumbo type," I said.

"You said it yourself, Anita; most of us don't have your talent with the dead. We get what help we can."

I looked at Edward. "Do you have help?"

He shook his head.

I looked at Olaf. "You?"

"Not stones and magic."

"What then?"

"The cross is blessed by a very holy man. It burns with his faith, not mine."

"A cross doesn't work for you, personally?" I asked, then almost wished I hadn't.

"The same man who blessed the cross told me I am damned, and no amount of Hail Marys or prayers will save me."

"Everyone can be saved," I said.

"To be forgiven, you must first repent your sins." He gave me the full weight of those eyes again.

"And you're unrepentant," I said.

He nodded.

I thought about that, that his cross burned with the faith of a holy man who had told him he'd go to hell unless he repented. He didn't repent, but he still wore the cross that the man had given him, and it still worked for him. The logic, or lack of it, made my head hurt. But in the end, faith isn't always about logic; sometimes it's about the leap.

"Did you kill him?" Bernardo asked.

Olaf looked at him. "Why would I kill him?"

"Why wouldn't you?"

Olaf seemed to think about that for a moment, then said, "I didn't want to, and no one was paying me to do it."

There, perfectly Olaf, not that he didn't kill a priest because it would be wrong, but because it didn't amuse him at the moment, and no one had paid him. Even Edward at his most disturbing wouldn't have had the same logic.

"We're talking in front of you too casually," Edward said. "Why?"

"Perhaps you simply feel at ease."

He shook his head. "You've got a permanent spell of some kind on the room, or house."

"All I have cast is that people may speak freely if they desire to. Apparently, your friends feel the need, and you do not."

"I don't believe confession is good for the soul."

"Nor do I," she said, "but it can free up parts of you that are blocked, or help soothe your mind."

He shook his head, then turned to me. "If you're going to have her do something with the medallion, do it. We need to go."

I fished the second chain from underneath the vest and all. I'd tried carrying the cross and the medallion on the same chain, but there were too many times when I needed the cross visible, and I got tired of people asking what the second symbol meant. The image on the metal was of a many-headed big cat; if you looked just right on the soft metal, you could discern stripes and symbols around the edge of it. I'd tried to pass it off as a saint's medallion, but it just didn't look like anything that tame.

I held it out to Phoebe. She took it gingerly by the chain with only two fingers. "This is very old."

I nodded. "The metal is soft enough that it bends with pressure, and some with just the heat of the body."

She started walking toward the door that her daughter had come through with the tea. I expected us to go all the way to her altar room, but she stopped us in a small, bright kitchen. Her daughter, Kate, was nowhere to be seen.

Phoebe answered as if I'd asked out loud, "Kate had a date tonight. I told her she could go after the tea was served."

"So she missed the metaphysical show."

"Yes, though many gifted in the area might have felt something. You do not call down such evil and such good without alerting those who can sense such things."

"I don't usually pick up stray stuff," I said.

"But you are not trained for it. Tonight's show would have attracted either the untrained, who cannot block it out, or the trained, who are open to the alert."

I shook my head. "Are we here for me to get lectured or to cleanse the charm?"

"So impatient."

"Yeah, I know, I need to work on it."

She smiled, then turned to the sink. "Then I will not waste more of your time." She turned the water on and waited a few moments for it to run, while her eyes were closed and she looked upward at nothing that I could see or feel.

She passed the charm and chain under the running water.

She turned the water off, then held the charm in her hands and closed her eyes again. "It is cleansed, and ready for use."

I gave her a look.

She laughed. "What, you were expecting me to put it on the altar and take you out to dance naked in the moonlight?"

"I've seen my teacher cleanse jewelry, and she does the four elements: earth, air, water, fire."

"I thought I would see if I could cleanse it doing something that you might actually do yourself."

"You mean just wash the bad stuff off?"

"I let the water run for a few minutes, as I thought, 'All water is sacred.' Surely you know that running water is a barrier to evil."

"I've actually never found that a vamp couldn't cross water to get to me. I've had ghouls run through a stream."

"Perhaps the stream, like your cross, needs you to believe."

"Why isn't the water like the stones, and works on its own?"

"Why should water be like stone?" she asked.

It was one of those irritating questions that Marianne would ask occasionally. But I'd learned this game. "Why wouldn't it be?"

She smiled. "I see why you worked so quickly and seamlessly with Michael. You both have a certain exasperating quality to you."

"So I've been told."

She dried the medallion carefully on a clean kitchen towel, then handed it to me. "This is not like your cross, Marshal. It is not an item that automatically keeps the bad things at bay. It is a neutral object; do you understand what that means?"

I let the medallion and chain pool into the palm of my hand. "It means that it isn't evil or good; it's more like a gun. How it's used depends on who's pulling the trigger."

"The analogy will do, but I have never seen anything like this. You do not know me, but I don't say that very often."

I looked at the dull gleam of the metal in my hand. "I was told it would keep Marmee Noir out of me."

"Did they tell you anything else about it?"

I thought, then had to shake my head.

"They may not have known, but I think as it keeps the Dark Mother out of you, it may also call things to you."

"What kind of things?" I asked.

"There's something very animalistic, almost shamanic, to the energy of the piece, but that's not quite it, either."

I wanted to ask, did it call the tigers to me? Was it the medallion itself that was causing me to be drawn to them? Would asking be giving her too much information?

"Why did you ask how good a witch Randy was?"

I felt the compulsion to simply tell her. She was right, I wanted to tell her, felt we should enlist some help from the local talent, but it wasn't my call. Edward was senior on this, and I bowed to his expertise. What could I say?

"The bad guys, or things, didn't go in for a killing blow. Their first strikes were to keep him from talking. He was a fully armed, fully trained, special teams guy. That's dangerous enough to just kill, but whoever struck the blows saw his ability to speak as more dangerous than the weapons."

"You asked me about a spell, but I can't think of anything that would force Randy to speak out loud. You saw Michael and what he did. His invocation was soundless."

"Yeah, but it takes concentration to do that kind of summoning, doesn't it? Could Randy call up that kind of energy in the middle of a firefight?"

She seemed to think about it. "I don't know. I have never tried to do a working in the middle of combat. We have other brothers and sisters who are soldiers. I can e-mail them and ask."

"Just ask if they've tried doing magic in the middle of a firefight. No details."

"I give you my word."

Had I said too much? It didn't feel like I had. "Let's say for argument's sake that your people tell you they can't do magic, silent and normal, during combat. What would come up against an armed unit, a SWAT unit, that Randy Sherman would have thought words, a spell, would be more effective against than silver-coated bullets?"

"Are you certain it was silver bullets?"

"It's standard ops that tac units like SWAT have silver-coated ammo to be carried at all times, in case one of the bad guys turns out to be a vampire or shapeshifter. They were backing up a vampire hunter; they'd have silver ammo."

"But you didn't check," she said.

I nodded. "I will, but I've seen these guys work, and they wouldn't make that big a mistake."

She nodded. "Randy would certainly not have made such an error."

"You haven't answered my question, Phoebe."

"I was thinking," she said. She frowned, rolling her lip under just a little. It looked like an old nervous habit that she'd almost lost. I wondered if it was her tell. Did it mean she was lying, or more nervous than she should be? Could she have some tie to what was happening? Well, yeah, duh, but it didn't feel right. But then, how much was her magic and the house itself with all its wards affecting my reaction to her? Shit, I wished I hadn't thought of that, or that I'd thought of it sooner. That I hadn't thought sooner meant I was being messed with again. Shit.

"The demonic, some evil spirits, as you saw with your Mother Dark." She frowned.

"You've thought of something," I said.

She shook her head. "No, it's just, it could be almost anything. You haven't even told me how they stopped Randy from speaking. I assume it was some kind of gag or damage that made speech impossible."

Honestly, for her to really be a worthwhile information source, she needed more clues, but Edward had expressly told me not to give her any. Crap.

"I know you don't trust me, Marshal."

"Why should I? You've got this house so wired with magic that you've taken most of our natural cynicism away. We've talked more openly around you than we should have already."

"Cynicism is not always conducive to studying and performing magic."

"But for cops, it's essential."

"I did not ward my house with the idea that police would come and question me."

"Fair enough, but how can we tell what was on purpose and

what wasn't? I can't even tell if we were talking too much before you redid the wards, or only after. If it was after, you did it on purpose to try to get us to tell you more about Randy Sherman's death."

"That would be a very gray thing for a Wiccan priestess to do, Marshal."

I smiled, and it was a real smile. "You did, didn't you? You used the emergency to tweak the spells so we'd be more chatty." I shook a finger at her. "That's illegal. Using magic on police in the middle of an investigation is automatic arrest. I could charge you with magical malfeasance."

"That would be an automatic jail sentence of at least six months," she said.

"It would," I said.

We stared at each other. "Grief makes me foolish, and I apologize for that, but I want to know what happened to Randy."

"No," I said, "you don't."

She frowned, and then her face clouded over. "Is it that awful?"

"You don't want your last"—I hesitated—"image of your friend to be the crime scene photos, and definitely not a visit to the morgue." I reached out to lay a comforting hand, but stopped myself. I was a little fuzzy on human psychic abilities. Did they grow with touch, like a vampire's? Mine didn't, but mine were pretty specialized. I let my hand fall back. "Trust me on this one, Phoebe."

"How can I trust you when you're threatening to put me in jail?" There was a thread of anger in her voice now. I guess I couldn't blame her.

I actually hadn't said I'd put her in jail. I'd just mentioned that I *could* put her in jail. Big difference, actually, but if she assumed it was a threat, fine. If it got me more information on the killings, or Randy Sherman, or anything, then even better. I wasn't here to win popularity contests; I was here to solve crimes.

There was movement in the doorway from farther inside the house. My gun was suddenly in my hand. Thought and action are one, grasshopper.

"It's my daughter," Phoebe said, but she was staring at the

gun. Staring at it like it was a very bad thing. I wasn't even pointing it at anyone, and already she was scared. From powerful priestess hooked up to deity and magic to frightened civilian in one move.

"Can I talk to you, or do you just want to shoot me?" Kate's voice held fury. A nice red wave of anger, tinged with fear, came off her. It made my stomach clench tight, as if I were still hungry, but I knew it wasn't that kind of hunger.

I stepped back from both the mother and the daughter. I put myself so that my empty hand would open the door, and I could get away from that tempting anger, if the hunger rose too fast and too hard to control. I had Wicked outside, and if I had to choose between the *ardeur* with him or psychic rape on a witch, then I'd choose sex and the vampire. At least he was willing.

"Are you afraid of me?" Kate asked, as she stepped carefully into the room. She'd added a short jacket over her jeans, and she had her hands stuffed in her pockets.

"Let me see your hands," I said, voice low and even.

She made a face, but her mother said, "Do what she says, Kate."

The girl couldn't have been much younger than me, five years or less, but she'd lived a different life. She didn't believe I'd shoot her, but her mother did.

"Kate, as your priestess, I tell you to do what she says."

The girl let out a breath, then took her hands, carefully, out of her pockets. The hands were empty. Her anger welled off her like some rich, thick scent, as if her rage would taste better than most.

"I won't let her put you in jail," she said, dark eyes all for her mother, as if I weren't standing there with a gun in my hand. I hoped I didn't have to shoot her; it would be like winging an angry Bambi. She just didn't know any better. The very naïveté of her helped me regain control of the hunger. I took deep, even breaths and thought soothing, empty thoughts.

"Kate," Phoebe said, "I let my grief get in the way of my better judgment. That is not the marshal's fault."

Kate shook her head hard enough for her brown ponytail to whirl around her shoulders. "No." Then she turned those angry eyes to me. "If I gave you a name of someone who could have done this, would you leave my mother alone?"

"Kate, no!"

"We don't owe him enough for you to go to jail, and what if he did have something to do with this? Then the next time he killed someone, it would be part of our karma, too. I don't owe him that."

"I was his priestess, Kate."

She shook her head again. "I wasn't." She turned back to me. "I'm dating a cop. He said something about the bodies being torn up, and not all of it was wereanimal. I mean, that always makes the news anytime you get a mutilated body. They always blame the local wereanimals first."

I just nodded. She was in a mood to talk, if I didn't spoil it somehow.

"But he said that some of the bodies were cut with blades. That the ME had never seen anything like it, and neither had you guys."

Her boyfriend was way too talkative, but if she'd give me the name, I wouldn't tell. I might try to find out who it was and tell him to keep his mouth shut, but I wouldn't rat him out. If she'd just say the name.

"Is that true?" she asked, at last.

"I'm not free to discuss an ongoing investigation. You know that."

"If it's true, then you need to talk to Todd Bering."

"He's off his meds again," Phoebe said. "You have to understand that. He's a good man when he takes his meds, but when he goes off . . ."

"What's he on meds for?"

"He was diagnosed with schizophrenia because he heard voices and saw things. He may have been mildly ill, but he is also one of the most powerful natural witches I've ever met."

"What does that mean, 'natural witch'?" I asked.

"Like you," Kate said, "your power just came, right? You didn't have to study, you could just do it."

"I had to have training to control it," I said.

"And that's what we tried to do for Todd." Kate didn't

sound angry now, she sounded a little sad. I was happy about the sad; it made the receding edge of anger less yummy.

"It didn't work?" I asked.

"It worked," Phoebe said, and she sighed, "but when he started getting sick again, he called up things that are never to be touched on our path. There are some things you cannot do and be a good witch."

I nodded. "So I've heard."

"He called a demon. It felt so awful, like you couldn't breathe past the evil of it," Kate said; she was looking at the ground, but her eyes were haunted, as if she could still feel it.

"I've felt the demonic before," I said.

"Then you know," she said, raising those haunted eyes to me.

I nodded. "I know."

"It had these big blade-like hooks for hands. As far as I know it's still inside the circle in his house, but if he gained control of it . . ." She shrugged.

I looked at them both. "The most likely scenario is that when it gets out of the circle, it just kills him and goes back to where it came from. How likely is it that this Todd Bering is powerful and sane enough to control something like this?"

Phoebe nodded. "He would be capable."

"You should have reported this to the authorities as soon as you saw it," I said.

"I thought, like you, that it would escape the circle and kill him. It would be instant karma. I didn't dream that he would be able to control it, or that he would attack policemen. Rumor says that it was that vampire serial killer and wereanimals. No one said demon or blades. The news reported that the police had been torn apart by claws and fangs."

We had a serious leak at the Vegas PD, and I would have to report it. Talking to your girlfriend is one thing; talking to the press is another. I couldn't take the chance that her boyfriend wasn't our Mr. Chatty.

"Blades, Mom, blades."

I didn't correct her that it was both. No need for me to share, too. "I appreciate the information."

"If you had simply told me that he was cut with blades—Randy, I mean—I would have told you about Todd."

"I know, but it's hard to know who to trust. I need his address."

They exchanged a look, then Phoebe got a notepad by the telephone and wrote it down for me. "May Goddess forgive me if he did these terrible murders."

I holstered the Browning and took the paper from her with my left hand. "I can't hide where I got the information from."

"They'll investigate us all!" Kate yelled, and took a step toward me. Her anger was just suddenly so there, so close, so . . .

I felt the door behind me opening, and moved so Edward could come through. "You guys all right in here?"

I shook my head, then nodded. "We have a crazy witch who raised a demon with blades for hands. The last time they saw it, it was inside the summoning circle. We need to see if it's still there."

"If it's still there, then he didn't do it," Kate said.

I gave her a look, and then had to look away, but sight wasn't what was sending her anger toward me like some sweet scent. My stomach clenched again, and I eased around the edge of the open door. "Just because it's in the circle now doesn't mean he didn't let it out and put it back," I said.

"You'll ruin our reputation. You'll ruin everything we've built; every good thing my mother has done will be lost in the news that one of our coven members raised a murdering demon!" Kate was yelling again and advancing on me.

I couldn't let her touch me because I wanted to feed. I wanted to suck all that anger off her. "I've got the address, and I need some air."

Edward gave me a look.

"It would be wicked of me to stay inside right now," I said softly.

"Go," he said, equally softly, then turned to calm the enraged girl and her sad mother.

Michael was being kept out of the kitchen by Olaf and Bernardo. No one was in handcuffs, yet.

I said as I walked past them all, "You should have told us

about Bering and the demon." I handed the piece of paper to Bernardo as I moved past.

He took it and said, "What is it?"

"The address to a demon with claws for hands."

"Anita," Olaf called.

I shook my head and was at the door. I felt the wards like a physical presence, almost like warm water or some thick bubble that clung to me as I moved. But it was designed to keep things out, not in, and I slid out of that warm, protective barrier to find the cool, desert night, and Wicked leaning against our car.

57

WICKED PUSHED AWAY from the car, almost coming to attention. Every inch of height was suddenly there, making the broad shoulders look even more impressive. He had a tan trench coat on over a suit of similar color. His blond hair was silvered with moonlight, the edges of it trailing over the shoulders of the coat. His face was almost painfully masculine, the moonlight and streetlights cutting the high cheekbones and dimpled chin into angles and planes, sharper and even more masculine than I knew was true. His eyes were blue and gray; in this light they were silver and gray. Those eyes widened as he felt me coming for him.

It didn't matter that he'd never been food before; it didn't matter that we'd never had sex. All my good intentions were gone by the time I crossed the yard and hit the sidewalk.

I heard the sound the key made to unlock the doors of the car, and glanced back enough to see Edward on the porch. He'd unlocked the car. Always practical, my Edward.

I turned back to the vampire, and he spoke in a voice that was already rough with the edge of my hunger. "Anita, what's wrong?"

I wanted to simply fall upon him like some beast. It was as if all the hungers I carried through the vampire marks, and my own magic, had surfaced in one huge swirling, drowning need.

I looked at that tall, handsome body and thought *food*. I thought *flesh* and I thought *blood*—and, only distantly, *sex*. I closed my eyes and tried to crawl into something resembling control. If I touched him like this, I wasn't sure whether I was going to try to fuck him or take a bite out of him—a real one.

The thought of sinking teeth into flesh until that hot, red liquid burst into my mouth . . . But vampire was cold food for that. The wind blew against my back, and I could scent Edward still on the porch. That was warmer. I started to turn around and stopped in midmotion.

I whispered, "Wicked."

"I'm here."

"Something's wrong."

"I feel your hunger. If you were a vampire, I'd take you to hunt now."

"Help me feed."

"Can you turn the bloodlust into the *ardeur*?"

"I don't know." And that was the truth. It scared me enough that I started taking my weapons off and dropping them on the ground. I called back, "Edward, get them after we're in the car."

"Done," he said.

I slipped the vest off last, and once its weight was removed, it was as if I could breathe better. My skin was running with heat, as if I'd burn when touched. Some lycanthropes spike a temperature before they shift.

"Anita," Wicked's voice said from much closer.

I opened my eyes and he was standing in front of me. This close the light fell full upon him, and I could see every line, curve, of his face. I could stare into those silvered eyes. Staring full into that face, inches from his body, and my gaze dropped to his neck, where the collar and tie kept it safe and neat. I stared at the side of his neck and searched for that pulse, but the skin was quiet. His heart didn't beat. I stepped back; this wasn't right. This wasn't what I wanted. I wanted something . . . hot.

I turned back to the house, the porch, the warmth. He grabbed my arm, pulled me hard in against his body. Something about the abruptness of it, the strength of it, startled me. I could think for a second. "Get me away from them, Wicked. Take me somewhere. Make me think of sex and not meat." I put my hands in the front of that button-down shirt and pulled, sending the middle buttons flying. I tore at his shirt until I could wrap my arms around his naked skin. The touch of that much muscled flesh helped me think of other things than what the blood in my friend's veins would taste like.

"Your skin runs hot tonight." He wrapped his arms around my waist, lifting me off the ground, and my arms slid to a part of his chest too wide for me to encircle. The next moment we were skyward. I felt the force of it like a solid push of something invisible against the ground, and my feet dangled in empty air.

Fear helped clear my head and tone down the hungers. I'd never flown by vampire, and I found that my fear of flying worked just fine this way, maybe worse than on a plane. I dug fingers into the shirt I'd ripped, hanging on for dear life. My pulse was choking me, and a scream bubbled in my throat. I pressed my face to his bare chest and fought that awful, perverse urge to look down.

I finally lost the fight, and did it. The desert stretched under us like some moving carpet. It wasn't as far down as I'd feared. I'd pictured tiny cars and toy houses, but we weren't that far up. Far enough that if he dropped me, I might only be crippled for life, not dead. Not a good thought. Then I realized the ground was getting closer.

"It's hard to land when you're carrying someone," Wicked said, his voice rumbling up through his chest and against my ear. "I'll roll to take the momentum."

"What?" I asked.

"Keep your arms where they are," he said. "You'll be fine."

The ground was coming very fast now, and I had seconds to decide what to do. I started to wrap my legs around him, but he said, "Don't tangle my legs!"

I stopped, but it left me with only my fear, and seconds to decide what to do with it. I closed my eyes to the rushing ground and held on to him.

I felt the jolt as his feet hit ground, and then he was rolling forward, letting the momentum carry us down and over. We ended on the ground, on our sides, with his arms wrapped around me, so that he took the impact. I lay there, trying to relearn how to breathe, wrapped in his arms, trapped against his body.

"Anita, are you all right?"

I wasn't sure how to answer it, but managed, "Yeah, yes." My voice sounded breathy and scared.

He eased off me, drawing away until he could look down at me. He studied my face, then smiled and laid his big hand against my face. "It has been a long time since I did that. I'm out of practice."

"Most vampires can't carry someone," I said, still in that frightened voice.

"I told you, Truth and I are very good at flying." He smiled again, and this time I knew what kind of smile it was. It helped that he leaned in toward me.

I stopped him with a hand on his chest. "I don't think I need to feed the *ardeur* now. You've scared it out of me."

He laughed, a deep masculine sound. Everything about him and his brother was so male. I tended to like my men with a little more feminine energy to them, but it was still a good laugh.

"Your skin is still hot to the touch, as if you're running a fever. Whatever happened back at the house has not left you. When the fear fades, the hunger will return." His face sobered. "You need to feed before that happens again, Anita."

My voice squeezed down again. "I wanted to go back to the house and feed, Wicked. I wasn't thinking that it was Edward, or people, just that they were warm."

He nodded, still above me, propped on one elbow, while his other hand traced the edge of my face. The touch was more comforting than sexual. "I need you to release the *ardeur* before the other hungers rise. You must feed."

"What's wrong with me, Wicked?"

"I don't know, but if you feed the *ardeur*, the other hungers will be satisfied."

"For a while," I said.

He smiled, but it was sad around the edges. "It's always for a little while, Anita. No matter what you need, you will need it again." He cupped the side of my face and leaned in again. He laid his lips against mine and kissed me for the first time. It was the most gentle of kisses, a bare touch.

He drew back, just enough to whisper against my mouth,

"Release the *ardeur*, Anita, feed, so you can get back to your police friends."

I thought about Edward and the rest going into a house with a demon, and me not being there to have his back. I would guard the back of any policeman that I went in with, but let's face it, it was only Edward that I'd never forgive myself for.

I stared up into Wicked's face. "How did you know that would make me do it?"

"You are loyal and honorable, and you would not leave your friends to find danger without you. Feed, and we will see you back to them."

"We?"

"I called Truth to join us."

I frowned at him, and it was so suspicious that he laughed again. "Why?" I asked.

"Because if we do it right, I won't be able to walk right away, let alone fly." The look in his eyes made me blush and drop my eyes, which put me looking at his bare chest where I'd torn his shirt. That embarrassed me more, and I was left pushing away from him. He let me sit up, but stayed on his side on the rough ground. I realized there was nothing but bare earth, sand, and rock as far as I could see. The side of a hill loomed over us, behind his back, and that was all. Well, not all, because above us was the night sky. It stretched perfectly black above us, with stars, so many stars. They seemed to burn with white light in a way that they never did in the city.

"How far out are we?"

"You mean from the city?" he asked.

"Yes."

"I don't know; it's hard to judge miles from the air."

"We're far enough that there's no light pollution."

He turned to gaze up at all that sparkling sky. "It is pretty, but then I remember when most of the sky was like this, almost anywhere you went. There wasn't enough light at night to hide the stars, no matter how big the city."

I stared up at the glittering blanket of stars and tried to envision a world where the night sky always looked like this, but couldn't do it. This was the sky over far desert, over open water, over places where people were not.

He touched my hand, a tentative play of fingers. I looked
down at him. He looked at our hands, where he traced fingertips
over my skin, a light, exploring touch. I could not see his eyes
or much of his expression. "Drop your control of the *ardeur*,
Anita, please. I am not powerful enough to force the *ardeur* to
rise, and you are not attracted enough to me for it to happen by
accident."

"It's nothing personal, Wicked. I see that you're handsome."

He looked up at me, and there was something I hadn't expected to see on his face: uncertainty. "Do you, Anita?"

I frowned at him. "I'm not blind, Wicked. I see what you
look like."

"Do you?" He looked back down, his fingers tracing up the
line of my arm. He found the hollow where the arm bends and
traced a single fingertip around that soft, warm spot. It made
me shiver, and my breath shook on its way out.

He smiled then. "Maybe you do." He kept playing over that
spot until I wriggled and told him, "That tickles now."

"I don't think it tickles," he said, and sat up. Sitting beside
me, he was still much taller. He put his hands on both of my
arms, and smoothed his hands up my skin. "Let me in, Anita,
let me inside."

The double entendre made me frown again, but his hands
on my arms distracted me from being unhappy with it. He'd
accused me of being squeamish on the phone; with his hands
playing on my skin and the weight of him so close, I realized
he was right. I'd fallen back into the habit of fighting the *ardeur*. I could go longer between feedings, so I kept pushing it.
I was still fighting it, even though I knew that Edward would
be calling the local police. They'd set up a raid on Todd Bering's house. They'd go in, and there'd be at least a demon,
maybe vampires, and they'd only have someone like Sanchez
with them for magic backup. Sanchez was a powerful psychic,
but he didn't know the dead, and I was pretty sure he didn't
know demons. If I wasn't there and it all went to shit, I'd always believe that I could have stopped it. I'd always believe
that I could have saved some lives.

All I had to do was have sex with the man beside me and
feed the *ardeur*, and then I could go save the day. It sounded

simple enough when you said it like that. Sex, feed *ardeur*, then hunt one demon, some vampires, and try to keep everyone alive. Yeah, simple.

But first, I had to let go. First, I had to be willing to be vulnerable with yet one more man. That part I didn't much like; in fact, I hated it. I didn't like being vulnerable, not to anything or anyone.

"I'm not powerful enough to get through your shields, Anita," he said in a quiet, neutral sort of voice.

Even now, I was back in control. I could just make him take me back to Edward and the others. But . . . what if I lost control in the middle of the raid on the sorcerer's house? What if the hunger rose in the car with Edward and Bernardo and Olaf? There were worse things I could do than have sex with my friends. I could tear their throats out and bathe in their blood, which was exactly what I might have done if Wicked hadn't taken me far away from them.

No, whatever was wrong with me, feeding the *ardeur* really was the lesser evil. A quick feed, and then back to solving crime. I looked at the tall, handsome man beside me and said what I was thinking. "I'm sorry that our first time has to be quick. You're worth taking the time, Wicked."

He smiled, and it softened his face. "That is the nicest thing you've ever said to me."

I smiled, too. "Once I release the *ardeur* after not feeding for this long, it can be a little rough."

"I'll be careful," he said.

"I don't mean that." I shook my head, and just took off the T-shirt that we'd gotten at Trixie's. I sat there in just the bra, in the strangely hot night.

Wicked gave me wide eyes.

"I mean we might end up ripping our clothes enough that we won't have anything to put back on."

He shrugged and started undoing his tie. "I'd have preferred a more sensual reveal, but you're the boss."

I sighed. "I wish that were really true."

"You say *Get undressed*, and I'm doing it; trust me, that makes you the boss." He had the tie off, and the trench coat went next.

"You wanted to get undressed eventually, right?" I asked, hands hesitating on my belt.

"I did." He took off the torn remnants of the shirt, and just seeing him bare from the waist up made me have to look away. That first nudity with someone I didn't know well always made me uncomfortable.

My rule used to be that if I was uncomfortable stripping, then maybe I should stop, get dressed, and go home. I'd told Jason, in St. Louis, that I was losing myself. Here I was, far away from home, and it wasn't the men in my life stealing me away from myself, it was the power inside me. And that, I couldn't run away from. It was like that old joke: everywhere you go, there you are. I couldn't leave myself behind, so I couldn't get away.

Hands came from behind to slide over my ribs, to hesitate at the base of my bra. I reached for the straps, to move them down my shoulders, but his hands got there first, and he lowered the straps, slowly, laying kisses on my shoulders as he bared them. His hands slid to the back of my bra, and unsnapped it. The underwire gave, and the whole thing slid down my arms, so that my breasts spilled out.

Wicked's hands slid over them, cupping them in his big hands, squeezing them, kneading them, exploring them. I felt myself grow damp, just from that. Those practiced hands drew a small sound from me. My hands slid to the unbuckled top of my pants, but his hands were there first, sliding down from my breasts, to unzip my pants and ease them open, so that his hand slid down the open front to brush the hair between my legs and reach for lower.

I laughed. "Your hand is too big, and the pants are too tight."

"We can fix that," he said, voice low and rough next to my ear. He pulled the pants down my hips in a harsh jerk that bared me to the tops of my thighs. My underwear had come down with the pants, so I was bare to the night.

His hand touched my bare ass, caressing, cupping, exploring. It sped my breath and put my pulse in my throat. "Wicked," I said.

"That's the way I want to hear you say my name." And his hands slid to the front of me as I knelt on the ground. His fingers slid between my legs, brushing that most intimate part, tickling, teasing, until I cried out. His other hand pushed the jeans down until he could spread my thighs wider, and those knowledgeable fingers could reach more, touch more, caress more.

He tried to reach farther between my legs, but the angle wasn't quite right. His hand was too big for the space he'd made. He made a low, frustrated sound in his throat and moved his hand to put a hand on either side of my jeans and jerk them down to my knees. Then he pulled me against the front of his body, and I could feel how large, how hard, how ready he already was, but his other hand went back between my legs. His finger slid inside me, and I cried out again. He pushed his fingers inside me, then slid them out, so he could play my own wetness against that small, sweet spot, near the front of me. His other arm tightened around my waist, pressing me against the hardness of him. It made me grind myself harder against him. His fingers played between my legs, caressing, teasing, until I felt the building weight of pleasure.

I breathed, "Close."

He changed the rhythm of his fingers, faster, over and over and over, until I gasped, "Wicked!" And his fingers spilled me over that edge, drove a scream from my throat, sent me spasming against the front of his body while his fingers played, and coaxed, and kept the orgasm coming, until I couldn't decide if it was all one big orgasm or if he was bringing smaller ones so fast, one after the other, that they blurred into one.

I screamed my pleasure to the shine of stars, and only after I collapsed in his arms did his hand stop moving, only then did he move me a little from his body, and I felt the head of him begin to push against me. My legs weren't working yet, so he held my weight with one arm around me, while the other helped him find the angle he was looking for. I said his name again, "Wicked." Then he laid me on the coat he'd spread on the ground and moved away from me.

"What's wrong?" I asked.

"Nothing," he said, "absolutely nothing." I lay there waiting for more of my body to work again, and watched him. He was fumbling through his clothes until he found a condom. I was on the pill, but the rule was that any of the men who weren't my main sweeties had to use a condom. If there was going to be an accident, it needed to be with someone I loved. That I'd forgotten that rule, and he'd had to remember it, said just how far gone I was tonight.

Wicked crawled back to me, the condom already spread down the length of him. He put his arm around my waist and lifted me off my stomach, so I was almost on my hands and knees. He went back to searching for that perfect angle; the feel of him brushing against me tentatively brought small eager noises from me. I said his name again. Then he found my opening and began to push his way inside, and I had no more air for words.

He spilled me forward onto the coat he'd spread, with my cheek pressed to the coat and the ground beneath, and the rest of me up, with him inside me. He pushed his way inside me until he couldn't go any farther, his body and mine meeting, stopping, wedded together. He hesitated like that for a moment, then he began to find a rhythm, in and out, pushing himself in long, slow, deep sweeps of his body, plunging into me until he couldn't go any farther, but gently, as if he were afraid of hurting me, then pulling out again.

I managed to say, "You won't hurt me."

"I'm bumping your cervix; I will hurt you unless I'm careful."

"I like it."

"What?"

"You've done the prep work, Wicked, it feels wonderful."

"Let the *ardeur* out, and I'll go faster." He kept that careful rhythm going, though I could feel the tension in his body as he fought himself.

"Harder," I said.

"Ardeur," he said, in a voice that showed the strain, like the trembling of his muscles, as he fought to be so careful of me. I didn't want him to be careful.

I did what he wanted, I did what I needed, I reached into that part of me that was the *ardeur*, and it wasn't a shield that came down, it was more like I simply stopped fighting it. The *ardeur* broke over us both in a rush of heat that made us both cry out.

"Fuck me, Wicked, just fuck me."

He stopped being careful, and used all that length, all that width, hard and fast, pounding himself into me until the sound of flesh hitting flesh was loud, and I screamed for him, shrieked for him, orgasming from the feel of him hitting that spot deep inside me, and having to stop, and still he wasn't done. He started again, this time a little more shallow, a little different twist of hips, and I felt the warm, heavy weight growing inside me again. I started to say his name, over and over, my words growing in the rhythm of my body and his, "Wicked, Wicked, Wicked, Wicked. God!" The orgasm screamed out of my mouth, left my hands scrambling at his coat and the ground underneath. If I could have reached him, I would have cut my pleasure on his skin, but I was left scrambling to find ways to get all that passion out.

He cried out above me, and his body lost that practiced rhythm and suddenly he was fucking me as hard and fast as he could. I'd thought he'd already done that, but he proved that even there he had been careful. I felt the impact of his body inside me, and without the *ardeur*, it might have been something besides amazing, but the *ardeur* took away anything but lust and the joy of it. He brought me one more time, and only then did he lose control. Only then did his body thrust that one last time deep into mine so that we cried out together, and I felt his body shudder inside me, and only then did I feed.

I fed on the thrust of his body deep inside mine, I fed on the feel of him spilling inside me, I fed on the strength of his body as he rose above me on his knees. I fed on his hand as it gripped my shoulder and braced him for one last shuddering thrust. It made me cry out again, and then he collapsed against my back. He caught himself with his arms, and was tall enough that he could bridge his body over mine, the dampness of his naked chest pressed to my bare back, his body still deep inside me, so that we knelt on all fours together, pressed as close as bodies could touch, our breathing thundering in our ears, and his heartbeat thudding against my back. His heart was beating for me now.

He pulled himself out of me, with a laugh and a shudder. I gave one last, soft cry, and collapsed to my side, with him curled around me. We lay there, relearning how to breathe, and only then did I look out into the night and see Truth standing in the starlight.

58

TRUTH STOOD THERE with his serious eyes, and his dark hair in contrast to his brother's. He stared at us with gray eyes and a face that was a match for his brother's under the partial beard that hid that nice jawline and let him be a little more invisible than Wicked.

I expected him to look away, our modest Truth, but he didn't. He looked at us, his face cold and pale in the starlight with that edge of dark hair. He looked at us, and there was something I'd never seen on Truth's face: hunger. He looked at us like a starving man, or maybe a drowning one.

Wicked ran his hand down the front of my body, uncurling my legs so that the front of me was bare to his brother's eyes.

I started to tell him to stop teasing his brother, but the words died unspoken because Truth was walking toward us. He threw his leather jacket to the ground, and his black T-shirt followed. Their upper bodies were almost identical, broad and strong; only a long curving scar, shiny with age, showed a difference. His hands were at his belt when I tried again to say something. It was when he dropped his gun, holster and all, on the ground without a backward glance that I knew something was wrong. Truth and Wicked were always careful of their weapons, always.

I started to say something, but his hands were at his belt and the pants were peeling back, and I found that it wasn't just their upper bodies that were almost identical.

I said, "Truth," and I felt it then. The *ardeur* wasn't gone. When I fed, it went back to sleep, always, unless it had spread to others in the room. But I had to touch someone to have it spread like that. Truth had been too far away, but even as I tried to think that logic all the way through, he was balancing on one leg to pull off first one boot, then the other, and he was in front of us, spilling his pants over his ankles and stepping out of them.

Still lying on the ground, held against his brother's body, I stared up at him. I had a moment to decide how I felt about that, and then he was kneeling beside us, reaching for me.

I managed to say, "Truth," and then he pulled me away from Wicked and spilled me to my back. I was left gazing up at him. He fell on top of me, putting his mouth to mine, and kissed me as if he would climb inside and flow down my throat. I kissed him back, kissed him with mouth and arms around his back, tracing his spine, spilling down to the swell of his body where waist ended and other things began. I couldn't reach beyond that; he was too tall.

He kissed me, long and hard, until soft, protesting noises spilled out of his lips, then he rose off me, too tall to both kiss me and make love to me. He spread my thighs with the strength of his hands. I had a moment to see all that hard, thick length, and then Wicked's hand was there, holding a condom.

Truth made a sound, low in his throat, but he took it and put it on. By the time he was finished he was making a sound that was almost a growl, low and persistent. Eagerness did not begin to describe that sound in a man's throat. He pressed all that safely sheathed length against me. I watched him push himself inside me, one inch at a time. Just watching him slide inside me threw my head back and made me cry out. I could see the night sky and a million stars dancing overhead as Truth pushed his way inside me.

He kept himself propped above me, back on his knees, so that almost the only thing that touched me was the long, slide of flesh that kept going in and out of me.

I cried his name to the stars, and he began to pound himself inside me, harder, faster, his breathing growing ragged as he began to lose his rhythm. I stared up at his body above mine, his eyes looking out into the night and not at me. I started to tell him to look at me, but the orgasm caught me unawares, and I was left screaming, shrieking, hands reaching for any part of him I could, tracing my pleasure in his flesh. He wrapped his arms around my waist and lifted my lower body off the ground as he made that last hard, shuddering thrust, burying himself as deep inside my body as he could, as he spilled inside me and the *ardeur* fed.

I fed not just on the sex and the soft sweat of him, but on the fear in him. He'd been afraid of the *ardeur* since Belle Morte gave him a taste centuries ago. So afraid, yet it had caught him again, caught him in the desert night under a shine of stars and the sweet scent of naked bodies. He collapsed forward, still on his knees, his hands locked around my body, his head falling forward against my breasts. I managed to touch his hair; it was finer than Wicked's, fine and silky under my hands.

I petted his hair while I learned how to breathe again, and my pulse climbed back into my throat, so that the clean, desert air was like champagne, cool in my throat.

His body started to shake, and I realized he was crying. I stroked his hair and said, "Truth, Truth, are you all right?"

He raised his face to me, tears glittering in the hard light of the stars. "I wanted to say no, but I couldn't. I could not resist you naked in the moonlight."

"Oh, Truth, I'm sorry," and I meant it. I knew what it was not to have a choice.

Wicked came to us, putting an arm across the other man's shoulders. "It's all right, she's not like Belle."

Truth pulled back from both of us. "The *ardeur* makes them all monsters in the end."

I sat up and, very carefully, very gently, went to him. He actually looked scared, and I wiped his tears away with my hands. He let me, but his eyes were wide, showing too much white, like a horse about to bolt. "Help me not to turn into the monster, Truth."

He frowned and looked at me, not like I was something to fuck, or something to be afraid of, but as if he were seeing me—whatever that meant.

"What do you mean by that?" he asked, voice still thick with tears.

"I mean, you tell me if I'm becoming a monster. You tell me if the power is turning me into something else."

"Jean-Claude will tell you that."

"He told me once that he trusted me to kill him if he became as heartless as Belle Morte. That he counted on my not letting him be a monster."

"Are you telling me to kill you if you lose control?" he asked, slowly.

I thought about it. "Not yet, but if the Darkness takes me, and there's no more me left, then yes."

"You don't know what you're asking," Wicked said.

"I know that everyone else loves me too much, but if all that's left of me is the *ardeur*, then I'm already gone."

The brothers exchanged a look, then gave me almost identical looks back. "How do we know when you're gone?" Truth asked.

I thought about that. "I don't know."

Truth touched a finger to my cheek and came away with a single trembling tear. "You mean it."

I nodded, and curled my arms around my knees, clutching me to myself. "I thought that it was the men. That living with Jean-Claude and all the others was making me lose control of myself, but they aren't here. It's me. It's me, Truth, don't you see? I don't know what's happening to me, and I don't know how to control it." I laid my head on my knees and cried. Knowing that I should get dressed, and there was a demon waiting, and I didn't know where Edward was, but all I could think of in that moment was that I didn't trust myself anymore.

Truth wrapped his arms around me, and Wicked came at my back, so that they held me between them while I cried. They held me while I confessed to them something I wasn't sure I could say to Edward, or any of the men I loved. How do you ask someone you love to kill you if you grow too powerful, too evil? Jean-Claude had asked it of me once, and I had cursed him for it. Now I let the two brothers hold me, and gave them my darkest fear.

Truth whispered against my hair, "If the *ardeur* takes you and you become as evil as Belle Morte, I promise . . ."

Wicked said, "We promise."

"We promise," Truth said, "that we will not let you be that evil."

"You'll kill me," I said softly.

They were quiet for a few breaths, and then their arms tightened around me, and they said in one voice, "We'll kill you."

And that was the best I could get, that if the *ardeur* or the Darkness took me, that Wicked and Truth would kill me before I could do whatever it was that either of the evil bitches of the West wanted me to do. It didn't matter that it might kill anyone metaphysically tied to me, because if Marmee Noir possessed me, or I became nothing but a vessel for the *ardeur*, whatever was inside me would spread to them eventually. The thought of what we could all do, if we became truly evil, truly without pity, was too awful to contemplate. We could rule the vampires and most of the wereanimals in this country, and then we could move on Europe. If Marmee Noir took me over and possessed all that belonged to Jean-Claude and me, there'd be nothing to stop us unless the two vampires holding me now could stop it early, stop it with me.

I sat there in the starry night, held in the arms of the only two people who I thought might be good enough, ruthless enough, and honorable enough to kill me if I asked. I'd once thought that Edward would do it if it needed doing, but I knew now that even he would hesitate. He loved me too much. But Truth and Wicked didn't love me, not yet, and if we were careful, they never would. I needed them to keep this promise. I needed to know that if I failed, utterly and completely, I had a fail-safe. A fail-safe made of swords and bullets, and two of the finest warriors that had ever walked the planet. As fail-safes went, it wasn't bad.

59

WE GOT DRESSED, because strangely, when the *ardeur* left and the grief left, the desert night was cold. Truth gave me his leather jacket; when I protested, he said, "I don't really feel the cold like a human." Duh, I so knew that, but the emotional revelations had shaken me a little. When he held the jacket out to me, I saw his arms. His lower arms had nail marks on them, some bleeding. I'd even managed to bleed the back of his right hand.

"God, Truth, I'm sorry."

He glanced down at the scratches as if he'd just noticed them, too. "It's nothing."

"I'm still sorry I didn't ask how you felt about nails."

He gave a small smile. "We didn't have much time to negotiate."

"I guess not."

"I count it as a mark of my service to you and Jean-Claude," he said.

I flinched a little. "Don't call it service, that sounds too much like . . ."

"Don't make more of what he said than there is to make, Anita," Wicked said. "He didn't mean anything by it."

I let the conversation die because it was all too confusing for me. Truth's jacket was large enough that my hands kept vanishing in the sleeves, and the bottom of the leather hung down to midthigh. I looked like I was five and playing dress-up in my dad's clothes, but I was warm. The fashion police could ticket me later.

I called Edward on Truth's cell phone. Mine was probably in Phoebe Billings's yard. I hoped Edward had found it. I called to find out where he was, and if I was too late to help him hunt demons.

"Anita," and he sounded half relieved and half frightened, not something you hear from Edward often.

"Are you okay?"

"I should be asking you that," and he lowered his voice, as if he were afraid of being overheard. "Last I see, you're carried off by a vampire, and I let him do it, and it's an hour and a half later, and you're not back. I'd think if you had to feed the *ardeur*, a quickie would have done it."

I fought not to glance at the two vampires. "Trust me, Edward, it was a quickie. Did I miss it? Was there a demon at Bering's house?"

"You haven't missed anything. Did you ever try to get a warrant based on a possible demon being in a house?"

I almost said yes, then had to stop and think about it. "No, actually."

"Well, we got a judge who thinks that demons are just evil spirits. He's arguing that demons couldn't possibly have killed our cops."

"Normally, he'd be right, but it doesn't matter. Our warrant of execution should get us in Bering's house," I said.

"Shaw didn't think so, and he's the undersheriff."

"Let me guess, Bering is rich, or connected, or something."

"His family has been a big deal around here for as long as Max has been in charge. He's the last of the family unless he breeds, which doesn't seem likely if we can ever get into the house."

"You can just press the warrant; it's federal, and that outranks local."

"I wanted to give you time to get back," he said.

"Shit, Edward, you didn't have to delay the investigation because I'm having a metaphysical breakdown."

"Put it another way, have you seen anyone else but you and me that you'd want backing you against a demon?"

I thought about that. "Lieutenant Grimes and his men are good," I said.

"They're some of the best, but I haven't seen them pray to the angels and have everything glow."

Oh. "Okay, tell me where you are, and Wicked will drop me nearby."

He was back at SWAT headquarters. "We've had the briefing about Bering's house. We're just waiting for the warrant, or for me to push the one we have."

"My weapons are stashed there; could you change out some things? I didn't pack with demon in mind."

"I've already repacked for you, and I found your phone in the yard with your weapons. I can list what I packed for you," he said.

"That's okay, I trust you to pack for me. Though, frankly, most of the time a demon isn't solid enough for normal weapons of any kind to work. The rare ones that do get solid enough to attack may only be solid for the second of that attack, so we'll have to be shooting around each other if it goes bad."

"See, none of their practitioners knew that, and neither did the priest they've got here that's been blessing our bullets."

"The priest has been doing what?" I asked.

"You heard right."

"Hmm, I've never tried that."

"Me, either," he said.

"I wonder if the bullets will glow?"

"We'll find out," he said.

I sighed. "Yeah, we'll find out."

"You don't sound so good," he said.

I opened my mouth, closed it, then said the only thing I could think of. "I'm tired of being a victim to my own metaphysical powers, Edward."

"Are you okay now?"

"I've fed the *ardeur*. I should be good for twelve hours at least, maybe twenty-four."

"Why double up?" he asked.

"Let's just say it was a good meal, okay."

"Okay," he said, "get here as soon as you can."

"So what, I walk in and play the Fed card and piss everyone off, so that you come off as reasonable and I'm the bitch?"

"I'd play the heavy if I could, but I've been too reasonable. I can't explain the change."

"So I *am* the bitch."

"Picture Shaw's face when you do it."

I smiled, and knew it wasn't a pleasant smile. "Well, there is that. Fine, I'll be the bad cop, but it's your turn next time."

"You don't damage your rep by doing this."

"And you might," I said.

"Ted is a very nice guy," he said.

"You know, it always creeps me when you talk about Ted in the third person."

He laughed, and it was a good Edward laugh. "Just get here as soon as possible. Do you have a badge?"

My hands went to my belt and found that the belt, badge, and empty holster had survived the night. "Surprisingly, yes."

"Then flash it, and come explain to everyone why we don't have to wait on Shaw and the judge."

"Isn't this going to make you and the other marshals look weak?"

"They already think we're pussy-whipped; why disappoint them?"

I shrugged, realized he couldn't see it, and said, "Okay, but please warn Bernardo and Olaf what we're doing so that they don't blame me."

"I'll tell them. Just get here." I heard noise on the other end of the phone, and his voice trailing away, "Hello, Detective Morgan, yes, it is Marshal Blake." Movement, then, "Ask nicely, and maybe I will."

Apparently, he asked nicely. "Where the hell are you, Blake?"

"Following up a lead," I said.

"What kind of lead?"

"Vampires," I said.

"And what kind of vampire lead would that be?"

"One that didn't lead anywhere."

"So you just wasted an hour and a half of our time," and his voice was hostile.

"Most leads don't pan out, you know that. Besides, it's not me that's trying to double-paper my ass."

"Just get your ass back here."

"You aren't my boss, Morgan. Put Ted back on."

"Is he your boss?"

"Closest thing Vegas has to one, yeah."

There was more noise, and movement, and then Edward came back on. "Sorry about that, Blake," he said in his cheerful Ted voice. I heard him walking, cowboy boots hitting some hard surface, and then he spoke in his normal voice. "Morgan didn't agree with Shaw going to a judge. He thought we should throw Bering to the wolves."

"So he's taking his mad-on at Shaw out on us?"

"Yelling at us won't get him fired or demoted."

"I'm getting really tired of being everyone's whipping girl, Edward."

"Yeah." He stopped walking. "Get here, Anita. We need this done."

I was left with a buzzing phone. Actually, I'd have rather tackled the demon in the daylight, but two problems with that. One, some demons didn't show up in daylight, so if you wanted to kill it or send it back, you needed it to be dark. Two, if the vampires were in there, again, I'd rather wait until daylight, but while we waited and played it safe, they might kill someone else. Not acceptable. So much of my job, lately, was just a choice of disasters. I guess that was true of a lot of police work, though.

I turned back to the vampires. "I need to get back to Vegas and help us push our warrant for a house."

"I thought your warrant covered any house you needed," Wicked said.

"It does, but we've got a pissy undersheriff and a judge who doesn't like the execution warrants. A lot of judges don't."

"Why would they not like it? It's only a nearly perfectly legal excuse to kill anything in your path," Wicked said.

"You sound like you don't approve."

"Not my job to approve or disapprove."

"Fine, Truth, you take me to Vegas."

"I didn't say I wouldn't do it," Wicked said.

"Then stop bitching. I've had enough of that from the locals."

His face softened. "I'm sorry, Anita, but I am a vampire, and the executioners could kill me tomorrow with almost no proof of a crime and no trial."

"Hey, at least you guys can't be killed on sight in this country; better than most of the rest of the world."

Wicked and Truth came to stand in front of me, giving me that mirrored look as if they were thinking the same thought. "We'll take you where you need to go," Truth said.

"Aren't you afraid to touch me?" I asked.

He shook his head.

I studied that serious face. "Aren't you afraid of the *ardeur*?"

"Yes."

Wicked answered, "He's not afraid of you, Anita. We know you meant what you said. Belle would never ask that of anyone. She likes being the monster."

I shivered, and it wasn't pleasure this time. "I've felt her touch." I thought about her dream visit. I was almost sure that she'd kept Victor the weretiger from doing something to me in the dream, but in return she'd done something to the *ardeur*. Had it been her who caused the *ardeur* to spread to Truth from a distance? I didn't know, and if I asked her, she'd lie.

"Whoever's up for it, let's fly me to Edward."

"She's afraid of heights," Wicked said.

"How afraid?" Truth asked.

"Pretty," he said.

Truth looked down at me, considering. "We would never drop you."

I waved the thought away. "It's a phobia, not logic. Just decide who's taking me before I lose my nerve."

They laughed, and it was like hearing it in stereo. Wicked said, "You may lose a lot of things, but you'll never lose your nerve."

"Pretty to think so; now who's pilot for the return trip?"

"Why don't you just order one of us?" Truth asked.

"Because I can't fly, and I don't know if Wicked is tired from carrying me here and then feeding the *ardeur*. So I trust you two to decide who's up for it."

Wicked smiled at me. "I'm almost more honored that you trust us, rather than order us, than I am about the sex."

I shrugged. "You're welcome, I guess. Now, whoever, but I need to get back to town."

"I'll take her," Truth said.

"I've had more recovery time," Wicked said.

"I'll take her," Truth repeated. The brothers looked at each other for a long moment. One of those unreadable moments that you can simply feel on the air like a weight of unspoken things, and you suddenly feel like a voyeur in someone else's life. I realized why Bernardo had said something similar earlier about Edward and me. He was right.

Finally, Wicked said, "As you like."

"I do," he said.

Again, I felt like I was listening to shorthand, and that there were a dozen things going on below the surface of those few words, but you're never supposed to let people know that you hear the unspoken things. It makes them nervous. I scare people enough without going all girl-intuitive, too.

Truth looked at me. "Are you ready?"

I took in a deep breath, let it out slowly, fighting to keep it from trembling, then nodded.

He closed the distance between us. He hesitated, then said, "I need to carry you."

I nodded again. "I know." My voice sounded just the tiniest bit unhappy. I could do this, damn it. It was just heights, and flying, and . . . Oh, hell, I did not want to do this, but we were too far out for driving, even if we had a car. This was the quickest way, and Edward had stalled for me long enough.

Truth picked me up in his arms, as if he meant to walk with me. Something must have shown on my face because he said, "It's the most secure way for you."

"It's just that Wicked carried me differently."

Wicked said, "I was afraid you might've started struggling with the hunger on you. Carrying you against my body, I had more control if you had gone . . . mad while we were flying."

Truth turned with me in his arms and asked, "You said *hunger*, not *ardeur*."

"The first hunger that came to her was blood and flesh. She had turned toward the humans when she asked me to take her someplace where she would not be tempted."

Truth looked down at me, his face blank and serious, which I'd begun to realize was his blank face. It was what he hid behind when he didn't want anyone knowing what he was thinking.

"What?" I asked.

He shook his head. "I will take you to your friends, but if the other hungers are rising more than the *ardeur*, then you need to be even more careful to eat solid food, and . . ." He faltered.

"What he's trying to say is that to make certain you don't try to attack your human friends, you need to feed the *ardeur* more regularly, as well as eat more real food."

"You think I should eat before I go to sleep tonight?"

"I think a midnight snack wouldn't be a bad idea," Wicked said.

"Agreed," Truth said.

"Crap," I said, "I really didn't want to do some of the people you brought from St. Louis."

"I think a little sex with willing men is the lesser evil here, Anita."

I nodded. Let's see, sex with more men, or trying to tear the throats out of Edward, Olaf, and Bernardo. Let me think . . . out loud I said, "I know it's the lesser evil, but I still don't have to be happy about it."

"If you were happy about it, you wouldn't be you," Truth said.

"But if you were a little more happy about it," Wicked said, "you'd have better control of the *ardeur* in the first place. You have to embrace your vampire powers to truly use them well."

"You know, if we're just going to chat, then put me down."

"I think the lady is tired of talking," Wicked said.

"Then to action," Truth said, and I felt that push of energy skyward. The sand and tiny gravel swirled upward from the force of it so that we left the ground in a cloud of it.

I had a dizzying glimpse of the ground falling away beneath his boots. A wave of nausea tried to crawl up my throat. I closed my eyes tight and leaned in against his chest. The nausea was less, though my pulse was still trying to crawl out the side of my throat, my heart beating so fast it hurt my chest. I fought not to tighten the arm around his neck too much. But I couldn't keep myself from getting a handful of his shirt, as if the thin T-shirt would really help if everything went to hell. But sometimes, when you're really scared, illusion is all you've got. Cling to it, baby, cling to it.

60

I WAS ACTUALLY able to open my eyes before we got to Vegas. I just had to keep my gaze very steady on Truth's shoulder or the sky. I could even admit that being up in the dark, surrounded by stars, was beautiful. It was the ground being so far away that spoiled it for me.

Truth had asked only once if I was all right. When I'd answered yes, he had let it go. I knew he felt the fear in my body. There was no way to hide my heart rate and pulse from him. But before we landed, those had both quieted. I was still scared, but I guess I couldn't stay at that level of fear without either a full-blown panic attack or fainting.

The stars began to fade, and at first I thought it was daylight, even though I knew the time was completely wrong for it; then I realized it was the lights of Vegas. They rose against the sky like a false dawn, draining the light from the stars, turning the black sky pale. The city rose above the night like a permanent dawn, always pushing against the dark, keeping the stars at bay.

Truth had to go higher just to keep above the buildings. Some of the roofs were so close, I think if I'd leaned out I could have touched them. As afraid as I was of heights, I still had that perverse urge to reach out. I made my hands cling tighter to Truth, and he seemed to think that meant I was more afraid.

"We will be there soon," he said, and his voice sounded strained.

I looked at him and almost asked if he was all right, but if he wasn't, what could I do? We left the tall buildings of the Strip behind and flew over normal houses and shops. We were flying over Anywhere, USA. Then the land began to open up, and the first thing I saw was the twinkling runway lights at the airport. For one moment, I thought Truth was going to use them, but then he began to angle toward buildings that were on the edge of it. I wouldn't have recognized the building from the air, in the dark. I was a little worried about that whole rolling-on-the-ground part, with concrete and buildings to hit. The ground rushed up, and I had to close my eyes or be sick. Then I realized it wasn't just the visual but the swooping feeling in my stomach. I opened my eyes to find a building at our side, and Truth hit the ground running. He stumbled slightly on impact, but kept moving forward, with me in his arms. The run slowed, and finally he was able to stop, still hidden in the shadow of the building. I had a glimpse of the street with a spattering of cars driving by, their headlights cutting the electric-kissed dark. Truth moved us back a short way into the shadow of the building, so we'd be less visible from the street. At our back was the open area that surrounded the airport.

He leaned his back against the building, as if he were tired, hugging me closer the way you would a child.

"You can put me down, Truth," I said.

He opened his eyes and blinked at me, as if he'd been far away in his head. He put me down and let me slide out of his hands. He leaned against the building, his chest rising and falling as if he'd been running. Vampires didn't always breathe, or have to, so the fact that he was breathing heavily meant either he was tired or something else.

I touched his bare arm with my fingertips. His skin was warm to the touch. "You're warm."

"Touch me where I wasn't holding you against me," he said, voice breathy.

I reached up and touched the side of his face. His skin was cool. "So it was just my body heat warming you up?"

He nodded.

"Why are you breathing like that? How much energy did this use up for you?"

He swallowed hard enough for me to watch his throat work. "Enough."

"Shit, you should have let Wicked bring me."

He shook his head, still leaning shoulders and arms against the building. "It wouldn't have mattered. You fed more deeply than I thought, that's all."

"What do you mean?"

He looked at me with those gray eyes that almost never looked as blue as his brother's. "Just as we can take less blood, or more, in a feeding, so with the *ardeur*. You were like a vampire that had not fed in too long. You needed more."

"But a vampire can only drink as much blood as his stomach can hold," I said. "The *ardeur* doesn't work like that, does it?"

He just looked at me.

Shit. "How hurt are you?"

"Not hurt, just tired."

"Fine, how tired are you?"

"You need to go to your police friends," he said.

"I can't leave you on the street this weak. You can't even stand up. If Vittorio's people found you now, you'd just be a victim for them."

His eyes went all vampire on me, gray light shining in his gaze. "I am no one's victim," and he was angry when he said it, and then his eyes went back to normal and he began to slide down the wall. I caught him, steadied him. He put a hand on my shoulder, and I felt his body fight to stay upright.

"I am sorry," he said.

"No, it's me that's sorry."

"Flying takes a great deal of energy, and carrying someone takes more. I had forgotten how much more."

"So it's not that I fed, but that you did something strenuous afterward," I said.

"Yes, it would have been good to simply sleep afterward, or feed myself."

"Would feeding help?" I asked.

He nodded, while his body trembled in an effort to stay leaning against the wall. Even with my hands to steady him, he was still in trouble.

"I can't leave you like this, Truth. Either you have to come with me, and let the cops keep you safe, or . . ." I did not want to open a vein for him. I'd done it once before to save his life when he'd been stabbed with a silver blade trying to help me

and the police catch a very bad vampire, but I didn't like playing walking blood bank. But there was no way that Grimes and
his men would want a vampire inside their place. How would
I explain him to the other cops, and how did I explain what was
wrong with him? When opening a vein is the lesser evil, you
need to rethink your priorities.

"Take blood from me," I said.

"You don't donate to anyone." His voice was rough, and his
legs began to give. I helped ease him to a sitting position, with
his back solid against the building.

"Not usually, but this is an emergency, just like me needing
to feed the *ardeur* on you."

He gave me fluttery eyes.

I held his face between my hands. "Damn it, Truth, don't
you dare pass out on me!"

His eyes opened wide, and I watched him fight to do what
I'd ordered. I did the only thing I could think of; I offered him
my left wrist. It would hurt more than the neck, but it would be
easier to hide from the other policemen.

"I am not vampire enough to cloud your mind. I can only
hurt you."

"Feed, damn it," I said.

He raised shaky hands and wrapped one of them around my
wrist at the hand, and used the other to scoot the sleeve of his
jacket away from the wrist. The sleeves were big enough on
me that he had no problem pushing the leather out of the way
and baring my lower arm.

I braced for the bite, then blew out a breath and tried to
relax into it. If I tensed up it would hurt more, just like a shot.

Truth opened his mouth wide, so I had a glimpse of fangs
before he struck. I tensed at the last minute; I just couldn't help
it. I was caught between the sharp immediacy of the pain and
the sensation of his mouth locked around my wrist, forming a
tight seal, while the fangs dug in deeper. The deeper part hurt,
but his mouth on my wrist, and the sucking, felt good. I'd been
feeding Jean-Claude and Asher more often in the last few
months, and apparently my body had started translating feeding into pleasure. I'd started associating it with sex, because
with Jean-Claude and Asher, we'd made the blood part of our

foreplay, and sometimes part of our intercourse. I hadn't realized until this moment how much that had colored how I felt
about this whole thing.

I stood there, caught between pain and pleasure, while my
body tried to decide which box to put it in. Truth sat up, away
from the wall, his hands so strong around my arm, his mouth
feeding harder, his throat swallowing, swallowing me down.

I had to put a hand on the wall to keep me kneeling and not
falling over, because my head had finally decided that it felt
good. Good enough that I was getting weak-kneed.

It was Truth who stopped, pulling his mouth away from my
wrist. He kept his hands on my arm and laid his forehead
against my skin. I leaned into the cool concrete of the wall,
heavier, fighting not to give into that weak-kneed feeling. I was
wet, my body prepped for what usually came afterward. When
was the last time I'd let a vampire take blood when sex wasn't
involved? I couldn't remember. I didn't donate blood outside
sex. Shit.

Truth's voice was still rough but not breathy, a little deeper.
It wasn't sickness or tiredness that deepened his voice. "You
taste . . . your energy . . . You didn't taste this way when you
fed me last."

"You were dying. You just don't remember."

He raised his face and looked at me. His eyes glowed flat
silver-gray in the dimness. "A vampire doesn't forget the taste
of blood, Anita. Something has changed in you since we first
met." He licked the wound on my arm, one long, sensual
movement. He closed those shining eyes and licked his lips, as
if to catch every drop of blood. The wound was still bleeding,
and would for a while, because of the anticoagulant in vampires' saliva.

"Let go of my arm, Truth," I said, and my voice was a little
uncertain. He wasn't acting like himself, and I didn't like the
idea that my blood tasted different. What did that mean?

He opened his eyes but didn't move his hands. He stared up
at me with his eyes gone blind with vampire powers. "I feel
amazing, Anita. Your blood has more kick to it than a shapeshifter's does."

"Let go of me, Truth, now." My voice was firmer this time.

He smiled and let me go.

I pushed away from him, using the wall to stand. I'd never seen Truth smile, not like that.

He just sat there against the wall, smiling up at me.

"Are you drunk?" I asked.

"Maybe." He smiled happily.

I'd seen only one vampire react like that, and that one had taken a feeding from both Jason and me. Werewolf with a chaser of necromancer had made Jean-Claude giggling drunk.

"I need to go, Truth."

"Go," he said, his smile wide.

"I need to know you're all right before I leave you."

"Oh," he said, and he stood, in one of those too-fast-to-see movements. One minute on the ground, the next standing. Vampires are quicker than human-normal, but for the standing trick, they have to use vampire mind powers to appear that fast. If I'd had a gun, I'd have tried to aim it, just out of habit.

I had moved back out of reach, but after that speed, I knew that it did me no good. "Shit," I said.

"I didn't mean to frighten you, but as you can see, I'm very all right."

My heart was in my throat. "That wasn't mind tricks," I managed to say.

"You mean the speed?" he asked.

"Yeah, the speed."

"No," he said.

"I've never seen a vampire that could move quite like that."

He gave a little bow from the neck. "High praise from you, but it was a trait of our bloodline."

"You mean the speed without mind tricks, all of your bloodline could do it?"

"Yes."

"No wonder you were the warrior elite. That's faster than most lycanthropes."

"Once, if the vampire council wanted shapeshifters killed, they sent our bloodline."

"But now you and Wicked are the last, right?"

He nodded.

"I've seen you fight; you weren't this fast."

"I haven't felt this good in a long time." He stretched his arms skyward, making the muscles in his arm bunch and move. "I feel made new. I feel"—he looked at me, as his eyes drained from silver glow to normal—"like I did before we killed the head of our line." He frowned. "You bound me to Jean-Claude with your blood and his power. What have you done, or what has been done to you, since that last feeding?"

"I don't know what you mean by that," I said.

He was frowning harder, thinking harder. "I mean, Anita, that I feel born again, as if our old master should walk down the street and greet us." He moved toward me, and I moved back, keeping our distance. It made him stop. "Are you afraid of me?"

"I don't know what just happened, so let's just say I'm being cautious."

He nodded, as if that made perfect sense to him. "I will see you safely to your friends, and then I will go back to the hotel."

"Good," I said, and then because it was me, I couldn't leave it alone. "No offense, but you don't seem bothered that I'm nervous about you now."

He shrugged those broad shoulders. "I startled you, and I don't know what happened just now, either. Until we know whether it was your blood, your power, or mine, caution is not a bad thing."

"Okay," I said, "then just watch me walk around the corner, and you can go."

"Agreed." He gestured me forward. I walked wide around him, and we sort of circled each other until we got to the corner of the building. All I had to do was walk around the corner, and a few yards away were Edward and all the rest. A cluster of cars whirred by on the street, oblivious to what we were doing. It was almost startling to see the cars and know there were people just over there, as if we'd been in some little pocket world of our own for the last few minutes.

One thing I noticed in the circling dance we were doing was that Truth's gun in its belt holster showed without the leather jacket. The black T-shirt wasn't long enough or wide enough to hide the gun.

Did he have a carry permit for this state? I didn't know, but

I did know that being a big guy all in black, flashing a gun, could make some eager cop stop him. Being a vampire would not help him when it happened.

I took off the leather jacket and held it out toward him.

He shook his head. "I told you, I don't feel the cold like you do."

"It's to hide your gun," I said, "I'd rather not have you stopped by a cop for brandishing."

He almost touched the gun at his back, but stopped himself in midmotion. He took his jacket, being careful not to touch me while we made the exchange. That let me know that the fact that I was still spooked showed. Oh, well.

He took the jacket and slipped it on. He hugged the leather around him. I thought he was cold for a moment, then realized he was smelling the coat. Smelling me on it. Again, it was more a shapeshifter gesture than a vampire one. I stared at him in the stronger light of the streetlights, and he looked rosy cheeked and healthy. If I hadn't known what I was looking at, even I might have said human. What the fuck?

I stood on the sidewalk and asked, "Did your bloodline have any other superpowers?"

"We could pass for human, even to witches."

"Anything else?" I asked.

"A few, why?"

"Nothing. I'll see you tomorrow night."

"Aren't you planning to be home before dawn?"

"I wouldn't count on it."

"I feel torn, Anita. I should be by your side, guarding you, yet I must let you go into danger without me. It seems backward."

"It's my job, Truth."

He nodded. "I will await you at the hotel. I hope you get home before dawn." He turned and said over his shoulder, "You're still bleeding."

I looked down to find blood trickling down my hand to drip on the sidewalk. I put pressure on the wound and held it up. How had I not felt that?

"How are you going to explain the wound?"

"I'll think of something. Now go, Truth, just go."

Classical music played, a little high-pitched but recognizable as Beethoven. Truth reached into his jacket pocket and drew out his cell phone. He answered with, "Yes."

I waved good-bye and started for the corner.

Truth called, "Anita, it's for you."

I stopped and looked back at him. "Who is it?"

"Your marshal friend, Ted Forrester."

I went back to him, taking the phone he was holding out to me. "Ted, I'm just around the corner from you."

"I don't think so," he said. I heard noises.

"Are you in your car?"

"We got a call out."

"What's happened now?"

"Club invaded by vampires. They let some of the customers go but kept all the dancers. The released hostages described a vampire that fits the holy water scars that you described on Vittorio."

"Shit," I said.

"You said he'd up the body count tonight, Anita. You were right."

"Believe me, Edward, I didn't want to be right on this one."

"I'll give you the address."

"Is there anyone home to drive me?" I asked.

"It was an all hands, Anita."

"Shit."

"Don't you have transport?"

"Yeah, Truth is still here. I'll let him bring me to you."

"Make sure he sets you down well behind the police barriers. I wouldn't want the uniforms on the barriers to see a vampire flying with a woman in his arms tonight."

"I understand."

"We're here, but I can't wait for you, Anita. They sent the ear of one of the dancers out with the customers they released. The vampires are threatening to send the rest of the dancer out, a piece at a time."

"I will be there ASAP, Edward." But I was talking to empty air. He'd hung up.

"Fuck," I said, and put a lot of feeling into it.

"I heard most of it. What's the address?"

I told him. He asked for his phone back, and did some things on the screen. I peered at the screen and found a little map. He studied it for a few minutes, then said, "I've got it. Are you ready?"

"I can't feed you again this soon, Truth."

"I feel fine, Anita; trust me, I won't need to be fed when we land."

I just had to take his word for it. I let him pick me up again, and I had to keep pressure on the wrist bite instead of holding on to him. I was hoping if I kept pressure on it, the bleeding would stop before we landed. If it did, it would be the only thing that had gone right tonight.

61

I TUCKED MYSELF in against Truth's body as hard as I could without being able to hold on to him, but finally I couldn't stand it anymore. I stopped pressing on my wrist and wrapped my arms around his neck. I held on and buried my face against him. He felt warm now, warm with my blood, my energy. There was a pulse in his neck to move against my cheek as if the beat of his heart were calling to me.

The bend of his neck smelled clean, fresh, like clean sheets that had been dried outdoors in the wind and sun. It was almost like his skin held a hint of all the sunlit days that he would never see again.

I felt something change in the way Truth held me. It made me move my face so I could see. There were flashing lights and a lot of cops down below, but not too close. Truth took us down on the far side of a darkened strip mall. He had to run a little to take up momentum, but it was smoother than the last landing. Either he was getting in practice, or he just felt better.

He stepped into the thicker shadows by the darkened store and looked up the street toward all those flashing lights.

"The police barricades are just up ahead."

"You can put me down now," I said.

I got a flash of his smile in the dimness. He put me down without a word. "Are you still bleeding?"

I looked at my hand and found the blood drying. "No."

"Good."

We stood there for a moment awkwardly. There was a tension like you get on a first date, where you don't know if you should kiss or just hug. This was wrong; I'd never felt like this around him before. He leaned down toward me, and I stepped back. "I'm sorry, Truth. I don't know what's happening, but I don't think it's voluntary on either of our parts."

He stood straight, looking at me, his face still mostly in shadow. "You think I'm bespelled by you."

I shrugged.

"But it's not just me, Anita; you feel the pull, too."

I remembered something Jean-Claude had told me once. "A lot of Belle's line of vampire powers cut both ways, and it only cuts as deep as the vampire is willing to be cut."

"Then you must be willing to be cut to the heart," he said.

I didn't know what to say to that, so I hid behind work. "I have to go. You have to go." I shook my head. "Go, Truth, just go, be somewhere else."

One moment he was there in the shadows; the next he was skyward, blowing my hair across my face.

I turned toward the crowd and the police barriers. I'd have to get through all that before the uniforms would let me through to talk to SWAT. I wanted to find Edward, not for police work or practical reasons, but because I needed a friend. I needed a friend who didn't want to fuck me or fall in love with me. I needed someone who didn't want anything from me. The list was getting smaller every night.

62

I WAS ALMOST to the edge of the crowd when a man in a gray hooded sweatshirt turned and blocked my way. I opened my mouth to say, *Excuse me, sir,* but I got a glimpse of the face in the hood and the words froze on my lips.

I had a glimpse of dark brown eyes, black hair, skin darkly pale, a handsome, masculine face, until he turned into the light and the burn scars on his right side showed.

My hand reached for the Browning, but it wasn't there, nothing was there. I was unarmed, and he was standing in front of me.

"Do not contact your vampires via mind; I will sense it, and I will tell my vampires to kill the temptresses inside the club. And, yes, I knew you were unarmed. I did not think you would ever be that careless, but it gives us a chance to talk."

I licked suddenly dry lips and did the only thing I could think of: stepped back, gave myself room, for all the good it was going to do me.

"Why take the club? Why give the police time to trap your vampires?" I asked, voice still calm. Point for me.

"It was bait, for you, Anita."

"Gee, and most men just send flowers," I said.

He looked at me with solid brown eyes. I couldn't read his expression completely, but I think my reaction wasn't what he expected, or maybe not what he wanted. "If you call for help in any way, I will have the vampires that I control start killing the harlots."

"They're dancers, not prostitutes," I said, "but I get it, you're master enough to contact your people mind to mind," I said.

He nodded. "As are you," he said.

I took a deep breath and fought to get some control over my pulse and heart rate. I didn't know what to say to that, so I let it go. I rarely got in trouble keeping my mouth shut.

He was staring me up and down, not the way a man will a woman, but like he was looking over a car he planned to buy. It was definitely more purchase than date, that look.

I tried to get him talking, "Fine, you want to talk to me, let's talk."

"Come with me, now." He actually held one large, long-fingered hand out to me. It was a big hand, bigger than I liked, but graceful, like his voice.

"No," I said.

"I will have them kill the whores we have taken unless you come with me."

I shook my head. "You'll probably kill them anyway."

"If I give my word?"

"I know you mean that, but you're also a serial killer and a sexual sadist; sorry, but that makes me not trust you." I shrugged and started thinking furiously in Edward's direction, not magic, just that wish in my head that he would look this way, come this way, notice. But I was too short and the crowd blocked the view. I realized that the vampire in front of me was blocking the view even more. I doubted it was an accident.

"I see your point," he said. He moved the hood more from his right side. "Take a good look, Anita. See what the humans have done to me."

I tried not to look, because I wasn't sure if it was a distraction technique, but some things are hard to look away from. Asher's facial scars were just on the side of one cheek, trailing down to the chin. The entire right cheek of Vittorio's face, from where the hood hit it to the edge of his mouth and the tip of his chin, was all hardened scar tissue.

He let the hood drop back to hide his face, and I realized he had his left hand held out to his side, for all the world as if he expected someone to come take his hand. A young girl reached for him. I thought for a moment she was another vampire, but one look into those wide, gray eyes and I knew better. She was dressed in tramp chic, skirt too short, midriff showing, small breasts as mounded as she could get them. Before it became the style I'd have said hooker, but so many of the teenage girls were wearing this kind of shit, it made me wonder what the real hookers were wearing.

He smoothed her straight brown hair back from her face. She smiled dreamily up at him.

"Leave her alone," I said.

He caressed her cheek, and she cuddled into it like a kitten. He turned her face to me, so I could see how young the face under the makeup was: fourteen, maybe fifteen, no more. It was hard to tell in that much makeup and the clothes. It tended to make you add years that the girls hadn't earned.

"I said, leave her alone." My voice wasn't shaky anymore; it held the first edge of anger. I embraced that, fed the anger with sweet thoughts of vengeance and what I'd do to him when I had the chance.

"If your beast rises, I will tear her throat out." He drew her in against his body as he said it.

I had to master my anger then, swallow it down, because he was right; I couldn't guarantee with this much stress that anger wouldn't tip me into some kind of lycanthrope problem. If I could have shifted for real, it would have given me weapons, but it wasn't a weapon for me, it was just one more problem.

He reached his other hand out, and a man came to it. He was tall, taller than the vampire. His gray eyes were almost a match for the girl's; even his short hair was the same shade of brown. He gazed forward, seeing nothing.

Vittorio began to unzip his sweatshirt, exposing his chest. I knew what it would look like, because that was the worst of Asher's scars. But again, it was worse. The holy water hadn't just scarred the skin, it had eaten into the deeper tissue, exposing ligaments and the bones of his ribs. It looked like his body had tried to regrow some tissue over it, but the right side of his chest and stomach looked like a skeleton with a hard covering of scars. His stomach was a little concave, where there'd been no bone to support the healing.

If he had wanted to hurt me in that moment, he could have, because I was mesmerized with the damage and that he'd survived it.

"If I could have died of infection, I would have, for there were no antibiotics when they did this to me."

"If you want to die, wait here, I'll get a gun and help you out."

"There was a time when that was what I sought, but no one was powerful enough to slay me. I took it as a message that I was death, because death could not touch me."

"Everything dies, Vittorio," I said, and I couldn't keep my gaze from flicking between the daughter and the father.

"So fragile, humans, aren't they?"

"Did you bring them with you to use as hostages?"

"I found them in the crowd. I thought at first"—he hugged the girl—"she was a whore, but she is only pretending." He kissed the top of her head, and she snuggled against him. "She reeks of innocence and untried things."

"What—do—you—want?" And I let each word hold the anger that I was really having trouble fighting off. I'd have given almost anything in that moment for a gun.

He stared down at the girl as she cuddled against him, her arms deep inside the sweatshirt, wrapping her arms completely around him. She gazed up at him like he was the best thing since sliced bread.

"She sees what I was before. I was beautiful once."

"Then you do the big reveal, and that's part of the thrill for you. I get it."

He spoke looking at me, not her. "I can leave this place with this family or with you. Will you trade your freedom for theirs?"

"Don't do this," I said, voice softer.

"You will come with me to save them?"

I looked at the man, with his unseeing gaze, and the besotted girl. "You don't kill children or men. Unless the men are strippers. These aren't your victims of choice. Let them go."

"Should I wake the father up enough to see and know what we do to his daughter?"

"What do you want, Vittorio?" I asked.

"You," he said.

We stood staring at each other. He had a slight smile on his face; I didn't. "Me, in what way?"

He laughed, and it was a bitter sound. "Oh, your virtue is safe, Anita; the Church took care of that long ago."

"Is it about your vampires in St. Louis? Is that why you wanted me here?"

"Revenge is for the small-minded, Anita. You will learn that I think larger thoughts, grander ones."

The girl began to kiss the ruined side of his chest. She began to make small eager sounds in her throat.

He'd done something else to her, mind to mind, and I hadn't felt it. I was standing feet away from him, and I hadn't felt a damn thing. I hadn't met a vampire in years that could do that to me.

"I have spies in Maximillian's camp. He knows, and I know now, that Jean-Claude has not given you the fourth mark."

I fought to keep my face blank and knew I failed by a widening of the eyes, a catch of the breath, a speed of pulse.

"Your master has left the door open for others, Anita. Bibiana wants Max to walk through that door. She believes that if you loved Jean-Claude you would have allowed it and married him by now. She sees your indecision as proof that you haven't found your true love."

"She's old-fashioned that way," I said, because what else could I say? He'd know if I was lying. Vampires and wereanimals are like walking lie detectors if they're powerful enough, and he was.

"But do not worry about Max and his bride, for I have decided it is my door to open, not his."

I blinked up at him, the anger dying under the confusion. I'd thought of a lot of things this nut-bunny could have wanted from me; that hadn't been one of them. "You want to make me your human servant?"

"I do."

"Why?" I asked, "Everyone knows what a pain in Jean-Claude's ass I am. Why do you want to deal with that?" I couldn't call for help in any way, or someone else died. I couldn't go all lycanthrope, because it wouldn't help me. What could I do? What the fuck could I do without a gun?

He laughed again, but this time it was lower, more attractive, more seductive. "The power, Anita. You are the first necromancer in centuries, and with so many other powers." He moved a little closer, drawing the girl with him. The man followed a step behind like some kind of robot.

Vittorio reached out with the hand not wrapped around the girl. I stepped back. All vampire powers increase by proximity, and especially touch. He'd done things that were almost impossible; I did not want to find out what his touch could do.

"Anita, you will make me the most powerful Master of the City in all of the new world."

"So you take me, and then we take Vegas from Max?" I was thinking furiously, going over my options. There didn't seem to be a lot of them. I only knew I wasn't leaving the area with him. One rule with serial killers: make them kill you in public, because whatever they'll do to you in private will be worse. I also couldn't let him leave with the girl and her father. But he couldn't fly with two people; he'd have to simply walk away. I could stop that, couldn't I? *Shit. Think, Anita, think.*

"Tiger is my animal to call, Anita. We slay Max and his wife, and it is over."

"Victor, you'd have to kill their son, too," I said.

He smiled, and he moved toward me again. I moved out of reach again.

"Yes, of course. What a queen you will make for our empire of blood and pain." His voice was cheerful, as if we weren't talking about murder.

"Allow me but a touch, just to lay these fingers alongside your cheek." He held the hand up, like a magician; nothing up my sleeve. Riiight.

"Don't move." It was Edward's voice. It took almost everything I had not to turn and search for where he was, but I kept my eyes on the vampire in front of me. Help was here, if I didn't fuck up.

The father moved up beside Vittorio, and I'd have bet everything I had that he was blocking Edward's shot.

"The man's bespelled, Edward," I said, and again had to fight not to look for him, but Vittorio was too powerful to look away, for even a second. I wasn't sure what his touch would do to me. Maybe nothing, or maybe something bad. I was faster than human-normal, thanks to Jean-Claude, so if I just kept looking at him, I could stay out of reach, or that was the plan.

"My friends, come to me," he said, and this time I felt the smallest tug of power. The crowd at the barrier turned toward us and spilled out toward him.

"He's bespelled the crowd!" I started to turn to run, but the girl was still in his arms. It made me hesitate. The crowd spilled around us. They shielded him from any gunfire, but they also tried to grab me. It was as if they were zombies, sightless eyes, reaching hands, no thought. How had he mind-rolled this many people? How the fuck had he done it?

I tried not to hurt them, at first, but when I realized they were trying to hold me down by sheer numbers, I stopped being nice. I kicked a knee and felt it give. A man screamed and then said, "What's happening? Where am I?"

I hit the nearest face, seeing my target as the opposite side of that face, the way you're taught in martial arts. He simply went down and vanished in the crowd. I brought down two more with joint hits and one bloody nose. The pain brought them out of it, and they crawled away, no longer a threat, but I'd waited too late, and there were just too many.

I yelled, "Pain, they snap out of it when they hurt!" I wasn't sure anyone heard me, until I heard cries of pain from the outside of the mob. Someone was coming, someone on my side. But the hands held me down, the sheer weight of all the people, and I couldn't move.

Vittorio knelt by my head. He laid his hand on my face. I tried to keep moving, but there was nothing I could do. His eyes filled with brown fire. I knew what he was going to do.

I screamed, "Edward!"

One moment I heard bodies hitting the ground, the next there was nothing but the touch of the vampire and his eyes, like brown glass flame, hovering in front of my face. They pressed against my face. I closed my eyes and screamed.

63

I WAITED FOR that flame to sink into me, to take me over, but nothing happened. The hands were still holding me down, I could still feel the press of power, of that brown flame, but that was it. I opened my eyes a slit, and the brown-gold of the flame was dazzling, but it wasn't coming closer.

A gunshot sounded so close that I was deaf for a second. Then the flame was gone, and Vittorio's face was above mine. I thought he meant to kiss me, but realized from the way he held himself that he was ducking. Another shot sounded, and then the people who'd been pinning me let me up and moved to form a human shield by the kneeling vampire.

"Another night," he said, and he was suddenly standing and running in a movement that I couldn't follow with my eyes. I sat up, watching him go, my heart in my throat. I'd seen only one other vampire that could move like that without mind tricks: Truth.

Men were yelling, "Fuck, where'd he go! There! Did you see that!"

Edward was suddenly standing above me, his hand held out. I took it, and he lifted me to my feet. I swayed a little, and he steadied me.

"You all right?" he asked.

I nodded.

He gave me a look.

"He tried to mark me, but he couldn't get past my shields in the time you gave him."

Olaf loomed over us. "Is she hurt?"

"I'm fine," I said, and forced myself to let go of Edward's

hand, when what I really wanted to do was collapse into his arms and hold on.

Green uniformed SWAT guys were there now, moving the crowd around as the people began to wander around, asking what happened.

Hooper was there, his face the only pale thing in the outfit. "What the hell happened, Blake?"

"The hostages, the club, it was a trap."

"A trap for what?" Hooper asked.

"Me."

Georgie came up beside his sergeant. "Nothing personal, Blake, but then why didn't he kill you?"

"He doesn't want me dead."

"What does he want?" Hooper asked.

"Me, as his human servant."

"You already belong to the master in St. Louis, right?" It was Cannibal, coming up from the other side of the dispersing crowd.

What was I supposed to say? "Something like that."

"Then he's too late," Cannibal said.

"He thinks he's powerful enough to take me away."

Hooper was standing there, not moving but watching my face. "Is he?"

"Not tonight, he wasn't."

Hooper's mouth made a small movement; maybe it was a smile, maybe not. "Let's not give him another night."

"Amen to that," I said.

I turned to Cannibal, alias Sergeant Rocco. "Some heap-big psychic you are. Didn't you sense Vittorio working the crowd?"

"Sorry, Anita, but I only do memories."

"Shit, can't any of you sense this kind of thing? Where's Sanchez?" I asked.

"Why?" Olaf asked.

"I thought he might have sensed the metaphysics."

"He's with the second team. They're going to scout Bering's house," Edward said. "Grimes wanted his practitioners to see if they could sense the demon."

"Why aren't you with Sanchez?" I asked Rocco.

"My ability is touch and memories. I'm not touching a demon on purpose, and I don't want those memories."

Edward said, "They're trying to see if they can sense the demon, so we can make entry closer to the targets or farther away from them, depending on what they find."

"Give me a gun, and let's get out there."

Edward was beside me; he handed me my own backup gun from a pocket in his tac pants.

Rocco said, "You have vampires right here; why chase demons?"

"This is a hostage situation. I'm not a negotiator."

Bernardo came up. He had blood running down his face from a cut on his forehead; apparently someone had hit back.

The people from the crowd who had tried to beat the hell out of police officers were being given blankets and hot drinks by Red Cross workers. The team doctor was checking them out, with his med tech by his side. I heard a man say, "I knew what we were doing was wrong, but I couldn't stop. I had to do what the voice in my head told me to do. I wanted to stop, but I couldn't."

I stepped in front of Rocco, and he stopped, looking at me. "If Sanchez and the other practitioners can sense the demon, it can sense them. If it's what killed the other operators, it could come out and trail them by their own magic."

"Most demons aren't that bright," Edward said.

"We're aware that some preternatural beings can sense psychic ability, Marshal. We've got them warded so their"—he made a waffling motion with his hand—"signature is garbled."

I was impressed and said so.

"Psychic ability is just another part of the job for us," he said. His radio crackled to life, and he turned to listen. He started to do a slow jog, and the rest of us just fell into step with him. All right, the men slow-jogged; I had to fast-jog. My legs were shorter. "The vampires have given up. They've freed the hostages, and they surrendered."

"What's the catch?" I asked. If anyone heard me, they didn't answer, but I knew there was a catch; with vampires there was always a catch.

64

SOMEONE HAD HIT the lights in the club so that it was bathed in bright lights. Lower-rent strip clubs are not meant to see bright lights; they reveal all the cracks and bad paint patch-up jobs. They show the illusion for what it is: a lie. A lie about sex, and the promise of having it, if you just pay a little bit more money. Nathaniel, my live-in sweetie, had explained to me that dancers make their living on the customer's hope that real sex is possible. It's all about advertising but never really selling. Under the harsh overhead lights, the scarlet women looked like even if they were selling, you wouldn't want to buy.

The dancer who had lost an ear was being rushed to the hospital, with the idea that they might be able to sew the ear back on; the wound was fresh enough. The other dancers were in the back rooms being interviewed, because we had the vampires in the front area between all the little stages. The vampires were chained in shackles with the new special metal that some of the bigger, more well-funded police forces had for preternatural criminals. It was some uber-space-age metal. I hadn't seen it put to the test yet, so I'd wait before putting my faith in it too completely.

The vampires sat in a sad-looking row, their hands held awkwardly in front of them because the chain went to their waist and their ankles. I had to admit that even if they broke the metal, they probably wouldn't be able to break enough chain to attack before we could get a shot off. Maybe just shackles were a good idea, though you had to get up close and personal to shackle a prisoner, and to my knowledge, the only person in this room who was immune to vampire gaze was me.

Olaf was circling the chained vampires. He was staying out

of reach, but he paced them, like a cattleman looking over a herd that he was thinking of buying. Or maybe that was just me projecting. Maybe.

Edward and Bernardo were interviewing the dancers. Why was I with Olaf? Because the dancers knew a predator when they saw one, and even after an evening of being held prisoner by vampires, some of them spotted him for what he was, and it wasn't helping to settle their nerves. For a good interview, Olaf needed to be elsewhere. Why didn't I interview the women? Because I could get as up close to the vampires as possible and not risk being bespelled. My specialty led me squarely to the other room. But Edward had said something to Sergeant Rocco, aka Cannibal, because either he or one of his men were at my side at all times. They were careful not to give the vamps direct eye contact, but they stayed close. Frankly, Rocco made me a little nervous after our encounter at SWAT HQ, but the first time he moved his body between me and Olaf—subtly, but just enough to make the bigger man have to walk wide around me—I just enjoyed that someone had my back.

"Okay, guys, this is the drill. We're going to escort you one at a time into another room and ask you what happened. Don't talk amongst yourselves while we're gone. Marshal Jeffries and some of the nice SWAT operators will still be in the room, so mind your manners."

They all promised like eager kindergarteners. There wasn't a vampire in the room that I would have been afraid of, one on one. But there were ten of them, and ten was a lot. Ten of any kind of vampire would have been scary. Hell, ten human beings all rush you at once and you won't get them all.

Officers helped the first vampire up to shuffle into a small room behind the bar. It was where the liquor was kept, and they put him in a chair that they'd found just for this. I knelt by the first vampire and found myself gazing into the face of a slightly plump man with pale brown eyes and hair to match. He smiled at me, careful not to show fang. He was trying to be all harmless, friendly, helpful, but I knew that of all of them, he was the oldest. I could feel him in my head, like an echo of time. He was three hundred if he was a day. He was dressed neatly, too neatly for the heat, for the town, for what he was pretending to be. He had pale slacks and a slightly darker tan shirt tucked in and buttoned up. The belt was good leather and matched the shoes. His nondescript brown hair had been cut recently and well. The watch on his wrist was gold and expensive, though once it doesn't say Rolex, I can't tell you what it is, but thanks to Jean-Claude I know quality when I see it.

I smiled at him. He smiled back. "Name?"

"Jefferson, Henry Jefferson."

"Well, Mr. Henry Jefferson, tell me what happened."

"Honestly, officer, I was in the casino, playing poker, and he came to stand by the table, just outside the ropes."

Ropes meant he'd been at one of the high-end tables, where a hand could start at five hundred, or ten thousand, or more. "Then what?" I asked.

"Then he made me cash out and told me to come with him." He looked up at me, and there was puzzlement and a hint of fear on his face. "Maximillian is a powerful Master of the City. He protects us, but this guy just came out of nowhere and I couldn't say no."

The next vampire was a lot younger in every way. Maybe only a few years dead, and barely legal when he crossed over to undead land. He had healed needle scars at the bends of his elbows. He'd been clean a long time. I had a hunch.

"Church of Eternal Life, right?" It was the vampire church, and the fastest-growing denomination in the country. Want to know what it's like to die? Ask a church member that's gone on. That's what they call it, *going on*. Church members wear medical ID bracelets, so if they're in a life-threatening situation, you call the Church and have a vampire come and finish the job.

The man's eyes widened, and his mouth opened enough to flash fang before he remembered. Boy, he was new. He recovered and tried to do what all the older vampires tell you to do when talking to the police: play human. Not pretend to be human, but just don't be vampire.

"Yes," and his voice was whispery, so frightened, "how did you . . ."

"The needle tracks. The Church got you off drugs, right?"

He nodded.

"What's your name?"

"Steve."

"Okay, Steve, what happened?"

"I was at work. I sell souvenirs just down the street. People like buying from a vampire, ya know."

"I know," I said.

"But he came up to the stand, and he said, *Come with me*, and just like that, I did." He gazed up at me, his eyes wide and frightened. "Why did I do that?"

"Why does a human being go with you once you bespell them with your gaze?" I asked.

He shook his head. "I don't do that. The Church rules . . ."

"Say no vampire gaze, but I bet you've tried it, at least once."

He looked embarrassed.

"It's okay, Steve, I don't care if you've played slap-and-tickle with the tourists with your eyes. Did this vampire catch you with his eyes?"

He frowned up at me again. "No, I would swear it wasn't his gaze. It was almost as if he said, *Come with me*, and I had to do it."

"So, was it his voice?"

Steve didn't know.

None of them knew why they had done it. They'd left their jobs, their dates, their money on craps tables, and just followed him. Sometimes Vittorio had spoken; sometimes he'd simply stood close to them. Either way, they'd followed him and done what he said.

The girl looked about nineteen, but except for Henry Jefferson, she was the oldest of them. Two hundred years and counting was my guess, and it wasn't a guess. Her hair was long and dark and had fallen over her face, so she was trying to blink it out of her eyes.

We'd already been through name, rank, and serial number, when I said, "Sarah, do you want me to get your hair out of your eyes?"

"Please," she said.

I moved the hair carefully out of the wide, blinking gray

eyes. She was the first one to ask, "You're looking me in
the eyes; most humans don't do that. I mean, I wouldn't roll
you or anything, but cops are trained not to look into our
eyes."

I smiled. "You aren't old enough to roll me with your eyes,
Sarah."

She frowned up at me. "I don't understand." Then her eyes
went wide, and what little color she had to her skin drained
away. You don't get to see a vampire go pale very often.

"Oh my God," she said, and her voice held terror.

Rocco stepped up. "What's wrong?"

"She's figured out who I am," I said, quietly.

Sarah the vampire had started to scream. "No, please, he
made me. It was like I was some human. He just rolled me.
Oh, God, I swear to you. I didn't do this. I didn't mean . . . Oh,
God, oh, God, oh, God. You're the Executioner! Oh, my God,
oh, my God, you're going to kill us all!"

"You might want to step outside. I'll try to calm her down,"
Rocco said, having to yell above her screams.

I left him to the hysterical vampire and went back out into
the main part of the club. Hooper and Olaf were arguing,
quietly but heatedly, in the corner of the room away from the
prisoners. There were still plenty of guards on the vampires. I
walked by them and found them watching me. The looks were
either hostile or scared. Either they'd heard Sarah screaming
or someone else had figured it out. Of course, there was one
other possibility.

I got close to the two men and caught snatches, "You son of
a bitch, you are not allowed to threaten prisoners."

"It was not a threat," Olaf said in his deep voice. "I was
merely telling the vampire what awaits them all."

"They're telling us everything we want to know, Jeffries.
We don't need to scare them into confessing."

They both looked at me and made enough room so I could
join the little circle. "What did you tell the girl?"

"How do you know it was a girl?" Hooper asked.

"I'll do you one better, I'll tell you which girl. The one with
long, wavy brown hair, petite."

Hooper narrowed his eyes at me. "How the hell did you know that?"

"Otto has a type," I said.

"He was talking low to her, but he made sure the others could hear. He told her he was going to cut her heart out while she was still alive. He told her he'd make sure and do her after dark, so she'd be awake for it all." Hooper was as angry as I'd ever seen him. There was a fine trembling in his hands, as if he were fighting the urge to make fists.

I sighed and spoke low. "Did you also mention who I am?"

"I told her we were vampire hunters, and we had the Executioner and Death with us."

"I know Blake is the Executioner, but who's Death? You?"

"Ted," I said. I glared up at Olaf. "You wanted them afraid. You wanted to watch the fear on all their faces, didn't you?"

He just looked at me.

Hooper asked, "What's your nickname, Jeffries?"

"I do not have one."

"He doesn't leave survivors," I said.

Hooper looked from one to the other of us. "Wait a minute, are you telling me that these vampires are all going to be executed?"

"They are vampires involved with the serial killer we were sent to destroy. They are covered under the current warrant," Olaf said.

"The human crowd at the barricades attacked police officers, but when they said the vampire took them over, we believed them."

"I believe the vampires, too," I said.

"It doesn't matter," Olaf said. "They took human hostages, threatened human life, and are proven associates of a master vampire that is covered under an active warrant of execution. They have forfeited their rights, all their rights."

Hooper stared at Olaf for a second, then turned to me. "Is he right?"

I just nodded.

"No one died tonight," he said, "and I want to keep it that way."

"You're a cop; you save lives. We're executioners, Hooper; we don't save lives, we take them."

"Are you telling me that you're all right with killing these people?"

"They aren't people," Olaf said.

"In the eyes of the law, they are," Hooper said.

I shook my head. "No, because if they were really people under the law, I'd have another option. The law, as written, doesn't make exceptions. Otto is right; they have forfeited their right to live under the law."

"But they were under the power of a vampire, just like the human crowd."

"Yes, but the law doesn't recognize that as a possibility. It doesn't believe that one vampire can take over another vampire. It only protects humans from the power of vampires."

"Are you telling me that there's no other option for these vampires?"

"They go from here to the morgue. They'll be chained to a gurney with holy objects, or maybe these new chains will do, I don't know. But they will be taken to the morgue and tied down in some way, where they will wait until dawn, and when they go to sleep for the day, we kill them, all of them."

"The law does not say we must wait for dawn," Olaf said.

I couldn't keep the look of disgust off my face. "No one voluntarily does them while they're awake. You only do that when you're out of options."

"If we do them as soon as possible, then we can move on to help Sanchez and the other practitioners."

"They radioed in," Hooper said.

"What happened?" I asked.

"House was empty. The house had been torn up by something, and Bering, or what we assume was Bering, is dead. He'd been dead for a while."

"So, a dead end, no pun intended."

Olaf said, "I thought they were only to scout the house psychically, and wait for the rest of us to enter it."

"They sensed nothing in the house. They radioed in and the lieutenant made the call." Hooper turned back to me. "If we could prove that these vampires were telling the truth, could you delay the executions?"

"We have some discretion on when to put the warrant into force," I said.

"Cannibal can get their memories."

"He'll be opening himself up psychically to vampires. That's different from playing around in human brains," I said.

"It doesn't matter why they did what they did," Olaf said. "According to the law, they will be executed, regardless of why."

"We're supposed to protect all the people in this city." Hooper pointed back at the waiting vampires. "Last I checked, they qualify as people."

"I don't know what to tell you, Sergeant. No jail will take them, and we can't leave them for days chained to a gurney with holy objects. It's considered cruel and unusual, so they must be executed in a timely manner."

"So it's better to just kill them than to leave them on the gurney?"

"I'm telling you the law, not what I believe," I said, "Frankly, I think putting them in cross-wrapped coffins for a while would keep them safe and out of the way, but that was considered cruel and unusual, too."

"If they were human, it wouldn't be."

"If they were human, we wouldn't be talking about putting them in a little box and shoving them in a hole somewhere. If they were human, we wouldn't be allowed to chain them to a gurney and remove their hearts and their heads. If they were human, we'd be out of a job."

He stared at me, a slow dawning look that was almost disgust. "Wait here, I'm going to talk to the lieutenant."

"The law is the law," Olaf said.

"I'm afraid he's right, Hooper."

He looked at me, ignoring Olaf. "If there were another option, would you sign off on it?"

"It depends on the option, but I'd love to have a legal recourse for moments like this that doesn't include murder."

"It's not murder," Olaf said.

I turned to him. "You don't believe that, because if it wasn't murder, you wouldn't enjoy it as much."

He gave me those cave-dark eyes, and there was a hint of anger down in the depths. I didn't care. I just knew that I didn't want to kill Sarah, or Steve, or Henry Jefferson, or the girl that he'd made cry. But to keep Olaf from being alone with the women, I'd take them myself, but not while it was dark, not while they could see it coming, not while they were afraid.

"You really don't enjoy killing them, do you?" he asked, and he sounded surprised.

"I told you I didn't enjoy it."

"You did, but I didn't believe you."

"Why do you believe me now?"

"I watched your face. You're trying to think of ways to save them or to lessen their suffering."

"You could tell all that from one look?"

"Not just one look, a series of looks, like clouds passing over the sun, one after another."

I didn't know what to say to that; it was almost poetic. "These people are innocent of any wrongdoing. They don't deserve to die for not being strong enough to resist Vittorio."

"Ted would say that no vampire is innocent."

"And what do you say?" I asked, trying to be angry, because it was better than the shaky feeling in my gut. I didn't want to kill these people.

"I say that no one is innocent."

Hooper came back with Grimes beside him. Grimes said, "We have a lawyer who's been wanting to try for a stay of execution in cases like this."

"You mean like that last-minute call from the governor in the movies," I said.

Grimes nodded. His so-sincere brown eyes studied my face. "We need an executioner to write it up and sign that he or she thinks that executing these vampires would be murder and not in the public good."

"Let Cannibal read some minds, make certain we haven't been fooled, and then I'll sign it."

"Anita," Olaf said.

"Don't, just don't, and you stay away from the prisoners."

"You are not in charge of me," he said, and there was the beginning of anger. Great.

"No, but I am," Grimes said. "Stay away from the prisoners until further notice, Marshal Jeffries. I'll tell the other marshals what we're doing."

They walked toward the back room and the ex-hostages and Edward. Olaf said what I was thinking. "Edward won't like what you're doing."

"He doesn't have to like it."

"Most women value their boyfriend's opinion."

"Fuck you," I said, and walked away from him.

He called after me. "I thought you didn't want to."

I kept walking. The vampires on the floor stared at me as if I were Vittorio, or something else equally scary. There was hatred in a few eyes, but underneath it all was their fear. I could taste it on the back of my tongue, like something sweet that held a bitterness to it, like dark chocolate that's a little too dark.

The far door opened and Cannibal was helping Sarah the vampire walk through the door. She caught sight of me and started screaming all over again, "She's going to kill us! She's going to kill us all!"

Usually she'd be right, but maybe, just maybe, we really could save everyone tonight.

65

IT WAS LESS than two hours before dawn. I was so tired I ached, but the vampires were all still alive. They were chained to gurneys in the morgue, and since the morgue had a room designed for only one vamp at a time, the coroner and all of his people hadn't been too happy to see ten of them, but Grimes had used his own men to act as extra guards. The guard duty was volunteer only, but his men had looked at him like he was crazy; if he said it was a good thing, it was. Besides, he'd explained it like this: "No one died tonight; if we do this, no one dies tomorrow either."

Edward hadn't been happy with me. Bernardo had been amused. Olaf had left me alone, caught in his own thoughts that I wanted no part of. I'd actually let Sergeant Rocco drop me at my hotel because Edward didn't offer. Normally, it would have hurt my feelings, but not over this.

"I've never tried my talent on a real vampire before," he said in the quiet of the car.

"How different was it?" I asked, still gazing out at darkened buildings on the street. Like most streets in most cities, everything was closed on this street. Just before dawn, even the strippers get to go home.

"They're still people, but it's as if their thoughts are slower. No," he said, and something about how he said it made me look at him. His profile in the light and shadow of the streetlights was very serious. "It was like those insects frozen in amber, as if the memories that were clearest to them were old, and what happened tonight with our killer was mistier for them."

"I'll bet that was only true of Henry Jefferson and Sarah," I said.

He glanced away from the road to me. "Yeah, how did you know?"

"They were the oldest. You know how with some people, when they get old, the past is more clear than the present to them?"

He nodded.

"I think for some vampires, it's like that, too. The ones who haven't succeeded but just survived. I think they look back on their glory days."

"Does your vampire boyfriend do that?"

I resisted the urge to ask, *Which one?* and played nice. "No, but then he's the master of his city."

"You're saying he's happy now."

"Yeah."

"Henry was wearing a watch that cost more than this truck. He's not doing bad, so why was his most vivid memory of a time when women wore long dresses and curls, and he was in vest and suit with a pocket watch and a top hat?"

"Did he love the woman?" I asked.

Rocco thought about that, then said, "Yes." He looked at me again. "I've never been able to pick up love images before, Anita. I'm good at violence, hate, the dark stuff, but tonight I got soft images and had to work at the harsh. Did you do something to me when I read you?"

"Not on purpose," I said, "but I tend to have an effect on vampire powers."

"I'm not a vampire," he said.

"We're alone, Rocco, and you wanted to talk to me alone, so no more lies. You know, and I know, and your men know, that you feed on the memories you gather."

"They don't know."

"Cannibal is your call sign. They know; at some level, they know." I settled back into the seat, and we turned onto the Strip, and I suddenly knew where everyone was; they were here. The street looked the same at hours before dawn as it had closer to midnight. "I thought New York was the city that never slept," I said.

Rocco laughed. "I've never been there, but the Strip doesn't sleep much." He glanced at me again, then back to the bright lights and the animated billboards. "You fed on my memory, too."

"You showed me how."

"By me feeding on one memory, you learned how to turn it on me, just like that?"

"Apparently," I said.

"Where are you staying?"

"The New Taj," I said.

"Max's place." He said it like it was a bad thing.

"Max knows if he lets anything happen to us, it might be a bad thing. He'll keep us safe to keep the peace."

"Your boyfriend that big in the vampire world?"

"We do okay," I said.

"That didn't answer the question."

"Nope, it didn't."

"Fine." We were at the light in front of the Bellagio, with the fake skyline of New York close by and the Eiffel Tower in sight. It was like the world had been pared down and squished into one street.

"Ask the question you wanted to ask, Rocco."

I half-expected him to protest, but he didn't; he finally asked, "You're like me. You feed from your power."

"From raising the dead? I don't think so."

"It's something to do with sex or love. I feed on violence, the memory of it, but you feed on softer emotions, don't you?"

I debated on how to answer; maybe I was just tired because I told the truth. "Yeah."

"Am I going to keep seeing softer things?"

"I don't know. It's like we traded a little power." I looked at the pirate ship, the fire, and it was surreal, unreal, like some dream where nothing makes sense.

"Have you ever shared power like that before?"

"I can act as a focus for psychic ability for raising the dead."

"What does that mean?"

"I can share power with other animators, and combined we can raise more, or older, dead."

"Really," he said.

"Yeah, I wrote it up for the magazine *The Animator* a few years back."

"E-mail me the back issue, and I'll read up on it. Maybe practitioners here can do something similar."

"Your abilities aren't very similar."

"Ours weren't either."

"We're both living vampires, Cannibal; that's similar enough."

He glanced at me, and it was a longer look. "The law hasn't expanded to psychic vampires yet."

"They don't want to understand it enough to regulate it."

He grinned. "Too many politicians would be on the wrong side of it."

"Probably," I said.

He gave me that glance again. "You know any?"

"No, just being cynical."

"You're good at it."

"Why thank you, always high praise from a cop." I had the feeling that he still hadn't asked all of his questions. I waited in the bright neon silence, punctuated by darkness between the lights, as if the night were thicker anywhere the light didn't shine. My mood was showing in my head.

He pulled into the big circular drive at the New Taj. I realized I should have called ahead and had some of our people meet us. I'd expected to be dropped off by Edward and the boys, and I would have been safe enough. Now it was just me.

"You want me to walk you up?"

I smiled at him, hand on the door. "I'm a big girl."

"This vampire has a serious hard-on for you, Anita."

"You ask all the questions you wanted privacy for?" I asked.

"Anyone ever tell you that you're blunt?"

"All the damn time."

He laughed again, but there was an edge of nerves to it. "Do you ever get tempted to feed on more than you should?"

The doorman, or the valet, or someone, was at the door. I waved them off. "What do you mean, Rocco?"

"I can take a memory, Anita. I can take it and erase it from their mind. I did it accidentally a few times. It's like it becomes my memory, not theirs, and it's a high. It's a rush. I think if I let myself, I could take it all, every bad memory they've ever had. Maybe more. Maybe I could take everything and leave them blank. I think about how it might feel to take it all."

"Tempts you, doesn't it?" I said.

He nodded and wouldn't look at me.

"Have you ever done it?"

He gave me a look of shock, of horror. "No, of course not. It'd be evil."

I nodded. "It's not about being able to do something, Rocco. It's not even about thinking about doing it. It's not even about being tempted to go too far."

"Then what is it about?" he asked.

I looked into that very grown-up, very competent face, and watched the doubt in his eyes. I knew that doubt. "It's about deciding not to do it. It's about being tempted but not giving in. It isn't our abilities that make us evil, Sergeant, it's giving in to them. Psychic ability isn't any different from being good with a gun. Just because you could walk into a crowd and take out half of them doesn't mean you will."

"I can lock my gun up, Anita. I can't take this out of me and put it somewhere safe."

"No, we can't, so every day, every night, we make the choice to be good guys and not bad guys."

He looked at me, hands still on the steering wheel. "And that's your answer: we're good guys because we don't do bad things?"

"Isn't that what a good guy is?" I asked.

"No, a good guy does good things, too."

"Don't you do good things every day?"

He frowned. "I try."

"Rocco, that is all any of us can do. We try. We do our best. We resist temptation. We keep moving."

"I have to be older than you by a decade; why is it that I'm asking you for advice?"

"First, I think I'm older than I look. Second, I'm the first one you've met that you thought might be tempted in the same way. It's hard when you think you're the only one, no matter how old you are."

"That sounds like the voice of experience," he said.

I nodded. "Sometimes, sometimes I've got so much company I don't know what to do with it."

"Like that," and he nodded toward the window. It was Truth and Wicked, patiently waiting for us to finish our conversation. Had they been watching for me, or had they just known I was here? Did I want to ask? Not unless I was ready for the answer.

"Yeah, like that. I turned back to him and offered him my hand. "Thanks for the lift."

"Thanks for the talk."

We shook, and there was no magic between us now. We were both tired, our fires dimmed behind use and emotion. He got out and helped us unload the car. The overeager bellman was allowed to touch my suitcase and nothing else. Most of my really dangerous stuff was still locked up at SWAT, but there was enough here that I didn't want the staff carrying it. Wicked and Truth took the extra bags. Sergeant Rocco offered his hand to them. They were surprised by the offer, though he probably didn't see the signs of it. They shook his hand. He said good night to me, and "See you tomorrow."

"We'll start in the area where he found all his vampire victims tonight."

"Yeah, maybe his lair will be in the area." He got in his truck. We went for the doors. I wished I felt more secure that Vittorio only hunted near his lair. It seemed like an obvious mistake, and he didn't strike me as the kind to make those.

Wicked and Truth didn't say much until they got to the elevator and we were alone. "You seem tired," Truth said.

"I am."

"You fed on both of us, and you're tired already," Wicked said. "Should we be insulted?"

I smiled and shook my head. "It was a stressful night, and no, it's no reflection on either of you. You know just how good you both are."

"A backhanded compliment, but I'll take it," Wicked said.

"I wasn't fishing, I was just saying you seem tired."

"Sorry, Truth, sorry, just a long damn night."

They exchanged a look, which I did not like. "What was that look about?"

Wicked said, "Requiem is waiting in your room."

"I figured that my room would have the coffins, or the adjoining room."

"That's not what he means," Truth said.

"Look, I'm beyond tired, just tell me."

"He's waiting to feed you," Wicked said.

"I fed on both of you less than"—I squinted at my watch—"less than six hours ago. I don't need to feed the *ardeur*."

"Jean-Claude gave instructions that you needed to have food available more often if you wanted it."

"Did he now?"

The elevator doors opened. "He's worried that you'll lose it with the police as your only food, Anita," Wicked said.

I thought about that and couldn't argue that it wouldn't be very bad. "I do not feel in the mood, guys."

"We're just giving you a heads-up, Anita," Wicked said.

"Did you guys tell him I fed on you both?"

They exchanged that look again.

"What?"

"We came through the door, and he said, 'She fed on you. She fed on you both.'"

"How did he know?" I asked.

They shrugged, and it was like a mirrored gesture. "He said he could smell you on our skin."

"He's a vampire, not a werewolf."

"Look," Wicked said, "don't shoot the messenger. But he's waiting in your bed, and if you turn him down, I don't know how he's going to take it."

I leaned my back against the wall between two doors that were not ours. "Are you saying he's jealous that I fed on you guys?"

"*Jealous* may be too strong a word," Wicked said.

"Yes, he was jealous," Truth said.

Wicked frowned at his brother. "You don't have to live up to your name all the time."

Truth shrugged again.

"And this is exactly why Jean-Claude put you in charge during the night shift, and not Requiem," I said.

"Because he's a moody bastard," Truth said.

I nodded. "Yeah." I pushed away from the wall and looked at my watch. "We've got an hour until dawn. Shit." I stopped walking, because I was in the lead. "Gentlemen, I don't know what room we're in."

Wicked led the way, and Truth brought up the rear, with me in the middle. We got to the room. Wicked used the little key card, pushed the door open, and held it for me.

It was a nice room. Big, a little too red and lush for my tastes, but it was a nice suite. We'd have no complaints about Max's hospitality on rooms when we got back home. The outer room was a real living room with a table for four near the windows that looked out over the brightness of the Strip. There was a coffin near the door, but only one.

"Where are you sleeping?"

"Our coffins are in the other room for tonight. You have less than an hour; enjoy." They put my bags by the closed door that had to lead into the bedroom, and then they left.

"Cowards," I hissed.

Wicked stuck his head back around the door. "He doesn't like guys, and neither do we."

"You didn't mind an audience earlier," I said.

"We don't, or I don't, but Requiem does. Good night." He closed the door, after taking the privacy sign with him. I realized that Jean-Claude hadn't put Wicked in charge of just the vampires at night but me, too. I guess, in fairness, that Requiem wasn't the only moody bastard still in the room.

But this kind of thing was exactly what had gotten Requiem moved lower down the food chain for me. He was like one of those boyfriends that the harder you try to break up with them, the harder they hang on. This was also the kind of thing that made me want to go back to my own house and leave most of them somewhere else.

I just wanted to get some sleep before I had to get back up and go out and hunt Vittorio again.

The door to the bedroom opened, just enough to show the

line of his body, one hand, an arm, a spill of long, thick, dark hair. In the dimness of the room, with the backlight, the waist-length hair looked very black. It was hard to tell where the black robe he wore ended and the hair began. The skin that showed at chest and neck and face was pale as the first light of dawn, a cold beauty like snow. The Vandyke beard and mustache were black, darker than the hair. They framed his mouth the way you would frame a work of art, so that your eye was drawn to it.

I let my eyes rise higher, because that was my real failing. I was an eye man, or woman. A pretty pair of eyes really did it for me, always had. His eyes were blue and green like Caribbean seawater in the sun, one of the most startling shades of blue that I'd ever seen outside contact lenses, and his were natural. Belle Morte had a thing for blue-eyed men, and she'd tried to collect him, as she had Asher and Jean-Claude, so she'd have the darkest blue, the palest blue, and the greenest blue that was still blue. Requiem had fled the continent of Europe so he didn't become another of her possessions.

A minute ago, I'd wanted to say, "I've been hunting serial killers all day, honey, can't I take a pass?" Now all I could do was stare at him, and know that there was nothing to do but admire the artwork.

I dropped the bags in my hands and went to him. I slid my hands inside the half-opened robe to caress that smooth perfection of skin. I laid a kiss on his chest and was rewarded with the sound of his breath sighing outward.

"You were angry with me when you first came in the room."

I gazed up at his six-foot-even frame, hands on his chest. I was still wearing too much weaponry to fall into his arms. "Then I saw you standing there, and I realized that you'd worried all night. You'd wondered where I was, and what was happening, and I didn't call. You were left wondering if dawn would come and you still wouldn't know I was safe."

He nodded, silently.

"I'm a bad husband, Requiem, everyone knows that."

His hands found my shoulders, traced my upper arms, as he said, ". . . the heart's tally, telling off / the griefs I have undergone from girlhood upwards, / old and new, and now more than ever; / for I have never not had some new sorrow, / some fresh affliction to fight against."

"I don't know the poem, but it sounds depressing."

He gave a small smile. "It's a very old poem; the original was Anglo-Saxon. It's called 'The Wife's Complaint.'"

I shook my head. "I'm trying to apologize, and I don't know why. You always make me feel like I've done something wrong, and I'm tired of it."

He dropped his hands away. "Now I've made you angry."

I nodded, and started moving past him into the bedroom. No one was pretty enough for this level of need. I just didn't know what to do with it. I kept my back to him while I stripped out of the vest, the weapons, all the paraphernalia of my day. It made quite a pile on my side of the bed. It was the side I slept on when there was only me and one man in the bed. Lately, that hadn't been often. I didn't mind being in the middle, God knew, but some nights there were too many, and this was one night when just one more was feeling like too many.

I heard the robe on the carpet; silk has such a distinctive sound. I felt him just behind me, felt him reach for me. "Don't."

I felt him go very still behind me. "I know you do not love me, my evening star."

"I have too many men in my life that I love, Requiem; why can't we just be lovers? Why do you have to remind me constantly that you love me, and I don't love you? Your disappointment is like a constant pressure, and it's not my doing. I never offered love, never promised it."

"I will serve my lady in any way she will have me, for I have no pride left where she is concerned."

"I don't even want to know what you're quoting; just go."

"Look at me and tell me to go, and I will go."

I shook my head stubbornly. "No, because if I see you, I won't. You're beautiful. You're wonderful in bed. But you're also a pain in the ass, and I'm tired, Requiem. I am so tired."

"I didn't even ask you how your night had gone. I thought only of my own feelings, my own needs. I am no true lover, to have thought of only myself."

"I was told you were here to feed the *ardeur*."

"We both know that's a lie," he said, voice soft and close.

"I'm here because it broke my heart to know that you slept with the Wicked Truth."

I started to say something angry. He said, "Hush, I can't help feeling the way I feel, my evening star. I have asked Jean-Claude to find me a new city, one where I can be someone's second-in-command rather than a distant third."

I turned around then and searched his face. "You're telling the truth."

He gave that slight smile. "I am."

I hugged him then, molding our bodies together the way you do with someone when you've lost count of how many times you've been together. You know each other's bodies. You know the music of their breathing when sex perfumes the air. I hugged him to me and realized that I would miss him. But I also knew he was right.

He stroked my hair. "It helps to know that you will miss me."

I raised my face to look into those blue eyes with their flash of green around the pupils. "You know I find you beautiful and amazing in bed."

He nodded and gave that sad smile again. "But all your men are beautiful, and all of them are good in bed. I want to go somewhere that I have a chance to shine. A chance to have a woman love me, Anita, just me. You will never love just me."

"I'm not sure I will ever love just anyone," I said.

He smiled a little wider. "That is something, to know that you frustrate Jean-Claude, too. I never thought to see anyone who could resist him."

I frowned up at him. "I haven't exactly resisted."

"You are his lover, his human servant, but you are not his."

I started to step back, and he hugged me closer. "He said almost the same thing on the phone. Do I have you to thank for that little talk?"

"I told him why I needed to leave, and he agreed. That is why I am here in Las Vegas, to see if I would like to visit."

"I don't think it's your kind of town."

"Nor I, but it is a start. I will see their show, and I will dance, and women will think me beautiful, and they will want me, and eventually I will want them."

"There isn't enough of me, Requiem, not to date all of you.

I can have sex with this many men, but I can't be everyone's lady love; no single woman could."

He nodded. "I know. Now, kiss me, kiss me like you mean it. Kiss me like you'll miss me. Kiss me, quick before dawn, because when you finish hunting your killer, I won't be going back with you. If I don't like Vegas, then the Master of Philadelphia is looking for a second, and she's requested a man of Belle's line if she can get it."

I looked up into his face and realized this really was it. He meant it. I went up on tiptoe, and he lowered his face to mine. I kissed those lips, gently at first, like you'd touch a work of art, afraid to scratch it, and then I let my hands and mouth kiss him the way he was meant to be kissed. Kiss him the way you kissed someone when the touch of their mouth, the weight of their hands, the rise of their body was like food and drink to you. I couldn't give him my heart, but I gave him what I could, and it wasn't a lie. I loved his body, and the press of his sad poetry; I just didn't love him. God knows I'd tried to love them all, but my heart just didn't seem to stretch that big.

He drew away first, laughing, eyes bright with the attention. "It is too close to dawn for me to do justice to such a kiss. I know you do not let even our master sleep in your bed once he dies for the day, so I will go to my box. I will send warmer bed partners to you, so that you will not be alone, and you can feed when you wake."

"Requiem," I started, but he touched fingertips to my lips.

"She walks in beauty, like the night / Of cloudless climes and starry skies; / And all that's best of dark and bright / Meet in her aspect and her eyes."

I wasn't sure why, but I felt the first hard, hot tear trail down my face. He moved his fingers from my lips to catch my tears. He kissed them from his skin, then kissed them from my face. "That you would cry for my parting means much." Then he left, closing the door gently behind him.

I went to the bathroom and started getting ready for bed. I'd wash the tears away. I wasn't even sure why I was crying. I was just tired. I heard noises and turned off the water, to have Crispin call out. "It's us, Anita."

I had a moment to wonder who "us" was, because Crispin

didn't know any of the other wereanimals who had come from St. Louis, or not well enough to bring them to bed with him. I'd found that heterosexual men are very picky about who they bring to bed, boywise. It's more about friendship than sex. More about trust, than lust. I thought about peeking out and seeing, but it seemed like too much trouble. So tired. Crispin and whoever would still be there when I was done. I came out of the bathroom wearing the robe off the door, which covered me from shoulder to my toes. The two men in my bed were wearing nothing but the bedsheet at their waist. Two naked men in my bed, both cute enough. Problem was, one of them I'd never seen nude.

CRISPIN WAS AS lean and muscled as I remembered him. He sat up with a smile, the sheet pooling into his lap, so that I could see the side of his hip, and knew for certain there was nothing between him and my sheets. His short, curly white hair was backlit by the lamp, so that the light played in the curls, forming a shining halo of white. He gave me that crooked smile that dimpled just one side of his mouth. He might look like an angel in my bed with his halo, but if it was an angel, it was fallen.

Domino lay on his back on the other side of the bed, one arm stretched over the pillows, touching where I would have to lie. His black and white curls were framed against the white of the pillow. I realized that his hair was mostly black. Hadn't it been closer to an even mix before? His eyes were brilliant orange, the color that fire can have, but fire doesn't have veins of gold running through it. Fire doesn't blink long lashes at you, and try for a neutral face when its eyes give it away. The eyes held need, longing.

I waited to be mad, but I wasn't. Suddenly, of all the people in Vegas, I couldn't think of any two other men that I'd rather have curled up between. I'd told Truth that Belle Morte's line can only be as powerful as the vampire doing it is willing to be cut, but it was more than that. I could only go as deep into someone's heart as I was willing to let them dive into mine. I had all this power, and no idea how to protect myself from having that two-edged blade cut me to the bone.

All I could think when I saw them was *home*. A deep feeling of contentment, that Crispin hadn't earned yet, and Domino was a stranger to me. But sometimes you meet a stranger, and from the moment you see him there is a connection, almost a memory, as if that skin, that scent, has been on your sheets before, like an echo. I should have fought it, argued with it, but I was so tired. My eyes burned with it.

I said the only thing I could think to say. "I don't need to feed yet." My voice sounded small and uncertain. I cleared my throat sharply, tried again. "Nothing personal, but I'm . . ."

"Tired," Crispin said, "we know. We can feel it."

I looked past him to Domino. I could feel his uncertainty, and how much he wanted this to be all right. I didn't have anything left to fight with; it felt fine, good, strangely okay. For once in my life, I didn't question it. I didn't ask, *Can you both behave yourself if we're all naked?* because they were were-animals, and naked doesn't mean sex to them. It just means you aren't wearing any clothes. It was my human mind that made it dirty.

I undid the robe's sash and walked toward the bed. Crispin smiled, but Domino watched that thin line of my body that he could glimpse as I moved. Maybe being naked wasn't just not having clothes for him in that moment?

He spoke, and his voice was rough, so that he had to clear his throat before he finished. "Sex would be wonderful, but I feel your tiredness like some great weight pulling you down, and pulling at us. Let us hold you, Anita, just hold you."

I studied his face for a breath or two. He lifted his hand from the pillows and held it out to me. I let the robe fall to the floor and crawled onto the bed between them. Crispin helped me slide under the covers, then slid his body along my side, so that I could feel that it wasn't just Domino who was going to have trouble sleeping.

I stared up at Crispin, where he lay propped up on one elbow, grinning at me. "There's this beautiful naked woman in bed with me, and I'm a guy."

That made me smile. Then the bed moved, and it made me turn to see Domino moving toward us. His face was uncertain, as if he wasn't sure he'd be as welcome. Neither was I.

He had more bulk to his upper body than Crispin, and with them both propped up on elbows, I realized that the few inches of extra height Crispin had were all in the waist. Domino was keeping a few inches of distance between us rather than rubbing his body against me like Crispin. I appreciated the restraint.

I reached up to touch his hair. The curls were soft, but not as soft as Crispin's white. "Wasn't your hair more evenly white and black before?"

He smiled. "I've shifted to black tiger between then and now; when I come back to human form, my hair reflects the fur color of my last shape."

I stared up at him. "You can shift to white tiger *and* black?"

He nodded, rubbing his head against my hand, so that I stroked his curls more, the way you'd pet a cat that rubbed against your hand. It moved my hand from his hair to the side of his face, and he laid his cheek against my hand, pressing, so that I held his face. His eyes closed, and his face went almost slack, as if some weight had suddenly gone from him.

I rose up to kiss him, but it closed that small distance between us, and I could suddenly feel that he was not only happy to be in the bed, but so hard and eager that it made my breath catch in my throat and a small sound of surprise escape me.

He drew away from me. "I'm sorry, Anita, I can't help the reaction."

I shook my head. "It's not . . . Oh, hell, don't apologize for being male, Domino. I like it."

He smiled, almost embarrassed.

I found my hand sliding down the front of his body. His eyes closed again, and his head went back, as if it had been a long time for him.

Crispin seemed to read my mind. "The White Tiger Clan prides itself on being pure-blooded. Our queen is happy to find black tiger blood, but most of the females of our clan won't risk bringing a nonpure offspring into the world."

I stared up at the man who was still looming a little over me. My hand had frozen at his upper stomach. He still had his eyes closed, but he started to turn away, started to roll over.

I stopped the movement with my hand on his shoulder and chest. "There is nothing wrong with you, Domino. You're beautiful."

He shook his head. "No."

"Handsome, then," I said.

He gave me an almost shy look. "I can't believe that."

"Why not?"

"Because no one who's ever mattered has treated me like it's true."

In that moment I knew, tired or not, I couldn't be that tired. "I'm going to say something I will probably never say again."

He looked at me, all cautious again.

"We only have time for a quickie."

He grinned in surprise.

I smiled back. "I really do need to sleep before the police call me and we have to hunt the bad guys again, but I want you to know that it's no reflection on you. You are handsome, and if what I just felt against my hip is any indication, all the body is pretty damn good."

He actually looked embarrassed, dunking his head. I'd have estimated him at about thirty, but he was acting younger. Maybe in this one area he was, through sheer lack of experience.

I touched his face, turned him to look at me. "Make love to me."

"Making love takes time to do it right," he said.

I grinned. "All right, fuck me."

He looked startled.

Crispin said, "Her pillow talk is usually straight to the point."

I turned my head so I could frown at him.

He shrugged the one shoulder in the air. "Well, it's true."

I frowned harder, then turned back to Domino. "Whatever word you want to use."

"Just like that?" he asked.

I nodded. "Just like that."

"Why?"

"Because I want that lost look out of your eyes."

"Why do you care what look I have in my eyes?"

"Because the wound cuts both ways."

"What does that mean?"

"Shut up," Crispin said, "and take the offer, so we can all sleep."

Domino flashed him a less than friendly look, then looked

back down at me. "I've spent my life not being able to trust the women around me. Only the survivors would touch me, never my own clan."

"I'm a survivor," I said.

He shook his head. "No," and he leaned down over my hair and took a long, deep breath. "No, you smell like me: dark and light, all at the same time."

I slid my hand farther down his body and found that he wasn't trembling as hard as he had been; all the talking had softened things. I wrapped my hand around him and squeezed gently. It fluttered his eyes shut and sent his breath out in a sigh.

"Enough talk," I said.

He had to swallow before he could whisper, "Okay."

I continued to work him with my hand as he came down for a kiss, and suddenly he was kissing me. He kissed me as if my lips were food and he were starving. My hands were on his back; my legs slid down his thighs to wrap around his lower legs. He laid his full weight on top of me while we kissed, fiercely, completely. His body was back to that trembling hardness. Just the feel of him on the outside of my body, pressed between us, made me cry out.

Crispin was standing beside the bed with a condom in his hand. "Anita made me promise, after the first time we were together."

Domino and I came out of the kiss, gasping. I stared up at Crispin as if I didn't know who he was or what he was saying.

Domino went up on his knees, and I could suddenly see what I'd been touching. It brought an, "Oh, my God" from me.

Domino took the condom and slid it over himself. He went to all fours over me. He glanced at himself, then at my face. "We haven't done any prep work on you, and I'm . . ."

I finished for him, "Not small."

He shook his head.

Crispin said, "She's tight, but she'll be wet."

I frowned at him.

"Do you need foreplay for this?" he asked, hands on hips, as if chastising me.

I thought about it. "Foreplay is lovely, but"—I looked down Domino's body, and all I could think of was—"no, I want that inside me."

"I don't want to hurt you, not our first time."

"I'll tell you if it hurts, but," and I stopped, because no man wants to hear that you have other lovers more well endowed than he is, especially not at this moment, "Please, Domino, just fuck me. Now."

He didn't ask again. He let his body fall on top of mine, spreading my legs a little wider with a movement of his hips and thighs. He had to use his hand to guide himself in, but once he started, he didn't need any more help. He was wide enough that he did have to work his way in, the first few strokes.

He started above me, on his hands, his lower body pressed between my legs, so that I could look down the line of my body and watch him push his way in and out of me. Just the sight of it made me cry out, again.

"God, you're right, she's so tight, but wet."

Crispin had gone back to his side of the bed, and was simply watching. "I told you."

Domino's body worked me a little more open, and he could suddenly find his rhythm. I watched his body slide faster, smoother, deeper, inside mine. This was a position that if the man was of any size, it usually hit the spot, and he was, and it did.

I felt that growing weight between my legs. I whispered, "Oh, God, almost."

"Almost what?" he asked, but not like he was really listening to the answer. His voice was breathy, and his eyes were shut with concentration.

Then between one stroke and another, that weight spilled up and over, bathing my skin in warmth and pleasure. It tore a scream from my mouth and dug my nails into his lower arms. He froze above me.

Crispin's voice, saying, "Don't stop."

He started again, but he'd lost just that edge of ground. He gasped out. "I thought I'd hurt you."

"She's a screamer," Crispin said.

I might have frowned at him, but Domino was back to that

rhythm above me, and I didn't care about anything else. He fought to keep that rhythm, trying for another orgasm for me, I think, but his body began to lose the smooth motion of it. His breathing grew ragged. He fought, one stroke, two, four. That weight built between my legs again.

I gasped, "Close, close again."

He fought his body to keep pumping, and forced himself back into a smoother rhythm. I pushed myself up on my elbows, so the view was even better, and the angle a little sharper, and that was it. He spilled me over the edge again, and I screamed the pleasure of it at the ceiling.

He didn't stop this time. His rhythm changed, but it didn't matter now, as long as he continued to go in and out of me. The orgasm grew, and flowed from one sensation to another, as his rhythm grew more desperate, his body moving harder, faster, and he finally lowered his body so that he could use all that length and bump the end of me. It was a different pleasure, but he'd worked me enough that it was pleasure.

I gasped, "Harder, deeper."

He didn't ask if I meant it this time; he just took me at my word. He pounded himself into me, as hard and deep as he wanted, as I wanted, the weight and strength of him pinning me under him, pinning me to the bed, while his body shuddered above mine. He opened his eyes, suddenly, inches above me, and we stared into each other's eyes as his widened, and his breathing grew ragged again, and his body began to buck, fighting for one more rhythm. Then he hit me deep enough, and it was just pleasure. I screamed and dug my nails down his back, wrapped my legs around his waist, and painted my orgasm down his body in blood and screams.

He cried out above me, a thick, throaty gasp of, "Oh, yes." Then he thrust inside me one last time, as deep as he could go. That made me come again, so that our bodies trembled together, and I buried my mouth against his neck, muffling my screams with his flesh.

He lay on top of me, his heart pounding against my body, the pulse in his neck thudding in my mouth. I let go of his neck because I had the sudden urge to bite harder. I could already taste sweet metal and knew I'd bled him.

I lay back on the bed and held him with my arms, my hands, my legs still wrapped around him. I held him inside my body, as close as I could.

He finally rose up, and I unwrapped myself from him so he could spill himself into the middle of the bed, beside me. He lay on his back, trying to relearn how to breathe, having trouble swallowing past his pulse.

"If that was a quickie," Crispin said, "I can't wait for a longie."

Domino smiled, eyes still half-closed. He managed to say, in a breathless voice, "I wanted it to be good. Didn't want to disappoint."

I lay on my side of the bed, his side of the bed, unable to move anything below the waist and unwilling to move much else. I managed a shaky laugh. "Disappoint, hell, I can't wait to see what it feels like to do that with foreplay."

"So you do want me again?" And his voice was hesitant, his face lost.

I patted his stomach because that was the easiest thing to reach. "If I could move yet, I'd give you a kiss and tell you that every woman who ever turned you down was a fool."

He patted my thigh. "I think that's the sweetest thing any girl's ever said to me."

For some reason that struck me as sad, but I didn't say that part out loud. When we were able to walk, we cleaned up and crawled back into bed. They put me in the middle, and that was fine with me. I'd found that heterosexual men who are willing to have sex with another guy in the bed are still not usually secure enough to sleep with one of them in the middle. I valued the men in my life who didn't sweat stuff like that, but I didn't fault the others. I didn't like to sleep naked with another woman right beside me, as I'd discovered with some of the wereleopards in St. Louis. It was just a big naked puppy pile, or rather kitten pile, but still, I preferred to be sandwiched between beefcake, not cheese cake. So, who was I to bitch?

Some men spoon better than others; I'd found that Crispin was a stomach sleeper, so spooning really didn't work for him. But Domino curled up against my back and wrapped all that tall body around me, as if I were his favorite teddy bear and he couldn't sleep without me. I thought it would be awkward to sleep with a stranger. I mean, sex is one thing, when it's a new friend, but sleep . . . that's helpless. I don't like being helpless around people I've just met. But his body felt like it had been made to fit against mine, his arm tucking me in tight against him, the way Micah did at home. I had a thought for my leopard king. I missed him. I missed Nathaniel. I wondered how Domino would get along with them? I chased the thought away; one problem at a time. I had to kill Vittorio before I could go home. To do that, I had to find him. Later, Rocco and I would start looking for him.

But I didn't have to find Vittorio; he found me.

67

BUT HE DIDN'T find me first. She found me. I stood in the room where I knew her body lay. She looked small under the silk sheet; no, shrunken. For the first time, she looked like a corpse under a sheet. I waited for her to move or to hear her breathe, see movement, but there was nothing. She was gone.

Then I was in a night long ago, with the scent of jasmine and rain on the air. The air was hot, but not muggy, as if there wasn't a lot of moisture in it. But there was that edge of rain, and you could almost feel the ground underneath your feet, eager for it, like a lover waiting for an embrace.

She'd stepped into this night as a woman's figure, and as the night itself, but now she was a voice whispering against my skin. "Necromancer, they are coming to kill me. They are coming with modern weapons and things I do not understand. I have abandoned the shell in the room. That they may have it."

The smell of jasmine grew stronger, as the rain blew closer, a thick, clean smell. "What do you want?"

"You, necromancer. I want your body."

"No," I said.

"No, because you have kept me out. You and your ties to your men. But I need power, enough to survive when my shell is consumed. I cannot take your body, Anita, but I think I can feed through you."

"Feed how?" I asked, and felt the first tightness in my gut. The first hint of fear.

"The tigers, little necromancer, did you think they found you by accident?"

"No, I knew you had done something to me."

"Simply feed on all the colors of their rainbow and give the energy to me. It will give me enough strength to survive until I can find a host."

"Are you asking me or telling me to do this?"

"Would asking make you do it?" the voice asked.

"No."

"Then I tell you to do it."

"No," I said.

"I can make you do it, necromancer, but it will be less pleasant."

"I won't help you find another body, just because you can't have mine."

"Remember, necromancer, I gave you a choice. You have chosen the path of pain. Now, if you become pregnant, it is too late to help me."

"What did you say?"

"When I realized I could not get inside you, I tried to have you pregnant by one of the weretigers, but you stayed too far away from them for too long. Now you lie with two of them, and have a blue tiger close at hand. A color even I thought was lost. There are even two kings of two different pure bloodlines within walking distance of you. I would have given you a choice to use your protection when you fed for me, but if you will not do it willingly, then I will do what I did when you first met the white tiger."

"Wait," I said, because now I was afraid. I'd met Crispin in North Carolina, when he'd been traveling for a VIP bachelor-ette party, and I'd been a guest at the same hotel. I'd woken up two days later, naked, bruised, scratched, sore, with three naked men passed out around me. One had been Jason, but the other had been Crispin, who I'd just met, and Alex, who was just an innocent reporter covering the wedding, who also happened to be a red tiger. I could suddenly taste my pulse in my throat.

"Don't," I said.

"Either feed on the tigers voluntarily and let me take the power, or I will take you again. I will not make it days, though; as I said, pregnant now does me no good. So the sex will be quicker."

"Why me pregnant by a weretiger?"

"Because I was a necromancer in life, Anita, like you, and a wereanimal. The tigers are the most powerful cat left on this earth. I thought if the baby was part weretiger and part necromancer, I would have a greater chance of taking its body."

I was still scared, but the first anger was there, too. "You had no right."

"You've been inside my mind, little necromancer; do you really believe I care about right and wrong?"

The scent of jasmine was thick on my tongue. "No," I whispered. The rain was almost here, the wind cool with it. The night was so dark.

"This is your last choice to make, Anita. Is it willing you are, or is it force?"

"If I help you, you'll use the energy to escape the assassins and hide in someone else's body. You'll take them over and escape."

"Yes," she said.

The rain blew the thin dress against my body. I was wearing sandals that I'd never owned. My hair blew across my face. All I could taste was jasmine, as if I'd drunk perfume. The first spatters of rain rode the wind.

"Time grows short, necromancer. Your answer?"

I knew what the jasmine on my tongue meant. It was her power growing in me, like the trigger on a gun with a finger on it, already moving to squeeze.

I swallowed, and it was like it hurt to swallow past the sweet taste of it. "I can't help you take over another person's body. I can't sacrifice someone else to save myself."

"They would be a stranger to you," the voice in the dark said.

I shook my head. The wind hit me, and the rain came like a wall, so that one moment I was dry, and the next I was soaked to the skin. The rain was cold, and the world tasted of jasmine.

"I can't," I said.

"Oh, you can, and you will, necromancer. You will feed me. You will save me. I am the Mother of All Darkness; I will not die because one stubborn girl said no."

I stood there in a desert night that had existed longer ago

than books or cities. I shivered in a cold rain that hadn't fallen for thousands of years. I tasted jasmine on my tongue and felt her cut off my breath as she slid her power down my throat.

I managed to say, "No means no, bitch!" Then there were no more words.

68

THE RAIN STOPPED abruptly, like someone had turned a switch. The jasmine retreated from my throat. I drew a huge gasping breath. The world didn't smell like rain anymore. There was still the scent of flowers, but the rain had gone. The air was dry, and a wind came off the desert that the palm trees hid from view. The desert that I'd always known was there in this vision.

A whirlwind blew in from the sand. The Mother of All Darkness whispered in my ear, "No, it cannot be."

The whirlwind stopped a few feet away; as the wind died, Vittorio was revealed. But it was not the Vittorio that I'd seen in Vegas. This one pointed a handsome, unmarked face to the moonlight. His clothes were embroidered and rich, but matched the thin dress and sandals I wore. His short hair was long again, and he walked out of the wind, like some fairy-tale magician appearing in the nick of time. He had helped me; why? I didn't even care how, but why?

"I know you are still here, Dark Mother. I can feel you, hovering in the night, like some evil dream."

The voice came. "Father of the Day, you look unchanged. I see your little pets are back with you."

He made a motion and something appeared beside him. It was almost as if I couldn't see it, but from the corner of my eye, there was a huge man standing behind him. It wavered, and moved like a bad image on a screen that you needed to adjust, but it was there, in the dream, at least.

"Can you only call the people of the wind in dream?" she asked.

"No, the powers that you stripped from me return more

every day. As you grow weak, you lose control of that which you stole from me. It returns to me."

"I should have killed you."

"Yes, you should have. I would have killed you."

"I was too sentimental," the voice said.

"It wasn't sentiment that saved me, Dark Mother. I remember your words, very well. You said, 'If I were certain there was a hell, then I would kill you, so you could be tormented for eternity, but since I am not certain, I will leave you alive, to walk this earth, in your own private, powerless hell.'"

"It is too long ago; I do not remember my words exactly," she sighed.

"You were always careful what you remembered of your own deeds."

I wanted to say something, but was afraid to draw their attention to me. I wondered if I could break the dream and simply wake up?

"Do not go, Anita," Vittorio said, as if he'd read my mind. "Don't you want to see what happens?"

I swallowed and said, trying not to sound nearly as afraid as I was, "It sounds like you two have a lot of things to catch up on. I'll just leave you to it."

They spoke together. "No, necromancer, you will not go." "No, Anita, I can't let you go."

Shit.

"Does daylight not hold you prisoner?"

"You always did envy me that. You could never do it."

"As you could not raise the true dead."

"As you could not call the wind to your hand."

"We both had our armies of slaves, Day Father."

"You had your shambling hordes, and I had my army of jinn. I will have my army again, but you will not." His voice had gone low, and evil, somehow.

I wanted to ask if *jinn* meant *genie*, but I didn't want the answer enough to have him turn on me.

Her voice held that first thread of fear. "You would keep me from saving myself."

"Oh, yes, my love, I would."

"We both loved power more than anything else. It was not

sentiment that kept you from striking the first blow, my love," and she made the endearment sound like an insult.

He raised his hands and spoke words that I did not understand, but the hairs on my arms rose anyway, as if a part of my brain that I couldn't understand anymore knew exactly what the words meant.

He touched a ring on his finger.

"You speak the words, but the ring is what makes it happen. You are not strong enough yet to command them without it," she said.

"Not yet, but thanks to your plans, I will be soon." He spoke the strange words again, and my body shivered with it.

"They are almost here."

For a minute I thought she meant the jinn, and then I felt her look backward, as if there were a window I could not see behind where her voice was coming from. I had a moment to glimpse a slender, dark girl, and then the wind hit her. The wind held blades like a silver whirlwind; it surrounded her and cut her to pieces.

She shrieked, "Necromancer, do not trust him!" Then she was gone, but it wasn't the blades here. I felt an explosion rock in the pit of me, as if my body were the room where it had gone off. I fell to my knees with the sharp, burning pain of it.

"They've used modern explosives. She is dead," and he was triumphant. The wind of blades died down, as if it had never been, but I had another image of a second large figure behind him. There were two of them. Were they genies? If so, it was nothing like the cartoons except that the ring on his finger helped him control them. That was straight out of the old children's stories.

He turned to me, smiling, but it wasn't a good smile. It was the kind of smile that snakes would give if they could, just before they eat the mouse.

I decided I had nothing to lose by asking questions. "The jinn killed the policemen, didn't they?"

"Yes; my daytime servant shares some of my ability through the vampire marks."

"He just takes the ring," I said.

"No, the ring never leaves me."

"If you didn't have the ring, would they turn on you?"

"They are slaves. Slaves always resent the chains."

"I'm going to break the dream now, and wake up," I said, and tried for my voice to sound as sure as I felt.

He laughed, and it was a good laugh, but compared to Jean-Claude's it wasn't ordinary. Again it was as if he read my mind, because he said, "Belle Morte's line has powers that neither she, nor I, possessed. Belle was something new. All the others descend from us, but her and the Dragon. She was never human to begin with, so she was always different from us."

"So you don't share Belle's line of power," I said.

"I am oversharing, but it has been so long since I've had anyone to tell the truth to."

"It gets lonely," I said.

"It can, but I have my servants returning to me, and my magic."

"Bully for you. Now can I go, please?" I hated to add the *please*, but if it would get me the hell out of here, I'd say worse.

"The Dark Mother was always a good strategist. It's why she defeated me. It's a good plan."

"What plan?" I asked.

"Your feeding on all the colors of the tigers, and a vampire siphoning off the energy. It would have been enough power to save her, and it will still be enough to return me to my former glory."

"You're short two colors of tigers in Max's clan. You need yellow and red," I said.

"You saw the signs, Anita; there is a red tiger performing in Vegas. He was loaned to Max's clan for this year."

"But Max doesn't own him."

"I'm not calling only the tigers that belong to Max, Anita. I had many names, but one was Father of Tigers. I will call them to your room, and you, and they, will do what I want."

"You're still short a yellow one," I said, past the pulse that was trying to crawl up my throat.

"Don't you understand, Anita? You are the yellow tiger. It was a yellow tiger that struck you."

"But that makes me just a survivor, not pureblood. I'd shapeshift to a normal tiger."

"No, Anita, you wouldn't. How do you think the clans began? Do you actually believe the stories of tigers mating with humans and having offspring? No, fairy tales. They were all survivors of different strains of tiger. They have convinced themselves they are better because they breed true, but they have forgotten their own truth. They were once as you are, nothing more. They smell the gold tiger on you, Anita. The gold clan ruled them all, once, and they still respond to the power. If you were not true golden tiger, then they would not react to you, as they do."

"No," I said.

"I don't need you with child; in fact, that would complicate things, so we will make it quicker. I just need you to feed on them and to bring all the lines into their powers. For that we need a full feeding of Belle Morte's powers."

"Aren't you going to give me a chance to cooperate with you?" I asked.

"Why would I do that? I see my death in your mind, Anita. Lucky for you, I need you alive. Now, feed me the power that was once mine before the Darkness stripped me bare."

I screamed at him, "No!" Then there was nothing but the dark, and this time there was no voice in the blackness; there was nothing.

69

I WOKE UP in the dimness of a bed, sandwiched between warm bodies. I thought I was home, between Nathaniel and Micah. I sighed, content, and cuddled tighter in against Micah, pulling Nathaniel tighter against my front. It was how we usually slept, but the man behind me was too tall for Micah and just felt wrong. The man in my arms was too short, and didn't have the muscles or shape of Nathaniel.

My eyes suddenly opened wide, my body tensed. I couldn't see who was behind me, but the man in front had short, dark hair. He had his face buried into the pillow so I couldn't see his face. I held my breath and started moving my arm slowly away from his waist. I'd still have to move the arm at my waist from the other man, but one problem at a time.

"He won't wake," a voice said.

I jumped, and looked around the room. I saw a third man on the far side of the bed, one arm dangling. That one I knew was Crispin, nude sleeping on his stomach above the covers.

"You'll have to rise up to see me," Victor said again.

I started easing up, holding the second man's arm by the wrist so I wouldn't disturb him.

"Honestly, Anita, they won't wake. Everyone on the bed will have to sleep off the change. That won't happen for hours."

I could see him now, in the big chair in the corner. He'd put on one of the bathrobes that came with the room. His short white hair was tousled, as if he'd been running his fingers through it, or maybe it was bedhead.

Then I had an image, not of sight, but touch. I remembered running my hands through his hair, and forcing him to look in my eyes as we . . .

"Oh, shit," I said.

He nodded. "That would about cover it."

I was sitting up now, my back to the leather headboard. I could see the man on the other side now. He had long, dark hair that spilled over his face and went past his shoulders. He was muscled, and tall, and I didn't know him.

"Who are they?"

"You should recognize one of them."

I kept my voice low, as if they were just asleep. "I don't know the one at my back."

"You've probably seen him on the billboard outside the Taj. He's our guest star for the next month, and then he is to go home. Your Requiem is taking his place for a month."

I pictured the flashing image of the smiling redhead with the words, "Come watch the beefcake turn into kitty-cats," and the sign morphed from human to a red tiger.

"Oh, no," I said.

There was a noise from nearer the door. I couldn't see anything, but I remembered in North Carolina that there'd been one tiger on the floor. A man sat up, with a groan. He had straight black hair that fell around his shoulders, and a face that had uptilted eyes, like Bibiana's, but his skin wasn't pale. He was tanned and looked like the outdoors was his thing. He laid his face in his hands and groaned again. "What happened?" he asked.

"What do you remember?" Victor asked him.

He looked around the room until he saw me sitting in the bed. "Her."

Victor nodded. "Yes, her."

"I didn't do this on purpose," I said. I was remembering a dream. A dream with Vittorio in it and the Mother of All Darkness. The dream was coming back quicker than whatever had happened in this room.

"The Father of Tigers did it," the man on the floor said.

I stared at him as Victor said, "Who?"

"Vittorio," I said, "it's one of his old names. How do you know that title of his?"

"I was his tiger to call."

"Was?" I asked.

Victor just suddenly had a gun in his hand, pointed at the man. It was one of my guns.

"He called me from halfway across the world. I had to answer him. He was my master before, and when he regained enough power, I could not resist him." He seemed to be staring at nothing, but the look on his face said that whatever he was remembering wasn't anything good. "I thought I was free of him forever, but there's no escape, not if he wants you."

"He came into the hotel," Victor said. "He touched me, and I had to come here. I didn't even hear him come up to me. I heard nothing until he touched me, and then I just did what he wanted. I couldn't stop it. I couldn't ask for help. I couldn't say no to him."

"No, it's like you're his slave, or puppet. He can make you do such horrible things, and you can't stop."

"Who are you?" I asked.

"To him, I'm Hong, but to myself and for centuries, I've been Sebastian."

"All right, Sebastian, you said was, as in past tense, you were his animal to call. What changed?"

"You changed." He stood up, and he was as unself-consciously nude as all the wereanimals. I had a sudden memory of him above me, his body spasming, head back, lost to orgasm, and the sensation of him inside me. It made me have to take a deep breath and blow it out, slow. He was short, about my size. I looked at his hands; they were small, almost as small as mine.

"He may have fed on the energy of what we did in this room, but the moment we had sex, the moment I felt you feed on me, it was like you broke something in me. You broke his hold on me."

"That's not possible," I said.

"The Dark Mother did it centuries ago. It was one of her specialties to be able to break bonds between masters and servants. She would strip other masters of their power, and keep that power for her own."

"Victor, toss me a gun," I said.

He looked at me.

"Just do it."

He checked for the safety, which I liked, then tossed me my

Browning. I caught it and pointed it at Sebastian. "Did you kill the SWAT practitioner?"

He just nodded. "I might hate the master, but I gained powers, as of old. I could control the two jinn he had found, and the police wizard knew a very old spell. It would have lost me the control over them. The jinn hate to be slaves, and if they get the chance they will turn on their masters."

"Like a demon," I said.

"Yes, sometimes."

I had my knees up, resting the gun on them, still pointed at him. "I know you murdered a cop. I should turn you in, but I also know you had no choice. He can make you do things. Things you don't want to do."

"He smells of the truth, Anita," Victor said.

"I agree."

"What will you do?"

"I don't know yet. Tell us about the jinn."

He stood there, his hands at his sides, trying to be very still as we pointed guns at him.

"Tell us about the jinn."

"Do you mean genies?" Victor said.

"If what I saw at Vittorio's back was a genie, then the movies and storybooks have it all wrong."

"I take it they don't grant wishes," Victor said.

Sebastian and I both laughed, but not like we were happy. We looked at each other, and I realized that his eyes were the same color as Domino's, like fire carved into eyes. I asked, "Where's Domino?"

"At the foot of the bed," Victor said.

I nodded. "Okay, now tell us about the creatures."

"They can be attached to or trapped in an object, and then they can be forced to do the bidding of a sorcerer or magician. That much of the stories is true," Sebastian said.

"Like his ring," I said.

"Exactly."

"If he lost the ring, would he lose control of the jinn?"

"Yes, until he is restored to full power. Once at his full strength, he can call them out of the air without magical aid. It is his gift."

"There was wind, and then they appeared," I said.

"They are a second kind of people, Anita, created from air, as we were created from earth. They are very powerful spirits, so powerful that King Solomon destroyed them as a people and made them slaves to his bidding, and they were reduced to servants, or only spirits, whose greatest abilities lie in whispering evil in our ears to manipulate us."

"King Solomon had a seal made that he used to imprison most of their race, or something, right?" I said.

He nodded. "Yes. Some stories say that he used them to build his great temples."

"If we can get the ring from him, then will the jinn turn and kill him?"

"They might, or they may simply flee. He is to their race what the bogeyman is to yours."

I noticed he said *yours*, like it wasn't his. I skipped that and tried to decide what to do with him. He had killed a member of SWAT and helped kill others. But I believed that Vittorio had made him do it, just like the vampires at the club last night and the humans in the crowd.

"We have to kill him before he regains all his powers," I said.

"Agreed," Sebastian said.

"How?" Victor asked.

"I know his daytime resting place," Sebastian said.

I lowered the gun, and Victor followed my lead. "Turn on some lights, find some clothes, and tell me the address. Tell me all the addresses of anywhere he's stayed in Vegas since you got back with him."

"Happily, does this mean I'm not going to be executed?"

"Yeah, I think it does."

"You won't tell them about me?"

"I'll try not to."

"Thank you."

"Don't thank me, help me kill him before he becomes the Father of the Day again."

"Yes," Sebastian said. "If he regains his full powers, he will be able to conjure armies of the jinn from the very air we breathe."

Victor said, "I have pen and paper."

"Tell him the addresses." I started to crawl out over the other man in the bed, but crawling let me see his face better. "Oh, Mother of God, no," I said.

I fell off the foot of the bed, landing on Domino, who gave a grunt and woke up. "Anita, are you all right."

"You broke her fall," Sebastian said.

I got to my feet and was staring down at the bed. Crispin was still there, and the red tiger/stripper, whose name I didn't even know, but the third man wasn't a man at all. He was a boy. It was the blue tiger, Cynric, who was all of sixteen.

70

THE ONLY THING that kept it from being one of the most socially awkward moments of my life was that the boy didn't wake up. I got dressed in the bathroom, and told my reflection in the mirror that hysterics would not help the situation. My reflection did not believe me, but I won the argument.

When I came out, dressed in black from head to toe to match my mood, Crispin was awake and so was the redhead. Okay, not red, like human red, or even orangey tiger red, but red. His hair was actually more red than Damian's, my vampire servant back home. Yes, vampire servant, you heard me. To our knowledge, I'm the first human servant to ever manage that. Damian's hair was the red of not having seen sun for centuries, but with lamps lit, the tiger's hair was the red of a Crayola crayon. It was the red that they tell you in school is red, except there was an edge of black to it, like someone had thrown a little bit of extra color into the pot.

The face was a little long for my taste, but he was hand-some enough. His eyes were yellow, as if someone had melted autumn leaves into his face. It was when he turned and I saw all that muscled grace walking toward me, that I blushed and turned away. I got busy putting on weapons.

Crispin came up to me and hugged me briefly. "You okay?"

"No."

"My father and mother are missing," Victor said.

I turned to him. "What?"

"The Master planned on taking them. I told Victor, but it's too late, they're gone."

"How the hell did he take Max and Bibiana? I mean, your parents aren't exactly easy pickings."

"He said he would wait until he was powerful enough to take them both together."

I looked at Sebastian. "How much has he regained?"

"I do not know."

The red tiger came over to me. I wasn't embarrassed anymore. I was too worried for that. "I'm Hunter," he said.

I nodded. "Good for you, sorry I don't remember much. It'll come back to me."

His face went from arrogant to disappointed. "You don't remember?"

"Look, Hunter, if that's your real name and not a stage name, do you understand that the Master of the City and the head of the local tigers are missing? I'm about to call SWAT and go vampire hunting."

"Sorry, just trying to be nice."

"We'll be nice tomorrow. Today, let's stay alive, okay?"

He looked a little hurt, and I wondered how bright he was—or how unbright. But, again, not important this minute. I asked Victor, "Do you want me to tell the police about your parents, or do you guys want to handle it yourself?"

"Don't tell them yet. If he's got them at the daytime lair, great, they'll be rescued, but we may want to be a little less legal in the search."

"Okay, it's got to be your call; I'll leave it out for now." Then I called the first number in my phone that I'd put in for SWAT. It was alphabetical, so it was Lieutenant Grimes.

"Marshal Blake, we've been trying to call you for about an hour; are you all right?"

"Yes, in fact I've got the daytime resting place of Vittorio."

"Give me the address," he said.

I did. "We can roll a team now. The other marshals are already here."

"Shit, I'd rather you wait for me."

Grimes spoke to someone off the phone, then came back on. "Ted seems confident that we can move without you."

"Really? Okay. Can you put Ted on the phone for just a second?"

Edward came on. "Forrester here." He sounded cold and not himself.

Fuck it. "Edward, Vittorio isn't his real name. It's the name he took after the Mother of All Darkness stripped him of his powers and cast him out. He's originally the Father of the Day, or the Day Father. He's as old as the dark, and he's been gaining powers as she's been losing them."

"How do you know all this?" he asked, and he didn't sound mad now.

"He visited my dreams last night, and so did she."

"Anita, are you . . ."

"Okay, for now. Someone else took your job, and I think they blew her up last night."

"Can he walk in the day?"

"Not last we know, but if he can't, he's close, but that's not the worst part." I told him about the jinn.

"If he gets all his power back, we'll have a vampire in this city as powerful as the Mother of All Darkness," he said.

"Yeah," I said.

"Grimes sent Rocco and Davey to check on you. I wish we had Davey going in with us if the jinn show up."

"Why, what's his skill set?"

"He can do weather change, but what he really does is move air."

"What?"

"He can harden air to make temporary shields that are bulletproof."

"Well, fuck, that's nifty," I said, "like a combination of weather magic and telekinesis."

"Yeah, but what would happen if he hardens the jinn, if they're really made of air?"

"Good question, I'll think on it. When they get here, we'll head your way."

"Do that, and Anita . . ."

"Yeah."

"I'm sorry."

"It's all right, Edward."

"See you there."

"Save some for me," I said.

"I read the reports from St. Louis. At least one female vamp and a human servant male."

"Yeah."

"Gotta run."

"Bye," but I was listening to nothing. He'd hung up, but he'd apologized. It might be a first.

I decided to check on my bodyguards next door. I actually called Haven's number. He answered, "Anita, thought you'd be busy all day. If you wanted a party, we have enough men over here." He sounded disgusted.

"Some bodyguards you are, I spent the morning being mind-fucked by Vittorio."

"What?"

"Didn't you think it was weird, all the weretigers going into my room?"

"You came to the door and told me that it was fine. You invited them all."

"Didn't you notice I looked weird?"

"No, you looked fine, normal. I swear."

"I would not have agreed to everyone that came in here."

"You mean the teenager," he said, and so matter-of-fact, it pissed me off.

"Yeah, the illegal one."

"Hey, first, sixteen is legal in Vegas, and second, as long as it's legal, what's wrong with young?"

"Ah." I handed the phone to Victor. "Tell him the bad news about your family."

I went to Sebastian, who was still nude. "Does anyone have clothes left?"

"It looks like someone ripped me out of my clothes," he said.

"Then get a robe." He turned obediently toward one of the bathrooms. "Wait, is there any other plan, or something you should tell me about Vittorio?"

"The policemen in the hospital who are asleep. Vittorio could see through my eyes when they attacked, and he ordered me to kill the witch, but he said to only incapacitate the others. It gave me enough room to put them to sleep."

"Is there a way to bring them out of it?"

"Yes, love's kiss."

"What?"

"They just need a kiss by someone who loves them."

"You mean like Sleeping Beauty?"

He nodded. "Yes, it's the original power that started Belle Morte's line: a vampire power that was powered by love." He frowned. "I really thought that someone's wife would have kissed them by now, just by accident."

"Does it have to be on the lips?"

"Yes."

"Does it have to be a thorough kiss?"

"More than a peck, and some emotion to it."

"Like think of how much you love them, or lust them?"

"Yes."

Every time I thought I'd heard the weirdest vampire power, I was wrong. I started to reach for my cell phone so I could call SWAT and tell someone, but the door sounded.

I went for it, but Crispin got there first. "Let me check, Anita."

He was right. So I let him. He turned from the peephole, smiling. "It's SWAT. Do you want us to hide?"

"Yes."

They hid. I told them to get dressed and not to leave Sebastian on his own. I opened the door to Rocco and Davey. "We have a daytime lair address for them."

"Shit, did you call it in?"

"Yes, and we'll meet them there, but I got other news." I locked the door behind me, checked to see it closed, and walked off with the two operators listening to me fill them in. I got a glimpse of Haven's Cookie Monster–blue hair around the cracked door. I nodded at him, and that was the best I could do. Haven had a police record and had been until lately a mob enforcer. You couldn't play with him and the cops. We'd try legal first; then if that failed us, there was always going outside the law. I kept that thought to myself as I filled in Rocco and Davey on the morning news.

Davey grinned. "For bullets, it's not a hundred percent reliable yet."

"What's your percentage?"

"Eighty."

"Seventy," Rocco said.

"Still, in a pinch, nifty."

He grinned, making that lovely mouth into just a happy smile. It made him look younger, fresher, somehow. "But a monster that is made of air, that I think I can mess with."

I was happy for him, and seventy percent success was good for some of the rarer talents, but frankly, I wasn't sure I wanted to go up against a giant that could rip apart someone in body armor, or cut someone to pieces with a whirlwind of blades. Seventy percent sounded like good odds until it was your life on the line; then not so good. But frankly, what else did we have? Then I realized I was being stupid. I knew that the practitioner who had died had had a spell that Vittorio had feared.

I started searching my phone for Phoebe Billings's number. If her coven member knew the spell, then chances were that as his high priestess, so would she, and I was standing with two other practitioners. If we could all learn it, we had a chance.

71

I WAS SITTING in the passenger seat of Rocco's car when I got a glimpse of something. I thought at first I'd seen it out the window in the bright Vegas sun, but then it moved across my vision again, and I realized it was in my head.

"I'm seeing things," I said, out loud.

"What kind of things?" Rocco asked. Davey leaned forward on the backseat. It was a good question; I didn't have a good answer.

"I don't know; it's gone now, but it was bright."

"Tell us when and what you see."

"Will do." I was secretly hoping not to see anything else, but it was just nice to be working with police who didn't think I was crazy for being psychic.

My phone rang, and it was Phoebe Billings returning my message. She started with, "No police have come to my door. You didn't involve me and my group."

"Didn't see a purpose to it, but I found out what killed Randy, and what he was doing when he died." I explained.

"Jinn, truly, in America?"

"Honest."

"Wait a minute, and I'll look it up. I know the spell you mean, but it's very old, and it's in a book here. Randy was always very into the history of our craft. I remember a night that we talked about the jinn and how much of the legend was true." I heard her moving around. "Here it is. Do you speak Arabic?"

"No."

"Randy did; it was one of his specialties in the army. Does anyone else on the SWAT team speak Arabic?"

I asked that out loud to the others.

"Moon does, but then his mother's family is from Saudi Arabia," Davey said.

"I can read it," Rocco said, "and Moon says my pronunciation is okay."

I handed the phone to him, and Phoebe repeated the spell to him. He repeated it back, and it made the hair on my arms stand up, like in my dream. "She wants you to write the spell down."

"I can't write Arabic."

"Just write it as she tells you, one letter at a time. She's going to try to give it to you the way it's pronounced. She wants to see if saying it without knowing what it means will still work."

"Oh, like a real magic word, that has power even if you speak it by accident," I said.

"Yes."

"Those are really rare," Davey said. "Most spells don't work at all without some power behind them."

I was letting Phoebe dictate letters to me, one at a time. It didn't make any more sense made into mock English than it did in Arabic, but I was willing to try. When I had it all, I repeated it back to her.

"Now, read it faster," she said.

I read it faster. There was no tingle; it was just noise.

"Tell me what it's supposed to do," I said.

"It sends them back through Solomon's shield. It traps them outside our reality again."

"It's a banishing spell, like for a demon."

"Yes, that will do."

I tried again; thinking what it was supposed to do, I put intent into the sounds that were supposed to be words, and it still didn't work for me. I handed the notes to Davey, and again there was that hair-raising energy. "I think you're not pronouncing here and here right," he said.

I kept practicing as we drove, hard and fast, trying to catch up with everyone. We had Davey, and we had a spell. Guns wouldn't stop these things.

"Call Moon," Rocco said, "give him the words. He'll know how to pronounce it."

Davey made the call.

I asked Rocco, as he screeched around a corner and I clutched the door, "What made you learn to read Arabic?"

"I wanted to be able to read the Qur'an and the Bible for myself without translators messing with it. Most people don't realize that some of the original books of the Bible were written in Aramaic."

"I knew that, but I don't read it."

"I also read ancient Greek for the same reason."

"You must be a heavy churchgoer," I said.

"Every Sunday, unless I'm on a call."

I smiled at him. "Me, too," I said.

"I'm Lutheran, what are you?"

"Episcopalian."

He wasted a smile on me. "Fat Henry's church."

"Hey, I know my Church history, and I'm okay with it."

"As long as you know, it's cool."

"Yeah, my church exists because Fat Henry couldn't get a divorce as a Catholic."

I heard Davey repeat the syllables over the phone. It danced down my spine. "Wizard died trying to say those words," Rocco said.

"Yes, he did."

"This one's for Wizard."

"For Wizard," I said, and though I'd never met him alive, I meant it. Of course, I had the weretiger who had cut him up in my room, but he was as innocent as the vampires we were trying to save, and the humans we'd let go last night. Somehow I didn't share Sebastian with Rocco and Davey. What would I have done if it had been Edward on a gurney, and the were-animal said he had no choice, he was forced to do it? Easy answer: I'd have killed him.

72

WE MISSED THE party. There were three dead human servants lying on the ground with their hands and feet shackled. You shackle everyone, even the dead, just in case. It's SOP. Edward, Olaf, and Bernardo came out with more blood on them than on the other operators. But then it's a bitch to put the coveralls over all the weapons, so you get blowback. Olaf had the most blood on him.

Bernardo said, as he walked past me, "He staked his vampires, and de-fucking-capitated them. Ted and I shot ours." He kept walking, as if he didn't want to be around Olaf right that moment.

Edward said, "Vittorio wasn't there, Anita. There's a coffin that's empty, but he's not there."

"Shit!" I got another glimpse of something. I saw someone in white, kneeling.

Edward grabbed my arm. "Anita?"

"Did you have another vision?" Rocco asked.

"Someone in white, kneeling. I'm tall, much taller than I am. I'm seeing through someone else's eyes, I think."

"Who?"

"Vittorio," Edward said.

"What?" Rocco said.

"He messed with you, right? He wants you to be his human servant."

"Yeah."

"You know how it is when a vamp messes with you, Anita. The more they play, the more likely you are to acquire their powers, at least temporarily."

"Yeah, she did that with me," Rocco said.

Either Edward didn't catch that the sergeant had implied he was a vampire, or it didn't matter to him. "Concentrate, Anita, try to see it."

I closed my eyes and thought about Vittorio. I thought about the look of his face, the depth of the scars on his chest and stomach. The world wavered, and I was looking at Bibiana, chained and gagged on the floor, beside a bed. Vittorio turned his head, and Max was tied spread-eagled on that bed, covered in holy objects. The bed was red velvet and huge. I knew that bed. I knew where they were. I fought not to be excited but to be calm. I fought to break away, without him knowing.

"Don't go yet, Anita; stay, and see who else I have." He turned toward the kitchenette area. Rick the guard was chained with his arms above his head. His naked upper body was already bloody. "Don't feel so bad for Maximillian; they had the hooks in the ceiling. I'm betting that he's put his share of enemies here." Beside him was the stripper who had offered to give me a lap dance. Bri-something, Brianna. Vittorio held up a small butane torch. It burned blue-hot.

"She's nothing to me."

"Then you won't care that we ruin her beauty."

"Why? You know we know where you are now."

"Are the police with you?"

"Yes."

"We have one more guest, Anita." He turned and I saw the big table that I'd slept on with Victor. Someone was tied to the top of it. He walked closer and it was Requiem. My stomach fell into my feet, and only Edward's hands kept me from my knees.

"Fuck."

Vittorio moved so I could look down with him at those sea-green eyes. There was tape across the mouth I'd kissed only hours ago. He was bound with chains and holy objects. They'd stripped him of his shirt, as they had Rick, so that he was nude from the waist up. But whereas Rick was already hurting, Requiem was still untouched, pale and perfect against the wood.

I finally whispered, "His coffin was in my room."

"But did you check to see he was in it this morning?"

Shit. "No."

"We brought him out in a large bag while he was dead to the world, while the rest of you in the room were very busy. But I woke him up. I used to be able to wake any vampire early. I'm glad it's returned as a power. So much better when they can scream." He touched Requiem's face.

Requiem jerked away, and Vittorio backhanded him, casually. A cut opened on his cheek. Vittorio looked at the big ring on his hand. "This will make a mess of that pretty face, but I wouldn't want to damage the ring. Not when I have something so much better for the task." He reached into his suit coat pocket and drew out a small vial of holy water.

I couldn't stop myself. "Don't."

"Say *please*."

"Please."

"Good, then if you want to see him whole again and the others alive, come into the back room alone, and unarmed. Leave your holy objects behind, too."

"Why would I do that?"

"Because you know what I'll do if you refuse me, and I can feel that you care about him, that it would hurt you to see him burned."

I repeated what I saw, what he said. Rocco said, "We won't let her go in alone."

I repeated, "They won't let me."

"The police, I think they might." He walked to the door that opened into the main part of the club. There were dancers, customers; it was full. "I came last night, and detained them all." He turned toward the only two doors that led out, and the air shimmered before one, and there looked like there were swords floating in front of the main door. Something moved on the stage, like a shimmer of summer heat. It was a third jinn, and we didn't know what this one did. Shit.

"If the police do not let you come in alone and unarmed, I will have my servants kill all these nice people. You come to me, and I will release all the customers."

"You release the customers, and I'll come in."

"Not alone," Edward said.

"Can I bring one person in with me?"

"By all means, but not one of your marshals—one of the SWAT. They seem to die easily enough."

"No," Edward said.

"Oh, that's Death, I know his reputation. He isn't allowed inside."

I repeated what he said.

"Pick carefully, Anita; it will simply be another hostage to use against you, but by all means help me torture you more." He sounded so cheerful about it, and I realized he was; he had a room full of victims. What more could a serial killer ask for than that?

"But you'll release the customers first."

"Agreed, as soon as I see you outside with your SWAT friend. Now, I think I will shut this down between us. I thought to control you, and I did peek this morning; quite a show."

I was too scared and too angry to be embarrassed. "Then you know what happened to your other servant."

"Yes, you broke my hold on him, just like the Darkness could do. Her talents as a human were very similar to yours; I should have thought, but you don't expect to meet two necromancers of such power in one lifetime."

"Lucky you," I said.

"I will leave you with a parting image, to inspire you to do exactly as I've asked." He went back to the other room, and I didn't want him to, because nothing he was about to do would be good.

He went to Requiem, as I'd known he would. He unstoppered the little vial of holy water. "I'm coming, damn it, you've made your point."

"Oh, I'm not doing this to make my point, Anita. I'm doing this because I want to, and because it will hurt you, and because he is beautiful and I hate him for it."

"Vittorio!"

He trickled the water along Requiem's ribs. It smoked instantly, and Requiem's spine bowed, a scream coming even through the tape.

Vittorio capped the vial. "I will wait on the rest. You have a half hour to arrive, Anita, or I will try a more tender piece of him."

"I'm coming, you son of a bitch, I'm coming."

"Temper, temper."

"This isn't mad, Vittorio, you haven't seen me mad."

"Nor you me, Anita, nor you me." He pushed me out, closed the link down, and left me blinking in the sunlight, clinging to Edward's arms.

"Who's going in with you?" Bernardo asked.

"Cannibal is," I said. I looked and found Rocco. He met my gaze, no flinching.

"What do you want me to do?"

"Speak Arabic for me, and then we eat these sons of bitches."

A smile crossed his face, it was pleased and slightly Olafish. I knew that smile, because there's something about having an ability when you always have to be good that makes you wonder what it would feel like to be bad. I was about to give Cannibal the chance to be as bad as he wanted to be, as bad as he had the stomach to be. There was more than one way to skin a cat; well, there was more than one way to eat a vampire.

73

GRIMES DIDN'T LIKE me going in, and he sure as hell didn't want Rocco to go in with me. Edward didn't like me going in without him. But we had the arguments in the cars, so we could argue on the way and make the half-hour deadline.

"Lieutenant," Rocco said, "I can say the spell that will banish the jinn, and Anita can't."

"I know her pronunciation isn't good enough."

"I speak Arabic," Edward said.

"But you're not a practitioner, and we need a little magic with the words," Rocco said.

"What aren't the two of you telling me?" Grimes asked.

We both fought not to look at each other, and it showed. "What are you planning to do in there?"

"The phrase you're looking for, sir," Edward said, "is plausible deniability."

Grimes frowned at us. "Are you planning to do anything illegal?"

Again, we fought not to look at each other. "No, sir," Rocco said, "everything will be perfectly legal."

"Promise," Grimes said.

"It's legal," I said.

"But I don't want to know anyway, is that it?"

"What answer will get me in there with Sergeant Rocco?"

"Well, at least that's honest. Max's inner room at Trixie's interferes with electronics."

I didn't ask how he knew that, just accepted it as true. It didn't surprise me; as Vittorio said, the hooks in the ceiling for hanging people up had been in the ceiling when he got there. I was betting this was where Max did some of his dirty work.

"So you're going in there with no way to call for help," Grimes said.

"If we need to call for help, Lieutenant," I said, "you won't be able to get to us in time."

He studied my face. "I think you mean that."

"I do."

"You seem calm."

"I've got my goals."

"Your objectives," he said.

"If you like."

"And they are?"

"Rescue my friend before he gets more hurt. Save all the civilians. Send the jinn back to where they belong. Rescue Max and his charming wife, their bodyguard, and any other weretigers who are good guys. Oh, and kill Vittorio before he can manifest enough power to make a nuclear explosion over Vegas look like the better idea."

"Is he really capable of that much damage?"

"Think of an army of the things that killed your officers loosed on the city. Think of Vittorio able to broadcast his mind control over the populace."

"You think he's that good?"

"Not yet, and we have to keep it that way. I believe that we have to do everything within our power to make certain he dies today."

"You might be interested to know, Marshal Blake, that the governor signed off on the stay of execution for the vampires at last night's club."

"That's good, Lieutenant. I mean that; they don't deserve to die."

"Your report carried weight."

I nodded, but was already looking up the street to the police cars, the barricades, and the next fight.

74

ROCCO AND I were standing outside Trixie's with our hands clasped on our heads. We'd stripped down to T-shirts, pants, and boots for him, jogging shoes for me. A man who looked human but talked like Vittorio had his hand up his ass was saying, "Turn around, slowly, so we can see."

We did what he said to do.

The man seemed to be listening to something in his head. He nodded, and walked forward. He patted us down, thoroughly, top to bottom. "You have no weapons, very good," he said, but it was Vittorio's inflections. "Now, come join us."

"Let the customers go first, like you promised."

"Oh, yes, I suppose I did." The man was speaking, but it was really Vittorio using his body to do the talking. His ability to manipulate humans had grown more complex, more complete, in less than twenty-four hours. He had to die.

The man walked back through the doors. A few minutes later, people ran out. Dozens of them spilling out into the street into the arms of the waiting police, who hurried them to safety.

The man was in the door. He motioned toward it. "After you, Anita, and Sergeant Rocco, you said."

"Yes."

"Come on down," he said, in a mock announcer voice.

"Let the man go, too," I said.

"I said customers; he works behind the bar," the man said, talking about himself in the third person. He even had the smile Vittorio had used in the dream. It was an unsettling echo on the stranger's face, like a face on the wrong person.

The body he was using held the door for us. "Come inside, out of the heat."

Rocco and I looked at each other; then we lowered our hands, slowly, and went for the door. Neither of us looked back; we wanted to give our eyes as much time as possible to adjust to the darker interior of the club.

The dancers were huddled in the center of the room, at the chairs where the customers usually sat. They looked up hopefully as we entered, but the jinn with the knives was in front of us, and that got our attention. It was tempting to have Rocco say the words now, but I was certain if we did that, he'd kill some of his other hostages. Our goal was to get them all out, not just part, so we waited for a better moment. I admit that staring into the nothingness that was holding all those blades was hard. Turning our backs on it was harder, but we followed the man.

I felt the air move close to me and jerked back instinctively. I felt the passage of wind. A different jinn had tried to touch me. The man said, "You avoided his touch; not many humans are fast enough or psychic enough for that, but then you aren't human, are you?"

I ignored the question, but I swear that the jinn's attention wasn't as neutral now. I'd almost say hostile, but maybe that was just nerves talking. Maybe.

Rocco whispered, "I don't think they like you now."

"You feel it, too."

"Oh, yes."

The man opened the door and held it for us, with a smile. I moved ahead of Rocco, as we'd discussed. Vittorio wanted me alive; he didn't have the same feeling about the sergeant. So he had to bite his pride and let me take the most chances. Besides, we needed him alive to say the words over the jinn.

The back room was as I'd seen it through Vittorio's eyes. Rick and Brianna were on their feet, arms stretched to the ceiling, where they were chained. Brianna was crying; her robe had come undone, and she was as naked underneath as she had been that first night when Ted and I were here. She stared at me over the tape that cut across her face. I could feel her terror coming off her in waves. It stirred the beasts inside me, and I told them to be quiet. For once, they listened. Rick wasn't afraid, he was pissed. In fact, he was so angry, I wondered why he hadn't shifted yet.

Ava was near Rick. She had a knife in her hand and played it along his skin as I watched. She didn't cut him, just caressed him with it. There were weretigers scattered throughout the room. Their energy hummed through the air like wires stripped down, so you could feel the bite of it if you got too close. Most of them looked blank, as if waiting for instructions. How many people could he control at once, and how well?

I forced myself to see the room slowly, and not go straight to Requiem. I didn't want to give Vittorio any more reason to hurt him. The more I cared, the more danger Requiem was in.

But Vittorio wasn't standing by the table; he was sitting on the edge of the bed with Max and Bibiana. He'd stripped from the waist up so that his scars were very, very visible. They'd transferred Bibiana to the bed, she was tied with her hands above her head, around one bedpost, so that her body crossed one of Max's arms, where his one arm was still tied to the one post. Her feet were chained to one of the bed legs, but she was short enough that her legs didn't cross her husband's body at the legs. She looked pale and delicate, a cliché princess waiting for rescue. Max was missing his shirt. Apparently, we'd had a little striptease while they waited, but he had kept his word. There was no new damage to their bodies, just some of their clothes.

"We're here. Now what?"

"I want what I've wanted since I invited you to Vegas with my gift."

"You mean the human head in a box?"

He smiled happily and nodded.

"Next time, just send a box of chocolates," I said.

"Oh, but any man can do that. I thought my gift would be unique."

I smiled, and could feel that it wasn't a good smile. "Actually, I did receive a head in a basket once, as a gift."

The smile was just gone, like it hadn't existed. The old ones could do that—expression, then nothing in the blink of an eye. "Well, then, Anita, I will have to do something to prove myself unique among your admirers."

I would have given a lot to take back that smart-ass comment. It had been true, but I could still have kept it to myself.

"Oh, trust me, this invitation was unique."

"No, Anita, you're right, I must try harder." He was angry with me, as if I'd insulted him. "Let us play a game."

"We came here to negotiate for the release of hostages," Rocco said.

"And so we shall, Sergeant." He patted Max's bare stomach. "Come closer so you can see."

We hesitated.

"Here is the first rule. When you make me repeat myself, something happens to one of your hostages."

There was a sound from the other side of the room. Ava was carving a new cut down Rick's chest. He didn't scream, but a small sound had escaped him. Ava raised the blade to her mouth and licked the blood delicately away.

I turned back to Vittorio.

"You are not frightened or even impressed. I take it you've seen something similar before?"

I had, actually, more than once. Out loud, I said, "I don't know what reaction you want from me; just tell me and I'll try to give it to you."

"What is the first rule?" he asked.

"That if we make you repeat your requests, you'll have someone hurt."

"Here is the second rule. I will offer you a chance to do something pleasant; if you refuse, then I will do something painful to the person instead. Is that clear enough, officers?"

I said, "Crystal."

Rocco said, "Yes."

"Come over beside the bed, both of you."

We did it this time, no hesitating. We stood at the end of the bed on its raised dais, looking at Max and his wife, and the smiling sociopath beside them.

"Anita, give Max a kiss."

"If I don't?" I asked.

He drew a blade out from underneath the covers. "I will bleed him; one cut for one refusal."

I took a breath in, then out. It seemed a small request, but I was betting that the requests wouldn't stay small. "Okay, but if we do this, then you release one of the hostages."

"For a kiss, it would have to be some kiss."

I shrugged.

"If I refuse to free someone, are you prepared to watch me slice up the Master of the City?"

I thought furiously, and just didn't know what to do. Vittorio made a shallow cut across Max's stomach.

"I didn't say no."

"You broke rule number one. You hesitated. Now I'll ask you again: kiss Max or I cut him."

I just went to the bed, walked wide around Vittorio, and climbed up beside Max. I looked down into his blue eyes and said, "Sorry, Max." I leaned over and laid a kiss across his taped mouth.

"Well, you did do what I asked, but that is hardly worth the release of a hostage." He tapped the blade against his leg.

"Do you want me to kiss him better?"

"Take off the tape, and show me some of that talent I know you have."

Bibiana made a sound through her tape. I looked across at her. "Sorry, Bibiana." I took the tape off Max's mouth.

"He's going to kill us anyway, you know that."

"Now, Max, what did I say about talking?"

"You said no talking back to you. I'm talking to Anita."

"True." *Tap*, *tap*, *tap* went the blade against his leg. "Well, Anita, kiss him like you mean it, and I'll let your sergeant watch one of the dancers leave."

I bent over and kissed him full on the mouth. His mouth was still under mine. I looked back at Vittorio. "A dancer, freed."

"No."

"What was wrong with this kiss?"

"Kiss him like you mean it." There was no humor in him now, just a seriousness that I thought was more dangerous.

I stared down at Max. He was mostly bald, and round of face, but his biceps were huge, his shoulders deeply muscled.

He'd begun life as an enforcer, and he'd stayed in shape for it. I could see his strength, but he just didn't do it for me. I liked my men pretty and a little refined. Max was like a bully—big, scary, and nothing delicate about him—but I bent over him one more time. I touched his face, closed my eyes, and kissed him. Delicate, at first, then with more pressure, letting my arms slide over the hard, muscled bareness of him, and putting some body English into it. Max was absolutely still against me. Bibiana was making a high-pitched sound through the tape.

I turned to Vittorio.

"Very well, one dancer, but I want the next effort to be better, or the deal is off. Ava will choose who goes free, and Sergeant—Rocco, is it?—will watch from the door that the dancer gets away."

Ava went out, Rocco watched from the door, and apparently they let a dancer go because Rocco came back nodding yes.

"I'll give you a two-for-one deal," Vittorio said. "Let the little dancer over there give you a lap dance; if it's good, I'll free her and another dancer."

I walked over to Brianna without hesitation, but once I got there, I asked him, "What do you want to learn from making me do this?"

"Maybe I'm just like all men and have my little lesbian fantasies."

"I don't know what to say to that."

"Sit in the chair by Ava."

I sat in the chair; it didn't hurt me, and I didn't want to give them another excuse to hurt anyone. "Untie the girl."

Ava did what she was told. Brianna took her own tape off her mouth, then looked at me. Her makeup had run down her face like black tears. She rubbed at her wrists and took a shaking step toward me in her spike-heeled sandals.

"I'm offering you the best tip you will ever get, Brianna. Give the marshal a lap dance, and if it's good enough, I'll set you and another of your friends free."

Brianna took another staggering step toward me. I thought, *She's not going to be able to do it, she's too afraid.* He must have thought so, too, because he said, "If you refuse, or don't do a good job of it, I will use the torch on that soft, pink, perfect skin." He almost sounded bored.

Brianna dropped her robe to the ground and was in front of me. "Wait," Vittorio said. We both looked at him. "Sergeant, take Anita's place; let her dance for you."

Rocco just started walking toward us. I got up, he sat down, and Brianna started to dance. She had no music, but whatever was playing in her head was something with a beat. She started a little jerky, but then closed her eyes and found her rhythm. It was a nice rhythm. She moved her body in waves up and down Rocco—who had a death grip on the chair he was sitting in, because the rules are the dancers can touch you, but you can't touch the dancers.

Brianna ended up in his lap, straddling him, grinding her most intimate parts over the front of his pants. His face looked grim, and I was betting he was trying to think of baseball, taxes, dead kittens, anything but what the woman in his lap was doing.

I felt both sorry for him and happy it wasn't me.

With a last writhe, she bowed herself backward, completely, her legs wrapped around Rocco and the chair itself. She bent back in a graceful arch, her high, tight breasts spilling backward, proving yet again that they were real.

Vittorio actually clapped. "Very good, and the sergeant has held his composure admirably. Flee, little dancer. Anita, watch her go to safety; I don't think our dear sergeant can walk just yet."

Brianna picked up her robe and went for the door as fast as her high heels could take her. "Pick another dancer to go out with you, Brianna." She picked up the pace. I kept the door open and watched her go to the nearest dancer, grab her by the hand, and run out the door with her.

I did a quick head count. We had six dancers left. Six, and then we could get rid of the jinn and try to kill Vittorio. Just six more.

"I make the dancers entertain me before I kill them, Anita. I don't usually let them go, though."

"So this is part of your . . . usual." I stopped there because any word I could come up with sounded too much like an insult.

"Yes." He got up and walked to Rick. "I could control him, but only in part. I can't control him or Victor completely as I can the others. They are too dominant, too much tiger. I could make either of them my servant through marks, but I cannot own them as I own the ones in the corner." He moved so fast, it was barely visible.

Rocco said, "He mind-fucked me."

"No, he didn't," I said, "he's just that fast."

Vittorio was standing back where he started, by the time the blood started trickling down Rick's stomach.

"You didn't ask us to do anything," I said.

"So I didn't. Ava, let another whore go."

Ava just went to the door, and I watched as she tapped another woman. The woman ran out the door in a flashing square of sunlight. Five left.

"Anita, drink blood from the wound I just made on the weretiger."

I didn't like this one, but I went to Rick and knelt in front of him. The cut was just above the pants line, so I could reach. I was betting the placement hadn't been accidental.

I put my hands on his belt to steady myself, then leaned up and licked the wound. It was blood, hot, salty, metallic. I put my mouth against the wound and sucked. It was sweet copper pennies on my tongue. But it was more than that, it was belly meat, soft, above the muscles, and that feeling that just underneath were soft, tender things. My hands locked around the back of his body, and I fought to only suck the wound, not bite down, not take more flesh. I drew back from the wound with a shaky breath. I felt dizzy, disoriented. I realized for the first time that though I'd fed on all the men this morning, Vittorio had taken all the energy of it. Beyond that, he'd taken more of my energy, so I was actually behind the curve. Fuck.

I got to my feet, having to steady myself against Rick's body as I stood. I wiped my mouth with my hand, and knew I needed a rag or something to get the blood.

"Most people would have hesitated before drinking a lycan-thrope's blood," Vittorio said.

"If we hesitate, you hurt them."

"Ava, another dancer." This time Rocco watched the hos-tage leave. Only four now.

He paced in a circle, tapping the blade against his leg. "I must come up with things that displease you, or I will run out of hostages before I get to hurt anyone again." He turned to me with a huge smile. It tugged at the burned side of his face, so that the smile didn't quite work. "Suck on something else; you can pick any of the men, just bring them. To give you more incentive, I'll use the holy water on your fair friend again if you refuse."

I looked from Rick to Requiem. "May I ask a question?"

"You may."

"Has Requiem fed?"

"No."

"Then you know he can't go orally or any other way until he's taken blood."

"Then you are left with only two choices unless you wish to include the sergeant."

I fought not to look as uncomfortable as that extra sugges-tion made me. "Max hasn't fed this morning either, so it has to be Rick. You're only pretending to give me choices."

"Then do him." He was standing by Requiem now, and I realized that there was a line of holy water vials on the table above his head.

I went to Rick and started undoing his belt. Rick made a small protesting noise. I took a breath in, and blew it out. I whispered, "It's not a fate worse than death, Rick."

He went still in his chains and watched me undo his pants. I wasn't sure if the patient watching was less uncomfortable to me, or the struggles and noises. I got his pants unzipped and worked his pants down over his ass; I wanted the zipper out of the way both for his safety and mine. I'd kept his underwear in place, and only moved it out of the way once I was kneeling in front of him. He was as lovely below the waist as above, and there were no cuts here yet; I was hoping to keep it that way.

I looked up the line of his body and found him watching me. His blue eyes were angry, yes, but there was something else in them now, too. Apparently, he'd taken my *not a fate worse than death* to heart, because there was that darkness in his eyes that every man gets at about this time. I took him in my hands and lowered him to my mouth. He was already erect enough that I had to bring him down to me, because he was pressed against the front of his own body. He slipped inside my mouth, as full and smooth and good as any. I liked giving oral sex. I liked the feel of it in my mouth, and the look on a man's face while you did it. I liked the sounds they made, and the way their bodies reacted. I gave myself completely to the man in front of me, and the sensation of my mouth going over and around him. I kissed and sucked and licked, using my hand on him to guide and caress and squeeze. I let myself spill into the sex, and there was nothing else. I glanced up and found his eyes wide. His breathing quickened. He was so hard now, except for the soft smoothness of the tip of him. His body spasmed in the chains, and it wasn't pain this time. He closed his eyes, head flung back, and I worked him in and out of my mouth quicker, in and out, in and out, as fast as I could. I tasted the first hint that he was close; the texture changed, ever so slightly, like a preview of what was to come.

Vittorio's voice. "Two dancers, if you let him go on your breasts."

I didn't hesitate. I just yanked my shirt over my head and let it fall. I held him in my hand, working him, keeping him close; I didn't want to lose ground. I had to let go to undo my bra and throw it over my shoulder to the floor with the shirt. Then I plunged my mouth back over him, cupping, and playing, and teasing until I felt him tighten in my mouth. I moved off him just in time, stroking him with my hand as he spilled upward, outward, in a thick, warm rain of it. It spattered across my shoulders, my breasts, and I threw my head back, thrust my breasts more forward, and it also kept it out of my eyes.

Rick spasmed above me, rattling the chains, making small noises against the gag.

Vittorio was huddled against the counter; he looked at me, at Rick, at the show of it, with a look of eager horror.

I heard Ava and Rocco go to the door to let more of the hostages go. I started crawling toward the vampire, with my breasts hanging down, and the warm liquid beginning to drip. He pushed himself to his feet and screamed, "Kill them!"

My skin ran with that sibilant magic, and I knew that Rocco had said the words, and the jinn were gone. Ava screamed, and I risked a glance to find that Ava had buried her knife in Rocco's side, but he had her wrist, and I knew what he could do with that seemingly innocent touch.

The glance was a mistake. Vittorio used that blinding speed to be up and at Requiem's side. I couldn't move fast enough, but I had one power that was fast as thought. I opened the *ardeur* and thrust it like a weapon at the vampire. It might not have worked except he'd just had me do one of his fantasies. The idea of me and sex was already firm in his mind. He wanted to look.

I didn't run. I stalked, I writhed, I made everything work, and he couldn't look away. He was still staring at me when I wrapped my hand around his and cupped the vial of holy water, sending it to shatter harmlessly on the floor.

"I will ruin him," he whispered.

"That's not what you want."

"I can't have what I want," he said.

I put his empty hands on my breasts, and held his gaze with mine. His hands started smoothing the liquid across my breasts, as if he didn't realize he was doing it. "Your eyes," he said, "your eyes are full of fire, like cognac diamonds."

"Say it," I whispered.

He leaned his face downward, as I leaned upward. "Say it," I whispered.

"Release, I want release."

His mouth met mine, and we kissed. One moment it was gentle, the next he fed at my mouth, so hard his fangs cut my lips and filled our mouths with the sweet taste of blood. Blood made my hungers rise, but it was too late for any of the others; all that was left was the *ardeur*. I had denied it, tried to cage it, control it, but in that moment I understood why kings had offered Belle Morte their crowns, why women had offered everything for one more night with Jean-Claude; I understood what it meant to be Belle Morte's line. The *ardeur* wasn't something I had to feed to stay alive, it was the way I fed. It was my blood.

Vittorio made small eager noises against my mouth, his hands eager on my body. I felt the growing pressure of it build inside him, and I felt the *ardeur* mingle with the power of the beasts, all of it so warm and alive, so not vampire. His breathing quickened, his body tensed, and I drove the *ardeur* and the power of the tigers into him, like a seeking hand, and gave him, for a moment, a taste of it. I gave him the shadow of what he had lost, and his mouth tore away from mine in a scream, as his body spasmed against mine, his hands clutching at me. He collapsed to the floor beside the table, taking me, still in his arms, to the floor with him. He was crying and laughing. "How did you do that?"

"I am Belle Morte's line. I belong to Jean-Claude. We are meant to bring pleasure."

His hand searched the floor, and I knew what he meant to do before I saw the flash of silver. I rolled away from him, but he came for me, and he was simply too fast.

Then a white blur crashed into his side, and a second joined it. The two weretigers grappled with the vampire, and his speed did no good because they were already touching him. I pushed backward so I could see the bed, and the chains were empty. I didn't know where Max was, but I knew where his wife and Rick were. The other weretigers spilled out of the corner where they'd been frozen. I thought for one awful moment they meant to attack us, but they went for the fight and Vittorio.

Max appeared by the kitchenette. He handed me a towel. I stood up and began to wipe myself off. We both kept our eyes on the fight, but it was a blur of claws and teeth.

"You mind-fucked him, and that was the weakness I needed. The tigers are mine again."

Rocco came to me, holding pressure on his side wound. Ava lay behind him on the floor, staring sightless at the ceiling.

"How did it feel?" I asked.

"Good," he said. "She wasn't being controlled. She betrayed you, Max."

"I know. She felt we treated her as a second-class tiger, and she was right."

Blood sprayed out over the room. "That was arterial spray," I said.

"Fight's over," Max said.

I dropped the towel onto the floor, picked up my shirt and bra from the floor, and went to Requiem. I jumped up on the table and undid his chains. He ripped off his own gag. I hugged him and he gasped. I touched the burns, and felt my eyes grow hot. "I'm so sorry."

"You saved me."

I could only nod.

"Get dressed, Anita," Rocco said. "I've got to call the cavalry in and warn them that the tigers are on our side." I looked where he was looking, and found the white tigers, some in tigerman form, covered in blood. Vittorio was in pieces on the ground. Now that he was dead, they'd stopped feeding. Vampire is bitter meat, so I'm told.

I dressed and promised myself a shower later. Max offered to take Requiem to his own underground resting place until nightfall. I kissed Requiem, and turned toward the police as they spilled in through the door behind Rocco, but it was all over. This time Edward and the guys had missed the party.

Epilogue

REQUIEM SPENT THE rest of the day in the downstairs area with Max. Rocco and I had a lot of 'splaining to do. We left out some things. Ava attacked him and he was forced to use the maximum of his power. He probably could have stopped sooner, but why? She was dead either way because of the warrant.

Bibiana asked, in private, "You gave him his first pleasure in centuries; why did he attack you?"

Max and I exchanged looks, and he said, "He knew he'd do anything to have that feeling again. He knew that Anita owned him lock, stock, and barrel, and he couldn't have that."

"He'd rather have power than the pleasure?" she asked.

"He knew it would be a choice," Max said. "I think Anita's leash may be shorter than the one you keep me on." They had laughed good-naturedly and hugged.

Requiem suggested that we cut the burns away the next night, and try to heal it with sex, as we'd done with other fresh wounds in the past. It worked. He's perfect again. It makes the idea of trying it on Asher possible. But we'll start with a little piece of skin, just in case the deeper burns make it not work.

Denis-Luc St. John's sister never gave him my message. He called, upset that he'd missed it all, but his sister wasn't sorry—he was alive. I kind of agree with his sister.

Lieutenant Grimes said that if I ever get tired of being a vampire hunter, to let him know; I could test and see if I could become their first female member. I was flattered, really flattered. I actually didn't say no. I can't see living in Vegas, but I could see working on a SWAT unit like theirs. Their pilot program of using practitioners is successful enough that other cities are talking about it—not St. Louis so far, but I have hopes. Would I really give up hunting vampires? I'd still help hunt them, but the idea of working on a unit where the idea is to save lives and not take them is pretty appealing.

I took Crispin and Domino home with me to St. Louis. The redhead, I sent home to his clan. Their queen has requested a visit in a neutral city, since I keep poaching her males—one of them being her son, the first one, Alex. So far the red tigers don't seem as affected by me as the white or the black. Sebastian went back to his life. He is drawn to me, but he doesn't want to go back into servitude to anyone. I don't blame him.

Cynric was a different problem. Yes, he was legal in Vegas, and yes, his legal guardians, Max and Bibiana, were fine with it, so no court charges, but he is besotted with me. It's worse than Crispin, because he had fewer internal protections. He was just so young, so open, and because the tigers, or at least the white clan, try for monogamy, I was his first. The thought of a massive *ardeur* feed, with a group orgy thrown in, as anyone's first time just makes me ill.

They're keeping him in Vegas for at least a year, because next birthday he'll be legal in Missouri. I told Bibiana it doesn't matter, he'd still be a child, but she said, "You have made him your tiger to call, Anita, you must take responsibility for that."

"I didn't mind-fuck him, Vittorio did."

"But you are who he pines for."

I made the mistake of asking, "What do you want me to do about him?"

"Let him come visit next year."

I told her we'd discuss it, but really, not only no, but hell no.

The SWAT operators in the hospital are all awake. They found a girlfriend, or wife, or child, or parent to give them a kiss of love. It all worked, though one operator had never married, parents dead, and so they finally brought his dog in; one good face-licking later and his master was up and around. Ain't love grand?

Jean-Claude, Asher, and I have talked about what happened in Vegas, with the *ardeur* and Vittorio at the end. We agree with Max about why he attacked me, but why did sex disrupt all that ancient vampire ability? Jean-Claude finally said, "Everyone believes that Belle Morte's line is weak because our power is love, but really, *ma petite*, what is more powerful than love?" I could have argued that I'd seen hate kill love, or violence, or . . . but in the end, maybe he's right. I know that Vittorio wasn't beaten by power. He was beaten by the offer of love. "'Twas beauty that killed the beast," the old movie said. 'Twas love that killed this one, or maybe lust, but sometimes I'm not sure there's as much difference as we like to think between the two. Not if you mean it.

I wasn't lying when I offered the *ardeur* to Vittorio. In that moment, I wanted to give him back what he'd lost because I could feel his need, feel the great sorrow of it that had turned to such rage. I wanted to hold him and make it better, and I did, and he tried to kill me for it. Men—who knows what they really want?

New in hardcover from
#1 *New York Times* bestselling author
LAURELL K. HAMILTON

FLIRT
An Anita Blake, Vampire Hunter Novel

Anita will face the most dangerous of clients—one who won't take no for an answer.

When Anita Blake meets with prospective client Tony Bennington and learns that he is willing to pay top dollar to have his recently deceased wife reanimated, she feels a lot of sympathy for his loss. But she knows that what she can do really won't help. What could step out of the late Mrs. Bennington's grave would not be the lovely blonde Mrs. Bennington, but rather a zombie...

M578T1009

The all-new Anita Blake, Vampire Hunter novel
from #1 *New York Times* bestselling author

LAURELL K. HAMILTON

BULLET

The triumvirate created by master vampire Jean-Claude, necromancer Anita Blake, and werewolf Richard Zeeman has made Jean-Claude one of the most powerful vampires in the United States. He's consolidating power in himself and those loyal to him, doing in America what Belle Morte did in Europe when she was at the height of her power. She almost owned Europe, and there are those who are determined to prevent Jean-Claude from doing the same in America.

Assassins are coming to St. Louis to kill them all.

penguin.com

AVAILABLE IN PAPERBACK
FROM BERKLEY BOOKS
An Anita Blake,
Vampire Hunter novel

BLOOD NOIR

by

LAURELL K. HAMILTON

#1 *New York Times* bestselling author

A favor for Jason, vampire hunter
Anita Blake's werewolf lover, makes
Anita a pawn in an ancient vampire
queen's new bid for power.

M169T0509